THE UNEXPECTED VACATION of GEORGE THRING

Alastair Puddick

Published by Raven Crest Books

ISBN-13: 978-0-9926700-8-5
ISBN-10: 0-99-267008-X

DEDICATION

For Laura

CHAPTER 1

GEORGE Thring ran away from home. By accident. It happened like this.

ON a crisp February Tuesday evening, as a heavy orange sun hung low in the sky and the cool, grey dusk settled down around the buildings and houses, blanketing them like a soft, warm duvet, George Thring drove straight past his own house.

He left his office at the usual time; took his usual route home from work, which took as long as it usually took; and he turned into the street where he lived at the usual time. Yet as he neared his house, instead of turning into the small, grey, rectangular driveway where he usually parked his car – for some reason his foot stayed on the accelerator, his hands held the steering wheel straight and he drove past his little house and right out the other end of the street.

Actually, it was not unusual for George to do this. Every now and again, whilst sitting in his little grey car on the way home from another particularly unsatisfying day in his particularly unsatisfying job, George would find himself thinking. He'd think about all the things he'd done that day: all the people he'd spoken with; the various tedious events that had taken place and he would just sort of drift off. Lost in a fog of contemplation, his autopilot would take over and he would just drive and drive, oblivious to the world around him.

The first time it happened George had naturally been quite concerned. He'd driven out of the office car park; found himself thinking about something and nothing; drifting off into a melancholy fog and pootling along at an average speed. When he finally came round – that's what he'd come to call it as that's the only way he could rationalise it, as if he'd fallen into a dream and suddenly woken up – he was 27 miles from home, doing 67mph down the motorway.

He'd had to carry on for five minutes until the nearest junction, turn himself around and then he'd finally arrived home an hour and a half late. Not that he was really late, as such, as he had no real plans to speak of other than watching the usual drivel on TV and eating his dinner. But he was later than he would usually be.

It had certainly troubled him: how his mind had become swamped and his body had simply carried on driving, swooping him up out of his life and whisking him away on a strange little adventure.

He'd been worried enough to think about going to the doctor. It couldn't be normal, after all, getting lost in a cloud of thought and driving without realising it. So perhaps he ought to get his head checked. But, then, he'd heard horror stories about that type of thing. You'd go to the doctor complaining of funny

1

dreams or insomnia, or some mild complaint, and before you knew it they'd have you on anti-depressants, talking to a counsellor about your problems once a week and keeping a journal of your dreams.

And that was just the mild cases. If they thought there was something really wrong with you, the men in white coats would be round quick-smart, helping you into the fancy jacket with the buckles round the back and whisking you off to your own luxury padded fun-house.

So, just in case there was something seriously psychologically wrong with him, George thought it was probably safer to remain tight-lipped and simply hope for the best.

The eventful evening blackouts and strange psychological mystery tours continued, on and off. He could never tell when they were likely to strike. He would simply leave work, set off in his car and hope to get home sooner rather than later. There seemed to be no rhyme nor reason as to when they'd occur; he'd just find himself halfway down some country lane, caught in rush-hour traffic on a mysterious ring road or, as on one occasion, parked up in somebody else's drive in a completely unknown town – much to the consternation of the middle-aged woman who'd stood staring at George from her kitchen window, holding up a rolling pin to demonstrate that she was armed and not scared to use it.

On average it happened once or twice a month, and each time George found himself slightly further from home. Once he'd driven for 47 minutes in the wrong direction before suddenly realising where he was. It had then taken him a full hour and a half to navigate his way back, meaning it finally took nearly three hours just to get home from work. He was so tired when he eventually got through the front door that he just had a cheese sandwich for dinner and went to bed. Which turned out to be a bad idea, because the cheese gave him a rather disturbing dream about drowning in strawberry yoghurt.

And so George drove on. Thinking about his day and getting further and further from home.

On this particular day George had filed away files; answered phones; written reports; updated his spreadsheets; and, tried to muster up some enthusiasm for the data he was supposed to be analysing. And, when that failed, he just analysed the data anyway.

George had read 102 emails that he didn't want to read and replied to 37 e-mails he didn't really want to reply to. He'd purposely left the replies slightly longer than he should have, partly so that he'd look busier than he really was and partly because he knew that the person expecting the reply would be getting irate and frustrated at his tardiness.

He had checked the clock one hundred and thirty-seven times and each time had been mildly disappointed that it was earlier than he had hoped it to be.

George had thought about quitting his job and going off to write a novel. He had then decided that he'd probably just get bored doing that as well.

He'd had sexual thoughts about Paula Tredcott from accounts. He had then spent a painfully embarrassing four minutes and thirty-two seconds clamped in behind his desk, silently willing an unwanted erection, protruding very obviously in his trousers to "please, for the love of God, go away before anybody sees".

George had secretively surfed the internet looking for answers to the crossword he couldn't quite finish. He had then gone for a pointless five-minute walk around the building in order to stretch his legs and to waste five minutes of the day.

He had drifted off into a daydream whilst waiting for the automatic drinks machine to dispense his cup of watery coffee, briefly imagining how he would react should a giant lizard have broken in through the wall and started gobbling people up at random. He imagined himself flying into action: ripping off his shirt; tying his tie Rambo-style around his head; and leaping at the beast with nothing to protect him but a shatterproof ruler and a hole-punch – a modern day superhero, sure to have the women swooning at his heroism.

He then decided that in reality he would probably not have been heroic at all and likely would have merely run away and hidden under a table.

His watery coffee had come out in the surprising form of weak tomato soup. He contemplated drinking it anyway, then thought better of it and left it on the side in case someone else fancied it. He returned two minutes later and placed a Post-it note next to the cup. It said: 'Free Tomato Soup. It was supposed to be coffee. I did not spit in it.'

George had sat in front of his computer, getting irate and frustrated at the length of time it took some people to reply to his e-mails.

George had spoken to Linda (the Business Services Administration Manager and also his boss's boss's boss) or, rather, Linda had spoken *at* him about the annual company barbeque he hated going to each year but had to attend as it was a mandatory team-building exercise. She had explained that she was far too busy to organise the event this year so she was delegating the task to him. Which would have to be done in his spare time, to prevent him from falling behind with his daily reports. Apparently George's Team Leader, Anton, had volunteered him for the task knowing that he would be unable to say no and hoping it might reflect well on him in retrospect.

George had drunk seven cups of coffee (having figured out that to achieve coffee from the machine he had to push the button marked 'Still Lemon Drink'). This was more coffee than he suspected was good for him but lately it was the only thing that kept him from getting too drowsy in the afternoon. He'd then read a report on the internet about how too much caffeine was bad for you and worried about the effect that each and every sip of those seven cups was having on him.

George had spent several minutes thinking about the task of organising the barbeque and wondering whether a broken limb would be sufficient excuse for passing the planning on to someone else. He then thought about all the ways in which he could conceivably break an arm or a leg, and the pain and complications that would no doubt be involved. He remembered the scene from

'Escape To Victory', where one plucky young lad agreed to have his arm broken on purpose so that Sylvester Stallone could play in goal. He remembered it looking particularly painful.

And broken arms didn't always end only with broken bones, did they? Couldn't the veins and arteries also get damaged? One could conceivably set out purposely to break a limb so as to get out of some dreaded task, and end up with major complications leading to internal bleeding, the loss of a limb, or even death. These sorts of things happen all the time on television.

George decided that he was probably going to have to organise this year's company barbeque after all.

George had spent a very bored thirty minutes in an exceedingly warm, dry meeting room, trying to stay awake through a particularly dull meeting about statistical analysis, again imagining the giant lizards crashing in through the wall and gobbling up his superiors. Under these circumstances, George knew he definitely wouldn't have leapt to their defence.

He had taken his usual 20-minute mid-morning 'sit-down' in the toilet. For lunch he ate a disappointing ham salad sandwich, a bag of salt and vinegar crisps, an apple and a bottle of orange Lucozade.

This was all pretty standard for George. A very usual day indeed. And as he continued to drive, going nowhere in particular and not even really noticing that he was still driving, George started to think about all the things that he hadn't done that day.

For example, George hadn't sent an e-mail round the office telling everyone just how much he hated the annual team building barbeque that he was forced to attend each year and, as it had fallen to him to organise it this year, he had decided that he was cancelling the event, to save everybody the tedium of attending and instead would be dividing equally the allotted funds from petty cash between each member of the office – £11.63 each – and letting them decide for themselves what they wanted to do with it.

He hadn't been given the pay rise he'd been expecting 'any day now' for the last six months. He hadn't stormed into his boss's office and told him to stick his job up his bum, then marched out of the building to the rapturous chorus of his fellow employees' approval.

George hadn't had a passionate encounter with Paula Tredcott from accounts in the third floor stationery cupboard. He had thought about it: imagined the feel of her hot breath on his neck; her hands running through his hair; her lips on his lips. He'd even imagined the discomfort of the racking pressed into his back and the dull pain in his left buttock as each thrust pushed him back against a freshly-sharpened box of HB pencils. He'd thought about it, but he hadn't done it.

He hadn't been quite brave enough to try the exotic sounding brie, bacon and tomato sandwich he often saw on the shelf at the local sandwich shop – and always quite liked the sound of – so instead stuck with the safe, disappointing option of his usual ham salad.

When Linda from Statistical Configuring had stormed over to his desk and demanded a very important set of figures by the end of the day, he didn't tell her how much he wanted to poke her in the eye with a rusty fork.

He hadn't poked Linda in the eye with a rusty fork.

These were not unusual things for George to think about. He often considered the things he hadn't done that day, and wondered why he hadn't done them. He wondered what might have happened if he had done them. And as he lost himself in a dreamy world of 'what ifs' and 'maybes', thinking about all the things he could have done, and should have done, and might well do if he ever worked up the nerve, he invariably drove past his own house.

Naturally, George had wondered what might be causing these 'blackouts'. Of course he'd Googled it, triple-checked Wikipedia and surfed various medical websites. Having read through countless pages online and created a number of fanciful self-diagnoses, George had decided the closest match seemed to be something called a 'Dissociative Fugue State'.

Apparently, sufferers of Dissociative Fugue can lose their sense of personal identity and have been known to wander impulsively or travel away from their homes or places of work. Although George didn't think he had any problems with his sense of identity – he knew who he was: boring old George Thring – the impulsive travel certainly seemed to be a good fit.

In most cases, 'episodes' were triggered by a traumatic event. Again, George had trouble thinking of any traumatic events in his life – not since that time at the wildlife park and that had been so long ago that it couldn't be a cause. George's life now was so unexciting that the 'tomato soup' incident was about as traumatic as things got. And he was sure he had enough mental fortitude to cope with something like that without flipping out and driving halfway to Wales.

Deep down, George wondered whether there might be another cause for his random, unplanned journeys. He simply did not want to go home.

Sometimes he just couldn't face the echo round the cold walls of his house as the key scraped in the lock. He couldn't bear walking into a dark, empty house with no-one to greet him and ask about his day, kiss him lightly on the cheek and tell him dinner was nearly ready. No kids' hair to ruffle and no homework to be helped with. Only a small, empty flat; a fridge full of unappetising food; and a television to talk at him from the corner of the room. And so sometimes George would just drive, subconsciously putting off the inevitable.

But it was more than the empty house. How can a man go home and be satisfied with his life when he is so full of regret at the simple things he hasn't done in a day? How could he walk through his front door, sit on his sofa and pretend that his life was adequate; that he wasn't dreaming deep down in his heart that he were somebody else, doing something different, living somebody else's life?

So George would drive past his house and just carry on driving. Secretly, he liked the soothing nature of it all; the way his mind could drift off; the subconscious way his body would take over the driving. His feet on the pedals;

his hands on the steering wheel; his eyes watching the road; all seemingly separate entities from his brain. His arm somehow simply knew to change gear at the right time, without George's brain having to tell it. The body would drive the car, leaving George with plenty of time to sit and contemplate; to ponder and wonder and not really have to think too hard about his surroundings or his place among them.

He liked the gentle rumble of the tyres on the road; the soft deep hum of the engine; the warm air blowing slowly from the vents on the dashboard. He liked the calming nature of it: how it cocooned him from the world; the gentle heartbeat of the car carefully rocking and soothing him; like some kind of psychological return to the womb – if you wanted to think of it in those terms, which George never did because that all seemed a bit deep and involved and it made him think of a new-born baby all covered in blood and sticky stuff, which made him feel uncomfortable and a little bit queasy.

It didn't matter where George drove to – whether he got stuck in traffic on a busy dual carriageway or cruised effortlessly along a scenic country lane – he would just drive. Drive and think, and try to come to terms with his life. He would reconcile his day in his head, with all the disappointments and lost opportunities, and make a secret pact with himself that tomorrow would not be such a disappointing day. He would definitely do the things he wanted to do and not end the day driving past his own house thinking about all the day's disappointments. "Carpe Diem," he would recite to himself, like some demented mantra.

"Seize the Day, George," he would order himself, staring into the eyes reflected in the rear view mirror. "Be bold, George. Be bold and brave, and make things happen."

And then the 'episode' would end. He'd turn the car around and go home satisfied that tomorrow would be better. It would be the tomorrow that George deserved.

Either that, or he would suddenly realise that he was actually very hungry and he should probably eat something soon because he didn't want to get low blood sugar levels and pass out at the wheel and accidentally plough into a group of girl scouts on a hike or something. So he'd better go home and have a spot of dinner and think more about things a bit later on. Except he'd go home, have some dinner, get stuck in front of the television and completely lose his train of thought. Until he was driving home again the next day.

But this was no ordinary day. For as George drove past his house, as he had done so many times before, he started to think of lots of other things he hadn't done that day. He started to think about how he hadn't taught anybody how to scuba dive that day. For that matter, he hadn't learned how to scuba dive himself.

He hadn't gone to a bullfight, nor had he gone on an international treasure hunt. He hadn't made a killing on the stock market. He hadn't killed another person – though he had to admit that he was actually quite glad about that because he probably wouldn't have wanted to kill another person, not without a really good reason anyway. But nevertheless it was another thing he hadn't done.

He thought about the fact that he hadn't eaten the biggest hamburger in the world, or the tastiest piece of cherry pie. He hadn't run off with the circus to become a lion tamer – though again George thought this probably a wise move as he wasn't really that fond of any animals, let alone the type likely to bite your head off should you stick it into their mouth.

And, of course, there was that other business with the lion when he was just a boy, that he didn't like to dwell upon.

He hadn't bought a motorbike. He hadn't bought a sofa.

George hadn't eaten five Mars bars in a row. He hadn't set off the fire alarm for a prank. He hadn't gone to the pet shop at lunch, bought 20 hamsters and let them loose in the office, causing mass hamster-related panic. He hadn't taken all his clothes off, painted his willy blue and run through the office shouting, "Help, I'm being attacked by a Smurf!"

It seemed to George that there were a great many things that he hadn't done that day. Yet the more things he thought of, the more came, until he felt like he was trapped in a great whirlwind of ideas, crashing, whizzing, zooming and spinning around him in his tiny little car.

And as George continued to think about all the things he hadn't done that day, he carried on driving, getting further and further from his house. A house that, for whatever reason, had disappeared completely from his mind. And, most unusual of all, George didn't even feel the slightest bit hungry.

CHAPTER 2

TUESDAY

GEORGE Thring woke at exactly 7.13am, a full two minutes before his alarm was set to wake him. This happened every day. George would wake up two minutes earlier than his alarm clock was primed to go off. He'd never actually get up at 7.13am, of course. The alarm was set for quarter past and he didn't see why he should get up earlier than he needed to. So instead he'd just lie there, thinking.

Thinking about life. Thinking about how life could be, or should be. He'd lie there contemplating the cruelty of his brain stealing those two minutes of sleep from him. The frustration of being awake two whole minutes before he actually needed to be.

Recently, George had actually come to enjoy those two minutes. Instead of seeing them as stolen moments of sleep, he'd come to regard them as a gift. It was his two minutes of peace, when his world-weary brain could happily ignore the rest of existence. He could linger there, halfway between sleep and awake. He needn't worry about his life, or work, or the commute into the office, or what to make for dinner that night. He could simply lie there and think about whatever he wanted to. He could imagine himself as anyone he wanted to be.

Some days he was a brave fire-fighter: tackling blazes; climbing ladders; rescuing helpless kittens from trees – always with a wink for the ladies who seemed to love him in that uniform. Other days he was a high-flying stockbroker on Wall Street, trading stocks, nipping out for champagne lunches, making millions in a day and driving expensive cars.

He'd been a pilot, an astronaut, a world famous surgeon, a secret spy with a license to kill, a stand-up comedian who always left people in stitches. In those two minutes every morning, George had led some of the most incredible lives.

His favourite fantasy, however, was to imagine himself as a simple, happy family man. He wasn't even sure what his job was in this dream. It never really mattered, as the whole thing focused around him helping a smiling, fair-haired boy with his maths homework and watching a giggly, long-haired daughter demonstrate her latest ballet lesson before tucking them both in and reading them a bed-time story. It was as simple as that, but it was the one that made him smile the most.

As varied and fanciful as George's fantasies were, one thing was always the same. He always had a beautiful wife to come home to. Someone there to ask about his terribly exciting day. Someone to curl up with on the sofa. Someone to make mad, passionate, steamy love to – providing he wasn't too tired from his day's various adventures. And someone to wake up next to – which always made George feel just a little sad, when he finally woke up to find he was, like every day, alone.

And so George lay there, on that cold Tuesday morning, thinking and waiting. Enjoying that brief recess before the rest of the world came calling.

Finally the harsh buzz of the alarm clock blared out: stabbing at his ear drums; smacking him cruelly in the face. He reached out a weary arm, patted around on the dresser and found the clock's off button. For a second his thumb contemplated the big, enticing oblong snooze button, with its promise of just a few more moments respite from the world – nine minutes of peace before the new day fully tumbled down on top of him.

But where does that ever really get you? Thought George, his hand sliding down his body to scratch absentmindedly at his crotch. Aside from putting off the inevitable?

And so the alarm clock was halted for good, and with a heavy sigh George lifted his head and threw back the duvet.

It was dark in George's bedroom – practically still night – and the cold February air leapt at him, stinging his bare toes and making him shiver. His legs ached slightly as he climbed out of bed. With eyes still only half open, he staggered his way across to the bedroom door, bouncing off the same wall he bounced off every morning and tutting the same tut he tutted every day.

He made his way to the bathroom, climbed into the shower and after a few minutes of rejuvenating water splashing on his head he began to come out of his zombie-like fog. His usual washing routine – working the soap downwards in exact concentric circles across the surface of his skin, then back up to allow his fingers to savagely massage his face – lasted the same six minutes and forty seconds it always did. Another sixty seconds standing idly to allow the conditioner to do whatever it did to his hair, and George methodically rinsed and climbed back out of the shower, brushed his teeth then went to the toilet. All as regular as clockwork.

He stood looking at himself in the mirror, the face staring back at him slightly distant and unfamiliar. How had he come to look like this? The grey hair at his temples was increasing daily, spreading back over his head in two silver streaks, and at least five or six years before he thought he probably should have them.

His face wasn't exactly wrinkled but it looked heavy and tired, the skin sagging slightly, pulling his features downwards. How had he become so old? It was a world away from the tight-skinned young man with thick, lustrous blonde locks that he remembered. Or did he remember? Maybe he'd never looked like that, just imagined it. Perhaps he'd always been this tired, greying 36-year-old man that stared back.

George had never liked his face, not really. He'd always thought it seemed far too serious for him and he could never really make it smile properly. The mouth always looked forced when he tried: held in place by the correct muscles but never looking quite right. All teeth and dry lips forced over a clenched jaw. Happy and unhappy, all at once. And his eyes always looked so sad. He didn't exactly feel sad, but one look into his own eyes was enough to depress even himself on some days.

George trudged back to the bedroom, opened the wardrobe and dressed in one of his standard grey suits and white shirts. He had four suits all exactly the same make, fit and colour. He didn't particularly enjoy wearing suits, so he thought: why bother having different colours? Why add the extra choice? With only one suit to choose from there was no decision to make.

Some of the guys in his office seemed to wear a different suit every day of the month. How they could cope with deciding, day-in, day-out, which one would be right for each particular day? George's suit was smart and seemed suitably appropriate for sitting behind a desk all day. And with four suits all the same, he could easily rotate usage of jackets and trousers, ensuring even wear and making them all last that little bit longer.

Not that he worried about money, of course. He'd never had to worry about money. He just didn't relish the prospect of having to go shopping again before it was absolutely necessary.

With his white shirt, George opted to wear a red tie with little pictures of penguins dotted about at random intervals. It was quite a jazzy tie, George thought. He liked jazzy ties. Where he was quite happy to wear the same dull, grey suit and standard white shirt every day, he did like to make an effort with his ties.

He had a lot of ties, in many colours, with a variety of patterns. Some were comical, some geometric, some simple and understated. Some were positively garish and outlandish. He liked to think his ties reflected his personality to a certain extent – his one piece of style and flair amid a fairly unobtrusive outward appearance. He hoped people would notice the effort he made with his ties and realise he wasn't actually as dull and boring as he assumed they found him to be.

Of course, he'd never actually got around to wearing any of the really vibrant ties. He would really like them when he first saw them. He'd like what they said and what they could be made to say about him. He imagined the startled reactions as he strolled into the office: "Hey, have you seen George today? What's with that crazy tie? My God, that guy's got personality!" They made him smile. They made him feel warm inside and he thought they might project some of that warmth at others.

Of course, whenever he actually went to put on the tie with bright red-and-yellow check; or the garish orange number with big purple flowers; or, his very favourite, the blue tie with characters from Wallace and Gromit repeated across it; he was instantly struck with a fear that he'd end up drawing too much attention to himself. "Have you seen that guy George?" he imagined people saying. "Who does he think he is, wearing a tie like that?"

And so he would invariably replace it on his fancy electric tie organiser and opt for a safer pattern. Nothing that would get him noticed too much.

But today George felt different. He couldn't quite put his finger on why, but, seemingly without any real thought at all, he found himself pulling out his red penguin tie, sliding it carefully around his neck and tying it in a perfect double Windsor knot. He smiled at himself in the mirror and for once the smile looked right.

He made his way downstairs and turned on the television to watch the breakfast news. He had a cup of coffee with two slightly burned pieces of wholemeal toast, lightly spread with a type of margarine that was supposed to help lower cholesterol. George had no idea whether or not he actually needed his cholesterol to be lowered but he'd seen the worrying adverts on the television and he wasn't taking any chances.

******

George had a very boring job. It was so boring that George often wondered if he must be a very dull person himself for having such an uninteresting job. But he didn't think so. He didn't feel like a boring person. He knew quite a few boring people, and he knew he wasn't like them, so he thought it safe to assume that he was not boring himself. No, George had a happy soul – an exciting, vibrant soul, full of life and bursting with energy and all the possibilities of the world. Only people could never see it, because, in fairness, George was not that good at expressing his bright side.

Deep inside George was vivacious, commanding, debonair, exciting. Only, on the outside, he didn't really like to make too much of a fuss. He was happy hovering in the background, just out of sight, keeping out of the way, trying not to be too much of a bother to anyone else. Not that he didn't sort of dream of being the centre of attention, earning people's respect and admiration. And neither did he feel as though he was not deserving of the same respect and admiration. It was always just easier, somehow, when people left him to get on by himself.

No doubt people thought George a little dreary, but little did they know. Little could they see the dreams and thoughts in his head; the desires; the emotions. All they saw was a meek, timid little man, always friendly and polite, always happy to help, always there but not really there. Like a plant or an office fixture, George was always there when people needed him – when they wanted reports, or favours, or sandwiches from the shop. But when they didn't he wasn't really that noticeable. He blended into the background.

George worked in a modest office, as part of a small team, and for the most part it was fine. The work was easy enough and, as long as he kept his head down and his output to the required level, and tried to stay out of everybody's way, he could put up with it.

That's not to say that George liked his job. George did not like his job. He found the work boring and far beneath his levels of capability. He didn't really like the company of his fellow employees – not that they were bad people of course; it's just that George never really got to know them and they had made little effort to get to know him.

He was a very organised person. He liked order and he liked routine. One year, at his annual staff appraisal, George's boss made a special note of George's organisational skills. *George Thring*, he had written, *is a very competent worker and is very organised.* At the time George had been quite pleased about this accreditation, for being competent and organised were surely two elements any worker would be pleased to list among their own unique skill-set.

But George had often looked back at that recommendation. Clearly it was not a bad statement. There was no rebuke there, nor any sentiment of dissatisfaction stated. But, thought George, was that really how he was seen? Were those the nicest things that could have been said? Were those the two attributes that George most clearly demonstrated?

He imagined how other people's appraisals might have read:

Gloria is very passionate about her work and tackles every opportunity with enthusiasm and a clear head.
Carol is a real character around the office and everybody loves her.
Jim is incredibly smart and an asset to the team.

George was 'competent' and 'organised'. Not the highest praise he could have hoped for and not what he wanted for himself. He wanted to be known as 'a character'. He wanted to be loved. He wanted to be seen as enthusiastic. More than that he wanted to actually *be* enthusiastic. But just how enthusiastic, thought George, can a person ever really be about a job they have little enthusiasm for?

******

At exactly 8.15am George picked up his car keys, turned off the television, exhaled a long, slow, breathy sigh and walked out the front door of his house.

It was a bitter February Tuesday morning, and, although a big, yellow sun hung tantalisingly in the sky offering promises of warmth and summer and happiness, a cruel icy wind whistled around George's ankles and scooted up under his jacket, pinching his legs and slapping at his belly. He shuddered slightly as he noticed the ice on the windows of his little grey hatchback, before unlocking the door and retrieving the luminous-green plastic ice-scraper.

Five minutes later and George was finally inside the warm, womb-like confines of his little car as the heaters worked overtime, blowing air into his face. He reversed out of his drive, made his way to the end of the road, turned left onto Cromwell Street and directly into the depressing queue of cars he would sit in for the next 35 minutes as he crawled slowly towards work.

George had often wondered whether he'd be quicker riding a bicycle to work, weaving in and out of the traffic, blasting through the gaps at speed, laughing at all the poor souls stuck in their little tin boxes as he advanced daredevil-like down the road with not a care in the world and nothing to stand in his way.

But it was cold mornings like this, and the fact that he hadn't really worked out properly in quite some years, that made him glad of his little car. Better to sit in traffic and get there gradually than to arrive at work red-faced and panting, sweating profusely and chancing the inevitable coronary. Not to mention risking life and limb on the roads.

Eventually the traffic eased and George made his way into the dark, soulless, grey industrial estate where he worked. What a joyless little pocket of depression it was. A cramped cul-de-sac of big grey buildings, seemingly all with blanked-out windows. A few grimy motor repair workshops; a couple of warehouses; the huge green We-Store-For-U storage facility; and then, at the end of the row, four nondescript office blocks, each as lacking in identity as the next.

George pulled into the car park outside his own office building, parked and made his way in. He nodded, as he did every day, to Sheila, the middle-aged receptionist who sat behind the expansive desk in the lobby. He received, as he did every day, no more than a contemptuous frown in return. He wasn't sure whether she was this disengaging to everyone who worked there or whether she had taken against him personally and gave him extra special treatment.

Bypassing the small silver elevator, George opted to take the stairs up to his fifth floor office. It was a quite a number of stairs to tackle, but George didn't take the lift. Not since the time he got trapped in there with two overweight builders and had to spend 45 minutes crammed in the tiny silver box, which seemed to be getting smaller with every second, trying not to think about hanging – literally – by a wire over a huge chasm; gripping his hands into tight fists in his pockets and trying to avoid descending into a full-scale anxiety attack. Besides, he reasoned, the exercise would probably do him good. Maybe help to get that cholesterol down a bit.

Slightly out of breath, and trying not to show it, George made it to his desk at precisely 8.59am, a full minute early. This still didn't seem good enough for the rest of his 'team', who'd all no doubt been in since 7.30. As if synchronised, they all looked at their watches as George sat down.

George offered his usual friendly good morning to Clive, Louise and Anton. The three returned an impatient "Morning" without actually looking up from their screens, pausing only slightly before returning to the incessant tap-tapping on their keyboards.

George turned on his computer. He sat quietly as he allowed it to warm up, absent-mindedly stroking the tip of his red penguin tie. All that fuss, all that fear, and no-one had even noticed it.

The screen burst into life with a mechanical tune and George noticed that he already had 17 e-mails waiting for him in his inbox. He deleted them all without reading them, then stood up and walked to the vending machine for a cup of coffee.

******

George had always felt slightly out of place as a member of the team. And, in truth, he was rather out of place. He didn't share the enthusiasm, the drive, or even the interest the other guys did. He had no intentions of arriving early in the morning or staying late in the evening. A day's work was a day's work, and whatever you couldn't fit in between 9am and 5.30pm could surely wait for the next day.

Not that it was ever a problem. George prided himself on always managing to do the task at hand in the allotted time. And he always managed to clear his desk before he went home in the evening. It seemed odd to him, as he watched Louise typing frantically, surely making more mistakes than if she were to take her time over the task, how she allowed herself to get so frazzled and always desperate to meet deadlines. He couldn't understand how Clive, even though having turned up a good hour early for work, would invariably spend all afternoon complaining that there just wasn't enough time to get everything done, before sighing, "Looks like it's gonna be another late night for me." Were they just very poorly organised?

Anton, the team leader, took great joy in pointing out where they were all going wrong and how they could improve their time management. He once even subjected the whole group to what he called a time-and-motion study, pulling apart every small detail and offering ingratiating, condescending advice on the areas in which they might improve. Because Anton was never flustered or rushed, he always seemed far more in control. Yet, despite being the most organised and professional of the group, Anton also seemed to spend more time in the office than anybody else.

At just 23-years-old, Anton was by far the youngest of the team. And it was quite a bone of contention with the other two that he had been elevated to the status of team leader – a position they had both coveted greatly. They hated that he held that slight fraction of power above their heads. George could actually hear Louise's teeth grating when Anton would give one of his team-leader speeches. He could see Clive's face reddening, as if it were about to explode.

Anton was a thin, wiry man, with pointed features and long, gangly limbs. George always thought he looked a bit like a stick insect, only thinner.

And he looked young. He was young, of course, but he looked even younger, like he was on work experience from the local comprehensive. Which, again, really seemed to annoy the other members of the team, who had to listen to his management drivel.

He had slicked back hair; wore a cheap suit with different-coloured garish striped shirts; and was one of these new executive types that shunned the wearing of ties. Too busy to tie it in the morning, no doubt, so eager was he to get into the office. George wondered whether, being so young, perhaps nobody

15

had ever taught him how to tie a tie and he didn't wear one simply because he couldn't.

The whole combination resulted in someone who looked like they'd been dressed by their mum, and been assured that it made them look really grown-up. Which it did not.

But, as Team Leader, Anton thought it necessary to show a shining example of leadership and would always be first in and last to leave. He'd arrive at the office earlier than anybody, then make sure to send a group e-mail to the rest of the team – something tedious about projected targets, or upcoming meetings, nothing that couldn't have waited to be said in person – just to make sure that the e-mail's time-stamp acted as physical authentication of when he had arrived at work.

On a really good day he'd be able to think up something with the slightest relevance to the managers above him, so that he could copy them in on the email and his early appearance in the office would travel up the ladder to those in charge. Sometimes, if he'd made a gallant effort to stay particularly late, he'd e-mail an end-of-day report to the team, just so they knew how dedicated he was in staying later than everybody else.

For a short period, both Clive and Louise fought back, trying their hardest to stay on later and arrive earlier in the morning. But it never worked. No matter what time they made it in, Anton would already be behind his desk, smiling that satisfied smile. Whenever they tackled his evening resilience, hunger or tiredness would always overcome them and they just couldn't match him.

Finally, they'd all heard the rumour that one day, in order to really stamp his authority, Anton had apparently shown up at the office at 5.30am. It was so early that Geoff, the night-shift security guard, refused to let him in and he'd had to sit in his car in the car park, working from a laptop, until Geoff finally unlocked the doors to let the cleaners in and couldn't refuse him any longer. After that the other two knew they were beaten and quickly gave up.

George, of course, was never interested in competing. Nine to five-thirty was more than enough time to spend in the office, thank you very much. And he had no interest in trying to prove his devotion for his job to those around him because, in truth, he had no devotion to his job. And he was fairly certain that Clive and Louise, and probably even Anton, would rather have the extra sleep than trawl themselves into work in the middle of the night. They just couldn't be seen to lack dedication and drive, not if they were going to get on in the company.

George felt a bit sorry for Anton. He was very ambitious, and George had no doubts that he would go far and be very successful indeed. He clearly had his sights set on bigger things and was the very model of a perfect employee: courteous and complimentary and always agreeable. Always desperate to prove he could be that little bit better than everybody else, even if it meant denigrating others' achievements and capabilities in order to further accentuate his own successes.

But what kind of a life did he have? At 23 he should have been enjoying himself. Living for the weekends, binge-drinking and clubbing until the early hours. Drinking on a school night and coming in the next day unshaven with an un-ironed shirt. Not turning himself into this corporate robot, this work-obsessed, goal-oriented clone. No doubt he would become an achiever, but at what cost?

Louise was every bit as aggressive and ambitious as Anton. She had a bit of a chip on her shoulder, George always thought. A feminist convinced the higher male powers were always trying to keep her down; trying to thwart her advance through the ranks just because she was a woman. "If it wasn't for what I've got in my bra," she often told George, "I'd be running this company by now. But they're just too afraid to let a woman in the club. Too afraid I'll expose the inadequacies they've been hiding all these years."

And in a way they were afraid, but not for the reasons she assumed. She made no attempt to hide the fact that she thought she was better than those above her. She made no bones about wanting to take their jobs from under them at the earliest possible opportunity. And so it really wasn't an issue of gender; she was a victim of her own success. They kept her down, precisely because they didn't want her to succeed and edge them all out. Much better to promote someone like Anton – keen, eager, hardworking, successful and, above all else, easy to keep in his place.

Clive's motivations for success were born primarily out of fear. At 52-years-old, Clive was well aware that this was probably his final job. With so many eager young Antons out there, with more qualifications than Clive had ever achieved and with the added bonus that they'd work for less money, Clive knew it was only a matter of time before he became obsolete.

He'd been with the company for 14 years, headhunted from his previous employer, and although he knew a fair redundancy would await him, the offers were unlikely to come flooding in after that. And where would that leave his all-important pension? He had no real drive to make the company successful any more, he just didn't want to be forced into early retirement before his pension had reached full maturity. And for that reason he worked harder than anybody. And carried twice the stress.

His belly was expanding at an astonishing rate due to the sugary foods he packed in throughout the day and the energy drinks he quaffed to keep up his momentum when dealing with the younger, fitter members of the squad. And his hair had definitely receded more – possibly due to the way he would run his hands through it; pulling it back and tautening his wrinkled forehead in moments of severe worry. A balding, increasingly obese, red-faced worrier; constantly perplexed and anxious, aggressive and bitter; on the rise and fall of various sugar highs.

They were the marketing department. A strange little group with not an ounce of friendship between them. They shared four L-shaped desks, carefully conjoined in a big square formation. It had not escaped George's attention that viewed from above it would probably resemble a giant swastika. The connotations of that made him smile a little.

To the right of George sat Louise, to the left sat Clive and diagonally across from him sat Anton. George didn't really like sitting in such close proximity to the others but he reasoned that if it had to be this way, at least he benefited most favourably from the arrangement. With Anton so far away he had no need, like the other two, to purposely angle his computer monitor away from Anton's view.

Both Clive and Louise were aware that Anton sometimes secretly shifted the angle of their screens so that he could effectively monitor what they were up to throughout the day. He'd no real need to do it, of course, as neither of them ever did anything outside the bounds of strict work protocol. Even at lunchtimes they denied themselves the supposed pleasures of Facebook, Twitter and eBay, just in case they gave any ground in their little three-way war.

George also really didn't mind sitting next to Louise. She was a very attractive woman – George guessed about 28 or 29 years old – always very presentable, with long blonde hair tied back to make her look more professional, and thin-rimmed glasses that gave her that sexy secretary look. Not that George would have dared say that to her face, for fear of being slapped for mentioning the S-word – 'secretary' not 'sexy'! She was an executive, and God help anyone who didn't afford her the proper respect. A sexy executive, nonetheless.

In summer she'd wear low-cut lycra tops that really accentuated her shapely figure and prominent breasts. And while George never openly gawped or leered at her, he did reason that there were certainly worse things that he could have occupying his peripheral vision.

In fact, one quiet Thursday afternoon, when Louise was deeply ensconced in a particularly long and important phone call and the power-saving function on her computer had turned her monitor to black, George looked over and realised that the 'anti-Anton' positioning of her screen had left it at the perfect angle to reflect right down the front of her top. He'd felt a little embarrassed at first, suddenly able to gawp at her cleavage, and instantly looked away. But he soon found himself having a little peek again, moments later.

Now he often actually looked forward to her long phone calls, when the monitor would transform into his secret mirror. Not in a pervy way, of course! But because it was his little secret; something to smile about, something to break the monotony.

In truth, George didn't know what 'marketing' actually was and he had no idea how he'd become a Marketing Analyst. He was an accountant, really, and was used to working with numbers and figures. He was more a kind of back-up to the marketing team: the analyst who assessed the figures from the various contracts and projects and reported back to the creative elements of the group.

George had started in the accounts department of the company and somehow found himself transferred across to work with these new people, none of whom had much respect for George's role within the department but all of who were more than happy to ask for his advice or help when dealing with the trickier parts of their own jobs. 'Numbers Man,' Anton had taken to calling him. George really didn't like it.

"You're my main man, George, when it comes to dealing with these pesky numbers," Anton had once said to him.

Yes, and you're my main man when it comes to being a weaselly, bum-licking, self-important little prick, George had thought – but been too well-mannered to actually say.

Four desks in one; everybody else's paperwork threatening to avalanche onto George's pristine work area. George had nightmares of actually drowning in facts and figures; being washed away, kicking and screaming, spluttering and wailing, in a tidal wave of spreadsheets and statistical analysis.

But the thing that really annoyed George about the others was the horrendous marketing buzzwords that they used. They left George cold and confused. "F.Y.I., George," they used to say. F.Y. what? Why can't these people just speak in plain English?

"George, can you let me know the state of play with that data?" State of play?

"George, I need those figures by the end of play today?" What play? It's not a game. There's no play here. Play indicates fun, doesn't it? This isn't fun. Tedious, boring, mind-numbing, dull. These are all words that could describe working in that department. George couldn't honestly see how 'play' came into it. Did these people actually think this was fun in some way?

As far as George could see, nobody was having any fun at all.

******

With the hot coffee burning his hand, George settled back down at his desk, jogged the mouse to upset the screensaver and looked at the various tasks he had set out to tackle that day. None of them looked particularly interesting so he closed his eyes, counted to ten, then opened them up again, deciding to work on the first file his eyes landed on. *'Statistical Analysis of Marketing Mail Shot to Company Directors in Greater London',* the file name seemed to yawn back at him. George double-clicked the icon, sighing softly under his breath, as a heavily detailed spreadsheet sprang open before him.

He had no idea what the figures referred to and he wasn't sure exactly what he was supposed to analyse. But then he didn't really care either. He probably should have known what the data was about. No doubt there would be a boring meeting at some point, up in the hot, stuffy, oxygen-draining meeting room, to outline what the data was and why it was so important.

In fact, it was entirely possible that George had already sat through a meeting explaining why the figures in front of him were so important and he just hadn't taken any of it in. George clicked a few boxes, opened up another blank spreadsheet and titled it *Findings*. He then sat back and sipped at the chemical-tasting coffee in the small plastic cup.

It was doubtless going to be another boring day. No different to any other. No excitement, no enjoyment, nothing of any particular worth or merit. Just the usual looking at spreadsheets; balancing figures; writing dry, uninteresting reports. And he had a couple of meetings scheduled as well.

It was warm in the office, and George was already feeling a little drowsy from the lack of oxygen.

CHAPTER 3

THE sun was almost gone. Only a bright, golden, orange-and-pink haze lingered on the horizon beneath the increasingly dark, thick crust of night sky. The little grey car hummed and sighed wearily as it coursed along on its mysterious journey. George gazed blankly out of the windscreen at the road ahead; seeing and not seeing, taking nothing in, still lost in a cloud of thought.

The longer that George drove, and the further he travelled away from his house, the more he thought about all the things he wished he had done that day and all the things he wished he could and would do. The things he should be doing.

He should be writing a book. He should be doing an online Open University course in quantum physics. He should be having an office romance with a busty, blonde secretary; sending her racy emails throughout the day and sneaking off with her at lunchtimes for intimate encounters in the car park behind B&Q.

He should be playing practical jokes on co-workers: super-gluing phones to people's ears. He should be leaving spurious faked documents containing details of everybodys' salaries in the photocopier for people to find, or filling peoples' desk drawers with jelly beans.

He should be engaged in industrial espionage, selling company secrets and financial records to interested third parties. He should be embezzling company funds and anonymously donating them to a donkey sanctuary. He should be using company time to work on a secret project to build a time-travel machine.

The possibilities were endless. So why was he doing none of them?

Slowly the whirlwind of thoughts and ideas and dreams subsided and George could think clearly again. An epiphany, thought George. That's what I'm having. A revelation. A wake up call.

And as these thoughts permeated his brain and started to settle into something almost like a logical plan of action, George started to notice his surroundings. Or more accurately, George started to notice that he didn't recognise his surroundings. He glanced at the little digital clock in the dashboard and the bright-red neon digits flashed out at him: 22.27. Hmmm, thought George, nearly half past ten.

Nearly half past ten! It took a few seconds for the thought to register fully. Hang on, he interrupted himself, it's nearly half past ten. It was nearly half past ten and George had absolutely no idea where he was.

As if slapped in the face with a big wet hand, George sprang back into life. He suddenly became very aware that he was sitting in his little car. He gazed around and noticed the dark outside. Cold black had crept in unannounced, snuck up behind him and turned everything to night.

He'd left the office at 17.30 sharp, as he did every day. He'd crossed the car park in the average 2 minutes and 17 seconds it usually took, climbed into his car, did his usual checks of safety belt, gear stick and petrol levels, and set off. All of which meant that he'd been driving non-stop for almost five hours.

How had he not noticed how long he'd been driving? How had his bum not become numb and his legs very stiff?

Then George thought about his legs and his buttocks and he realised that he did indeed have stiff legs and a very numb bum. A dull ache tingled in his lower back, slowly, quietly stretching up his spine. The skin on the sole of his right foot had become completely nerveless, almost melded to the pedal throbbing slowly beneath it.

Somewhat anxiously, George scanned the horizon. He looked around him, trying to pick out the slightest clue to where he was: a landmark, a road sign, anything. But everything looked the same. The road in front of him looked very much like any other road. On either side were fields and trees and it was dark, so nothing of any significance stood out. Where the hell am I? He thought.

George didn't even know which direction he'd been driving in; what roads he'd driven on; or even how busy those roads had been – so absorbed had he been in what he was now starting to think of less as an epiphany and more as a nervous breakdown.

I could be literally anywhere! He thought, growing slightly more concerned with each passing second. Or at least, anywhere in a five hour driving radius of where I set off from.

George had seen plenty of police shows where the officers involved were tracking a criminal or trying to catch up with a missing person. They would always calculate roughly what distance someone might have travelled since last seen, then draw a huge circle on a map on the wall, sticking brightly coloured pins in specific locations.

Of course, none of that really helped George as he didn't actually know how far he was likely to have travelled in five hours. Neither did he have a big map on which to draw a large circle. Or any brightly coloured pins.

But he did have numbers. He knew the numbers could help.

He had set off five hours ago and, from what he could remember, he'd been travelling at a pretty steady speed. He didn't remember being on a motorway, so he could assume that he had driven out into the countryside. Okay, this is working, he thought, as his pounding heart rate gradually eased and the heat of his blush-red face began to subside.

Since these were country roads and he'd been travelling at around forty or fifty miles an hour, then in five hours he might have travelled 250 miles. That did seem a lot. But then, these were country roads not straight motorways, so if he could find his way to a motorway he may well find that he was only a few hours' drive from home. And if he did find a motorway then he was sure to find a motorway service station, where he could stop for a coffee and a Ginsters and, depending where he was, maybe even a night in a travel lodge.

George exhaled a heavy breath, calmed at having come up with a plan. All he had to do was carry on driving; keep an eye out for signs; find his way to a motorway; and he'd be fine.

And then something quite unexpected happened to George. As he trundled along, mapping in his head the various locations he might feasibly have ended up, looking out at the twinkling cats' eyes dotting the road ahead and the tall dark trees lining the verge, stretching right up into the black of the night, he realised that not knowing where he was didn't actually scare him. When he really thought about it he wasn't scared at all. Not really. He was, if anything, just a little bit excited.

A few weeks ago, a few days maybe, possibly even just hours before, not knowing where he was would have worried George very greatly. But as he continued to drive, and continued not to know where he was, George realised something. He realised that he had now something new to put on his list: something that he *had* done today that he had never done before. Today George had driven non-stop for five hours, without knowing where he was going or in which direction, and had ended up completely unaware of his surroundings. Okay, he hadn't actually meant to do it, but it still counted.

So often had George thought about breaking with his routine: doing something on the spur of the moment; something outlandish and unexpected. He'd dreamed it, imagined it. But every time he'd come to actually do it he was struck with fear and lost his nerve.

But now he'd done it, he'd actually done it! This was an accomplishment. And as he thought these things, and continued to drive, George realised that he was smiling. A great big grin slapped right across the middle of his face, all teeth and happiness.

It was a while since he'd smiled like this. He couldn't remember the last time anything had given him reason to smile such a glorious, face-cracking, beam of a grin. Not since Emily. She'd made him smile. She could always make him smile, even when she wasn't trying. Even when she didn't know that he was looking at her. But that was all in the past and there hadn't been much cause for smiling since.

As George looked out ahead of him, smiling his big smile, he allowed himself to drift off slightly again and dream about what other good things might come. Could this be the start of something exciting? A new chapter to the adventures of George Thring?

Surely, weren't all the possibilities he'd spent the last five hours imagining just that little bit closer to his grasp? Could he actually start doing the things he'd spent so much of his life dreaming about, hoping for, scared to try?

Then George noticed a funny clunking noise coming from the car's engine. A horrible, clanking, banging, grinding sound, mechanical and unhappy. The car started to jolt and lurch, stopping and starting and stopping again. It bunny-hopped along the road for a few more feet before finally signalling its total disapproval and coming to an exasperated, crunching, belligerent halt at the side of the road.

Oh dear, thought George.

It seemed that for the second time that day George was experiencing something of a breakdown. He could see the irony in it, but he didn't much appreciate it.

******

Sitting at the side of the road, the little grey car slumped unhappily on the thin grass verge, George could feel his heart rate suddenly shooting up again.

Oh dear, he thought. Oh dear, oh dear. What's happened? He scanned all around him, looking at the steering wheel, checking his mirrors, glancing at the streak of different coloured lights on the dashboard. For some reason he even found himself looking down at his feet on the pedals, before his eyes rested on the fuel level indicator. And, most notably, the angry-looking little orange light adjacent to it. Oh dear.

George had been driving for so long, not paying any attention to the instruments and indicators in front of him, and the car had simply run out of fuel. And now he was stranded on a cold, dark country road, miles from home and in a completely unknown location. The gleaming smile fell from George's face and a furrowed brow of worry and confusion blinked back at him from the rear-view mirror.

George was not a mechanically-minded person so, when he stepped out of the car at the side of the road, he really didn't know what to do. It was quite dark now and the only light was coming from the car's headlights. Fortunately, George had remembered to keep a torch in the car for precisely this type of emergency. Unfortunately, he hadn't thought to test it out when he'd bought it. He just assumed it would be all right and put it straight in the emergency box in the car.

And so, guided by a light equivalent to that he assumed you'd get from one of those pen lights that doctors use to check your eyes, he strolled carefully and thoughtfully around the grey, sad looking little car, gripping his chin between thumb and index finger, umming and aahing, confused as to what conclusions he was supposed to reach. He made a full circle of the vehicle, inspecting things as closely as he could in the dark: peering at the wheels; checking for smoke or steam escaping from underneath; making sure nothing seemed horribly amiss.

He considered opening the bonnet to look at the engine because that's what other people seemed to do in such circumstances. And that's what he assumed you were supposed to do. But unless the problem was extremely obvious and jumped right out at him, George didn't think he would have known what to look for. He didn't, in all honesty, know what all the different parts of the engine actually were and still had to refer to the little instruction book when it came to putting in oil or windscreen washer. And even if George did manage to figure out what was wrong with the car, he wouldn't actually have known what to do to remedy the situation.

Still, he felt honour-bound at least to investigate, so he reached in under the steering wheel, pulled at the little release lever and walked back round to lift the heavy, metal bonnet.

Two minutes later, after a thorough inspection of the various dark, dirty metal things, and all the mysterious tubes and pipes and bits of wire, George closed the bonnet again, still none the wiser. He was, of course, 99% certain that the car had simply run out of petrol, as he had been when he looked at the car's petrol gauge. But you never know, and he felt a little better – almost manly – for having at least had a look. Best phone for the breakdown people, he thought.

He reached into his pocket and retrieved his mobile phone, which, rather typically, was indicating that it had no signal. George again looked around, surveying the landscape. One long narrow road, almost pitch black, enclosed on either side by hedge-lined ditches and long, empty fields beyond.

It was starting to get cold, George noticed, as little white clouds of breath drifted from his mouth and flew up into the sky like lost balloons. Now what is it they say, George thought, about when you break down? Stay with the car.

Or is it stay *in* the car? Or maybe *don't* stay in the car? Either way, it was only going to get colder and, with no engine, there wouldn't be any way to make the heaters work. Would there? He was sure you needed the engine on to make the heaters work. Didn't you?

It was all academic anyway because he still had no way to let anybody know what had happened or where he was. He could take the chance of waiting around and hoping someone might wander past and find him, but another quick glance at the road told George this was not really the type of road that people just wander past on.

With his hand clamped tightly to the small torch, George took another full circuit around the car, sighing softly, and decided to go in search of a petrol station. He couldn't remember having passed one on his way there, but then he couldn't actually remember much of anything on his way there. So he decided that, as with most things in life, the best option was to keep going forwards.

He turned off the car's headlights and flicked on the hazard warning lights, making his surroundings even darker, and ever more eerie as the road and trees ahead flashed orange with each blink of the little car's distress beacon. With a deep sigh he headed off in the direction in which he'd been travelling.

25

CHAPTER 4

THE road ahead was long and dark and seemed simply to stretch on and on until the hedges on either side met in the middle. As the small torch penetrated the thick darkness, lighting up only the smallest areas at a time like a laser beam tunnelling into the night, George edged his way carefully along the road, checking every few steps that he wasn't wandering too close to the ditch at his side.

It was a cold night and George couldn't help but wish that he'd remembered to bring his big anorak with him that morning. He could see it now in his mind's eye, carefully hung in the cupboard under the stairs — left there because it was just too thick to fit comfortably under his seat belt in the car and he'd thought he could do without it.

Now, as the cold bit into his cheeks and his nose grew more numb by the second, it seemed a foolhardy error he couldn't believe he'd made. Oh well, thought George, at least I can thank my lucky stars that it isn't raining. And with that thought still wandering slowly through the corridors of his mind, George felt a rather large, rather wet, drop of rain slap down onto the top his head.

Moments later George was soaked through as the heavens opened and a wild, thrashing storm cascaded down upon him. He turned to look at the car, briefly considering dashing back, locking himself inside and escaping the downpour. But he was already soaked and by the time he'd made it back to the safe, dry confines of the car, it would be too late anyway. He knew it was better to push on and hope he found shelter where he could make a phone call and find rescue. But what if shelter was still far away? He could be walking for miles, caught in this terrible storm, risking pneumonia or hypothermia, or something even worse.

Backwards or forwards? Carry on, or run for shelter? George stood there, dithering in the rain.

Just then, somewhere in the distance behind his car, George saw the outlines of two bright, white beams of light bending around the corner of the road. A car! It must be a car, thought George, thankful that rescue had managed to find him.

He started back in the direction he'd come from, waving his arms wildly, trying to catch the attention of the forthcoming vehicle. And as he started running, anxious not to let the car speed past without seeing him, waving his tiny torch as fast and wide as he could, he momentarily took his eyes away from where he was walking.

George's foot landed on a large, sticky-soft patch of mud. He slipped, losing his footing. His heel shifted under his weight and slid out from beneath him. His weight and speed carried him forwards, tumbling and stumbling, crashing down onto the soaking muddy floor before him. He skidded, the rain-slicked floor fuelling his momentum, as he slid headfirst into the cold, wet, dank, muddy ditch at the side of the road.

He landed hard on his back, all the air whooshing from his lungs in one loud grunt. The sound of the approaching vehicle grew louder.

George flailed, winded and disorientated, slapping around in the mud, trying to heave himself up. The rumble of the car got closer, the air vibrating slightly with the engine sound.

George knew he had to get back to the road. He had to stop the car.

Muddied, cold and drenched, his eyes foggy with dirt, George managed to pull himself back out of the ditch, clawing at the slick, sticky thatch of soaking earth and grass before him. He fought to catch a foothold, slipping and sliding several times. The light grew stronger as the car got closer.

With one final, heroic thrust, George heaved himself up out of the ditch, clambering to his feet and lurched into the centre of the road, waving his arms wildly, shouting loudly. And then it occurred to George that he was essentially just a dark, muddy mess, not very visible and standing in the middle of the road as a speeding car came hurtling towards him. A car that would, more than likely, drive straight into him.

George very quickly took a few well-timed steps to the left and stood at the side of the road, still valiantly waving his arms and shouting, very loudly, desperate to be heard over the rain.

To his great relief, the car came to a very abrupt stop a few feet on from where he stood.

******

"You're soaked through," the man said, none too helpfully.

"Er... yes... that does seem to the be the case," returned George, still soaked through, covered in mud and getting wetter by the second in the pouring rain.

The man craned his neck out through the driver's side window, peered back to the shivering little heap of George's car, then spun round to look at George again. "What happened then?" he asked. "Car break down?"

George fought the urge to applaud the man on his apparent excellence in stating the obvious, and chose instead to reply with, "Yes, right again. I don't suppose you'd have a phone I could borrow, to call for help?"

"Phone? I can do better than that. There's a town just along the road. Little garage there. I'll give you a tow and you can get your car fixed."

"Oh, thank you," said George, the rain trickling down his face and running into his mouth. "That's so kind of you."

"No problem, chief. So what happened then, alternator gone? Blown gasket?"

"Erm…" hesitated George, not wanting to admit his ignorance on the subject. He was, of course, also keen to hide his own ineptitude in having allowed the car to simply run out of petrol. "Yes, the… er, gasket, I think."

Ten minutes later and George's car was hooked up to the back of the man's vehicle. George sat in the passenger seat of the stranger's car, still soaked and shivering, but grateful to be out of the rain. He held his hands out to the little slatted grille in the dashboard, rejuvenating heat breathing out onto his skin, drying the rain and bringing life back to his numb fingers.

He was a big man, the stranger. Much bigger than George had expected; his full height and girth hidden by the dark night and his seated position in the car.

He was tall, a good deal over six feet, and heavy built. Not fat, exactly, just big. So big, in fact, that had George seen him simply walking down the road towards him, he might have felt a little fearful, wondering if this giant of a man might just pick him up and… well, George wasn't entirely sure what an unprovoked attack from a strange huge man might entail. But he was sure it wouldn't be nice.

He spoke in a warm, gravelly London accent, in a pitch just slightly higher than George would have expected. It sounded soft and a little squeaky and made George think of a clown squeezing his rubber nose. It also had the effect of slightly reducing the scariness of the man.

He smiled when he spoke, with a slightly cocky, derisive curl to his lips, as if he was making fun of George. It didn't come across as insulting, however. It was friendly, a gentle mocking, as though he'd immediately accepted George as a friend and he was pulling his leg in a matey kind of way. It gave the man a certain charm and George couldn't help but smile back, instantly liking him.

His hair was jet black, combed high into a vibrant, bouncy quiff and he had two thick, bushy sideburns clinging to his cheeks. He looked like he might have felt more at home in a different era – perhaps the 60s or even the 50s.

As George looked more closely, he noticed that the man was wearing a high-collared black shirt with one of those black leather tie straps, fixed with a brooch-like medallion that one only ever saw on cowboys and country and western singers. A ten-gallon hat would not have looked out of place perched on his head and George had to fight the urge to scan the back seat to see if he had one hiding there. He did sneakily try looking at the man's feet to see if he was wearing cowboy boots but it was too dark in the foot-well to see properly.

"So what brings you out this way so late at night?" the man asked, the words gliding from his mouth in that friendly, cockney drawl. "I mean, you are pretty much in the middle of nowhere."

"Am I?" replied George. "Oh dear. Well, I was just out for a little drive really. But I guess I must have driven further than I realised… where exactly are we?"

"Well, we're not too far from London, but kind of out of the way, in the countryside. Just near the Sussex coast. Give it five minutes and we'll be in a little town by the sea. Nothing special, and not too big, but the people are nice."

"Oh. What's it called?" asked George.

"Chidbury. Well, Lower Chidbury to be precise, but everyone just calls it Chidbury nowadays. You know, after what happened to Upper Chidbury."

"Upper Chidbury?"

"Yeah, well, there used to be both, you see. Upper and Lower Chidbury. Lot of history there. Used to be a lot of trouble, years of warring and fighting between the two."

"War?"

"Yeah, well historically, you know. Hundreds of years ago there were wars, disputes about land, angry farm-owners, that sort of thing. Upper Chidbury had the whole of the coastline, you see. Kept it for themselves, and that created a fair old dispute between the 'Coasters' and the 'Landers'.

"That all ended, but there were years of animosity. Some things are never forgotten, I suppose, and the people of the two Chidburys always kind of hated each other. Not exactly full-blown enemies but, you know, rivalry. The Uppers and Lowers would try to outdo each other in competitions. There were always disputes between the two; the councils trying to impose different laws. That sort of nonsense. All over now, though, thankfully."

"Oh good," smiled George. "So what happened? Did the people of Upper and Lower Chidbury resolve their disputes and make peace?"

"Not quite," replied the man, his gravelly voice coughing out a small laugh. "Upper Chidbury fell into the sea."

"Oh," said George, the satisfied smile instantly running off his face. "The whole town fell into the sea?"

"Yeah, well, it is slightly unusual, I'll grant you. About 20 years ago now, it was. Big storm came in off the coast, all of a sudden like, causing havoc, lifting roofs, toppling trees. Carnage everywhere. The noise of the wind was so loud it sounded like God himself was screaming the place down. Woke up in the morning and Upper Chidbury was gone. Just gone. Not there anymore. Fallen in the sea."

"Really? That's awful."

"Oh yeah. It was sad, don't get me wrong. No matter how much you dislike a place, and the people that live there, you wouldn't wish that on anyone."

"And all the people that lived in Upper Chidbury died?"

"Died? Oh God, no. There were only 47 people living there anyway. It was, by far, the smaller part of Chidbury. Thankfully, they were all rescued before it finally went crashing down."

"So what happened to them?"

"Couldn't tell you. Of course they were offered places to stay and could have found homes in Lower Chidbury. But feuds run deeper than you might think. No way they were gonna come and live in the town they'd been at war with. Of course, they did try and blame the folk of Lower for what had happened. Claimed we'd somehow managed to sabotage the border between the two towns and push theirs into the sea. Nonsense, of course," he said, flicking George that devious wink, with a furtive smile.

"Yes, of course."

"No, so they just cleared out. The feud was over and we all ended up that little bit closer to the sea."

The car wove swiftly and carefully round the bends of the wet, moonlit country roads, coming to a stop in the small, quiet town of Lower Chidbury at 12.13am.

"There's a garage down the road, though they won't be open 'til tomorrow at least," said the man. "But there's a small hotel just here," he continued, pulling into the side of the road. "Can't guarantee you'll get a room, mind. It is a very busy week here. But they're good folks that run it, so I'm sure they'll sort you out."

With that the man climbed out of the car and disappeared round to the back, unhooking the coupling between the two vehicles. George climbed out of the car, following him.

"Oh right. There's no way anyone could look at the car tonight?" asked George, still not wanting to admit that it probably just needed refuelling. "I mean it might be a very simple thing to fix. And then I could be on my way."

"Sorry Chief," replied the man, opening the boot to his car and putting his towing gear away. "There'll be nothing doing till tomorrow, at least. You're best getting your head down for the night and get it sorted tomorrow."

"Right, yes, I guess that's probably the best idea. Are you sure they'll still be open?"

"Oh yeah, there'll be someone up." The man climbed back into his car, turned over the engine then wound down the window again.

"Just pop in there and get some kip," he said, pointing at a small, dark looking building with a faded blue *Hotel* sign just visible in the light from a streetlamp. "By the way, my name's Jeff and it's my garage down the road."

George felt instantly embarrassed that he hadn't even thought to ask the man's name.

"I'll pop round in the morning, and see if I can't get it going. If I don't see you, leave the keys on the wheel and I'll take a look.

"And don't worry," he said winking at George and flashing that cocky, toothy smile, "I'll bring a can of petrol with me. Just in case."

He revved the engine and peeled away, pulling out into the road and disappearing down a dark hill.

CHAPTER 5

GEORGE looked up at the ominous dark building and shivered slightly. A barely-lit, blue sign hanging from a post in the middle of a sodden lawn said *Hotel* in large, curly letters. It didn't look much like a hotel. It was an old, dilapidated building, with more than an air of haunted house about it. But George was pretty thin on options. It was either this or sleep in his car. Without a working heater.

At least if this place had a room going spare he could get a decent, warm night's sleep and then re-evaluate his options in the morning. So, with a deep breath, he did what he could to brush down his filthy, wet suit, crossed his fingers and strolled cautiously down the cracked black path to the large front door.

Happily the door was unlocked, so George pushed it slowly open and ventured inside. The entrance hall was dim and poorly lit from a small lamp on a reception desk. The air inside was slightly damp and George could taste the thickness of it in the back of his throat. The décor was dated and hadn't been attended to, or possibly even cleaned, since it was first put in place sometime in the late 70s. This was certainly no premier hotel.

The hallway was quiet. George approached the small desk carefully and quietly, sneakily almost, feeling like an intruder in somebody's home. He lifted each foot stealthily, placing it back on the floor as lightly as possible, despite their weighing twice as much as usual thanks to the excess of water and mud. He made it to the desk, peered over the edge, and found it quite deserted.

He scanned the hallway and heard a noise to the left, coming from a door to the side of the desk. It sounded like people laughing; glasses clinking. A bar? George took a big breath, pushed the door open and stepped through.

Inside was possibly the smallest bar George had ever seen. In a room not much bigger than an average single bedroom, or a small poky office, was what appeared to be a tiny version of a pub.

A wide, brown bar ran the length of the room and looked very professional, as if in a real pub. There were proper beer pumps, offering three types of lager and two of bitter. Authentic bar towels and beer mats emblazoned with various logos and brewery names littered the dark wooden surface. There was a shelf just above head height housing an array of glasses. On the back wall there were several large bottles hanging upside down, their necks squeezed into optics, offering a generous variety of different spirits. It was exactly like a real pub, only much smaller.

There was even a dartboard up on the wall, although players would have to stand outside the building and throw the darts in through the small, rectangular window on the opposite wall to reach anything like the official playing distance.

Wedged into the corner of the room were two small, round tables; each with their own two stools orbiting like satellites, offering the most meagre leg-room. In front of the bar were three wooden high stools, each home to a different bottom, the owners of which were now looking intently at George, quizzical expressions hanging from their faces.

George looked back, slightly embarrassed, feeling like a gate-crasher at a party who'd been discovered. He didn't like suddenly being the centre of attention.

A short, podgy, grey-haired man at the far end of the bar finally broke the silence. "Hello, looks like we've got a straggler." Then squinting his eyes to take a proper look at George, followed with, "And he looks like a right dirty bugger, too." He burst into laughter, and the old lady, and even older looking man sitting beside her at the bar, followed suit.

"Oh, yes," said George, looking down at his mud-caked shoes and trousers, and his ripped and dirtied shirt and jacket. "I'm terribly sorry, I have had a rather unfortunate evening."

"Goodness, dear, you have been in the wars, haven't you?" said the old lady.

"What happened?" cackled the grey-haired man. "You been out mud wrestling or something?"

The whole bar giggled again.

"No, I got a little lost," said George. "Then my car broke down and, well, it started raining. And then I fell down a ditch…" He ran a hand through his wet hair, feeling more than a little sorry for himself. "Is there any chance you might have a room available?"

"A room?" barked the old man closest to George at the bar. He was slightly overweight, more portly than fat, with a round, ruddy face that looked like the result of too many years of drinking. The top of his head was bald and shiny, round and pink, and glinted softly in the light. The sides of his head were adorned with two fluffy white plumes of hair, overgrown and uncombed, tumbling down over his ears and making him look like an angry clown.

He started to stand, keen to assert himself as proprietor of the establishment, but suddenly seemed to think better of the idea. Perhaps realising he was drunker than he'd thought and that his legs might not hold him, he slumped back down onto the stool. "This is our busiest week, you know." His voice sounded crotchety, almost angry, and George thought he looked a bit like a bulldog.

"Oh, leave off, Clive," said the old lady, poking the man in the arm. "You'll have to excuse my husband," she said. "He thinks he's funny, but he's the only one."

Her voice was soft and comforting, and George found it quite warming. "You're in luck, though, as we do have one room left. It's not the biggest, or most fancy, mind. But it's warm and dry."

"Oh thank you," said George.

"But first, let's get you a drink. Warm you up a bit. The old lady looked behind the bar then called, "Alice."

A previously unseen door, hidden in the panelling on the back wall of the bar, opened and a young woman walked through it. "Yes, mum," she said, somewhat irked at having been summoned.

She was quite simply the most beautiful woman George had ever seen. He guessed her to be about 30 or 31 – not that much younger than himself. She had medium-length brunette hair, which played about the sides of her face, and a messy fringe that caught gently on her long, black eyelashes. Her tight black top and slim blue jeans showed off her gym-toned body and ample chest, and she had cute, petite hands and shiny, sparkling fingernails.

Her face was simply beautiful; crafted perfectly. The soft, warm skin was unmarked by any lines or wrinkles, with pink curved cheekbones and an adorable little button nose. But it was the eyes that really caught George. They were the deepest, most soulful, hazel coloured eyes George had ever seen. When they looked back into his he was instantly struck by a dull, intense pain in his chest. He felt weak suddenly, as if all the air was being sucked from his body.

Everyone else in the room simply melted away and only the two of them remained, locked in a stare that George felt could have gone on forever. He was shocked, stunned, like something immense was happening to him.

George had read about things like this; people falling instantly in love. He'd seen it on television shows and laughed at how unrealistic it all was. That never really happened. People didn't really get swept up in these sudden intense rushes of emotion. He certainly didn't, at any rate.

So what was this? Could this be that moment, the one he'd believed to be Hollywood fantasy? Had George accidentally stumbled upon the love of his life in a tiny old hotel in the middle of a strange little town he'd accidentally found himself in, on what should have been a simple drive home from work?

Was he really standing there, open-mouthed and gawping at the woman who could finally fill the hole in his life; be the person he'd spent this whole time waiting for? The person he'd all but given up on ever really finding. Was this pain in his chest, love?

Or was it just a touch of indigestion? He hadn't had any dinner, after all.

It had been an eventful night, very confusing and rather tiring. And not for the first time that evening, George had to question his own mental fortitude. Perhaps he was just cracking up. The stress and strain had finally got to him. It had all just become a bit too much, and the rubber band holding his brain together had finally snapped, leaving him a gormless, staring idiot, unable to speak or move.

"Alice, can you pour a large brandy for Mr...?" The old lady looked at George inquisitively. "Mr...?" she repeated, slightly louder, trying to wake George from his trance.

The old lady's voice finally penetrated George's consciousness. He then very quickly became aware that he was, in fact, a gormless, gawping idiot, standing staring at a poor young woman who was now starting to look slightly uncomfortable.

His name. She was asking his name.

"Oh it's… it's…", oh my God, what was his name? He couldn't remember his name. It just wasn't coming.

"Erm… erm… erm…" he mumbled. This was intolerable. The more he tried to remember, the more ridiculous it seemed that he couldn't. How could he not remember his own name?

The room was silent now, all four people staring intently, suspiciously, waiting for an answer.

"Erm…" A small bead of sweat trickled slowly down the side of George's forehead. He could feel his face starting to redden; that unmistakeable burning sensation rising up from his collar; inching its way up his neck; creeping into his cheeks. Oh God.

And then: "Thring!" He almost shouted it, jubilant at suddenly having remembered his own name. "My name is Thring!"

"Thring?" interjected the grey-haired man at the end of the bar. "What are you, a cash register?"

The whole bar fell about laughing at what George thought was a pretty weak joke at best.

"Erm, my name is Thring. George Thring," he said much quieter, looking down at his shoes, trying to hide the embarrassment.

"Alice," the old lady continued, "can you get Mr Thring here a large brandy. Poor love's had a terrible time of it. He's absolutely wet through."

"No problem," said Alice, spinning round to pour the drink from the large bottle on the wall behind.

George lifted his head again and couldn't help but take a quick look at her bottom. It was quite possibly the nicest, most shapely, most perfectly formed bottom he'd ever seen. He then suddenly realised how intrusive he was being and flicked his eyes back to the ground, hoping nobody had seen what he was looking at.

Alice turned again, reaching over the bar and handing George the freshly-filled glass. She smiled briefly, the warmest smile George had seen in a long time, and George could have sworn he felt the lightest flicker of electricity tickle through him as her finger lightly touched his hand. He looked down at the dark, brown liquid in the glass. It didn't look very appealing.

"Oh thank you," he said, "but I don't really…"

"Go on, get it down ya," offered the man at the end of the bar.

"Go on," said the old lady, backing him up. "You need something to warm you up, or you'll catch your death." She sounded quite forceful now, like his mother always had when insisting he swallowed spoonfuls of cough syrup.

He looked down at the glass almost fearfully. George very rarely drank, and certainly not spirits. He'd have the odd glass of wine, from time to time, but only one or two and not enough to get drunk.

He'd been drunk before, on a few occasions. One time he'd even drunk so much that he'd been sick in a pot plant and woken with the most incredible headache the next day. But he had never really seen the appeal of drinking. He certainly couldn't understand how so many people devoted so much time to doing it.

The loss of inhibition was pleasurable enough, to a certain extent, but George always found that alcohol made him more sleepy than anything else. And he'd seen so many people make fools of themselves whilst drunk at office parties that he'd felt even less inclined to take part.

He looked at the glass. He looked at the people in the bar. They were all standing there looking at him, expectantly. He raised the glass slowly to his mouth, pressing the rim to his cold, wet lips. He tipped it back slightly, feeling the warming liquid almost burning his mouth, trickling onto his tongue as he took the smallest sip he could. It tasted disgusting, and George wanted to put the glass straight down onto the bar in front of him.

"Go on," offered the grey-haired man, somewhat unhelpfully, "get it down you."

George, not usually a man to take against someone he'd only just met, couldn't help but wish he'd mind his own business.

"It'll help," said Alice softly, her deep, brown eyes opening wide as she smiled that soft, warm smile.

There was nothing else to do, so George gripped the glass tightly in his hand, raised it back up to his mouth and valiantly threw his head back, pouring the liquor straight down his throat. He instantly coughed, the brandy burning his lips, scorching his mouth with its dark, bitter taste. The pain of that one first tiny sip was suddenly magnified a thousand times.

It hit his stomach with a jolt, threatening to bounce right back up again. His whole body tensed, muscles convulsing, toes clenching as he fought to keep the drink inside his stomach.

Oh my God, the agony of it. People do that for fun? He thought. It was like poison. It was like drinking acid. It was like that scene where Dr Jekyll drinks his foul potion and collapses to the floor, screaming and wailing as his body shakes and trembles in revolt. Jekyll had it easy, George thought; he should try this horrible brandy.

Again he seemed to exhale all his breath in one quick burst, sucking back twice as much as he did his best to pretend that he hadn't nearly died from one simple drink.

Gradually the pain started to subside. His face unscrewed and he reached forward to place the glass down onto the bar, getting it as far away from him as possible, as he fixed a forced, flat, agonised grin to his face. And as horrible as the taste left lingering in his mouth was, he did have to admit to feeling quite a good deal warmer than before.

"Yeah, it's got a kick to it," offered his unhelpful friend at the end of the bar, obviously noticing George's discomfort.

37

"Mmm, yes. Nice," replied George, though he was certain nobody believed him.

As well as instantly warming him, the drink also seemed to have an equally speedy effect on George's brain. Again perhaps due to the lack of food, George instantly felt the effects of the alcohol. His cheeks felt flushed and, though he couldn't remember ever having specifically felt his nose before, he knew for certain that he couldn't feel it now.

Almost giddy, and very aware that people were still looking at him, George felt it best to extricate himself from the situation as quickly as possible.

"Thank you for the drink," he said, "but I really am very tired. Could I possibly take the room you spoke of?"

"Of course, my love," said the old lady. She seemed very kind and George instantly liked her. He couldn't tell her age, she just had that stereotypical old lady look. Her hair was pure white and fluffy like candy floss. There was no distinct style, it seemed just to sit there, perched on top of her head, in big thick waves and curls, like a small cloud had sunk too low and become stuck to her.

She had kind eyes, brown like the girl behind the bar, but old and tired. The wrinkles on her face made her look world-weary, but the eyes still sparkled with laughter.

"Follow me," she said standing up and stepping past George as she went out through the door. George smiled and said good night to the rest of the assembly in the bar. Nobody replied, they just smiled slightly and nodded, so George turned with a sigh and followed the old lady.

She picked up a set of keys from a board behind the desk, then ushered George up a flight of stairs and along a dimly-lit corridor. They reached a door at the end and stopped.

"This is you, then," she said. "Now, it's not the biggest room, as I say. But I'm afraid it's all we have. And you'll be comfy enough." She touched George lightly on the shoulder and smiled again. "There's a bathroom across the hall if you want to clean up. And if you need anything, we'll be in the bar for a short while yet, I shouldn't wonder."

"Oh thank you," George said, "you're very kind."

"Now, can I get you something to eat," asked the woman. "The kitchen is technically closed, but I'm sure I could get Alice to rustle you up a little sandwich or something."

Alice. The thought of seeing her again made George smile. The thought of having her deliver food up to his room had his mind instantly racing with thoughts he really shouldn't be thinking about a young woman he'd only just met. And then the mere thought of food itself made him suddenly feel a bit sick again.

"No, thank you," he said softly, "I think I'd like to just go to sleep. Thanks again."

"Okay, well you have a good night's sleep then. Breakfast is between seven and ten, down in the dining room. Goodnight then," she said and she disappeared down the corridor and back downstairs.

George unlocked the door. It creaked loudly as he pushed it open. He stepped inside, fumbling for the light switch on the wall, nearly tripping over the edge of the bed. Finally he found the switch, clicked it on and the room was not so much flooded in light as drizzled; a weak light bulb on the ceiling crackling slowly into life.

It certainly wasn't the largest room in the world. The old lady had been right about that. It was small for a single room, by anybody's standards; housing a single bed, wedged in under the window and barely fitting lengthways between each far wall.

A stretch of brown- and orange-patterned, tatty carpet led up to a rickety-looking chest of drawers at the far end of the room, atop which sat an ancient TV. It was small and dark, made of brown wood, with a panel of grey buttons on the left hand side. An old bunny-eared antennae perched on the top, which George felt sure probably weren't even manufactured anymore.

George walked into the room and sat down on the bed. It was way too soft. And lumpy, as if a series of hard, sharp springs were poking up intermittently through the worn material. He adjusted his position, shifting his bottom this way and that, being met at each point by another spiky spring sticking up and poking him.

George eased off his sodden suit jacket, hanging it carefully over the back of a chair wedged into the corner of the room by the chest of drawers. Sadly there was no Corby trouser press, as one might expect to find in a slightly better-quality hotel. Though, looking at the state of his torn, muddied trousers, George didn't think even the best trouser press would have stood much chance of resurrecting their ironed crease, not to mention removing the filth and grime. So he draped them over the seat of the chair, hoping at least to remove some of the moisture. Then he peeled off his shirt and red penguin tie, and climbed into bed.

The blankets were coarse and itchy. They were thick and heavy, and tucked in under the mattress with military precision, so tight that George barely managed to work his way underneath them. The sheets were crisp and hard, starched to within an inch of their lives, and the friction against George's legs made his skin creep; small jolts of electricity running the length of his body in tiny waves. The pillows were flat and lifeless, unevenly thinned-out and lumpier than the mattress; evidence of a thousand heads that had slept there – or at least had tried to.

Thankfully, the room was at least dark. The thick, brown curtains, emblazoned all over with faded red poppies, did a good job of keeping the light out. George reached over and flicked the light switch, the room instantly turning pitch black.

It dawned on George that his dream of getting some sleep in a nice, warm comfortable bed wasn't quite working out as he'd hoped. A night in a cold, lumpy, uncomfortable bed was as good as it was going to get. And he just knew his back was going to be an aching knot of crumpled, twisted muscle by morning. But he was so tired he just didn't care any longer.

He lay there, tightly cocooned under the heavy blankets, barely able to move. He thought of Alice again, of that warm smile and the way her lips curled up at the edges. He thought of that most brief of moments when their fingers barely touched, and the tickle of electricity he'd felt. He thought of how it had warmed him in an instant.

He smiled to himself as he closed his eyes, and just a few seconds later he was fast asleep.

CHAPTER 6

WEDNESDAY

GEORGE Thring woke at exactly 7.13am, just as he did every morning. He was still a little drowsy, only half awake, his brain slowly washing up on the shore from a sea of warm dreams. He lay there, gradually coming to, enjoying his daily morning respite, waiting for the shrill siren of his alarm and the new day to clatter down around him.

He didn't want to move. He didn't want to get up. As soon as he pulled back the covers, gave in to the cold morning air and incessant light trying to find its way under his tight-shut eyes, that would be it.

Another bloody day to endure. Anton, Clive and Louise's one-upmanship. Their petty squabbling and desperate need to be recognised. That horrible, stuffy office sucking the years and the life out of him. Spreadsheets to update, figures to analyse, energy-sapping meetings to attend.

And Linda bloody Cardigan pitching up at his desk, needling him about his daily reports.

He didn't need it. Not yet, anyway. In bed it was still warm, still cosy and safe. Nothing could get at him. He didn't have to get up until his alarm went off.

And as he lay there, slowly coming to, thinking about what fresh disappointments the new day ahead might bring, he got the distinct feeling that something was a little off. It was very quiet. Too quiet. Surely his alarm should have gone off by now.

The bed felt strange, too. It was a bit on the lumpy side. He couldn't remember it ever feeling this uncomfortable before. He shifted his weight, wriggling his legs, and a soft, dull ache throbbed in the small of his back. That's weird, he thought.

He moved his legs again and the crisp, starched sheets and coarse blanket scratched against his skin. What the hell has happened to my duvet, thought George, his mouth snapping open into a wide, gaping yawn as his hand slid down his body to absent-mindedly scratch at his crotch.

And then he remembered.

His eyes sprang open. He tried to sit up in bed, but the sheets and blankets were still so tightly tucked around him that he couldn't manage a full-bodied jolt and had to settle instead for lifting his head and scanning the room.

The dim hotel room, partially lit now by sunlight creeping in from around the edges of the curtains. His tattered suit lay muddied and crumpled, ripped and damp, on the chair in the corner.

It all started coming back to him. His mild psychological episode; the long drive; the car breaking down; the rain… then the hotel; the people in the bar; the brandy… the uncomfortable bed, in which he was still lying.

He heaved at the covers, gradually pulling them up until he could sit up in bed and fully take in his surroundings.

One hand scratched at the mass of unkempt hair sprouting up on the top of his head. The other reached behind and rubbed at his aching back. Much as he'd expected, one night on the soft mattress had done him no good. As he sat up it shifted beneath him, his backside sinking into a dip.

He sat there for a while, trying to take it all in. His car was still broken down and goodness knew how far away from home he was. And there was no way he'd make it in to the office on time.

He'd be late. George had never been late for work in his life. Not even when it snowed, and most people had taken the advantage to 'work from home', George had still arrived there precisely on time. Not a single minute late.

George went to climb out of bed, reaching across and retrieving the mobile phone in his jacket pocket. He should phone the office; let them know that he wouldn't be in on time.

But then he stopped. He wasn't quite ready to phone in. As soon as he did that, it would be admitting to what had happened. So far the only one who really knew what had happened the previous night was him. As soon as he confessed to his little lapse of consciousness it became somehow more real. His accidentally driving hundreds of miles away from his house would not be something that he could simply shrug off as 'one of those things', it would be a serious event. Something real and tangible. Something that he could not hide from any longer.

Of course he knew he should have done something about his episodes long ago. He should have called a doctor or seen a therapist. At the very least he should have written it down in a diary. But it had been easier to simply ignore it and hope it would all just get better. Now it had become serious. It had caused him to miss a day at work. The repercussions were visible to more people than just himself.

He looked at the phone in his hand. He couldn't do it. Not just yet. So he turned the phone back off and put it down.

He leaned over and parted the curtains slightly, a thin beam of light pouring in and illuminating a golden strip across his chest. He peeked out through the gap to the world outside. It was bright and sunny; the only remnants of the previous evening's storm the damp road and pavements. The light was so bright he had to view it through half-closed eyes. At least it was a nice day.

George's stomach rumbled and growled, and he suddenly realised that he was very hungry indeed. With no dinner the previous night, and only that foul-tasting, burning brandy consumed since lunch the previous day, George's stomach needed food. And it needed it now.

At the very least, thought George, he could leave his decision-making until after he'd had some breakfast. Perhaps he'd think more clearly once he'd eaten.

He yanked himself out from under the tightly-tucked sheets, climbed out of bed and stepped over to the chair in the corner of the room. His shirt was a state: a big black and brown streak of mud splashed right down the front. But at least it had dried out.

He pulled it on, trying to scrape away as much of the dirt as he could whilst buttoning it. The tattered trousers were still quite damp and badly ripped at the ankles. He shivered as he pulled them up his legs. They'd shrunk slightly as well, and felt just a little tighter in the waist than normal.

He pulled the jacket on. It was also still damp, and tighter under the arms than it should be. But despite the cold, wet feel and the close fit, it was at least still wearable.

And better than going to breakfast in his underwear.

He picked his favourite red penguin tie up off the floor and held it in his hands. It was completely ruined – ripped, sodden and smeared with mud. He looked at it with a slightly wistful smile, then curled it up into a ball and tossed it into the small wicker wastepaper bin at the foot of the bed. Shame, he thought. He'd only ever worn it once. Perhaps he should have been braver and worn it more often.

His stomach rumbled again, forcing a small, gassy burp to bubble up and pop in his mouth. Then he could taste the brandy again and he thought he just might be sick.

He took a series of quick, deep breaths, managing to compose himself. Then he opened to the door and stepped out to see what strange events would present themselves next.

******

George walked tentatively down the hall and descended the stairs, his eyes adjusting to the thick beams of light pouring in through the windows. It was so bright he had to keep his eyes half closed, and raised his arm up to try to block it out.

The check-in desk was no longer abandoned, as it had been the previous evening. Sitting behind it was the old man from the night before; the grumpy one from the middle stool that George took to be the hotel owner.

George looked up to nod a polite good morning and would have thought no more about it. But then he noticed something rather unusual. The man was dressed as Elvis Presley.

It was not that he was one of these old guys you sometimes saw with a faint resemblance to Elvis: the bouffant hairstyle and the thick, dark sideburns, like some ageing Teddy boy trapped in the past. This belligerent old man was actually dressed as Elvis Presley. Just standing there smiling as if there was nothing strange about it at all, decked out in a bright-white, poorly-fitting, full-length jumpsuit. The arms and collar were decorated with small red and blue plastic jewels. The collar hung low, cut to just above the navel, revealing the old

43

man's pale, hairless chest and obscene, wrinkly cleavage of saggy old man-boobs.

On top of his head he wore a jet-black wig, cut into an elaborate, giant quiff, jetting easily six or seven inches into the air. Attached to the wig were two big, bushy, black sideburns. They hadn't been stuck securely to the man's cheeks, and were consequently curling upwards slightly, as if trying to take flight.

In all, the combination looked somewhat shoddy and amateur, like a homemade fancy dress costume. But he seemed ever so pleased with himself. Gone was the curmudgeonly look and instead he actually appeared rather happy.

Things had certainly taken an unexpected turn over the last 24 hours and somewhere in the back of George's mind he knew he should have been expecting things to continue on that weird path. But he'd never have imagined this!

More in disbelief than shock, George simply couldn't take his eyes off the man. Like a pile-up on the motorway, or passing somebody in the street with an unfortunate facial deformity, that most base and voyeuristic side of his brain took control and he couldn't help but gawp.

The man looked up, noticing that he was being stared at. "Something I can help you with, my friend?"

"Erm… er… sorry," stumbled George. The one question he wanted to ask burned on his tongue like a hot chilli, but he was too scared to ask. Instead he opted for: "Erm, where do we go for breakfast?"

"Breakfast?" replied the man. His whole body jolted as if he'd been hit with a bolt of electricity. He swivelled his hips, threw his arms into the air and twisted around until both outstretched hands pointed in the direction of an open doorway. A sign above it read DINING ROOM. "Uh, just through there!" he sang, in a strange, mumbled American accent.

Did he really just sing that? Thought George.

"Oh," said George, still concerned the man might have brushed against a loose wire, or jammed his wet toe into an unused plug socket. "Thank you."

The old man simply stood there, pointing, his lip curled up into a snarl. George smiled, gave him a slight, affirmative nod and walked through the door.

"Uh thankyouverymuch!" the old man mumbled after him.

The doorway led into a small dining-room. There were seven round tables, each with four chairs. None of the other guests had come down for breakfast so George chose the table in the far corner and sat down. There was a menu with various cooked breakfast options and George looked it over, trying to decide which of the coronary-inducing combinations of sausages, bacon and fried bread would be least likely to arrive swimming in a pool of grease.

A door swung open at the other end of the room. Footsteps clomping in his direction. He concentrated harder, trying to decide what to have.

The footsteps drew closer and he looked up, ready to relay his order, when he was struck with his second strange sighting of the day: Elvis Presley. Again.

At first George assumed it was the same Elvis from the front desk. But this was a different Elvis. Shorter, skinnier, more bony.

The jumpsuit that this Elvis wore was red, and the plastic jewels were sewn into a rather more elegant pattern of lines and swirls around the collar and cuffs. There were no sideburns or giant bouffant wig; instead just a shaggy, curled plumage of thick white hair. Large golden sunglasses obscured much of the small, elderly face, like giant alien eyes.

"Morning my love. What can I get for you?"

And then George recognised the voice. It was the woman from last night. The little old lady that had been so kind in the bar and shown him up to his room.

George felt dazed, like a shock victim suddenly realising where they are and what's happening. "Erm... I... er..." he tried to say.

"The sausages are very good," the little old Elvis-woman said. "Got them from the butcher this morning. How about I do you a nice big 'Full English'?"

"Um, yes, okay," replied George, momentarily forgetting his aversion to eating anything too greasy. Again the question was burning a hole in his tongue, but he couldn't bring himself to ask.

What was going on here? Had he wandered into some strange Elvis Presley-themed hotel? He didn't remember seeing any sign when he'd checked in last night, and he was sure the old couple had been dressed a lot more normally. He had been very tired, so maybe he just hadn't noticed. But then, it did seem to George that no matter how tired you were, that's the sort of thing that you would probably pick up on.

Both she and the man behind the desk were clearly quite old. Maybe they were in the depths of some kind of senile dementia. Perhaps they had no idea that they'd come to work in second-rate Elvis costumes. Maybe they didn't actually work here; they'd broken out of a lunatic asylum down the road and wandered in off the street.

Or maybe this was just the way people dressed and behaved around here. George had heard strange tales of village life before, where the residents of really remote places were so far removed from the rest of civilization that they behaved very strangely. Like they were trapped in their own little world.

Maybe they'd have no idea that dressing and acting as Elvis Presley would be deemed by the rest of the country as somewhat eccentric. Of course it seemed a bit rude to ask, and George was, to be honest, a little bit afraid to. His mind suddenly filled with images of being set upon by an army of barmy Elvis-impersonators; him being strapped to a giant wicker Elvis and burned alive as the villagers whooped and cheered and swivelled their hips in some kind of deranged approval.

So George decided to simply sit quietly and not say anything.

"And would you like tea or coffee with that?" the old lady continued.

"Er... coffee... please," said George. Then, not wanting to seem totally rude by not even acknowledging what he'd seen, George stammered, "Erm... I like your costume."

The woman stopped dead, spun round and stared at George; her lips

45

tightening, her eyebrows raised, not saying a word – just looking at him. Oh God, thought George, here it comes. I'm done for.

A small grin spread quickly across her lips. "Thankyouverymuch!" she said, in a low, southern American drawl before turning and toddling off towards the kitchen.

She reappeared 15 minutes later carrying a plate piled high with sausages, fried eggs, bacon, fried bread, black pudding, mushrooms and a huge dollop of congealed baked beans. She placed the food down in front of George and it was as greasy as he'd feared.

Usually just the sight would have put George off, making him worry about heart disease, fatty acids and all the other paranoid health issues the TV and newspapers told him he should be fearful of. But he was so hungry he just tucked in, shovelling mouthfuls of oily breakfast into his mouth.

Ten minutes later and he was finished, washing the lot down with the strongest, sweetest cup of coffee he'd ever had.

The dining room sat silent, the rest of the guests having still not emerged from their rooms, or maybe just avoiding the less-than-healthy breakfast. George was secretly rather glad, though. Knowing what a state he looked, he was pretty sure he probably didn't smell too fresh either. He was glad to avoid all the stares and whispers he'd otherwise have endured.

He'd need to do something about these ruined clothes, he thought. And then he'd need to do something about his car. And he still had to decide what to do about work.

His stomach rumbled again, this time a deep, gurgling, satisfied salute to the food he'd enjoyed, and he sat back in his chair, patting his full belly. First, he thought, I'm just going to sit here for a minute and let things go down.

CHAPTER 7

THE morning sun glinted in through the window; a thin golden streak running across the breakfast table, warming George's hand and glinting off his butter-covered knife. It occurred to George, as he sipped his coffee and washed down his last mouthful of toast, that he had technically – although not purposely – run away from home. He'd climbed into his car and driven, just driven, until he couldn't drive any further; inching slowly away from his life, leaving everything behind him.

How funny, he thought. The number of times as a child he'd imagined running away to some mysterious magical land; leaving his sad, lonely little life behind and venturing towards a new, exciting, adventure-packed existence! All those times he'd sat tucked in behind his desk at work, wishing he had the courage to quit his job, jump on the first plane to anywhere and see where his adventure would take him.

And now he'd actually done it. Completely by accident.

Okay, it wasn't the magical land he'd dreamed of. Far from it. And it wasn't the exotic location he might have chosen to have an exciting adventure in.

Had he actually planned to run away, he'd probably have made sure he had enough petrol in the car not to break down at the side of the road. And he wouldn't have listed his dream destination as a small country hotel, stuck in a time warp and staffed by old-aged Elvis Presley impersonators.

Nonetheless, it wasn't home. It was a strange place, somewhere new and… yes, he had to admit it, just a little bit exciting.

George wondered if anybody else had ever run away by accident. Surely it must have happened to somebody else. At least one other person. Just going about their day-to-day business, doing what they normally do, going into a little bit of a trance – George had decided to think of it as a trance, rather than some kind of worrying psychological episode – and all of a sudden they'd run away from home. Ended up somewhere new and just decided not to go home again.

George hadn't actually decided whether or not he was going to go home, but as he hadn't decided that he definitely *was* going to, it seemed to him that the decision was still up for debate. And, as a result, it was perfectly plausible that he may well decide never to go home.

Then he started to think. If he wasn't going to go home, what was he going to do? Where was he going to go?

A small pain throbbed deep in the centre of his brain and a funny, sickly feeling swam in his stomach. His heart beat a little faster and his hands grew clammy, so he thought he'd best stop thinking about it. After all, it was a lot to take in. It's not often that one accidentally runs away from home. It was probably best to try and approach this a lot slower. The last thing George wanted to do was rush into things. He should take his time and try not to worry.

And as he tried not to think about things too much, and his breathing returned to normal, the small dull pain in his head started to subside. But the funny feeling in his stomach was going nowhere and George realised he was just going to have to get used to that for the time being.

Of course, running away from home, either purposely or accidentally, was bound to have repercussions. People were naturally going to miss him. When he didn't turn up for work they would probably become suspicious.

He didn't have any pets that needed feeding so that was one less thing to worry about. He did have a plant that would most likely die without him being there to water it. But then it had been a present from her, a long, long time ago. He hadn't even liked it in the first place and only carried on watering it as a matter of course, so he couldn't have cared whether it died or not. In fact – and it made him feel a little bit mean – he actually found himself rather hoping that it would die.

I mean, what is the point in plants anyway? He thought. You spend your whole life watering them, cleaning their leaves and making sure they get enough sunlight, and what do you get for your troubles? An ungrateful, thirsty green lump in the corner of the room. People always told him: you need to get some plants, brighten the place up a bit. Well why? What good did they really do? He couldn't think of a single plant ever thanking him for anything.

Work. He really should call work.

George reached into his pocket, retrieved his mobile phone, flipped it open to reveal the buttons and the screen and started dialling the numbers to call the office. He should let them know that he wasn't coming in; that was only polite. He didn't like to leave them in the lurch and he didn't want to appear unreliable by simply not turning up.

But if he phoned in, he would have to say *why* he was going to be late. And he really didn't want to phone Anton and have to explain that he was unlikely to make it in as he had suffered an as-yet-undiagnosed Dissociative Fugue State – or minor psychological episode – and accidentally ended up miles from home.

He could, of course, come up with some excuse. Some invented emergency doctor's appointment, or mystery illness that had overcome him. Should he put on a crackly voice to make it seem more authentic, or do people always see through that sort of thing anyway?

He could pretend a family member had died, or that he'd woken up to find his whole house had collapsed down around him in the night. And though that didn't necessarily mean he was unable to come to work, he would have rather a lot of sorting out to do.

He could claim to have been abducted by aliens, and – though he'd been returned safely, and the aliens had been mostly very friendly and polite – he was still feeling slightly liverish and unable to sit down for long periods, after a round of uncomfortable rectal probes.

Of course, none of those would work. George couldn't lie. He was no good at it. People always saw through him.

Somehow, dishonesty never sat well on George's shoulders. At the mere prospect of telling a lie, doing something dishonest or – God forbid – even breaking the law, he would immediately feel his heart start beating faster. The throbbing palpitations would vibrate harder until they became a large, pulsing, banging pain in his chest. His legs would turn to jelly, his palms becoming clammy, and he'd start to sweat. And not just a little. Thick, salty beads of perspiration would dot his forehead: building; growing; slowly turning into hot, dripping rivulets of sweat. His face would burn crimson: a brilliant red warning flare. 'Deceit, deceit, deceit!' flashing like a beacon, giving him away.

Then he'd crumble, red-faced and fearful; a horrible, sickly ache deep in his stomach; desperate to run away, hide; ashamed at having been caught out. His deceits shattering before him and tumbling to the floor like shards of broken mirror for all to see.

Billy Cornwell, now he could lie. Billy was George's best friend at first school and had a real talent for it. Seemingly with no effort at all, he'd be spinning yarns as tall as a skyscraper, as wide as an ocean; inventive and clever and devilishly corrupt. And, best of all, extremely entertaining.

Even though you knew there was no truth to them, Billy's lies were so magnificent, so preposterous, so delightful, that deep down, right down in the bottom of your heart, you were always so desperate for them to be true. Billy had an uncle in the SAS who single-handedly saved the world from evil geniuses on a weekly basis – James Bond, eat your heart out!

His family were richer than the Queen (despite living in a council house in the rougher part of town), though they chose not to flaunt their wealth and only went on the biggest, brashest spending sprees when – conveniently – nobody was around to see.

Billy had a pet alligator that lived in his bedroom. It slept on the end of his bed at night and could count to 10 with loud, lustrous snaps of its mighty jaw. Billy's Dad was a submarine captain, a helicopter pilot and a Navy general (he must have rotated each job on a weekly basis), and it only looked as if he was spending all day in the bookies because he was on a secret undercover mission.

Billy's Nan had a bionic leg. His sister was really a robot. He had met all the members of the A-Team and they'd been to his house for tea and biscuits.

And that was nothing compared to the incredible feats that he himself had achieved. You name it: Billy had seen it, done it, been the best at it. Of course, he'd never have offended people with demonstrations, or any tiny modicum of proof, but that's just the way Billy was. He didn't like to brag…

Billy had the imagination and a face bold enough to have listeners gasping with delight at his tall tales; living them along with him; gazing in awe and wonderment at the fantasies he laid out before them. Of course, everybody knew they were lies. Deep down they all knew. Children's lies – easy to spot and twice as easy to debunk. But that wasn't the point.

Other kids often fell foul of themselves, their lies spinning just too far out of control to be reeled back and maintained. They would be mercilessly mocked; a deluge of "liar", "chinny-reckon" and sometimes even "bullshit" hurled directly at them until they were red-faced, crying, or running away home. But never Billy.

In many ways, Billy's lies weren't lies at all. They were dreams. Dreams that everyone could all share in and enjoy. Dreams that all were equally as desperate to come true. And that's why nobody ever told Billy they knew he was lying, because if they did then the magic would be broken and they never could have come true.

Of course, the last George had heard of Billy he was doing two years for fraud. Apparently his criminal career started with his borrowing money under false pretences from friends (never with any prospects of repayment, of course) and progressed to small-time fraud; tax evasion; confidence tricks; and then, that one big score. The biggest lie of them all, that even Billy couldn't control. The lie that got away from him. The lie that saw him finally caught out. His bluff called and repaid with a hefty prison sentence. But then, that was always Billy's biggest problem: he never knew when to stop lying.

George typed in the last three digits of the number. But when he went to push the little green telephone button to make the call, his thumb just seemed to hover above it.

Perhaps he shouldn't call work after all. He wasn't entirely certain about the rules and etiquette of running away from home, but it seemed that phoning work and telling them that you weren't coming in probably wasn't the done thing. In fact, you probably weren't supposed to tell anybody, were you? Wasn't that the point of the running away part?

If he phoned anyone to let them know that he'd run away, then maybe that wasn't running away at all. Wasn't that more like a last minute holiday?

No, accidentally or not, he'd run away from home and it had proved to be one of the most liberating experiences of his life.

He hadn't felt this excited since he met her. Emily. That day when he looked up to be confronted by the most beautiful, deep, shimmering, green eyes he had ever seen. The long, flowing golden hair that seemed to move in slow motion, carried effortlessly on a breeze. The perfect, heart-warming smile that made George want to jump to his feet and burst out in song like some corny character in a cheap musical. That first heart-thumping moment when, within a single second, all the lovesongs, valentines cards and mushy sentimentalist nonsense of the world instantly made sense to him.

His life had been grey since her. Grey and cold and damp. But now he could see colour again, like a half-faded rainbow lighting up the corner of a dim, blackened sky. And he wasn't going to mess it all up now. He didn't want to lose this sense of newness. This excitement. Not just so as to avoid inconveniencing a group of people he didn't even really like, or care about.

He knew exactly what would happen. He'd phone work and Anton would come up with some incredibly important reason why George absolutely, definitely, positively had to go back right now. He'd feel so guilty, so beaten-down out of a sense of misguided loyalty that he'd instantly crumble, climb into his car and go home. And that tiny, faded little rainbow would drip down out of the sky and be lost forever.

George's thumb moved across to the little red phone key and pressed down hard, cancelling the call. And without giving George's brain any time to countermand the order, his thumb moved straight to the power button, turning the phone off altogether.

Now they wouldn't be able to find him at all. And, now that he thought about it, he actually quite enjoyed the idea of people not knowing what had happened to him.

Maybe they would be concerned. Perhaps they'd try phoning him to see where he was and what he was doing. And, when they couldn't get hold of him, perhaps they'd call round all the hospitals, like they always do in films, to make sure he hadn't been in a car accident, or thrown himself off a building, or endured some embarrassing sexual injury involving a Hoover attachment and an intimate personal area.

Perhaps they'd say, "Has anyone seen George? It's not like him to be late. I do hope he's all right..."

Or perhaps someone would say, "Hey, where's that guy that always wears those nice ties?"

Or maybe they'd say, "Where the fuck is George? I need those bloody figures he was working on. He'd better be dead, or I'm gonna bloody kill him..."

Deep down in his heart, however, George knew there was a much greater probability that they wouldn't even notice that he wasn't there. His seat would remain cold and untouched, tucked in behind his desk. His computer would sit quiet, turned off, and the people around may even subconsciously notice the lack of that almost imperceptible hum it made throughout the day.

His coffee cup, the navy blue one that said *ACCOUNTANTS DO IT WITH INFLATED FIGURES*, that he'd been given as a joke present from his old boss, would still be sitting in the cupboard.

And maybe they would be aware that something was a little off, not quite right, but George was convinced that nobody would actually notice that he had not turned up for work. Not until half past four, at least, when Anton would lean over and ask him for his daily reports.

So George sighed, placed the phone back in his jacket pocket, and signalled old Mrs Presley for another drink.

******

The coffee was only just warm, and tasted dark and bitter from having sat in the pot for too long. Had he been in a more up-market hotel, George might have asked for some fresh coffee to be prepared but he didn't really like to make a fuss and he didn't want to hurt the old lady's feelings. So he stirred in an extra spoonful of sugar to try to improve the taste.

It was nearly nine o'clock now and he noticed that nobody else had come down for breakfast. Was he the only guest staying here? He could have sworn the old lady had told him he'd been lucky to get a room.

He glanced up to the old lady – who was still eyeing him eagerly – and raised his head, opening his mouth as if to speak. Within seconds she was over. "Can I get you anything else, my love?" she asked, clearly eager to please.

"Oh no," said George, gazing over at the pot of stewed, tepid coffee on the side, anxious not to have to force another cup of it down. "Everything was lovely, thank you. No, I was just wondering where all the other guests are. Have they not come down for breakfast?"

"Oh a few have been and gone, sweetheart. The rest should be checking in throughout the day. The events don't start until tonight, so we should be filling up soon enough."

"Events?" asked George.

"Yes, the festival," she returned. "Of course, you won't know about that, will you? Oh, how funny. You must think we're all quite daft, dressed up like this."

"Erm, well…," replied George, a little sheepishly.

"This is the week of the festival. What a funny time to turn up in town," she giggled.

"Festival?"

"Yes, we have one every year. It's actually quite famous, you know. If you have time you should stick around for a while. There are lots of fun events and parties going on until Friday. It's the best week of the year. Anyway, you'll have to excuse me," she chirped, "must go and check on my sausages." She turned and pranced off towards the kitchen with a spring in her step.

A festival? As if this whole experience hadn't been strange enough, he'd somehow found himself marooned in a strange little town, right in the middle of their annual festival. This experience couldn't get much weirder.

He took another sip of his coffee, flinching at the bitter taste. There was no use just sitting there. George had a lot to think about. There was a lot of planning to be done and decisions to make. And he wasn't going to come to any conclusions sipping stale coffee at a breakfast table. Decisive action, that's what he needed. So he decided to go and sit up in his room for a bit.

CHAPTER 8

WITH the fried breakfast lying heavily like a brick in his stomach, threatening imminent indigestion, George sat on the edge of the bed in the small, dull room. Light shot in through the windows in thin beams, illuminating small, wispy clouds of dust. They congregated by his feet on the floor, making the rest of the room even darker by comparison. He glanced at the old television in the corner – a relic from the 1980s, with the bedraggled looking bunny-eared antenna perched on the top – and thought about turning it on. Then he decided he'd rather just sit in silence.

George had a lot to think about and he didn't need distractions. So he thought perhaps he'd just sit and think for a bit. He scratched his head and wriggled his bottom as he shifted about on the bed. He crossed and uncrossed his legs 13 times. He lay back and looked up at the ceiling. Then he sat back up, gripping his chin between his thumb and forefinger as he sometimes did when he really had to think.

He stood up, pacing the room, all the time thinking. But the room was only four paces long and he couldn't really build up a decent thinking stride, so he sat back down on the bed.

Soon it occurred to him that he probably wasn't going to get a great deal of good thinking done in the small dark room. Not with all that dust. He remembered reading that something like ninety per cent of all dust was actually made up of human skin cells that erode from the body over time, like chippings of rock that end up as sand on the beach.

Who's skin was it? It couldn't be George's; he'd only been there for a night He couldn't possibly have shed so many skin cells in one night.

All that skin, someone else's skin, just floating in the air. And George was sitting there amongst it, breathing it in.

Oh God, how much had he breathed in last night in his sleep? The very thought made him feel queasy and he worried that the heavy breakfast might yet see the light of day again. All of a sudden he needed fresh air. He had to get out of the room that seemed to be growing smaller with every second.

He jolted up from the bed, grabbed his jacket, and darted across to the door. He left the room, his heart beating hard, slamming the door behind him. His pace quickened as he descended the long staircase, nodding politely at the ageing Elvis Presley behind the reception desk before practically running out through the big, heavy front door, sucking in a great, fluffy gulp of cool, fresh air.

The light was even brighter than George had expected as he stepped out. And as he did, placing his heavy, tired feet onto the ground before him, his head feeling light and slightly dizzy, he had the oddest feeling; a sense that he was walking out into a whole new world. It was as if he'd left his old world behind last night and woken to find himself somewhere different. Somewhere new and interesting. Somewhere bright and shimmering, where possibilities could be endless and exciting.

Then the sun went behind a cloud and it all turned grey and gloomy again.

But it was different. George couldn't really put his finger on what exactly seemed different, or why, but the air seemed cleaner somehow. It was fresh, crisp, refreshing, almost sweet tasting. The light was brighter too, and he had to squint slightly as it stung his eyes. The streets and pavements before him faded into negative as his retinas slowly countered the effect. Then the small town came back into focus.

The hotel sat at the top of a hill: a long thin road, lined on either side by small shops leading down into the centre of the town. The road was quiet and only a handful of cars were parked along its winding pavements. Towards the bottom of the hill George could see a handful of people milling about, not busy and rushing; just ambling along at a sedate pace. He descended the stone steps at the hotel's front door and onto the pavement, setting off on a slow stroll down the hill.

After just a few paces, he wandered past his car, all sad and forlorn, parked where it had been towed to the previous evening. Out of petrol, thought George: how very unlike me! It was the first time George had ever run out of petrol in his life. He was usually so conscientious about checking the level and making sure that the tank was never less than a quarter full.

To his recollection, the small light that indicates you're about to run out of fuel had never even been allowed to blink. A pristine bulb: never once used; never even needed. There was something rather sad about that poor little bulb, never having been allowed to fulfil its one and only function. Never in its whole existence had it been allowed to shine. Rather like me, thought George.

And then, when it had finally illuminated – exclaiming to the world its sole message *"You're about to run out of fuel!"* – nobody had paid it the blindest bit of notice. "Lot of bloody good you were," George found himself saying out loud. Then he realised he was talking to a bulb on the dashboard of his car and felt slightly embarrassed.

George peered in through the driver's window of the vehicle, looking at the board of instruments and indicators, marvelling at the fact he'd managed to overlook such an important thing. He was sure the car had had at least half a tank of fuel as he'd left for work that morning. How far had he driven? And as he wondered about just how lost in his own head he'd been the previous night, his reflection in the window slowly came into focus.

His suit really was in an awful state: wrinkled and stained and still a little damp. Great dark patches of mud lined the trousers and the sleeves of the jacket. The left shoulder pad had burst; a small white candyfloss cloud of lining bubbling out. The cuffs were a good inch too short, where the rain had shrunk the material. His shoes were two hefty clumps of mud.

His face was unshaven for the first time in 36 years. His hair was a matted, uncombed thatch of confusion atop his head; the silvery-grey strands flecking the sides more prominent than ever.

And God only knew how bad his breath must have been. He considered cupping his hands together and breathing into them to check. But then, he thought, sometimes it's better to not know.

In the middle of all that mess – hidden amongst the rubble of George's battered, bedraggled face – those sad, tired eyes looked as lonely and lost as they'd ever been.

He felt dishevelled and dirty, unsettled and embarrassed. He was certain that had he been holding a paper cup, and accompanied by a scruffy-looking dog with a shoelace for a lead, kind strangers would probably offer him spare change. God, that he should be mistaken for some kind of homeless person!

George was highly practiced at not being noticed: everything he wore; the way he spoke; walked; acted. Everything about him was reserved and restricted, carefully underdone to aid him to blend in. Now he must have seemed highly conspicuous. Very noticeable indeed.

And what happens to noticeable people? They get noticed. George felt like all eyes were on him. He could feel them: staring; burning into him; jagging at him like sharp needles. He didn't like it. He wasn't used to it.

This wouldn't do at all. Immediate repairs and refurbishment were at the top of the list. A chemist and a clothes shop would have to be found, and found quickly. He reached into his pocket, fishing out his car keys and placing them on top of the front driver's side tyre as instructed. Then he started to walk.

******

It didn't take George long to walk down the hill into the town centre. And, when he got there and looked around him, it was so small he wasn't sure that he could necessarily call it a town at all. It was bigger than a village, he supposed, but quite possibly the smallest town he'd ever seen.

As he walked he tried hard not to notice the other people; avoiding eye contact; hoping they would not notice him. He glided stealthily along the street, head down; his gaze seeking any space without a person occupying it. He looked at his feet, he looked at shop signs; anywhere but at the people he passed.

Each shiny shop window bounced back the embarrassing image of his dishevelled form. A family butcher; a proper old-fashioned green grocer; and, a small convenience store appeared in succession as George meandered slowly along, taking in his new surroundings. It all seemed terribly quaint, and old-fashioned, like a theme village set 50 years in the past.

Of the few shops that did make up the centre of the town, George noticed that they all seemed to be independent. There were no chain shops at all: not a TESCO, McDonalds, HMV or WHSmith in sight. How oddly refreshing, he thought. But how bizarre that none of the bigger stores had penetrated this town, driving these littler shops underground with their mass-marketing and cheaper price promises.

A small, handwritten sandwich board, emblazoned 'CHIDBURY HERALD', stood in the street outside a diminutive newsagent. It read:

THE KING IS ALIVE!
FESTIVAL STARTS TODAY

How odd, he thought. The King is alive? What could that mean? Why had this story not appeared in any of the national press? And why would they be having a festival to celebrate it? George couldn't remember hearing of any royal celebrations taking place. So why would such a small town as this be the only place to participate?

George carried on along the pavement. He scanned the shop fronts until he came upon what he had been looking for: *H. K. MAXWELL, Gentleman's Clothier*. That should do very nicely, thought George, crossing the street and walking in through the door.

"Hello, Sir," said the tall, thin man standing behind the counter at the far end of the shop. "How can I help you to…" The sentence trailed off as George stepped fully into the light of the shop, revealing his degraded state. The man stood open-mouthed for the briefest of moments, before continuing, "Oh dear. We do seem to have been in the wars, don't we?"

The shopkeeper was exquisitely turned out, perhaps as well-dressed as any man George had ever seen. His suit was finely tailored; dark navy with the faintest pin stripe, matching waistcoat and long, thin trousers. His lilac shirt was set off with a very expensive-looking, carefully-stitched, patterned silk tie and his polished cuff-links glimmered just below the cuffs of his suit jacket.

He was well-spoken in a light, yet authoritative, voice; just this side of posh. He reminded George a bit of a butler, or at least the stereotypical butlers he'd seen on TV.

"Come in, Sir," he said to George, "and let's see what we're dealing with."

"Sorry," said George, "my, er… my car broke down. And then it started to rain. And my suit… well, I've ended up a terrible mess."

"Yes," said the man. "Well, I'm sure we can find you something a little less…"

"Perhaps just a new suit," said George. "And, of course, a shirt. And some shoes."

"Ah. Unfortunately," replied the man, gesturing around the shop with his hand, "I'm afraid I don't really have any suits in at the moment. At least, nothing terribly… traditional."

George's eyes followed the man's sweeping hand. On each rack, on each shelf, throughout the small shop hung nothing but strange, extravagant, brightly-coloured jumpsuits. Great, long flowing things; the type Elvis Presley became famous for wearing and which had subsequently become forever associated with him. The type of clothing that now took up residence in the wardrobes of all die-hard Presley fans and impersonators.

The range was truly incredible. There were white jumpsuits, red jumpsuits, powder blue, black, yellow. Every colour George could imagine. Some were simpler than others, with strong colours and lightly-patterned. Others were exquisitely designed: with huge swathes of pattern; hand-sewn words and logos; or, pictures of tigers; dragons; Elvis Presley himself.

George couldn't believe he hadn't noticed when he'd walked in: the shop sold literally nothing but Elvis Presley jumpsuits. A small shop, in the middle of the smallest, quaintest little town George had ever come across – and all it sold was Elvis Presley jumpsuits.

"Yes," said the man, noticing George's open-mouthed confusion. "It's because of the festival, you see? I moved all of my other stock into storage only yesterday, to make way for the more… specialist items. When the festival is on, this is all I can seem to sell, so I move my usual clothing out of the shop to make more space for these… items." The way the man said items led George to believe that he was not entirely happy about the clothing currently on sale in his shop.

"I'm sorry," said George, "the festival?"

"Ah, an out-of-towner. Yes, I thought so. And from the look of you, no offence, I'd wager that you're not here for the festivities?

"Erm…"

"Well, I'm afraid to say that you've landed in our little town right at the start of our annual…" The man's nose seemed to turn up slightly. "Our annual Elvis Presley festival."

"Huh?" said George.

The man explained. Apparently, every year the small town of Lower Chidbury, located on the Sussex coastline, held a week-long festival celebrating the life, times and work of Elvis Aaron Presley – the legendary Hawaiian/American pop singer who came to fame in the 1950s and grew to become arguably the best, most successful professional singer in musical history.

Legend has it, though no proof has ever been found – and historical logs would actually seem to prove otherwise – that in the early 1960s, in a bid to escape from his high-profile, decadent, claustrophobic showbiz lifestyle, Elvis Presley had sought peace and quiet and visited the town of Lower Chidbury, secretly holidaying there for one week.

He had kept pretty much to himself, though he had been very friendly and courteous to the folk of Lower Chidbury, even performing an impromptu gig in a local pub. He made such an impression, and ingratiated himself so closely with the townsfolk, that every year thereafter they held a small festival in his honour, celebrating his music and the friend they had all made in him, hoping to tempt him back for a more prolonged stay.

The festival carried on, year after year, with more events planned and eventually grew into a weeklong celebration. It grew in popularity, and each new year saw a greater number of Presley fans, impersonators and aficionados travelling to Lower Chidbury to take part and enjoy the festivities. And, no doubt, hoping for a glimpse of the great man himself should he respond to the Mayor's annual invitation and put in a surprise appearance.

When Presley sadly passed away in 1977, it was considered no better tribute to the man than to continue holding the festival each year, now as a memorial and celebration. So every year the town was transformed into a kind of living shrine. And though most of the original townspeople who claimed to have become friendly with Presley had now either passed away or moved on, the festival had become such an important part of the town's tradition (not to mention the added bonus of increased revenue from visitors) that the annual event carried on.

"Yes, so I'm afraid this is all I can offer," the shopkeeper said apologetically.

"Oh," said George, looking around at all the brightly coloured, figure-hugging, revealing costumes hanging around the shop. "I'm not sure this is really... I mean they're very nice but I... I wouldn't usually wear this sort of... I don't suppose there are any other shops, that..." George's voice trailed off, waiting for what he already knew the answer to be.

"Sadly, no," said the man. "We are a very small town, and there's not much call for more than my humble shop, I'm afraid. But I'm sure we can find something that you'll like."

George's heart started to race. His face flushed hot and red, and his head started to swim. After the events of the previous evening, this was a lot to take in. He spun round slowly, his eyes darting from one bright, garish costume to another. His worst clothing fears, manifest before him. He couldn't wear one of these. These were not his type of clothes. He would stand out in these. He'd look foolish in these. People would look at him and laugh.

Just like the ties in his wardrobe that he so liked looking at; so enjoyed picturing himself wearing; George drank in the joy and wonder that these outfits seemed to exude. Deep inside he smiled at the thought of himself dressed so garishly, so elaborately. But this wasn't him. He couldn't wear these things. This would not do at all.

"Are you sure you haven't anything else out the back?" he pleaded.

"I really am terribly sorry," said the man, "but this is all the stock I have at the moment."

George was all set to make his apologies, leave the shop and aim for another solution elsewhere, when he caught sight of himself in a long mirror on the shop wall. That suit: all torn and shrunken and covered in mud. Would it be worse to stand out for the garishness of his clothes? Or for the ragged mess looking back at him?

"Okay," said George. "Do you have anything quite plain?"

******

After a brief, almost too-familiar encounter with the shop owner's tape measure

– during which the man seemed to spin and whiz around George, the tape tickling and clinging to some of his most delicate, private and slightly podgy areas – George was presented with a selection of outfits, all finely tailored and crafted and presented in different bright and exciting colours.

"I believe these should all be a good fit," the man said. "Would you care to try them on?"

George looked at the suits in the man's hand. "Erm…"

Oh goodness, was he really going to have to do this? Was this all some kind of joke? He looked round quickly, hoping to catch someone hiding, waiting to jump out at him and tell him he was on television and how funny it would all be. But all he saw was an empty shop. An empty shop filled with Elvis Presley costumes.

He gazed at the selection in the man's hands. There was a white one, with a garish collection of multi-coloured rhinestones littering the chest, arms and legs, sparkling in the dim lights of the shop. Another was done in the colours of the American flag: red and white stripes running up the arms, with gold and blue stars peppering the high lapels.

There was a bright red one, covered in green and yellow palm trees, made to look like a Hawaiian shirt. One was black with long, ragged, orange stripes, like the skin of a tiger. George couldn't believe what he was seeing.

Where do I start? He thought. He'd asked for something relatively plain and, with the exception of the weird tiger thing, compared to the other garments he could see hanging around the shop the ones the man had selected were all relatively tame. But they were still incredibly bright. And they were all very figure hugging, with wide, gaping lapels, which would leave very little to the imagination. His heart beat faster at the very thought of going out into the world dressed in one of these things.

"How about this one?" said the man, pulling a suit out from the bottom of the pile. It was powder blue, with gold and white stitching running down the sides of the legs and arms in an elaborate pattern. "It's *quite* plain…"

"Erm… well…"

George took the suit and walked into a small changing room, pulling the curtain closed behind him. He slipped out of his muddy, shrunken, soggy suit and threw it into a pile on the floor. No need to take care of it now.

He looked at one of the garments hung out in front of him, assessing it, wondering exactly how one was supposed to get the damned thing on. There was a small zip, which seemed to go from what he assumed was the fly to half-way up the stomach. He unzipped it, opening the costume out fully.

I suppose you just… he thought, looking at it quizzically. Just, erm…

After several minutes of lifting legs, pointing toes and balancing himself against the cubicle wall, he slid one leg into the trouser part of the suit, followed by the other, and shimmied the jacket part up around his midriff. There were several minutes more of twisting, bending, stretching and squeezing himself into the costume and then he managed to get his arms into the arm holes, pop the jacket part up into position and zip himself up. He clipped on the accompanying belt, fastening the big metal buckle in the shape of an eagle, and walked back out into the shop, the flared trousers swishing wildly from side to side. He looked at himself in the mirror.

It was certainly a sight. Something George had not expected and had never imagined to see himself wearing. True to the shopkeeper's word, the suit was slightly less garish. At least from the front – until George made out the huge gold and white eagle immaculately stitched onto the back. But by that point he already had two full legs and half a buttock jammed into the trousers, and decided it was more sensible to keep going than try and take it off and risk falling and breaking his pelvis.

The collar of the thing was enormous. It must have been reinforced with cardboard to keep it so upright, and it seemed to extend half way up the back of George's head. The front felt very open indeed: the zip fastening about an inch above his navel, revealing a chest that he had always self-consciously worried looked conspicuously devoid of hair. The trousers ran down into a pair of audaciously wide bell-bottoms split on each side to reveal an inner lining of gold material, making them flare out even wider.

"Oh yes," said the shopkeeper, "that's a very good fit. How does it feel under the arms? Not too tight?"

"No, it feels okay."

"And how does the trouser feel?"

"Fine," said George, at once becoming strangely aware of how well-cushioned his bottom felt, as if two delicate hands were gently cupping each cheek. Then he caught sight of himself in the mirror, thinking that thought, and he couldn't look himself in the eye.

But he had to admit it was a very good fit indeed. Snug in all the right places, but not too tight. Loose in a few crucial areas and, although he did feel slightly embarrassed to have the majority of his chest and part of his stomach on display, the jacket was actually very comfortable. And although he wouldn't have said so out loud, and barely wanted to admit it to himself, he did notice that the blue of the jumpsuit did seem to bring out the blue of his eyes.

He swivelled slowly from side to side, watching himself in the mirror, taking in this daring new figure. He couldn't help but notice how the soft material of the outfit clung forgivingly to his slightly out of shape frame. It didn't make his belly look too big, and the sleeves and trouser legs all seemed to reach the right places comfortably.

Craning his neck nearly a full one hundred and eighty degrees, George was even surprised to see the outline of those two round buttocks – something his suit trousers always did a good job of flattening and hiding. He might not have wanted to admit it, but he was actually rather pleased and thought he looked pretty good.

He straightened up as he turned to face himself again. Standing slightly taller, his chest pushed out a little, he found himself endowed with perhaps just a little more confidence than usual.

George did consider trying on one of the other outfits, just to make sure that he was definitely buying the right one. But he looked again in the mirror and decided he really did like what he was wearing. It was quite stylish, he thought. He liked the way it fit, and he liked the way he looked in it. And to be perfectly honest, he wasn't entirely certain he'd be able to get it off again. "Yes, I'll take it," he said, handing over his credit card.

"Excellent, sir," said the man warmly. "And I take it you'll be wearing it now?"

George looked back to the changing room, where his old clothes lay in a forlorn pile on the floor.

"Yes, I think that would be for the best."

"And perhaps you'd like me to dispose of those?" said the shopkeeper, handing George his credit card and receipt and pointing to his old suit.

"Yes," said George, looking again at the new man reflected in the mirror. "Thank you."

"Very good."

"Oh, how about shoes," George said as an afterthought, looking down at his feet in just his socks.

The shopkeeper just smiled, holding up a pair of bright-white, high-heeled platform boots. "Size nine, I presume?"

"Of course," said George. "I should have guessed."

And so George stood in his new clothes, feeling excited and a little scared. He looked up at the entrance to the shop, preparing himself to walk out into the world.

"Here we go then," he said quietly to himself, taking a long, deep breath. And he opened the door.

CHAPTER 9

GEORGE stepped out of the shop into the cool fresh air of the day. The sun beat down with a harsh intensity, shimmering off the damp roads and bouncing back from the shop windows. In order to keep the glare out of his eyes he was forced to add the finishing touch the man had sold him for his costume, and he perched the thick-framed, gold sunglasses with the fat legs on his nose. They felt a little big compared with the more modest proportions of his skull, but they eased his vision and George had to admit that he did feel just a little bit cooler wearing them. Or, at least, he thought that's what it was – he'd never really felt particularly 'cool' before.

I should really go back to the hotel, thought George. He needed to find out if his car was fixed and he should really do something about phoning work. Or at the very least try to decide what he was going to do next. But he'd waited this long, he reasoned, so what was another half an hour? And he was curious to see what else this strange town had to offer.

He turned left out of the shop, wobbling slightly on the heel of his platform shoes, and headed off along the road.

It was a fairly inconspicuous town: the kind of picture postcard sort of place that typified that romantic tourist view of southern England. It did indeed feature a traditional butcher shop; a quaint little teashop; and a place that seemed only to sell postcards, ugly little ornaments and general assorted knick-knacks. George looked in all the shop windows as he walked down the hill, eventually coming to a short esplanade at the sea front, capped at either end by a collection of dark, black rocks jutting up out of the sea.

The barriers and paving were clearly newly-built and seemed to bring the road to a rather abrupt stop, as if a giant carving knife had come down from the sky, chopping a previously much longer road in two. In the centre of the railings was a large blue plaque, with a message commemorating the recently lost town of Upper Chidbury. It seemed terribly sad to George; a whole town simply disappearing overnight, fallen into the sea, never to be seen again.

He looked out at the waves, dark blue and gently rippling. A slight breeze caused light sprays of salty mist to dampen his face. He felt an enormous sense of calm, as though his cares were being washed away with each whoosh of the sea retreating from the coast.

"Terrible shame," he suddenly heard a voice say.

George turned to find not one but four Elvises standing before him. A father, mother, young son and daughter, all dressed in big, white, flowing jumpsuits and all adorned with the same sunglasses as George. The costumes were clearly more professionally made than the couple from the hotel and had a matching theme of gold braiding and detail. Each costume bore its owner's name, stitched onto the breast in gold lettering.

"Sorry?" said George.

"Terrible shame," said the man, pointing to the commemorative plaque. "A whole town. Gone, just like that."

"Erm, yes…" replied George.

The man looked to be a little older than George, maybe 40, and his wife was a few years younger. The young lad was maybe six or seven and clearly still revelling in the funny costume he wore; waving the slightly-too-long sleeves of his outfit and watching them rustle in the wind. His glasses were too big and looked like those oversized joke glasses that were briefly popular.

The daughter was maybe 11 or 12 years old, with a rather surly look on her face. The enjoyment she'd maybe once had for this fancy dress had clearly been lost and, unlike her brother, she wasn't enjoying it. She was just a little too old for it now, though that had apparently not stopped her parents from forcing her to take part. She was self-conscious and kept checking to see who was looking, preparing to be mortified at any second. George could certainly identify with that.

"Yes, we've been coming here for years," the man continued, "since before the kids came along. And though I wouldn't wish it on anyone, God bless them…" he raised his hand to half-shield his mouth and leaned a little closer to George, "…I do think things have been better since the Upper Chidburyians have gone."

"Yes?" said George.

"Well, they never really got into the spirit of the festival, the miserable sods. Just couldn't stand to see everyone else having fun."

His wife suddenly chipped in, cutting him off, presumably before he said something he might regret. "I do like your outfit," she said. "The stitching's really nicely done. Did you do it yourself?"

"Erm, no," said George. "I bought it from the shop."

"Ah well, it's very nice," she confirmed. "You'll be in with a good shout for a prize at the competition."

"Competition?"

"Tonight. At the pub," she said. "Ooh, this is your first time, isn't it? I could tell, couldn't I Pete?" she turned to her husband. "I said I bet this is his first time, didn't I?"

"Yes," replied Pete, a little annoyed at his wife commandeering the conversation.

"Well, it's tonight in the pub. You should definitely enter, shouldn't he Pete? You should."

"Right," said George.

"Well, maybe we'll see you there," Pete added, starting to walk away. "Bye now."

All four of them strolled off up the hill, leaving George alone again. He watched them walk away, still slightly baffled by the sight of a whole family of Elvis Presleys.

He scanned the rest of the street, where a few more people had started to emerge. They walked along the pavements, stopped and spoke to each other, looked in shop windows. People pushed prams, carried bags and generally just milled about. It was a very ordinary sight for a Wednesday morning in a small town. Aside from the fact that every single one of them was dressed as Elvis Presley.

It was like one of those moments in films where, had George been drinking from a bottle of wine, he'd have felt compelled to look at the label and check how strong the drink was. It was the strangest thing he'd ever seen.

He smiled to himself and then set off back up the hill.

******

As George reached the hotel, he was met by a strangely familiar-looking Elvis walking out of the door. His costume looked very professional and had clearly cost the owner quite a bit of money. This was no part-time Elvis; this guy did it for real – or at least enjoyed it so much that he'd made a decent effort.

The giant black quiff perched on top of his head was genuine too. Not a badly made wig, like most of the others George had seen in town. This had been lovingly grown over several years and immaculately groomed and styled into place. The big bushy sideburns were real too, clinging proudly to the owner's plump cheeks.

And then George realised why he looked familiar: it was the man from the night before. Jeff, the kind soul who'd stopped and saved him from a night trudging through the wind and rain. The man who'd brought him to this strange town in the first place.

"Ah, George," Jeff cried out, with a deep chuckle. "I see you've taken to the festival."

George looked down at his strange clothes. "Oh yes," he replied. "My suit was ruined from the rain. This was the only thing I could buy."

"Well, it suits you," said Jeff. "You should enter the competition tonight at the pub. I reckon you'd stand a chance of a prize. Well, that's if you stick around, of course."

"Sorry?" said George.

"Car's all fixed. That's why I'm here. I was gonna leave your keys at reception, but as you're here…" He handed the keys to George.

"Oh, thanks."

"Wasn't anything too bad. Just filled her with a bit of petrol, turned her over a few times and Bob's your uncle. Luckily there was no engine damage, but I wouldn't go running out of petrol too often 'cos it'll knacker the motor eventually."

"Oh that's great, thank you," said George. "How much do I owe you?"

"That's all right," said Jeff. "I've only put a can in, just to get her going. You'll need to fill up properly, but there's a petrol station at the other end of town."

"Oh great," said George.

"But listen, why not stick around for few days? Enjoy the festival. It's not the biggest or best but I think you'll like it. Besides, you've got the costume now."

"Oh, well, I really should be getting back. I haven't even phoned work yet. Are you sure I can't give you some money?"

"No, I wouldn't hear of it," said Jeff. "I'll tell you what, if you do stick around for the competition tonight, you can buy me a pint."

George smiled and nodded.

"And I wouldn't worry too much about work. Does us all good to chuck the odd sicky every now and again. Though don't tell the wife I said that!" He let out another deep, booming chuckle, gave George a hearty slap on the shoulder and strode off down the road. "Maybe see you tonight!"

So that was that, then. The car was fixed. George could simply climb in, start the engine and drive away. He was sure it wouldn't be too long before he found road signs to the motorway, or at least a major road. He could figure out where he was, plan a route home and be back in probably just a few hours.

Yet, as he stood there, staring at the tragic, lost-looking little grey car, he found himself hesitating.

What was he really going back to anyway? Back to work. Back to his quiet little house, and his quiet little existence. In the past 24 hours George's life had taken more unexpected turns, offered more surprises and greater adventure, than he'd experienced in the last 20 years. Was he really ready to give that up, ignore what had happened, try to forget his little adventure?

Maybe it had all happened for a reason. Surely it wouldn't hurt to see it out for just a little longer. At the very least, he was curious to see what other strange delights this weird little town would throw up next.

And so George decided to wait again. Just for a while. Until he'd had time to have a proper think.

He walked back up the cracked path and through the heavy door of the hotel. He didn't fancy going back up to his room, what with the clouds of dust and the cramped conditions. And then he remembered the little bar from the night before. Maybe he could spend some time in there.

It was unlike George to walk into a bar on his own. It was unlike him to walk into a bar at all. But he was getting used to doing things he wouldn't normally do, so he took a deep breath, ignored his own apprehension, and pushed his way through the door.

Seated at the far end, just as he had been the previous night, was the little grey-haired gentleman who'd seemed to take such delight in George's misfortune. He was sitting at the same angle, on the same bar stool and – had he not been wearing a change of clothes – George would have guessed he'd been there all night.

Instead of the brown trousers and white shirt he'd sported previously, he was now resplendent in a garish red Elvis Presley jumpsuit. It was possibly the most extreme version that George had seen so far, with sparkling gold trim lining the collar, cuffs and seams of the trousers. Shocking bright-yellow and orange flames danced up the sleeves and across the chest.

"Ah, Thring," said the man, "good to see you again. I see you got your clothes sorted. Very nice!"

He was beaming a large wide smile, his face red and mottled. Again, George might have assumed that was the result of alcohol. But something about that smile, the soft glow of the man's happy eyes, told George that he was just very pleased with himself. He'd seen that a lot, how these funny costumes somehow managed to bring out the best in people.

"Come in," continued the man, "sit yourself down."

George smiled back, crossed the room and sat down next to the man.

"We weren't properly introduced last night," said the man, "I'm Les. Les Wakeman." He thrust his hand forward, taking George's and giving it a tight, forceful squeeze. "I take it you're here for the festival, then?"

"Sorry?" replied George.

"The clothes?"

"Oh yes. The clothes. They were the only ones I could get. I'm afraid I don't know much about the festival. I didn't even know there was one. To be honest, I don't actually know where I am."

"Don't know where you are?" chuckled the man. "How's that then?"

George would not usually have been so candid but he found himself strangely comfortable in the man's company and, before he knew it, he was recounting the previous evening's events. He told him about the dull day at work; his minor nervous breakdown; driving for hundreds of miles without realising it; his car's mechanical failure; and, finally, ending up in quite the oddest town he'd ever been to, not even knowing where it was on a map.

"Went a bit cuckoo, eh?" the man laughed.

"Erm, well…" said George defensively.

"I shouldn't worry, mate. Happens to the best of us." He reached out in front of George, straightening three bar mats that George had absent-mindedly knocked when he sat down until they were perfectly aligned. He then moved a long, fluffy bar towel about a quarter of an inch, straightening it and ensuring it sat perfectly flush with the edge of the bar. "So, what are your plans now then?"

"Well," said George, looking rather thoughtful, "I'm not entirely certain I know what to do."

"How's that?"

"Well, my car's fixed. And I suppose I ought really to go home and… well, face the music."

"But you don't want to?" offered Les, standing suddenly, retrieving a discarded dirty glass from a table in the corner and placing it behind the bar.

"Well, I don't know. I should really phone work. They'll probably have noticed that I'm not there by now. And I should get home and get back to the house. And I should…"

"Sounds like a lot of shoulds," interrupted Les. "Just because you should, doesn't mean you want to. Or, in fact, that you actually *should*. So what do you *want* to do?"

"Well, I don't really know," said George.

Again Les stood. This time he walked over to the small window and moved the material of the curtain just slightly, eyeing it against the other curtain, apparently measuring their distance from each other. Satisfied, he came and sat back down.

"I've often found," he said, "that the best thing to do in these circumstances is to have a little drink and think it through." With that, he reached round to the other side of the bar and slapped his hand down onto a small circular bell.

The concealed door opened and in walked Alice. George's face instantly lit up. His heart beat just a little bit faster, his face becoming flushed with embarrassment. He fought the urge to smile, clamping his jaw shut and straightening his lips, holding an expression he was sure looked not unlike constipation.

"Yes, Les," she said, walking in and taking up position behind the bar, "time for another already?" Then, noticing George, she added, "Oh, hello Mr Thring. Didn't see you there."

"Alice, my love," said Les, "be an angel and pour me another pint. And Mr Thring will have a…"

They both turned to George.

"Oh, I'll have a… Oh, I'm not sure… perhaps I'll have a… a pint of the same please."

"Two pints coming up."

Naturally, she too was wearing a costume. It was white with blue detailing up the sleeves and down the legs, and sparkled with shiny costume jewellery around the low, yet tasteful, neckline. And where most people's outfits looked saggy and baggy and hung awkwardly in places they should have fit, or gripped too tightly in places they really shouldn't, hers looked absolutely perfect. It showed off her trim figure perfectly, clinging to her round, shapely hips, her flat stomach, the curve of her ample cleavage. And as she turned around to find two clean pint glasses, George noticed how well the costume showed off her lovely bottom.

"Alice," continued Les. "Old Thring, here, has a bit of a quandary. Can't make up his mind whether he should go home and back to work, or whether he should stay for the festival."

"Oh dear," replied Alice, placing a full pint down in front of each man. "Well, Mr Thring…"

"Oh, George, please," he said.

"Well, George," she continued, "it looks like you've already got the costume. Maybe you should stick around for a few days. It's quite good fun, really."

"Yeah," interjected Les, "it's loads of fun. There's loads of stuff going on.

Elvis impersonators from all over the world come here to perform. There's competitions, special themed nights at the pubs… There's even a few do's in here, aren't there, Alice?"

"That's right," she said, somewhat less enthusiastically, "though we're not really big enough to do the main events."

"Then," said Les, taking back over with the sales pitch, "it all gears up towards the big karaoke competition on Friday night. That's always good. Two competitions, you see, one for the pros and one for amateurs. We should put Thring's name down, don't you think Alice. I bet there's a right little performer in there, just waiting to get out."

"You could be right, Les," she said, smiling at George.

George blushed again, partly at the pretty girl smiling at him and partly at the terrifying thought of standing on stage singing in front of people. "Oh, I'm not sure about that…"

"Well, it would be very nice if you did stay around, George," said Alice. "If you like I can ask Mum to keep your room for you."

"Oh… um… thank you. Well, I'll think about it."

"Okay, well don't think too long," she said, "there'll be others looking for a place to stay later on. Just let me know if you want it. Anyway, best be getting on. Ring again if you want anything." She opened the door and walked out.

George sat there, dreamily thinking about that perfect smile. And that perfect bottom. It was a long time since George had found himself thinking about a girl's bottom.

"She's taken a shine to you, Thring," said Les, snapping George out of his spell.

"Sorry?" said George.

"Yep, she likes you all right," he said. "There's not many men get the time of day from Alice, let alone get her talking them into sticking around."

Les picked up the bar towel, mopped up a couple of stray spots of beer that had dripped down onto the bar, then lined it up perfectly again.

"Really?" he said.

"For sure. You know what? I'll bet you could phone in sick for the next few days. Even better, don't phone them at all. Keep them guessing. Stick around, for a bit. You never know, you might even enjoy yourself."

"Yes, but work."

"Jobs come, Thring. And jobs go. Sounds to me like you don't even really like yours anyway." He placed a reassuring hand on George's shoulder. "Go on, play hooky for a few days. I bet it'll do you good."

"I suppose I could," said George. "I bet they wouldn't even notice I'd gone."

He picked up the pint in front him, looked down rather ominously at it then raised it to his lips and took one almighty gulp. He then winced slightly; the bitter, acrid taste catching in the back of his throat. He swallowed it, bouncing the glass back down onto the bar in front of him.

Then he stood up, reached over the bar, rang the little bell and waited until

Alice poked her head around the door. "Oh Alice," he said. "Sorry to bother you but would it be possible to keep my room for another night after all?"

"No problem, George," she smiled back at him. "I've already asked and Mum says you can have it till the end of the week."

CHAPTER 10

THE stolen Ford Mondeo pulled up outside the dilapidated hotel at the top of the steep hill. It looked more like a pensioner's home, dated and poorly taken care of, than a place people would actually pay to stay. They'd have driven straight past it were it not for the beleaguered blue sign swinging ominously in the wind, as if it could come away from the post holding it at any second and tumble down onto somebody's head.

A tall, lean man climbed out of the front passenger seat. He was well dressed in a navy suit and looked stiff and starched from the perfect double-Windsor knot of his tie down to his shiny black shoes. His hair was combed into a neat side parting and a tidy moustache, impeccably trimmed and presented, sat above his top lip. He straightened himself up, brushing down his jacket and buttoning the top button, tugging both cuffs of his shirt gently into position. Finally, he straightened his tie, craning his neck forward, before taking a deep breath as he scanned the street.

He leaned down, peering in through the open window to talk to the driver, a stocky man with rough, messy hair and a large square jaw littered with angry, black stubble. "Right," he said, "we'll go and check in; you park the car. Looks like there's a car park at the back where you can get it out of sight."

A third man, shaven-headed with a crumpled face and dark, piercing eyes, exited the rear of the vehicle. He was brutish-looking, tall and stocky with broad shoulders. He was more tree trunk than man and the rear of the car visibly rose as his weight was lifted from it.

The two men walked through the hotel door, approached the check-in desk and rang the small circular bell. An attractive young woman appeared from behind the door to the side of the desk.

"Oh hello," chirped the well-dressed man, his tone posh and precise. "We have a couple of rooms booked. One single and a twin. Name's Fairview. Major Charles Fairview. And what should I call you?"

"You can call me Alice," she said.

"Alice," replied the Major. "Delightful."

Alice scanned the big white book in front of her. "Fairview... ah yes, here you are. Your rooms are all ready for you. Let me just grab the keys and I'll show you up."

Alice collected the keys from the board behind her. "Is there another member of your party still to come?"

"Just parking the car," said the Major. "You can show us up and I'm sure he'll catch up soon enough." He flashed a sycophantic smile, all teeth and too much charm, the way Alice thought a snake might smile at you just before lunging and biting your neck.

"Very well." She showed the men to their rooms and left them. There was something about the Major that she didn't like. He was creepy, and an uneasy feeling niggled in her stomach as she returned downstairs.

Another man passed her on the way up, obviously the third of the group. He was short and wide, all muscle and bulk. He looked scruffy, like he hadn't slept or washed in a few days. His hair was messy and uncombed and he wore dirty-looking jeans and a crumpled red shirt. He was carrying two large duffle bags, fully packed and bulging. They looked heavy, like any normal person would struggle to hold their weight. But he had them flung over one shoulder and carried them easily. He kept his head down as they passed on the stairs, his eyes fixed firmly on the floor in front of him.

He followed along the corridor, where he was ushered into a room by the Major. He dropped the two bags onto the floor, and sat down on one of the single beds next to the third man.

"Okay chaps," said Major Fairview, "step one complete. This is the scene of our little caper. So, let's go over the plan.

******

Major Charles Fairview was, of course, not really a Major at all. He'd never even come within two hundred metres of a military recruitment centre, let alone served any actual time in the forces. His claims to have been a formerly high-ranking army officer were entirely fabricated, as were many of his other tales. He wasn't really a gulf war veteran. He hadn't actually served for several years with the SAS. And he had certainly never been a security consultant at Buckingham Palace. His name wasn't even really Fairview.

He was Charlie Crowe, gentleman thief and conman. In fact, he wasn't even really a gentleman – at least not from the background and breeding he claimed to be. He'd grown up in Manchester, brought up by a mother who worked three jobs and shouted a lot, and a father who drank too much and shouted even more. From an early age he knew it wasn't the life he wanted. And it certainly wasn't the life he felt that he deserved.

He had always been clever, much more so than any of his classmates, and his teachers had high hopes for his future. However, they also lamented his lazy attitude and the fact that he always seemed happy merely to get by. He was content with average grades, never striving to excel at anything. He showed aptitude and ability but never seemed to have any ambition or interest in anything other than chasing girls and tricking the other pupils out of their lunch money.

He was finally expelled for stealing exam papers and selling them to his classmates. Considering he could have sailed through the test without a great deal of effort, the headmaster was baffled by why he'd done it. When asked, Charlie had simply replied that it had made the most sense. By stealing the paper he needn't bother revising and he could make a profit by selling it at the same time. The headmaster couldn't fault his logic exactly, but did ask whether he thought it was morally right?

"That's neither here nor there," argued Charlie. It was the easiest way to get what he wanted. And, surely, the easiest way was the right way, whether morals came into it or not.

At the age of 15, with an early release from education, no qualifications and few local prospects, he'd realised that life working in a factory, or manning a booth in a car park, were never quite going to live up to what he wanted for himself. He accepted a job in a supermarket and worked there just long enough to steal two and half thousand pounds from a till at the end of the day, which funded a late-night flit down to London.

There he set about making money as quickly, easily, dishonestly and as illegally as possible. Small scams and easy scores kept him clothed and fed but it wasn't long before he set his sights on bigger, more lucrative scams.

At 39, he was a full six years younger than the age he held out the Major as being. Having started to go grey in his late twenties, however, his hair held a distinctive salt-and-pepper look and he found he could easily pass for much older than he actually was. He'd modelled his look and style, including his neatly-cut suits, trimmed moustache and even his light-footed gait, on the ideal of the dashing 1940s Hollywood star. It was a classic look, which seemed to hold much weight in the minds of most people. He appeared charming, charismatic and, most importantly of all, trustworthy, before he even opened his mouth.

He'd worked hard on his accent, too, knowing that a twang of Received Pronunciation would gain him far more stead in most peoples' books than the whiny, nasal Mancunian accent he'd inherited from his parents. It had taken a fair bit of effort to iron out all the inaccuracies, but he'd worked hard, basing his research largely on films starring David Niven. After several hundred conversations with himself, mimicking Niven's voice, he'd worked up a passable impersonation.

And so Major Charles Fairview was born – the latest in a long line of fabricated personas.

Over the years he'd been Charles Montgomery, international businessman and creator of world-beating conglomerates. He had interesting investment opportunities to sell – only for the right buyers, of course. His preferred clients were those that wanted to make lots of money very quickly and didn't mind if a few laws were broken in the process. These were ideal for Charlie because, when the deals did in fact turn out to be too good to be true, and the investor's money disappeared without trace, along with a certain Mr Montgomery, they were hardly likely to go crying to the authorities. Unless they wanted to explain their own shady part in the proceedings.

He'd spent time as Charles Willerson, antiques dealer extraordinaire, with a unique gift for authenticating worthless tat as priceless memorabilia. He would then sell it on to greedy bargain hunters at grossly inflated priceless.

He set up a bogus record company, under the name of Charley Quinn, offering deals to naive fledgling bands and charging them printing costs for albums that never quite made the presses, let alone the record shops.

For six months he passed himself off briefly as The Reverend Charles Johnson, a kindly minister and former missionary who'd set up a charity for the starving children of Africa. He tirelessly shamed fame-hungry celebrities and the social elite into making hefty donations, in return for maximum publicity, of course. Then he cleaned out their bank accounts and disappeared without trace.

He'd even tried to pass himself off as the son of unknowing mentor, David Niven, when trying to woo a particularly wealthy widow with a penchant for vintage cinema and ridiculous spending sprees. He'd greatly underestimated how big a fan of Niven she really was. Faced with actually having to do research into the screen icon to keep up with her questions about his supposed father, he decided instead to simply pocket as much cash and jewellery as he could and disappear in the middle of the night.

Though the titles and surnames changed frequently, the first name was always a variation on Charles. He'd learned that tactic from watching James Bond films. People were always most likely to call you by your first name, so you had to adopt something that you couldn't fail to recognise. Not to react to someone calling you by your own first name would be a sign of complete idiocy. Or an indication that it wasn't really your name at all.

Each enterprise saw him adopt a different moniker, and he was always running away from one life straight into another persona and another devilish scam. He'd spent so many years pretending to be so many other people that he hardly even knew who he was himself anymore.

In reality, he didn't really need to be anyone. He'd found it so easy over the years to shed one skin and adopt another that he could simply create a new persona and become whoever and whatever he wanted.

The Major had been his most successful guise. It was one that worked particularly well in the pursuit of seducing rich, lonely widows, desperate for a distinguished man to spend their time and money on. The chances of making a great deal of money out of this gambit were limited, short of marrying the old dears and bumping them off. But that was all rather too distasteful. Say what you would about him and his disreputable character, but he drew the line at killing old ladies.

So he was unlikely ever to make his fortune from romancing desperate, rich women, but it put a roof over his head and kept him fed and clothed without having to work too hard.

Of course, all good things come to an end and sadly the Major found himself serving 12 months behind bars. Whilst romancing Katherine Winthorpe, a charming 62-year-old widow with a large interest in a haulage company in Norfolk which she'd inherited from her late husband, he'd sadly underestimated the latent greed of her grown-up offspring.

Naturally they viewed the Major with suspicion from the start, whilst claiming only to be concerned for the welfare, health and happiness of their still-grieving mother. Of course, they were far more concerned with making sure she didn't spend the late husband's money before they got their chance to appropriate it for themselves.

When the hate campaigns of carefully-guarded threats started, the Major — not one for confrontation at the best of times — decided the best course of action was to amass as much booty as he could before absconding and starting afresh a few hundred miles away. He convinced the darling Katherine to make him a substantial cash loan which he instantly divided into smaller amounts and moved from one bank account to the next until it was almost untraceable. Then he simply packed up his collection of tailored suits and expensive trinkets and made off in the brand new BMW she'd bought him as a rather expensive love token.

Of course, he should have left it at that. But, even though he knew he was asking for trouble, he couldn't talk himself out of stealing a rather beautiful antique diamond brooch that he was sure would raise a good price and fund his nefarious activities that little bit longer.

Sadly, he'd also rather underestimated Katherine's son, Howard, who'd anticipated the Major's early departure when he'd checked the accounts of the family business and seen a large sum of money unaccounted for. Howard had left the brooch unguarded in the hope that it would catch the Major's attention and thereby set a trap for him to blunder into. He didn't even make it as far as the end of the drive before the waiting police officers pounced.

Though he would usually ditch an identity as soon as it had been rumbled, he'd found it beneficial to carry on his act as the Major whilst inside. Though the Warden and prison guards all knew his true identity, he managed to pull the wool over the eyes of his fellow inmates. Through this guise he found he could sufficiently command their respect not to have to fear the shower block. In fact, he was so affable as the Major that many of the others seemed genuinely to like him.

He could certainly spin a yarn and there were few that didn't like listening to his stories, as he recounted his various fabricated military escapades. And though many were suspicious of his obviously slight frame (surely not the build of a military hero!), his tales of serving with the SAS, and all the different means he'd employed to kill people, seemed plausible enough that even the toughest prisoners were wary of calling him on it. So the Major served him well, and, on being released, he'd decided to keep up the charade for a little longer. At least until he'd had time to pull off one more job.

******

"So, if the job's not until tomorrow, why did we have to get here so bloody early?" asked the shaven-headed man, drawing the fat fingers of one hand down his stubbly chin.

"As discussed," replied the Major, "I thought it prudent to arrive early and make sure everything was in place. Cross all the t's and dot all the i's, so to speak."

"So, what are we supposed to do until then?" shaven-head humphed.

His dubious-looking companions were John and Steve Clefton, two thuggish brothers and small-time thieves. The shaggier-haired of the pair, John at 28 was the eldest by one year, though the younger brother Steve had grown and grown, ending up far heftier and meaner looking. Having come from a fairly average middle-class family, with hardworking parents and a comfortable upbringing, they had neither the 'underprivileged' or 'broken home' cards that most career criminals chose to play. They were simply two men who chose to break the mould and break the law.

Though not particularly bad-natured boys, when growing up the two Clefton brothers had never been particularly intellectually gifted. In school they were classic underachievers; always raising hell, fighting in the playground and generally misbehaving. This was aided by two main advantages: first that they were both bigger and stronger than the other boys (and many of the teachers); and second, that they were never averse to using these two characteristics in pursuit of getting what they wanted. Add to that a certain disdain for any kind of rules, and a propensity for breaking said rules to suit their own ends, and a life outside of the law was always going to be their best career option.

Petty crime came naturally to them and both grew adept at shoplifting, minor vandalism, assault on other youths and raiding the Woolworths Pick-&-Mix on a near daily basis. Their journey towards real crime came of age when, at just 14 years old, they robbed their very first Post Office, threatening the terrified counter clerk with a rounders bat they'd stolen from the school gym cupboard and an Action Man whose leg had been whittled into a rather nasty-looking shiv.

They made off with six hundred and twenty-four pounds and enjoyed one blissful afternoon of spending their loot on McDonalds, new trainers, Adidas tracksuits, a flash new Sega Megadrive and an expensive pro-performance football for a kick-around down at the local park. It didn't take police too long to catch up with them, however, as the Post Office they'd chosen to rob was located in the newsagents a mere two hundred yards from their family home.

They were awarded an extra prize for their first major crime, which came in the form of an eighteen months stay in a young offender's institute.

Growing up in a youth detention centre didn't see the boys grow any smarter but they did grow closer, teaming up together against the other inmates, prison guards and social workers. And, far from being rehabilitated and realising their potential in life, they simply came to realise their lack of potential for fitting into normal society and getting themselves real jobs. Like two ugly ducklings realising they were never going to grow into swans, the boys settled for using their two best assets to get what they could out of life.

More armed robberies followed, along with countless pub brawls, burglaries, car thefts and whatever other dubious opportunities came their way. Naturally, they'd endured various spells in prison throughout the years, but each stay only reinvigorated their goal that the next job had to be a big one, with a hefty pay-off, to really set them up. Maybe then they could branch out into loan-sharking, or set up some dodgy betting scams, or even just buy a nice little plot out in Spain and look into the possibility of a lucrative drug-smuggling outfit.

So when they happened to meet a certain debonair, fast-talking, recently disgraced former Army Major, who happened to be residing in the cell next door to theirs, they were more than keen to hear about his once-in-a-lifetime opportunity.

"Before we start worrying about the evening's entertainment," said the Major, "I suggest we go over the plan one last time, just to make sure we're clear on what everybody has to do."

"We know what we have to do," barked John, "we've been over this a thousand times. And it's not like it's our first time." He looked over at his brother, the two of them smiling rather self-satisfied grins.

"Yes, well," returned the Major, applying the more forceful tone that usually seemed to quell the mutinous uprisings in the siblings, "that may be the case. But if it's all right with you, I'd like to see if we could make it your first without getting caught."

The smiles slid off of their faces, as the Major raised one very taut, triumphant eyebrow.

"Now, as we know, the bank in town is usually equipped to hold around fifty thousand pounds in cash at any one time. But because of this delightful festival that they're having, and the rather large number of musically tasteless souls that will be pouring through here, tomorrow morning they will be taking delivery of an extra two hundred thousand in cash. Which means we should be able to get away with somewhere close to a quarter of a million pounds for ourselves, give or take. Split four ways, that should be a very nice little return each."

"I still can't believe we're giving away a whole quarter of the money," huffed John. "Three-way split would be much better."

"Yes, agreed, but let's not forget this job would not have come about without the help of our silent partner," snapped the Major. "He's provided some invaluable information, local escape routes, police response times, details on the comings and goings of the bank, and put the whole damn thing together. So yes, we will be splitting the proceeds four ways."

"That's another thing," replied John, "what's with all this silent bullshit? Why don't we get to meet this 'silent partner'? He's getting a quarter of our money, how come he don't want to show his face?"

"Let's just say he's the shy type, shall we?"

"Fair enough, if he's that shy, what's to stop us keeping all the money? If he don't wanna get his hands dirty, why don't we just renegotiate and keep his share as well?"

"Believe me, Jonathon," sighed the Major, weary and condescending, "this is not a man that you want to double-cross. He'd be very upset if you decided not to pay him his share, and there's no telling what the repercussions might be. But, trust me, it's not something you'd want to find out first hand."

"How do we even know there is a silent partner?" interjected Steve. "How do we know it's not just you trying to scam us for two shares all for yourself?"

"Oh, come now, Steven. Is that really what you think of me? I'm wounded. You know," he said, adding a rather stroppy chord to his voice, "if you'd rather not go through with the job, I'm quite happy to leave now. We can all go our separate ways and leave with nothing."

"No, he didn't mean that," John blurted, flashing a look of annoyance at his brother. "I think Steve's just a little frustrated that some mysterious character, who we've never met, is getting all that money that we're stealing. But if that's the way it is," he added, trying to placate the Major before all his toys went flying from his pram, "then that's the way it is. It would just be nice to know who this guy is, that's all."

"Well, you can't. Now shall we get back to the plan?"

"Oh, we already know the plan," said Steve, rolling his eyes, "we've been over it again and again."

"Yes, well we'll bloody well go over it again and again, and again, until I'm satisfied you two idiots aren't going to make a mess of things and land us all back where we've just come from." It was an unusually tense outburst from a generally very calm, relaxed man, and enough to see the two brothers suitably shamed into silence.

"Very well," said the Major, "let's continue."

The plan was fairly simple. They were going to rob the bank. It was to be an audacious robbery and the tactics lay more closely with the Major's flair for deception and misdirection than the brothers' usual penchant for brute strength and violence. They would enter the bank at precisely 1pm; the brothers would wave a few guns around to scare everyone into submission; and they'd grab as much cash from the vault and the tills as they could carry.

They would have approximately four minutes before the authorities from the local police station would be alerted and arrive on scene. As it was a small town, there would only be a handful of officers on site immediately and it would take at least a full 30 minutes to assemble back-up units from neighbouring police forces. As such, the job had to be swift and effective, taking advantage of the small town's primitive law enforcement.

The Major had every detail planned down to the second so that they would be able to swoop in, sweep up the cash and disappear before anybody even noticed what was happening. Of course, no matter how clever the plan, nothing instills panic and confusion quite like a big dose of fear, which is why he'd enlisted the unique skills of the Cleftons.

"So, I was thinking," offered Steve enthusiastically, "when we're in the bank... I mean, obviously we can't call each other by our real names, can we?"

"No, that wouldn't be advisable," replied the Major.

"So, what are we gonna call each other? I was thinking we could use code names. I saw this film where they did it. Called themselves Mr Black and Mr White and that…"

The Major raised his hand to his left temple, closing his eyes and rubbing it slowly as he let out a soft, exasperated breath. "If you remember what I said earlier," he said slowly and calmly, "I do believe we've covered this point. As everybody knows exactly what to do, and when to do it, there really should be no need to communicate at all. I'll deal with any instructions to the bank staff, which means you two needn't say a word."

"Yeah, but…" said Steve, "what if something goes wrong?"

"Nothing will go wrong, Steve," replied the Major.

"No, I know, but we could give it a try. I mean, I just thought it might be quite cool."

"Cool?"

"Yeah, you know. Like a really cool robbery in a film, or something. Oh, go on, it'll be fun."

The two brothers sat there grinning like a couple of young boys keen to embark on a game of soldiers. The Major couldn't imagine a more pathetic sight. How had he thought it was a good idea to enrol these two morons into his scheme? Still, they'd make themselves useful enough tomorrow, then he'd be rid of them when the job was done. Just think of the money, he reminded himself.

"Very well," he said, "I'll make you a deal. Should we need to communicate, and I mean really only if we absolutely, definitely have to speak with each other…" he pointed at Steve, "…you're Mr Dick. You're Mr Head," he said, pointing at John, "and I'm Mr Don't Give a Fuck! Now check the equipment, and try not to break anything. I'm going downstairs to check the rest of the hotel. Don't leave the bloody room!"

He walked out through the door, closing it sharply behind him, and set off through the long corridor and down the stairs.

CHAPTER 11

"SO Thring, tell me about yourself," said Les. He placed his pint down onto the bar in front of him and wiped the excess froth from his top lip with the back of his hand.

"About myself?" said George. "I don't think there's really much to tell."

In the case of many people, this would just have been false modesty. But when George thought about his life he really couldn't think of a great many things that were interesting. Certainly nothing that anybody else would find interesting, anyway.

"Oh, come on. Anyone who manages to accidentally drive hundreds of miles in the wrong direction on the way home from work, and then end up sitting across from me dressed as Elvis Presley must have something about them," insisted Les.

"Well, when you put it that way... what would you like to know?"

"That's up to you, Thring. It's your life. It's your story to tell."

George's mouth formed a mild grimace as he looked up into the corner of the room, pondering. Thirty seconds passed and still nothing came.

"Very well," interjected Les. "Family. Have you got any family? Wife and kids at home?"

"Oh no," said George, suddenly broken from his trance. "No kids. Never married. There was someone, a long time ago... and I had hoped that someday we might... but that didn't really pan out."

He looked down at the drink in front of him, a flicker of sadness flashing across his eyes. He could see that Les was on the verge of pushing him further on this but he wasn't comfortable talking about it, so he quickly continued, "No family at all, in fact. No brothers or sisters. No parents."

"No parents?" coughed Les. "So, you're what? An orphan?"

"Well, in a manner of speaking. My parents both died when I was 11-years-old."

"Both at the same time?" said Les.

"Yes."

"I am sorry. What was it, car accident or something?"

"No," replied George solemnly. "Lion."

"Lion?" blurted Les, incredulous. "You mean, like... a lion? Like a big cat? A lion?"

"Yes, my parents were eaten by a lion. At least, my father was."

******

The incident was still etched terrifyingly in George's mind. It had been a pleasant day. One of the few family days out that George could remember.

At his wife's insistence that he spend some quality time with his family, George's father, Lionel Thring, had packed them all into his prized burgundy Volvo 740 GLE and set out for a day at the local wildlife safari park.

Lionel was suitably unimpressed at having been forced to spend time with his family, what with all the other, far more important, things he could be doing with his time. Working on his prized model railway, for example. Tending to the household accounts or getting some work done. At the very least he could be doing something constructive. Time was far too important to be frittered away on these nonsense outings.

However, he was a man that realised his fatherly and husbandly duties. And, if only to save himself grief from his wife's inevitable lecturing and whining, he'd agreed.

With a comprehensive picnic of sandwiches, crisps, boiled eggs, pork pies and flasks of orange squash and tea packed away in the boot, and with George having been warned not to put his feet on the car's upholstery and to announce any signs of car sickness as soon as possible, they'd set off. The journey had been predictably boring; minutes seeming like hours and the hot weather thinning the air in the back of the car, making George sleepy. But with Mum's happy, jaunty music playing on the radio and Dad's usual gruff temperament apparently reined in for the day, George felt very content.

When they drove through the guided confines of the safari park, seeing all the animals grazing; lolloping; strolling around the car; everyone seemed happy. The park didn't have a huge array of animals but to George it was so exciting to see them at such close quarters.

The exotic birds were incredible. There were pigs and squirrels, hyenas and zebras, all of which George recognised from the pictures in his books. He had particularly liked the monkeys, which were allowed to roam free, jumping all over the cars that drove through the enclosure. All three had giggled and laughed at their crazy antics; the funny faces they pulled and their silly behaviour.

Lionel had become slightly annoyed when two of them climbed onto the bonnet of his car and he'd banged the window, shouted and beeped the horn to get them to move. George saw him raise his eyebrows in the reflection of the rear-view mirror, muttering something under his breath as he drove on.

When they drove into the lion enclosure, things took a turn for the worse. The car weaved slowly along the narrow, guided road, Lionel sticking fastidiously to the five miles per hour speed limit. All three passengers marvelled at the glorious big cats, lazing by the side of the road. Then, as the car edged its way around a tight corner, Lionel was forced to come to a complete stop. A large male lion stood right in the middle of the road, blocking the car's path and staring.

At first this caused a small rustle of laughter, as all three looked round at each other, amused at the obstinacy of the beast. Lionel gave a light parp on the car's horn, joining in the fun of the situation, and jokingly calling out, "Come on Mr Lion, out of the way!" Everyone laughed again.

The lion walked slowly towards the car and lay down in front of it. He then lazily opened his big jaws wide, and closed them down around the car's bumper.

"Hey, you," shouted Lionel, disgruntled that his prize possession was sustaining severe lion damage. I mean, was that something he could even claim for on his insurance? And what would it do to his no-claims bonus? "Hey you, stop that!"

The lion didn't move. It just lay there, chewing away at the bumper.

Lionel wasn't having this. Despite the express instructions from the safari park's guides to remain in the car at all times, he threw the car door open, climbed out and walked round to the front of the vehicle. "Hey, you there. Lion! Stop that. Stop that now!"

The lion, apparently not one to take much notice of middle-aged men screaming orders at him, simply continued his work on the Volvo's dense rubber bumper, chewing and scratching and clawing at it.

"You! Lion!" continued Lionel Thring. "That is a pristine condition Volvo 740 GLE with four cylinders and a 2.4 litre engine. And you are ruining the paintwork with your bloody great claws. I demand that you stop that now, or I shall be forced to stop you."

The lion stopped chewing on the bumper and looked up at George's father. Then, with a look that George could have sworn was sheer petulance, the lion stood up, lifted one of his giant, furry paws – extending the long, sharp, shiny talons – and batted it straight down onto the Volvo's bonnet. It then drew the paw back in agonising slow motion, leaving four perfectly-scored claw marks in the car's shiny maroon paint job.

"Right," yelled Lionel. "That's it!"

George couldn't quite believe what he was seeing as his middle-aged father, a relatively quiet – though distinctly belligerent, no-nonsense accountant – marched straight up to a lion in a safari park and kicked it in the leg. The lion did not seem to like this.

Lionel, having kicked the lion, took a step backwards, almost as if to allow the lion to acquiesce, realise its mistake and offer a full and frank apology for its wrongdoing. This lasted for about a second, as George's father looked down at the lion angrily and with complete intransigence.

His expression then suddenly changed as he realised what he had done.

The lion sat quietly for a few seconds, also seeming to take in what had just happened. Chances were that the lion, being a lion, and a resident of a quiet, peaceful English safari park, had probably never been kicked in the leg by a man before. His confusion, therefore, was quite justified.

His primal nature, however, also seemed to be registering that this strange new predator had just unleashed some kind of assault upon him. It wasn't the kind of claw-thrashing, teeth-bared, roaring, pouncing assault his upbringing as a lion would have taught him to expect. But it was an attack, nonetheless. And, as king of the jungle – or the very least king of a leafy Sussex safari park – he couldn't allow this.

All he was trying to do was have a bit of an old chew on the bumper of a Volvo 740 – something he'd rather taken to doing since they first started invading his territory at the beginning of the year and something that nobody had ever complained about before. And now he had some odd, thin, wiry, pink sack of meat actively attacking him for it. No, he couldn't let this pass.

His eyes fixed on Lionel, assessing him, trying to take in the measure of him. They looked at each other, eyes locked, before the Lion finally broke the tension by leaping forward, knocking Lionel onto his back with his great big paws, affixing his mouth to Lionel's arm and ripping it clean off with a pop and a squelch.

There followed a mad flurry of flailing arms, paws and legs. A dense blur of yellow fur, crimson blood and dark green sweater, as the lion bit, scratched, mauled, clawed, chewed. The whole thing was over in seconds, leaving poor Lionel Thring a bloody, scratched, chewed-up mess on the ground. Beaten, battered and, unequivocally, dead.

The lion stood up and very casually looked back over at the Volvo's remaining passengers as if to say, 'Well, I am a lion, what did he expect?' It then picked Lionel's arm up in its mouth, the expensive Rolex watch still glinting on its wrist, and sauntered off across the grass.

George and his mother sat lifeless in the car. Still, silent, open-mouthed. Neither could quite believe what they'd just seen: the horrifying sight of their father and husband ripped to shreds by a lion.

George's mother broke the silence, screaming out with a terrific, high-pitched, agonised squeal, "Lionel!"

She bolted from the car, running round to where her husband's mangled, shredded body lay crumpled and bloodied on the ground. Looking down at it she screamed again, wailing and bursting into tears, shivering with the shock. She went silent; the shaking stopped; and she just stood there, unbelieving, looking down at what used to be Lionel Thring. And then she collapsed, crumpling to the floor, dying from what George later found out to be an instant, shock-related cardiac arrest.

And so, what had started out as a memorable family day of fun, boiled eggs and animals had ended with George suddenly finding himself an 11-year old orphan.

The lion was destroyed a few weeks after the incident, which George thought was a terrible shame. It wasn't the lion's fault. Not really. It was only doing what lion's do, after all.

The story made all the national papers. And despite Lionel clearly having disobeyed the instructions not to get out of his car, the safari park's owners were deemed responsible for the circumstances of George's parents' death. After a short and private court case, they were ordered to pay George damages in the region of 3.7 million pounds.

He went to live with Uncle Clive, his father's brother, and his wife, Aunt Joan. Initially they were delighted to take him in and spent money transforming their loft into a cosy bedroom for him. They talked of new beginnings and a happy life and how good things can come from terrible tragedies.

Their enthusiasm at having him come to stay mysteriously disappeared, however, after discovering that the majority of the money had been put into a secure trust fund by the courts; locked away until George was 18 with just a modest monthly allowance paid out to cover food, clothing and general expenses. After that they treated George with a casual disdain and tried simply to ignore him.

So George had never really known the value of the money. He hadn't felt like spending much of it, considering the circumstances from which it had been bestowed. Over the years he'd dipped into it to buy a house and a car and a few of life's essentials, but the rest of it had been more or less forgotten about. George didn't actually know what amount it had grown to with interest over the years, but he assumed it must be a fair bit.

The safari park also returned Lionel's watch to George, along with the settlement. They'd found it several days after the incident, in the corner of the cage the animal had been locked in before it was put down. He kept it in a box in a drawer, never really wanting to wear it; partly because it would have brought back too many scarring memories of the final time his father had worn it; partly because he would have felt a little morbid wearing his dead father's watch every day; and partly because he didn't really like the thought of wearing something that had been through the digestive system of a lion.

******

"See," said Les, "you said there was nothing interesting to tell me. And then you come out with that. Parents killed by a Lion."

"Well, it all happened such a long time ago now," said George casually. "I've never really thought of it as an anecdote."

"No, I guess not," said Les. A silence hung between them. Les nervously fiddled with the bar mats in front of him: flipping them over; rearranging the order; then lining them up perfectly again.

"So what about this job you're so concerned about?" said Les. "What do you do?"

"I'm an accountant," said George. "Well, sort of. I mean, I used to be. I'm kind of a data analyst now, I suppose. Number cruncher."

"Sounds fascinating," chuckled Les.

"Well... no. It's pretty dull, actually."

"So why are you so concerned about going back? Forgive me for saying, but you don't seem like you particularly like it?"

"Erm... well... no. No, I suppose I don't."

"But you like the people?"

"No."

"The company?"

"Not really."

"So why the stress?"

"Erm… I don't know."

"I hate to state the obvious, Thring, but if you don't like your job and you don't like the people, why do you work there? Why don't you do something that you do like?"

George suddenly felt embarrassed, as if he'd been letting himself down all these years; not living life to the potential that he should. He wanted to say that he'd always believed in working hard; that his father had extolled the virtues of having a career and making something of himself. He wanted to say that he really loved working; was never happier than when he had spreadsheets to check and figures to analyse. He wanted to say that he was happiest when in the office: a real workaholic, who lived for his job and strived for success.

Of course, none of that was true. George really did hate his job. He hated working full-stop. And the worst thing was, he didn't even need to work. Technically, he had enough money that he never needed to go to work again. So why *did* he have a job?

He'd done it because that's what you were supposed to do. People were supposed to have jobs. That's what he'd been taught.

The fact that he had a lot of money in the bank had never really meant much to him as he'd never had any desire to spend any of it. It was ten years before the trust fund had released it all to him, and, rather than build up an insatiable appetite to fritter it away on trinkets and toys, he'd only grown apathetic towards it. He'd never wanted the money and he'd tried his hardest just to forget about it.

True, George's father had always tried to instill in him how important it was to have a career and to make something of himself. He'd told him how he needed to work hard if he wanted to achieve anything.

Now that George thought about it, he wondered how true that was. His father had worked hard all his life. And look what happened to him. Eaten by a Lion, trying to protect the paint job on a maroon Volvo.

George's job, it seemed, was more just a way of filling up time. Was he really so unimaginative that he'd spent so many years doing something he hated, just because he hadn't thought to try something better?

It hadn't always been that way, of course. He used to be more enthusiastic about life. But that was before. When he was with her. Emily.

Back then everything had seemed possible. The world was a bright and shiny place and the future was exciting. He'd had dreams and hopes and ambitions. But since she'd gone, George had just sort of stopped thinking of the future. He merely carried on with life, living one day to the next, trying not to think about everything he'd lost and might never get again.

At least he still had his job. It didn't make him happy but it stopped him thinking about her for a while. It gave him a chance to focus on something else. He didn't enjoy the work but he thought if he really worked hard then maybe it would get better. Or maybe he'd learn to enjoy it. So that's what he did. And before he knew it, the years had raced by. But nothing much else had changed.

George didn't want to think about it any longer and he didn't want Les to press him on it, so he changed the subject.

"Have you always lived in Lower Chidbury?" he asked.

"That I have, Thring. Lived here all my life – aside from the odd spell away from time to time."

The man gave George a curious wink, smiling to himself.

"And what do you do for a living, Les?"

"Well, strictly speaking," he replied, "I don't really do anything."

"Oh, I see," said George. "Retired?"

"Not quite," said Les, flashing that devilish smile again. "I've just got back from a bit of time away, if you see what I mean. At her Majesty's pleasure."

"Oh, I see." George's mouth dropped open, his eyes widening. He wasn't afraid, exactly, but this new information did put him slightly on edge. He'd never sat chatting with a convicted criminal before. He wasn't sure he'd ever even met somebody who'd been in prison. Certainly nobody who'd been so blasé about it.

"You're shocked, Thring," laughed Les. "Well, I don't blame you."

"What... er, what did you do?"

"Don't worry, Thring," he chuckled, "nothing too bad. I'm not a murderer, or rapist, or lawyer. I was a burglar, in effect. Career thief, you might say."

"A burglar? So you broke into people's houses and stole things?"

"Sadly, yes. At first anyway," said Les, his voice taking on a more serious tone. "Though I'm not proud of that, sneaking into people's homes. It's how I got started. I was a kid, really. Broken home, all that stuff. Not making excuses, mind, but there it is. Got myself mixed up with a bad gang and learned the art of housebreaking. Soon got caught, though, and ended up in prison. That was a real lesson, Thring, a real wake up call."

"It was enough to scare you straight?"

"Straight? Don't be silly. I learned more in prison about how to steal things than I'd ever known before. No, what I figured out was that crime really *does* pay. So long as you do it right, of course."

"Do it right..." repeated George, slightly confused.

"Yeah, you can't make money out of these Mickey Mouse jobs, Thring. TV here, stereo there, few gold chains and a bit of cash if you're lucky. What I learned is that you have to think big. I was a good thief, but I just had to make sure I was stealing the right things."

"The right things?"

"High end," George, "that's what it's all about. Pick your targets: rich people with plenty of stuff – paintings, jewellery, safes loaded with cash. These people have more money than sense and hardly even notice what you've nicked. Even when they do, they just claim it back on the insurance.

"So long as you've got a good fence to move the gear, you can't lose. Only need to do two or three good jobs a year and you've got more than enough cash. The fewer jobs you do, the less chance of getting caught. The rest of the time, I get to relax. Take things easy, live a good life. You can't tell me that doesn't make sense." He flashed that smile again, demonstrating how pleased he was with himself.

"Well, I suppose when you put it like that," said George, appreciating the man's reasoning. "But didn't you say that you've just got out of prison?"

"Yeah, well," replied Les, shifting in his chair. His head dipped slightly and he sniffed, looking a little embarrassed. "That's an unfortunate story."

George just looked back, eyes wide with intrigue, eager to hear what Les was less keen to impart.

"I have this condition," said Les, exhaling slowly, his eyes darting down to the hand holding his drink then back up to meet George's eye. "OCD the doctors call it. Obsessive Compulsive Disorder. I get these... urges, I suppose you might say. I just have to do these... things. Can't help it."

"All that tidying? Is that what you mean?"

"Oh, you noticed that?" said the man, slightly embarrassed. "Yes, of course you would have. Pretty bloody obvious, I suppose, isn't it?" he laughed. "I just can't stand mess. If there's any kind of mess, any slight thing out of place, dirty, broken, I just have to fix it. Sort it, you know. I can't leave it or I just think about it over and over. I get this kind of odd feeling in the centre of my brain and it doesn't go away until the mess is all cleared up. It's the bane of my bloody life, excuse my French. But I can't help it. So that's the way it is, I'm very tidy.

"In many ways, it was actually something of a bonus in my line of work. Meticulous, I was. Never left a single speck of dust out of place on any of the jobs I pulled. And where there's no mess, there's no evidence, is there?"

He smiled that smug grin again. "Not one fingerprint, not one hair left behind, nothing. That's why the police never caught up with me.

"Anyway, the last job I ever pulled was supposed to be a really sweet score. Big house in the city. The owners were out of town for the week, and stupid enough to leave a big stash of cash and jewels in their crummy little safe. Rich people really can be quite stupid about things like that. Mediocre security system, outdated safe – actually kept behind a painting on the wall, if you can believe it. I mean, do people not watch telly?

"Anyway, that sort of set up's no bother to anyone willing to put in the homework, so it should have been a walk in the park."

"So what went wrong?" asked George.

"Well, you can only account for so much planning when you're pulling a job like that. No matter how much preparation you've done, something can always go wrong."

"What happened, did you miss an alarm or something?" Said George, quite getting into the story. "Ooh, I know, the owners came back unexpectedly and caught you?"

"Are you taking the piss?" grumbled Les. "No, I told you: I was meticulous. No owners ever came back unexpectedly and I sure as shit would never have missed a bloody alarm!"

"Oh," said George, slightly deflated. "So what was the problem?"

"Well, I'd pulled the job; grabbed the stash out of the safe; wiped everything down; and I'm getting ready to leave. Only, as I'm giving the place the last quick once over – you know, just to double, double check I haven't missed anything – I back up too far and trip over a rug. Bloody thing shouldn't have been there in the first place. I mean who has a rug nowadays? Nobody with any bleeding taste, anyway…"

"And?" interrupted George, sensing this particular digression could go on for a while.

"Well, I tripped over the rug, fell backwards, crashed into this wall unit and pulled the whole bloody thing down on top of me."

"So you were trapped underneath?"

"Well, no…" said Les, wincing slightly and fidgeting with the drink in his hand. "The unit was light enough to lift off, so I crawled out and stood it back up. Only, when I looked down at the floor there was mess everywhere. Books strewn about, little glass ornaments smashed into a thousand pieces. Fucking mess everywhere."

"So?"

"So? I told you, I can't leave a mess, can I? I had to clean it up. Everything in my head is telling me to get out of there, do a runner, leave it. But I can't. I can't leave the mess. It'll stay in my head, gnawing away at me, eating me up. So I had to put it right before I left. Only, what with all the commotion, the neighbours have called the Old Bill and they bust in on the place while I'm down on my hands and knees with a bloody dust pan and brush!"

"Oh my God," George laughed. "So the police caught you breaking and tidying?"

The man's face dropped. "It's no laughing matter that, son. An affliction, that's what I've got!"

"Yes, sorry," said George, shamefaced. "So what happened?"

"That was it, Thring. Caught red-handed. Clear-cut case and I got five years, reduced to three for good behaviour. Luckily they couldn't pin anything else on me, though they bloody well tried. So I did my time – not exactly pleasant, but what you'd call an occupational hazard – and I got out four months ago." He raised his glass and drained the last of his pint.

"So, what now? Have you decided to go straight?" asked George.

"I never said that, Thring? Wouldn't do to dive straight back into a life of crime right after getting out of jail though, would it? I'd like to let the penal system think it had managed to rehabilitate me, for a short while at least. Be rude not to, wouldn't you say?"

"Yes, I suppose so."

"So I'm just… relaxing." said Les. "Resting up and biding my time until I think of the next move. But, first things first, let's have another drink." He reached round behind the bar and clanged the little bell again.

George and Les sat chatting for a few hours longer and George surprised himself by managing to drink a full three more pints of lager. He still hadn't quite got used to the taste but as time went on it seemed less and less offensive.

By half past four the beer had definitely taken effect and George felt rather drowsy. He wasn't used to drinking much, let alone drinking in the afternoon. His eyelids felt very heavy and though he wasn't exactly seeing double, the majority of objects did seem to have adopted a certain glow around the edges.

"Well, it's been lovely talking with you," he said to Les, trying hard to avoid slurring his words, "but I think I might just go and have a little lie-down."

"Good idea," replied Les, "you go and enjoy this new-found freedom of yours. Take it easy. And if you fancy another chat, I'm here most days."

George's knees wobbled slightly as he stood. Gathering his composure, he smiled briefly and left the room.

He made his way shakily back to his cramped room, the dust particles still dancing and twinkling in the glow from the sinking sun. He flumped down onto the bed, lying back as a warm, woozy feeling washed over him like a wave. Within seconds he was fast asleep and snoring loudly.

CHAPTER 12

"YOU know he talks to us like bloody idiots," Steve Clefton said to his brother in the cold, cramped hotel room. "Takes the bloody piss!"

John Clefton was busy fidgeting with the two packed duffle bags, removing large swathes of brightly coloured material and dumping them on the bed in front of him. He then carefully took out several small, grey metal canisters with thin ring pulls dangling from detachable square fasteners, and placed them on the floor.

He continued pulling out a series of other strange looking cans; lengths of heavy-duty mountaineering rope; five packs of Chinese firecrackers; three sets of shiny aluminium handcuffs; two medium-sized computer speakers; a tiny MP3 player; and three black, wavy-quiffed wigs with matching sets of stick-on sideburns.

"And what's with these stupid outfits?" continued Steve as John delicately placed two COLT M16A2 9mm submachine guns onto the bed. "I mean, we're gonna look like a right load of dicks!" he humphed.

Finally, John pulled out two Glock 17 (9mm) semi-automatic pistols, three back-up magazine cartridges and boxes of ammunition for each weapon. He threw the two empty duffel bags onto the floor.

"What are you bleatin' on about?" asked John, looking up at his brother.

"That posh git," he replied, "he's taking us for a couple of mugs. Treatin' us like hired help. I don't trust him. I'm sure he's up to something funny."

"Of course he is. I wouldn't trust that old bugger as far as I could throw him. No doubt he's already planning on taking all the money for himself, and leaving us in the shit. That's why I've brought these," he said, tossing one of the Glocks to his brother. "The Major ain't as clever as he thinks he is, you know. As far as he's concerned, we've only got the big 'uns. So, we keep these out of sight, and he's got no reason to know we've got them."

Steve looked back at him, eyes wide with a confusion, like a dog looking at itself in a mirror.

"So," continued John, "when the job's done, and we're splitting up the cash, we whip these out, hold the old bastard up, and take his share as well."

A thin, devious smile spread slowly across Steve's face. "I like it," he said. "Bloody brilliant! But he's not gonna like that."

"Course not, but what's he gonna do?"

"He was in the SAS, John. You know what those bastards are like. Hard as nails."

"He don't scare me. That was all years ago, wasn't it? If it's even true. I never saw him fighting inside, did you?"

"Well, no, but…"

"Nah, he's an old man. And you know what he's like: he won't carry a gun. That's why he wants us here, to do all the dirty work. Which means he'll be totally unarmed, won't he? I don't care how clever he thinks he is, he can't outsmart two of these."

He lifted the gun in front of his face, the light from the energy-saving bulb glinting dully on the cold black of the nylon-polymer shaft.

******

Major Charles Fairview crept along the narrow hallway and made his way downstairs, past the small check-in desk. He smiled sycophantically at the young brunette woman and strolled purposefully out the front door to the street outside. He looked around cautiously, scanning for anybody that might be watching.

With nobody in sight, he slid down the slim, dark alleyway running along the side of the building. He fished a small mobile phone from his jacket pocket then dialled the only number stored in the phonebook. The phone rang three times before being answered with an abrupt, gravelly, "Hello?"

"Ah, hello there," the Major said, "just checking in as requested. Everything going swimmingly here, so far."

"You can lose the accent, Charlie," the voice replied, "this is me you're talking to." The voice on the other end sounded gruff and weary, crackling like fire, the vocal chords straining under the stress of many years of heavy cigarette smoke.

"Ha, yes, sorry," said the Major, smiling, "old habits and all that."

His voice drifted into a softer, smoother accent. A generic southern twang, not as harsh and edgy as authentic cockney, but fast-paced and loose, all T's instantly dropped and words merging into each other in his mouth. Aside from his practiced Major routine, it was the most comfortable speaking voice he could slip in and out of. It had been carefully crafted and rehearsed to be completely indistinguishable and unmemorable. It was the sort of voice that could be from anywhere and wouldn't stick in anyone's mind.

He'd had so many different voices over the years, to go with so many different names and guises. He barely remembered what he used to sound like, or what he might sound like now if he hadn't worked so steadfastly to alter himself and the way others perceived him.

"Anyway," he added, "should you be using my name? Over the phone, I mean?"

"Oh, calm down, Charlie. We're not spies. We're just doing a simple job. Besides, the phones are clean and totally disposable."

"Yeah, well I'm still on parole, remember? One slip and I'll be straight back inside."

"Oh, keep your fucking knickers on, you big girl. I'm sure Big Brother isn't listening in to our phone call. Now, how are the brothers getting along?"

"They're all right. Pair of bloody idiots, but I'll keep 'em straight. They'll pull their weight fine tomorrow. So long as the plan runs to course, and they do what they're told, it should all be fine. Got them checking the gear now, up in the room."

"And they don't suspect anything?"

"Course not. If they've got two brain cells between them I'll be stunned. Just make sure you've got plenty of back up when we meet for the handover tomorrow. They might be stupid, these two, but they're big and angry, and that makes for a very dangerous combination in my book. I don't wanna be stood there holding my dick when these two realise they're being turned over."

"Don't worry, Charlie. Everything's in hand. Just do the job, get the money and make it to the rendezvous on time. I'll take care of everything else."

"And you're sure the timings are right? The layout? The numbers in the bank? Everything's down to the second and I can make sure things run like clockwork, but it all has to be exactly like you said. If not, the plan won't work. And if we get trapped in the bank, that's game over. There'll be no getting out."

"Don't you worry about the timings, Charlie. The information is bang on. Did most of the recon myself. Just make sure you're in and out within the times I've given you, and you'll be fine."

"And what about you? Where are you now?"

"Details, details, Charlie. That doesn't concern you. Just make sure you turn up to the meet on time and you'll see me soon enough. And don't even think about fucking with me, Charlie."

"Would I, dear boy?" the Major chirped, slipping easily back into character, his posh tones ringing out down the phone. "Pip pip, then. See you soon."

The Major hung up and slipped the phone back into his pocket. He sidled up the alley again, looking furtively around. With the coast clear, and satisfied that nobody had been watching him, he emerged from the dark alleyway and walked back up the path to the hotel.

CHAPTER 13

THE room was dark. A bright glow shone in from the streetlamp outside the window, casting a hazy orange lining onto the edge of the chest of drawers. It was cold, a chilled breeze blowing in from somewhere. It took George a few seconds to recognise where he was. His mouth was dry and tasted dirty, like rotten food.

He lifted his head to look around him, and was suddenly hit by a piercing, sickly pain drilling right into the centre of his brain. He clutched his head in his hands, dropping it back down to the pillow and groaned an agonised, breathy moan. He drew his knees up to his chest, rolling onto his side as his brain throbbed gently inside his skull.

George had slept for three hours and the drowsy, pleasant feeling the alcohol had given him had now turned into a sharp, stabbing hangover. He felt like someone had drained all the fluid from his body. His stomach was a nauseated knot, an angry pit in his centre.

All this from four pints? he thought. It was no wonder he'd steered clear of alcohol for all these years. Did people really get into this state by choice?

Slowly he straightened out, lifted himself up onto his elbows and swung round so that he was sitting, slumped, on the edge of the bed. He checked his watch: 7.57pm. So much for phoning work to tell them he wouldn't be coming in. The office would have been shut for over an hour now. Even the hardcore over-timers would have been sent packing by Geoff, the night-shift security guard.

George's hand went to his pocket, reaching for his mobile phone so he could check for messages. Then he stopped, deciding not to check after all. If anybody had actually left him a message, he wasn't sure he really wanted to hear it. He'd quite enjoyed the past few hours of detachment. He'd liked not being part of his own world and he didn't want to return to it just yet.

Finally, and more depressingly, he didn't want to check his messages because he was fairly certain there would be none to check.

George felt heavy, weighed down, as if his legs wouldn't be able to hold him. He wanted to lie back down on the bed and simply to go to sleep, as though all his problems could be solved by a good night's rest.

Paradoxically, that was about the last thing he wanted to do. He wanted to get out of the room. He wanted to explore this new world that he'd found. After years of stumbling along, not knowing where he was or what he was doing, it was as if a blindfold had suddenly been removed from his eyes. Life was going on outside that door and he wanted to go and join in.

But maybe he'd sit here for a few minutes longer. Just until his head stopped pounding so heavily.

From outside the door, George could hear a muffled noise. A dull, throbbing bass rumbling its way up through the floorboards. It sounded like music playing; people talking and laughing. He rubbed his weary eyes, ran a hand slowly through his hair. Then he slowly, tentatively lifted himself up onto his feet.

His legs wobbled slightly. He was struck with an almighty head rush, the blood suddenly shooting to his brain and threatening to send him crashing into a heap on the floor. He managed to hold his weight, gripping onto the side of the chest of drawers, and kept himself upright. A few deep breaths later, and he was slightly more stable.

He opened the door and a piercing bright light shot in at him, stinging his eyes and making his head hurt more acutely. The hotel that had previously been quiet and desolate now thrummed with activity. The rest of the bookings must have arrived, and now the atmosphere was positively buzzing.

Two young children ran past his door and disappeared up the corridor, the capes of their Elvis Presley costumes flapping and waving behind them. He could hear people chatting, doors opening and closing at random. Music rose like winding smoke from the ground floor up through the rest of the building.

George made his way down the stairs, past the empty check-in desk, and poked his head round the door of the bar. He could barely open it as the place was packed with people.

It was the largest number of Elvis Presleys he'd ever seen crammed so tightly together in one room. It was the largest number of Elvis Presleys he'd ever seen anywhere. The bar was a sea of brightly coloured costumes: white and blue, red, gold, orange, purple. People laughed and chatted. Glasses clinked and chinked as peopled drank and swayed, their arms rising and falling like waves on a turbulent sea.

There were people sitting at both tables; crammed into the corner; pushed far up against the walls. People mingled in the middle of the room, swaying slightly, bumping one another, and the bar was lined with people leaning, drinking and queuing. At the far end of the bar he could see Les, still sitting in exactly the same position as he had been earlier.

The room was hot and stuffy, the air thick with breath and the smell of alcohol, and it wasn't helping George's delicate stomach. Beads of sweat formed instantly on his forehead and he felt slightly dizzy. Instead of pushing his way in, he decided to retreat to a more relaxed environment, and crossed the hall to the small dining room. It was much cooler in there and a wave of fresh air soothed his woozy brain. He walked to the far end, sitting down at the table he'd occupied that morning.

Again the room was empty and he sat there for a few moments, enjoying the relative peace as the pain in his head slowly began to subside. He closed his eyes for a few moments, just to gather his thoughts.

He was jolted back to reality when he heard the creak of the door leading to the kitchen. It swung open and in walked Alice. She looked every bit as lovely as she had when he'd seen her that afternoon. Of all the people he'd seen wearing these funny outfits, she easily pulled it off the best.

Her eyes sparkled in the light and shone more brightly than any of the twinkling beads and sequins that littered her collar. Maybe it was his delicate state, but there was something majestic about the way she moved, as though she was literally floating towards his table.

"Hello Mr. Thring," she said. "Have you come down for dinner?"

"Erm... well," stumbled George. In truth he hadn't actually thought about dinner, and his stomach still felt a little unsettled. But then he hadn't eaten anything since the stodgy breakfast that morning, and the more he thought about it, the more he realised he really should eat something. "Yes, please. Dinner would be good. And please, call me George."

"Okay, George," she said, smiling that delicious grin. "Well, I'm afraid we don't have the biggest menu." She handed him a single sheet of laminated card displaying the limited dinner options and pub grub. "But it's all very good. Well, I would say that," she giggled. "I'm the chef."

He scanned the list, opting for the fairly safe sounding option of shepherd's pie, and Alice disappeared back out to the kitchen. When she returned ten minutes later, she was carrying two plates instead of one. She strolled back over to the table, placed one of the meals down in front of George, then put the other plate down on the table opposite him. She pulled up a chair and sat down.

"Hope you don't mind," said Alice, lifting a forkful of mince and mashed potato to her lips and blowing softly in the most sensual, erotic way anybody had ever blown on their food. "My shift finished at seven and I hate to eat alone.

"Besides," she giggled, "I wasn't sure you were going to get around to asking me out for dinner so I thought I'd beat you to it." She smiled, a devilish twinkle sparkling in her deep brown eyes.

"Oh, no," fumbled George. "No, I'd be delighted."

She smiled at him and he instantly felt at ease. His head felt clear, the throbbing pain dissipating, and the sickly ache in his stomach melted away. He smiled back at her, picking up his fork and digging up a scoop of mashed potato.

"So, George," Alice said, "you seem to be quite a hit with old Les. He's been coming here for years, on and off, and I've never seen him become so friendly with any of the other guests."

"Oh?" replied George. "I am pleased. He's quite an interesting man himself."

"Well, he certainly seems taken with you. He told me all about your little adventure, and how you ended up here, all covered in mud and... well, you know."

"Oh, he did?" said George, an embarrassed look crashing onto his face.

This was a disaster. What had he said? How could he have told her about his little episode? Now she'd think he was some kind of lunatic; some deranged mental case that accidentally runs away from home in the middle of a psychological breakdown. He couldn't look her in the eyes.

"There's no need to be embarrassed," Alice quickly interjected. "Life's full of quirky little adventures. It doesn't matter how you end up somewhere, only that you end up in the place you're supposed to be. Do you believe in fate, George?"

"Erm… well…"

"Just because you didn't mean to drive here doesn't mean you weren't supposed to come here. And just think, if you hadn't stumbled upon our little town, you'd never have ended up having dinner with me tonight."

There was something so genuine about what she said, and how she spoke, that George again found himself mesmerised by her; drawn in to those deep brown eyes. She laughed softly, and George found himself laughing along with her.

"When you put it like that," he said, "maybe it was less of an accident and more a stroke of luck."

She smiled back at him and he was rather pleased with himself. If he wasn't mistaken, that was actually quite a suave thing to say. He had no idea he could be so charming.

They sat and ate their shepherd's pie, and George found himself recounting the entire story again, leaving out the most embarrassing parts. He focused less on the schizophrenic elements of his journey and more on the delights of finding himself in such a quaint, quirky little town. She laughed in all the right places, where he attempted humour. She listened intently as he told his odd tale. She was interested in what he was saying. And George couldn't be entirely certain – after all it was a long time since he'd sat chatting with a woman – but he got the distinct feeling that she was flirting with him.

"Yes, this town certainly is quirky, all right," said Alice. Her tone sounded suddenly derisive. "You've come at the right time, of course. It's fun when it's busy, when there are people here. And the festival is an interesting time. But it's a bit of a morgue round here for the rest of the year. It's a one horse town, George, and the horse isn't looking too healthy."

"You don't like living here?" he asked.

"It's not that I dislike it, as such. It's just that there's not a great deal to like. There's nothing going on here. I feel like… I feel like life is going on all around me. Like out there things are happening, lives are being lived. And I'm stuck in this little town, just kind of existing. Does that make any sense?"

It made a great deal of sense. It was a feeling George had only just recently begun to realise he was experiencing himself.

"Don't get me wrong," she continued, "the people here are great, and I don't have a bad life, not really. It's just… it's a big world out there, George, and I've only seen the smallest, tiniest part of it. I guess what I'm saying is that there must be more."

There was definitely more. George had only driven a few hundred miles outside his lonely little life and he'd found a hell of a lot more already. And who knew what else was out there. "So why do you stay here?" he asked.

"That's the most tragic part of it, George. I don't even know."

******

It was true. Alice didn't know how she'd ended up staying so long in that claustrophobic, stifling, unimaginative little place. She'd always dreamed of moving on, heading out into the real world. She'd longed to see bigger things. She wanted to go to the places she'd seen on television: the bright lights of New York; the dense jungles of the rain forest. Even the busy streets and shopping centres of London, only a few hours' drive away.

Her favourite ever Christmas present, which she'd received when she was 12 years old, was the football-sized globe she'd begged her parents for. It sat proudly in her bedroom, just below the posters of Take That and Boyzone. It had been a constant reminder of just how big the world was; how vast some countries were compared with her home, and how many other interesting, exciting places were out there. She read books, finding interest in other cultures, growing ever more curious about what these places looked like; fawning over pictures, dreaming of stepping foot in these strange lands.

Though not consciously, her parents had always managed to discourage her. They'd never appreciated the virtues of travel or of experiencing new, exciting things. They'd always had everything they needed in Lower Chidbury and as far as they were concerned, Alice had everything she could want for as well.

They'd never been on exciting, tropical, adventurous holidays when she was growing up. She'd never been to Majorca, or Benidorm, or Disneyland, like most of her school friends. Her parents had always run their Hotel and they'd been staunch advocates of holidaying in Britain.

"Why would we want to go to Spain or Greece, or somewhere like that, when we've got everything we could want here in England?" her father had said more times than she could remember. "Besides, the food's all funny over there, and the people talk weird!"

So she'd never been abroad, actively discouraged from ever leaving the country. In fact, she'd never even seen much of her own country, her father having never taken a holiday – not wanting to pay relief staff to run his business. He made do with the odd weekend fishing trip, leaving the family to run the place. Alice's mother had taken her away for the odd week away, here or there, but that was generally to stay with aunts or grandparents, or old family friends, who all lived within a two hundred mile radius of her home.

Chidbury was what she knew, and it was pretty much all she knew. And as she grew older, finished school and settled into life, her dreams of travelling and seeing the world simply grew dormant in her mind. New dreams took their place: the things she was told she was supposed to want, like finding a job, finding a husband, buying a nice house. Her tired little town seemed less tired and she found herself less inclined to imagine what was outside of it.

She'd dated Michael since she was 15-years-old and simply found herself settling for the life that seemed to be unfolding before her. By 19 he'd proposed and at the time she'd accepted because she truly did want to marry him. They'd had a long engagement, and a turbulent whirlwind of break-ups and reconciliations, while they both took jobs and saved for a home and life together. They finally married when they were both 24-years-old.

Deep down inside, though she fought hard never to admit it, she was never really certain about the idea. She loved Michael, in her own way, and for a while she'd managed to convince herself that it was the 'real thing', or at least, the closest approximation to it that she'd ever known. But once the ring was on her finger, and the big book signed, it wasn't long before it dawned on her that she'd made a huge mistake.

The first year of marriage was actually okay. She and Michael got on fine. They bought a nice house and Michael was keen to start a family as soon as possible. And though Alice knew that was what she was supposed to want, like wearing a pair of shoes one size too small she knew it just wasn't right.

She spent the next year trying to talk herself into the life she'd already agreed to. She tried to convince herself that she'd get used to it. She really did love her husband, though not in the right way, and the last thing she wanted to do was to hurt him.

Then one day, whilst helping her parents clear out the loft, she came across her dusty old globe with the tiny stickers marking out all the destinations she'd imagined exploring. And it all came flooding back to her. Like an electric shock a sudden desire was reawakened within her. She wanted to see what the world could offer; to find out what life could be if she went out and found it. And in that very second she realised that the life she had just wasn't enough for her.

After that, a lifetime lived so slowly came hurtling back to full speed. It didn't take long before she'd moved out of the house, leaving Michael crushed and bitter. She wouldn't accept a penny from the divorce settlement, reasoning it was only fair after Michael had done nothing but be a perfect gentleman – even offering somewhat naively to take her back when she came to her senses and realised what she'd done.

She'd felt so sad then, to see him like that. He really did love her and if she could have managed it – could have flicked a switch inside her head and made herself love him – she'd have done it in a second. But life just doesn't work that way and it was far better to free them both than to go on pretending.

And so, at the age of 26, Alice found herself living back with her parents, working shifts in the bar and saving every penny she could. The stickers on her globe still shone out and the desire to see all these places burned more intensely inside her. As soon as she had enough money she'd be off and nothing was going to hold her back this time.

Somehow three years had gone by – had it really been three years already? – but now her savings were close to what she needed and her passion for escape had only grown stronger by the day.

And then one night this curious little man walked into the bar, soaking wet and covered in mud, with the most honest eyes she'd ever seen. He was cute, too: handsome and distinguished, in a strange 'dragged-through-a-hedge-backwards' kind of way. He had a kind smile and a certain warmth to him, and he was adorably shy and polite. She didn't know why but as he walked into the room that night, it was as if he'd come for her.

He'd looked so lost, like he'd been wandering for years with no idea where he was or where he was going. She couldn't explain it, but she instantly wanted to help him. She wanted to take him in her arms, give him the hug he so dearly needed, and take care of him.

This odd little man had blown in on a breeze and she wasn't sure why exactly, but somehow everything seemed different. She felt as though he must have been drawn there; drawn to her so that she could save him. Or maybe he was there to save her.

******

They sat looking at each other, smiling softly as they chatted and ate. George couldn't believe how calm he felt. There he was talking to this beautiful, incredible, interesting woman and he was perfectly relaxed. Usually he'd be nervous and uncomfortable, sweating and embarrassed. He'd be struggling to speak, terrified of saying the wrong thing, constantly worried about making a fool of himself.

In fact, chances are, he wouldn't even have been there. He'd have become flustered and made some excuse about having to do something urgent. But somehow the words were flowing easily and George was barely even thinking about what he said, just allowing the conversation to come to him.

She was a very engaging woman and he loved listening to her talk. He was intrigued by her and hung on every word she said, enjoying learning more about her. He felt very easy about opening up to her; telling her things that nobody else knew, as if it was the first time he'd ever managed to let anybody see inside the real him. Where he'd always remained at least partly guarded – just slightly closed off – with her he somehow allowed himself to just talk, to tell all there was to tell. And he got the feeling that she did the same with him.

They had a lot in common. They laughed and joked together, sympathised with each other's tales of woe, rejoiced in each other's triumphs and tales of joy. She'd laugh softly at something George had said, and in doing so, lean forward and gently touch his hand. It made him glow inside and his heart thudded each time with an extra beat. If he'd been feeling himself he'd instantly have panicked, fearing he was suffering from some form of cardiac arrhythmia. But luckily he wasn't feeling very much like himself. He was feeling a whole lot better than he'd ever felt before.

Before long they both had empty plates. "Well, that's dinner done," said Alice, placing her knife and fork down. "That was very pleasant. Thank you for your company, George."

"Oh, yes," replied George, looking rather deflated at the apparent end of their impromptu date.

She hesitated slightly, preparing to get up from the table and leave, not really wanting to go. The silence hung in the air between them, neither speaking, both of them wanting the other one to say something.

George wanted her to stay. He wanted to ask her to stay. He moved to speak. His mouth opened, a quick inhalation of breath, but nothing came. No words sprang forth. They were in his head, but try as he might he couldn't force them through to his tongue. His heart beat faster, his brain froze. His palms grew clammy, and he could feel a pain start to throb deep in his chest in preparation of her rejecting him.

The energy rushed out of him, fear taking over and quashing his enthusiasm. He sat there, poised on the edge of his chair, wishing he could summon up the courage to just ask her out.

Finally Alice broke the tension, pushing her chair back, picking up the two plates from the table and standing up. This was it. His chance was escaping from him. He knew if he didn't ask her now, that was it; he might not get another opportunity.

And still she hesitated, as if waiting, hoping for George to hold her back. But the words just wouldn't come. He sat there, frozen, unable to move or speak, just looking imploringly at her, hoping she might ask him instead. But she didn't. This was something he was going to have to do himself. He would have to take the risk.

Finally, she made to move. "Well, see you then," she said, sounding disappointed. She turned and started to walk off toward the kitchen.

"I don't suppose…" George finally managed to blurt out, launching himself to his feet.

"Yes?" she said, spinning round.

"Erm… well, I don't suppose you'd like to… er… go for a drink?"

He'd managed it. He'd actually managed to ask her out. He wanted to leap in the air and rejoice at his bravery. Then he realised she hadn't actually said 'yes' yet.

She stood there, silent and still, saying nothing. Every second seemed like a thousand. The blood rushed to George's head and he could hear it thumping loudly in his ears. His palms were positively soaking, his heart banging violently in his chest. Oh God, had he made some horrendous mistake? Had he misread the signs? She was going to say no. She was going to laugh at him, mock him cruelly for imagining that someone like her would ever be interested in a specimen like him. Oh, what had he done?

Her soft lips parted. Here it came…

"I'd love to," she chirped, a huge curly smile beaming across her face.

Oh thank God, he thought. THANK GOD! All the blood suddenly drained back out of his head, and he felt faint. His knees started wobbling and he thought he might fall over. Discreetly he leaned forward, steadying himself against the table.

"We could go to the costume competition at the local pub," said Alice. "Let me just go and get ready. I'll meet you back here in half an hour."

She turned and walked out through the door to the kitchen, leaving George alone again. He found himself beaming brightly, his cheek muscles aching with the effort of his hefty grin. He tried to calm himself, to restore order, but try as he might he couldn't stop smiling. He collapsed back onto the seat behind him, trying to take everything in. He had a date. A proper date. His first date in quite a few years.

His nervousness turned into giddy excitement. He'd have to go and get ready. He should have a quick shower, put on a nice suit. And then he remembered. He looked down at the sparkling blue outfit he was wearing.

Oh dear, he thought. He had his first date in years and he was dressed as Elvis Presley.

CHAPTER 14

"OKAY, I'm ready," said Alice, walking up behind George, as he stood patiently waiting for her at the front door. She looked incredible and for just a second George was unable to speak. She'd changed out of her Elvis costume and opted instead for a pair of tight, figure hugging jeans and a rather fetching, stretchy blue top with a low cut v-shaped neckline. The top showed off her cleavage to rather dramatic effect, and George literally had to clamp his head in place to prevent him from openly gawping at her.

Her shiny, brown hair was brushed back from her face, pinned in position behind her ears. She had dusted her face with a light sheen of make-up, her cheeks ever so slightly pinker than before and her lips sparkling and shiny with lipstick. And she smelled amazing; the light floral fragrance wafting across to George. She leaned in and gave him the softest, most delicate kiss on the cheek and he caught the coconut scent of her hair. She was quite the most beautiful thing he had ever seen.

George's transformation was a lot less dramatic, given that he hadn't changed a single thing about his appearance.

Had he been given adequate warning that the night was going to take a more romantic turn he'd have been able to prepare himself more fully. He'd have changed into a clean set of clothes: one of his less worn suits and a clean, freshly pressed shirt. He'd have put in plenty of time and consideration to pick out the perfect tie, factoring in all the variables from what best suited the tone of the occasion, to which colour he felt most comfortable wearing, to which style or pattern best reflected the mood he wished to convey.

For this particular outing he'd probably have gone for something fairly colourful and jazzy, to convey his fun, outlandish nature. But he'd have kept things contained and quite straight-laced within a simple striped pattern, so as not to appear too zany or quirky.

He'd have given his shoes two decent polishes, making sure they were as smart and shiny as he could get them, possibly even opting for a third quick buffing if he had the time. He'd certainly have showered, shaved, combed his hair, applied a generous amount of aftershave and made sure he looked as sharp and smart as he could. He might not have been the most handsome or enigmatic of characters but he would have done the best with the raw ingredients he had.

What he most definitely would not have done was dress up in a ridiculous Elvis Presley costume and go out on his first romantic date in years with uncombed hair, a five o' clock shadow and questionable breath.

Of course, when he'd retired to his room to get himself ready, he'd suddenly realised how little preparation he'd be capable of. Though he'd managed to clean himself up well enough that morning, he'd found himself side-tracked in the bar and completely forgotten about seeking out a chemist or local shop for cosmetic provisions. He didn't even have a toothbrush.

He couldn't take a shower, because his room came without an en-suite. The communal bathroom in the hall was most definitely in use, the occupant having returned a rather obscene tirade of foul language when George had innocently tapped on the door and enquired as to how long he intended to be.

The only real preparation George could undertake was to look at himself in the mirror and hope to make the best of a bad situation. He tried flattening down the black and white flecked hair which seemed, for reasons unknown, to have puffed out into a rather impressive bouffant. With no water source, he tried the old trick of licking his fingers and applying the spittle to his head – a procedure he'd endured his Grandmother administering to him countless times as a child. His saliva, however, clearly didn't have the same adhesive qualities and the hair just sprang back up, defiant and slightly sticky looking.

Although George had to admit that the outfit did suit him better than he'd ever have imagined, it was certainly not his first choice. It wouldn't have been his fiftieth choice, or even his hundredth, but it was all he had and that was that. He wondered whether there was any way to play it down: removing some of the sparkle, or attaching his own additions. But as the only materials he had to work with were the heavily starched sheets and pillowcases, and since he wouldn't know what to do with those materials anyway, he was stuck with what he had. He was dressed as Elvis Presley and that was that.

All he could do was to peer back into those tired, nervous eyes, try to assure himself that things would be okay and hope for the best. He rubbed his hand across his face, hearing the faint scratch of the newly-formed bristles on his chin, and let out a heavy, world-weary sigh. Oh God, he thought, please don't let me screw this up.

"You look lovely," said George, enthusiastically.

Alice blushed slightly. "Thank you, George. You look very nice, as well," she replied.

"Oh, yes…" said George, peering down at his clothing. "Sorry about the, erm… It's all I have, I'm afraid."

"On the contrary," she reassured him, "I think you look fab. And we *are* going to an Elvis costume competition after all. If ever there was a time to be dressed like that."

"You're not wearing your outfit?" George said.

"Oh, God no," she giggled. "Mum and Dad insist I wear that thing when I'm working. You know, to keep up appearances for the guests. No, I thought I'd go for something a little less ostentatious for this evening."

Alice could see that he still felt slightly ill at ease. "Seriously, though George, you look very handsome." Then she couldn't help but playfully compound his discomfiture by adding, "You should be a shoo-in for a prize!"

She opened the heavy, black front door. "Shall we then?" she said, and they both stepped out into the night and strolled down the cracked, broken path.

******

The pub was a short walk away and they ambled slowly along the pavement, Alice providing a commentary on the town as they walked. She gave George a history of the place; told him what each building was; who owned which shop, and what different things they sold. She told him about the seafront; the best place to get a cup of tea; the best place to go for lunch; and everything she knew about the town where she lived.

In truth she knew she was babbling, saying the first thing that came into her head just to break the silence. She always did that when she was nervous, spouting out any old thing, her mouth racing away faster than her brain could keep up. She knew she was talking rubbish and worried that she was boring the poor guy, but try as she might she just couldn't stop. The only interruptions came when she tingled slightly as their arms brushed against each other, the electric charge of it befuddling her, sending her momentarily silent as she fought to find words to again fill the quiet.

George ummed and aahed and said "Oh yes?" in all the right places, genuinely interested in everything she was telling him. He still could not quite believe that such a beautiful, vibrant, intelligent, consuming woman would choose to spend her time with him. It was like a dream, and somewhere buried in the back of his mind was the fear that soon he was going to wake up and it would all end.

They walked closely together, so close that their arms were almost touching, a few times actually even brushing against each other, which caused the most exquisite tingle in his stomach. He wanted to surreptitiously reach out and take hold of her hand, but he knew it was too soon for that.

What he didn't realise was that Alice was walking that closely to him, holding her hand still by her side rather than let it swing naturally with the flow of her walk, in the distinct hope that he might just take hold of it. But maybe it *was* still a little bit soon for that.

It was a clear night, the stars twinkling crisply in the sky, with the mildest breeze blowing in from the sea. It wasn't cold, but cool enough that, had George been in possession of a jacket, he'd have gladly removed it to drape around Alice's shoulders to keep her warm. Sadly, the best he could offer was the inadequately small cape from his costume and he wasn't sure it was even detachable. Once again, he cursed the silly outfit he'd been forced to wear.

They could hear loud music emanating from the pub as they approached. The whoops and cheers from the people inside echoed softly up the narrow high street. The pub was at the bottom of the hill, taking up prime position on the corner, so that half of the building faced into the town and the other half looked out over the softly rippling dark sea.

It was a large building, much older than the other 1960s era structures in the street. It was darker and more gothic-looking. The fish and chip shop next door looked like it had been bolted on: the red-bricked exterior standing in stark contrast to the dirty white plaster finish of the pub's walls. Heavy lead-framed windows – like big peering eyes – were brightly lit, illuminating the pavements outside. Colourful disco lights flashed red, blue, white and green against the glass, spinning and whirling, turning the street outside a different colour with each flash. Heavy half-dead hanging baskets hung intermittently from the thick, black guttering; limp, greeny-brown foliage falling down from the sides as if crying out for water.

The dirty red slate tiles of the roof were dishevelled and uneven, covered here and there with patches of dark green and black moss, giving the whole roof a slightly wavy, dilapidated look. On the sea-facing side of the building was a small fenced-off patio area housing two wooden tables, left unused due to the cold climate and the uproarious antics going on inside. Beneath an electric wall-mounted light-cum-outdoor-heater stood two overweight Elvises, their shiny costumes twinkling in the moonlight as they huddled together in the small pool of heat, thick spirals of cigarette smoke pouring from their mouths and snaking up into the cold night sky.

Above the pub hung a heavy white wooden sign, the words THE RED LION printed large and in thick lettering. On the pavement directly outside the front door stood an A-framed chalkboard with hastily-scrawled words written in chalk. The writer had clearly underestimated the length of their message, as not only did the words arc down slightly at the end of each line, but the letters started out large and grew smaller in order to fit in all the pertinent information. George could just about make out the message:

TONIGHT
THE RED LION'S FAMOUS ELVIS PRESLEY COSTUME
COMPETITION
FIRST PRIZE £100
ALL DRINKS HALF PRICE BEFORE 8PM
NO FOOD DUE TO CHEF BEING A BASTARD

"What does that mean?" George asked Alice, pointing at the rather confusing final sentence.

"Oh, Sandra will have written that," replied Alice. "She's the landlady. Fiery little woman. The chef is her husband. He recently ran off with the barmaid. Hence why they're not serving food at the moment."

"Oh, I see," he said.

George pushed the heavy wooden door open and it creaked loudly as a surge of heat poured out through the frame. Rock 'n' roll music played loudly on a jukebox inside, mixing with laughter, chattering and the clinking of glasses.

The pub was much larger inside than it appeared to be from the street, with an expansive bar running the length of the far wall. It was vastly more impressive than the small bar at the hotel. The place was dark save for the flashing disco lights which strained George's eyes, bringing a flashback to the headache he'd endured a short while earlier.

An array of tables and chairs lined the walls and much of the floor in front of a small wooden stage. A lonely microphone stand stood in the middle. The tables and chairs were all totally mismatched, as if every item had been bought individually from a different car boot sale. It was the sort of thing that would be very chic in London and trendy bars would probably pay extortionate fees to an interior designer to create that 'effect'. Here it was just furniture and it gave the place a kind of quaint, country feel.

The place was packed; an army of Elvis Presley impersonators populating every table, corner, standing space and stool at the bar. Aside from two or three people, everybody in there was dressed as Elvis Presley, in all forms, eras and outfits.

At the end of the bar stood a tall thin man, impeccably presented in a shiny, sparkly gold suit, representative of Presley's earlier years. Four guys gathered round a table all wore matching Jailhouse Rock outfits; the dark jeans and denim jackets offset by the black and white striped t-shirts. In the corner sat a couple wearing his-and-hers Hawaiian shirts with matching print and accompanying floral garlands.

On the other side of the pub sat a slightly overweight man who must literally have squeezed himself into a very tight looking pair of black leather trousers and matching leather jacket, much like the outfit from Elvis' 1966 comeback special. He looked painfully uncomfortable; the suit clearly too small. With his red face glowing brighter than the disco lights and thick, heavy beads of sweat rolling down the sides of his face, George wondered whether the man had made a wise choice in sitting so close to the open fire.

The most common costume was, of course, the same variety as George's. Long, flowing jumpsuits with wide-flared trousers, high starched collars and low-cut, chest-exposing lapels spread out as far as the eye could see, in a dazzling collage of bright colours. The whole room was like some ridiculous abstract painting, moving and swaying in time to the music which George now realised was, of course, an Elvis Presley song, albeit one that he didn't recognise. Which wasn't surprising, as George wasn't sure he really knew many Elvis Presley songs at all.

It was the most impressive, surreal thing he'd ever seen. There were white Elvises, black Elvises, Chinese Elvises. There were thin ones, fat ones, old ones, young ones. There were male Elvises, female Elvises, and some where George couldn't actually tell the difference. It was quite the most diverse group of Elvis Presley impersonators he'd ever seen.

He found himself wondering what the collective term would be. Elvises? Elvi? Elvis'? Elves, maybe?

George and Alice made their way through the bopping, gyrating crowd and found a spot at the bar. A short, harassed looking lady with fiery red hair was pouring a pint for the shiny-suited Elvis. "With you in a sec, love," she called out to him. It was then that George saw the hand-written sign hanging behind the bar:

SORRY WE DON'T ACCEPT CARDS. CASH ONLY.

Oh dear. Aside from the £2.43 he had left over from his lunch the day before, George had no cash on him at all. Since he'd arrived in Lower Chidbury, everything had been paid for on his card or had gone onto his room tab at the hotel. It hadn't even occurred to him that he'd need any cash.

"Oh dear," he said to Alice, pointing at the sign, red faced and embarrassed, "I'm afraid I've come out without any money. Is there a cash machine anywhere that I could…"

"You'll be lucky," she giggled back. "There is one, but it's always broken. I think they break it on purpose so that you have to go into the bank where they can try and flog you mortgages or insurance that you don't need. I'm afraid you're skint till the bank opens in the morning."

Could things get any worse? He was on his first date in years and he had no money to pay for anything. As first dates went, he was pretty sure that turning up dressed as Elvis, unshaven and scruffy, with questionable breath and no money to pay for anything was not the best of starts. He could feel himself starting to panic; his heart beating that little bit faster. He was messing it all up, just like he was sure he would. He could feel the heat in his cheeks; the beads of sweat starting to form around his hairline.

"Oh, you are adorable," laughed Alice, noticing the slight upset in his eyes. "Don't worry," she said, taking his arm in her hands and pulling herself close to him for a brief consolatory hug. "I've got plenty of money on me. I'll get the drinks."

"Oh, no, I can't let you do that."

"What, because I'm the girl? You've got a few things to learn, Mr Thring," she said with a mischievous smile. "You go and find somewhere to sit and I'll get us some drinks. Pint for you?"

Alice turned towards the bar and George wandered off in search of a seat.

******

"So, you really ran away from home by accident?" said Alice, smiling mischievously. "That's one of the funniest things I've ever heard."

They sat side by side at a table in the far corner, so close that their knees were touching. He could feel the warmth from her touch, that electric spark jolting through him again, forcing an involuntary smile. He'd read about these things on the internet: how it was a good sign, indicating that she was attracted to him. Touching was an indicator of attraction, either conscious or sub-conscious, and the knee touching thing was practically a green light. Or so the internet said.

Apparently, if she really fancied him, her pupils would be more dilated than usual. He looked closely at her, trying to identify any perceptible change. But as the light in the pub was practically non-existent, and intermittently laced with flashing colours, it was impossible to see. And considering he didn't actually know how dilated her eyes were usually, he couldn't draw any real conclusions.

"Well, I'm not sure you'd call it running away exactly," he said. "More like a surprise holiday – so surprising even I didn't know I was going on it. I suppose it is all rather silly, though. You must think I'm a bit odd."

"On the contrary, George, I think you're one of the least odd people I've ever met. A little bit lost, maybe, but on the whole, not odd. In fact, I think you're rather lovely."

She reached forward and took George's hand, squeezing his fingers in her warm grip, causing a slight flutter in his chest and an unexpected erection to swell in his trousers. He suddenly felt very embarrassed, utterly delighted and altogether too warm, all at the same time.

Had it really been that long since he'd had any substantial female contact that just holding hands with a pretty girl was enough to get him hard? He instinctively crossed his legs, trapping the offending article between his two thighs, and hoped desperately that she hadn't noticed it.

"It is quite funny though," she continued. "Did you not realise how far you'd driven?"

"No," he said. "I didn't really notice what was happening until the car broke down."

"Well, I think it's brilliant. The unconscious mind taking over, like you knew you wanted to get away but you just didn't want to admit it to yourself. So your brain takes over, kind of puts you to sleep for a bit, then whisks you away – almost rescuing you from yourself. It's like your brain knew you needed to get away and just did it without waiting for the rest of you to catch up. It's a very powerful thing, the unconscious mind."

"Hmmm, I didn't really think of it like that," he said.

"So, were you very unhappy? I mean, people usually run away from their lives because they're unhappy. Whether they know they're running away or not..."

"No, I wasn't unhappy exactly," he said, turning his eyes away in a deep, thoughtful motion. "But I wasn't very happy, either. I suppose that's life, isn't it? You spend so much time just getting on with things, assuming that's what you're supposed to be doing. Then you wake up one day and think: is this it? What exactly is the point of it all?"

"I think we all have days like that, George."

"Yes, but most people have an answer, don't they? They have a family to support, kids to feed. They have plans in life, goals, things they're working towards, jobs they love or holidays to save up for. They have dreams and ambitions, a sense of purpose. I don't really have anything like that. I just have me."

"Well, that's exactly it, George Thring," laughed Alice. "You can have whatever you want. You can be whoever you want to be. All you have to do is decide. I think somewhere along the way you stopped wanting and just accepted what you were given. Part of you probably thought that was alright, but the rest of you clearly wanted more. So you stole yourself away and came here. I'll sort you out, don't worry about that."

"Really," smiled George. "You think you can fix me?"

"You don't need fixing, just pushing in the right direction. The first thing we have to do is figure out which direction you want to be pushed in. So, what do you really want to do with the rest of your life?"

"Goodness," he chuckled, "can I have a few minutes to think about it. This is all still a bit new to me."

Alice beamed that warm, golden smile and squeezed his hand a little tighter. "Of course. But don't take too long."

"And what about you," said George. "Are you happy? What does the rest of your life hold?"

"Adventure, that's what I want. I was the same as you, George. I was a bit stuck in life. It was like everything around me was going at a hundred miles an hour and I was stood totally still, not quite wanting to catch up. It was like my life was racing away from me before I'd even had a chance to live it.

"I didn't know it but I wasn't very happy either; living here; letting life pass me by; getting married just because I thought that was what you were supposed to do. Then I guess I woke up too and realised I didn't want anything that I had. I didn't want to be who I was or where I was. So I had to think about what I wanted to do, who I wanted to be, and now I'm changing it. I'm going to see the world."

"Travelling?"

"To start with. You know, George, it's such a big world out there. When you look on a map and see just how small we are compared to the rest of the world, it's really quite incredible. There's so much to see, and I want to see and smell, and taste and touch and explore as much as I can. I want to see what the rest of the world has to offer. So, as soon as I have enough money, that's what I'm going to do. I'm going on an adventure."

"That sounds great. Where are you going to start?"

"No idea!" she announced triumphantly. "That's the whole point. It doesn't matter where I start. I'm just going to go to the airport and buy a ticket on the first available flight to anywhere that looks interesting. It could be America. It could be Russia. It could be China... I'm leaving it up to fate. Can you think of anything more exciting?"

"But what if you don't like it when you get there?"

"Don't be so negative, George. Why wouldn't I like it? And if I don't, so what? I'll just head on somewhere else, try and get some work if I can, or just keep exploring till the money runs out. That is kind of the point of an adventure," she smiled.

"Well, you're braver than I am," he replied.

"What's brave about it? It's just taking a chance, having a bit of fun. Besides, you've already done the hard part."

"Eh?"

"Well, you're here aren't you? You're adventure has already started. Okay, you didn't know you were going on an adventure, but you're smack bang in the middle of one, whether you like it or not. Now you just have to decide if you're going to give up and go home, or whether you keep on rolling and see what's around the next corner.

"And yes, you can have a couple of minutes to decide." She laughed, giving his hand another squeeze.

The fast-paced thump of the blues music suddenly ceased, replaced by the electronic thud of somebody tapping a finger onto a microphone. "Attention ladies and gents. Attention. Come on now, shut your mouths," announced a shrill Liverpudlian accent.

The whole room stopped, turning to look at the interruption. Behind the microphone on the small stage stood the red-haired landlady.

"Right then," she said, silence finally descending on the assembled Elvises (George had decided the plural definitely had to be Elvises).

"It's time for our fantastic Elvis Presley Costume Competition. Looking round the bar, I can see lots have you have really put in a lot of effort this year, and there are some great looking costumes out there." A lacklustre round of applause made its way around the bar like a Mexican wave.

"Of course," continued the landlady, "if I look a bit closer, I can see quite a few of you have put in hardly any effort at all."

The place erupted into nervous laughter, people quickly scanning the room, assessing their own costume against those of others.

"No, I'm only pulling your legs," she appeased the crowd, "you's all look lovely. It's just a good job I'm not on the judging panel." The crowd again hummed with laughter.

"Speaking of which," she said, "first things first: let's meet the judges. First up is last year's winner, and owner of our very own butcher's shop in the high street, Teddy McLeod!"

The audience clapped again, more generously this time, as a short, podgy man emerged from the crowd and made his way behind a table positioned to the side of the stage. He was dressed, much as George had expected, in a traditional-looking Elvis-style jumpsuit, quite possibly homemade, but clearly constructed with a great deal of care and attention. The material was navy blue and dull like suede or velvet. He spun round in an elaborate manner to reveal a highly-detailed sun motif, hand-stitched onto the back, before turning back, raising his hands triumphantly to the crowd and taking his seat.

"Our second judge comes to us all the way from the Texas, in America, and once played back-up second guitar with Elvis himself in Las Vegas. We're incredibly lucky to have him, so please give a huge round of applause for 'Little' Jimmy Douglas!"

A shorter, fatter man stepped out into the open. He looked to be in his late 50s and wore an expression of tired, misanthropic contempt. He was bloated and looked older than he was; years of unhealthy living having made their mark. The pub may have felt lucky to have his company but he clearly didn't feel as privileged to be there. He half-heartedly raised one hand in the air, tilting his head to the side with a glum, self-satisfied smirk, before joining his fellow judge behind the table.

The crowd went wild, or at least as wild as the clientele of a small seaside village pub could go. They clapped, cheered and one person excitedly whooped in the background. He might not have looked like much, or even been particularly famous in his own right, but the crowd absolutely loved him. Due to the simple fact that he had once played with, and by very definition actually met and possibly been friendly with their biggest idol, he was held in very high esteem. George guessed that he'd probably spent quite a few years living off his past association, attending similar conventions and festivals, adopting the role of the big star he could never become on his own. And it clearly didn't bring him much joy. Maybe he could have benefited from his subconscious mind rescuing him as well...

"Our third and final judge," announced the red-haired landlady, "is Chidbury FM's one and only breakfast show host: Vicky Swift!"

A slim young woman dashed out of the crowd, jogging on the spot and punching the air. She was dressed in a bright pink jumpsuit and had, in George's opinion, far too much enthusiasm.

"Chidbury has its own radio station?" George whispered to Alice.

"Sort of," she replied. "Hospital radio."

"Chidbury has a hospital?"

"Well, it's more of a doctor's surgery really."

George opened his mouth to speak, then closed it again. He thought it better not to ask. The radio presenter jogged and punched the air a few more times, then danced round behind the desk and sat down.

"So," said the woman on stage, "we have our judges. All we need now is our contestants. And this year's contenders are..." She held up a piece of paper and read from a list of names. The crowd cheered at each one.

George turned away from the action, looking back towards Alice. She had a curiously devilish smile on her face and he suddenly had a horrible feeling, as if he wasn't quite getting a joke.

"And last but not least," said the voice on the stage, "George Thring. Up you come."

CHAPTER 15

THAT was funny, thought George. For a second there it sounded like she'd said his name. The rest of the contestants moved towards the stage, lining up in an orderly queue, looking around as if waiting for a final straggler to join them.

"Come on George, let's be having you. George Thring!"

There it was again. She'd definitely said 'George Thring', he was sure of it. What an incredible coincidence. Not only had George found himself in this strange little pub, in this strange little village, that he'd happened upon quite by accident. But now he'd discovered there was another George Thring here as well. Seriously, what were the chances? He couldn't help but smile at the irony of it.

Nobody emerged from the crowd.

"George Thring, where are you?" said the now slightly irate landlady. "For goodness sakes, can someone check if he's in the Gents?"

This was all very strange. Where was this guy, who shared George's name? And why was he so reluctant to take to the stage. Unless…

Oh God. Oh no…

George looked at Alice again. "Next part of the adventure," she said.

She'd put his name down for the competition. It wasn't another George Thring they were looking for at all, it was him. Somehow she must have done it when he wasn't looking. "Go on then, George," she giggled, "your public awaits."

She then stood up, lifting his hand high into the air and shouted to the crowd, "Here he is."

George's heart started to pound in his chest, his face and neck immediately burning bright red. "Come on then George," said the landlady, "we haven't got all night, you know."

A small ripple of encouraging applause trailed its way around the pub as if trying to draw him out of his seat. This was definitely happening then. There was nothing he could do about it. He had two choices: he could hold his position and save himself the embarrassment of having to stand up in front of all these people, no doubt readying themselves to laugh at him. He could get out of the public performance, but in so doing he'd likely be ridiculed and shamed for not getting up. They'd laugh at him either way. And what would Alice think of him then? What would he think of himself?

The second choice, the most painful of the two, was that he'd have to go along with it. Succumb to the jeering crowd, brave it out and hope for the best.

Really there was no choice at all. He humbly acquiesced to the crowd's demands and, standing up on wobbly, uncertain legs, stepped out from behind the protection of the table and made his way to the stage. They gave a small, mocking cheer and George stared firmly at his feet, wiping a handful of moisture from his brow.

"Okay," said the landlady, "now that we have our judges in place and all of our contestants finally lined up, let's get started shall we?"

The contestants were called up onto the stage area. They were made to stand in the centre of a large, white spotlight to show off their costume. They would spin and parade in front of the judges, and then give an incredibly embarrassing twirl to the crowd. Finally, they had sixty seconds behind the microphone to say a few words about their costume: how it was made, what it was supposed to represent and to try to sway the voting judges in their favour. George was dreading his turn.

He'd never been one for public speaking or showing off in any way. When the class had to give presentations at school, he'd always managed to develop a sufficiently realistic set of flu-like symptoms to get out of having to attend that day. And, when his overbearing father had forced him into his school uniform anyway, telling him a few germs wouldn't hurt him and, "there's no use staying in bed, a good day's work and learning is the best thing for fighting off illness," he'd always managed to con the school nurse into letting him hide away in the sick bay.

At university, he'd always managed to put himself forward as writer, organiser or team leader; letting the braver, more socially adept members of the group deal with the verbal part of any presentations or demonstrations. And, whilst at work, on the rare occasion that he was called upon to speak in front of others in meetings, or deliver presentations, he'd developed a good technique of preparing everything in the form of engaging Powerpoint presentations. He could simply project everything up onto the wall for colleagues to see, making sure to pack it with sufficiently attention-grabbing charts and graphics, then stand at the back of the darkened room, where he could avoid direct eye contact.

But there was no getting out of this one. In just a few minutes time he'd be twirling and whirling and feeling utterly ridiculous in front of a room full of people. Then he'd have to stand in full, illuminated view and talk. In front of people. Their hungry eyes devouring him, waiting for any small slip, any tremble of the voice; desperate to ridicule him, like they had at school.

Like the time he'd been forced to read in front of the whole school, one Friday assembly. He'd been eight years old and had always been a quiet boy. Not shy exactly, just reserved – but quietly confident. Reading in front of people hadn't fazed him at all. He was a good reader, the best in his class, and was very pleased and proud to have been awarded the honour.

Everything had been going so well. It wasn't a long story and he'd read it seventeen times in advance so he knew where all the tricky words were. He knew the potential stumbling blocks. He'd practised reading it aloud in front of his Mum and Dad. Mum had been terribly proud, looking like she might have cried. Dad had been rather less impressed and made some comment about reading the paper every day and no-one ever told him how great he was.

So his assembly piece should have been perfect. And the first half of the story had been. But then came the one fatal mistake. Not a mistake at all, really. It was a simple spoonerism of two innocuous enough words, which shouldn't have been such a problem. Except for the fact that the two words in question were 'tall' and 'bits', which, when crashing together in George's mouth, unfortunately came tumbling out as 'ball tits'.

It was a delicious mistake for a room full of young minds and the whole room absolutely exploded in uproarious laughter. It was the kind of thing George would have relished himself, were he not the target of the humour.

It was Harry Markham who revelled in it the most, screaming out, "He said TITS! He said TITS!" The chant quickly escalated, soaring around the room, finding itself on the lips of nearly every pupil, the only abstainers the ones laughing too hard to manage to form the words. Teachers leapt up from their chairs, angry looks piercing the air; clapping their hands loudly, desperate to restore order.

George simply stood there, unable to take in what had just happened. One simple slip of the tongue and he'd become a laughing stock, a sea of merry faces cackling and pointing. Abuse and derision crashing over him like huge, devastating waves.

Finally the laughter subsided and an electric silence descended over the crowd; all eyes back on George, hungrily waiting for him to speak again. A pack of lions waiting to see which way their prey would run before leaping, claws and teeth flashing. But he was lost. His voice had retreated way back inside himself. The words in the book were a black smudge on the page. He just stood there, staring back out at them.

And then it happened. He tried so hard not to let it. He tried to hold it back. But the harder he tried the more insistent the urge became. He could feel his face burning; that overwhelming sickly knot of emotion spinning in his stomach; the warm salty water pooling in his eyes. And then it all came bursting out: the tears running in streams down his face, his breath catching in the back of his throat in short, sharp gasps. His shoulders juddering up and down as the emotion poured out of him.

He had just stood there, embarrassed and horrified, silently crying in front of the whole school as the laughter and jeers came hurtling back at him ten times harder than before.

Now, more than twenty years later, he could feel that ball spinning in his stomach again. Twisting and raging and picking up pace.

One by one, the contestants paraded to the crowd, turning and twisting, showing off their clothing. They waved their arms and legs to demonstrate the intricacies of the style; the stitching; the quality of the material; the bright, shimmering patterns. Then each one stepped behind the microphone, gleefully waxing lyrical about what they were wearing and desperately trying to outdo the previous contestant. All George could think about was the rapidly decreasing queue in front of him and the fact that it would soon be his turn.

His heart beat hard in his chest, a large lump forming in his throat. He felt sick. His head was hot and felt full of air; inflated like it might pop at any second. He was a wet, sticky, sweaty mess, and by the time he actually made it to the stage his costume would be little more than sodden rag. Nerves made his feet shuffle back and forth, side to side, where he stood. He wanted to run and hide. He wanted to get out of this – out of this pub, out of this village, back to his safe little life where embarrassing things like this never happened. And worst of all, he desperately needed a wee.

He looked over at the door and thought about running. It would be so easy. He could make it out of there in less than half a minute, probably before anybody even noticed he'd gone. And if they did notice – sure, they'd think he was a coward. They might even say it; call him names behind his back. But he'd be in his car, getting the hell away from this horror, and he'd never even have to hear it.

But then he looked over at Alice. She looked so happy. So excited; watching him, encouraging him, smiling that warm, delicious smile. She looked so beautiful and he knew he couldn't run. He could cope with everyone else thinking he was a coward, but not her. If he ran now, chickened-out and fled from the pub, that would surely be it for his chances with her. She was the one who'd set him this challenge and he couldn't fail it.

So he had to tough it out. He had to do what he least wanted. He turned back to see that the crowd in front of him had now disappeared. It was his turn.

Very gingerly he stepped forward, taking up position in front of the judge's table. His throat was as dry as a desert, in sharp contrast to the rest of him which seemed to be leaking fluid at a potentially dangerous rate. Sweat was streaming down his face; pooling in the elaborate 'V' shape at the front of his chest; running like a river down his spine.

He knew he was supposed to be proudly showing off – twisting and turning, strutting his stuff – but it was all he could to keep upright under all this pressure. He made one quarter-turn to the judges, as if to demonstrate that the costume had a back as well as a front, then leapt behind the relative safety of the microphone stand.

The bemused crowd looked on, anticipation rising. The dazzling spotlight burned down on him, making him wince even through the dark protective layer of his sunglasses. The crowd seemed to have multiplied ten-fold. What had previously been the capacity crowd of a small village pub now looked more like a sell-out at Wembley. He leaned closer to the mike. His lips parted. All he could think was: "Don't say 'Ball Tits'!"

"Er… hello…" he managed to spit out in a dull, choked, uncertain voice. "My name is George… er, George Thring." He looked round at the crowd. They looked back. Silence.

"My costume is… erm… well, my clothes were ruined, you see? Covered in mud and totally soaking… I had a little mishap with my car, after I'd driven quite a long…"

A small bead of hot sweat rolled agonisingly down his cheek. "Well, as I say, my clothes were ruined, and I didn't have anything to wear…"

Again he looked at the crowd. A sea of curious faces stared back. Silence. This was possibly not quite what they wanted to hear. It was certainly not as entertaining as the previous contestants. But at least he was talking.

"Anyway," he continued, "I had to go to the shop on the high street and the only thing they had was… well, this," he said, gesturing towards himself. "So I had to buy it…"

Bemused silence.

"It's pale blue," he added, sensing the crowd wanted more but not sure quite what to give them, "with sort of white and silver bits. I'm afraid I'm not really sure who made it."

He stood there for a few seconds, waiting for them to devour this insightful information. Coughs and deep, breathy sighs whispered across the audience, like wind racing across an empty desert. The bright, blazing heat of the spotlight burned deep into George's eyes: a great glowing hint to get off stage. Realising it was best to give up while the going was good, he shot across to hide behind the other assembled contestants.

He didn't get quite the applause the others had. A polite ripple of claps circulated the room, overshadowed by a very loud, very enthusiastic Alice standing on her chair, whooping and cheering and calling his name.

At least he hadn't been lynched. And, despite his worst fears, not a single person had laughed or made any kind of disparaging remark. Alice was so happy; so pleased to see him up there, egging him on and enjoying herself, he couldn't help but smile. It was one of the most excruciating things he could have imagined being forced to do and he'd come out of it actually smiling. This certainly was turning into an eventful few days for him.

The contestants were herded back in the stage area and made to wait while the judges gathered round and deliberated. They looked up every few seconds, scanning the row with critical intensity before reaching their decision. It was another tortuous four minutes before they delivered their verdict, revealing that George had come seventh out of the nine entrants.

Seventh? Okay, maybe he hadn't really given the best account of himself. And they may have taken his lack of performance as a lack of enthusiasm. But seventh? His costume, though slightly more sweat-stained than he'd have liked, was still far better than some of the other's homemade atrocities. Seventh? He definitely deserved better than that. It was a fix! He had half a mind to complain.

But thankfully it was over. And he'd settle for just being out of the spotlight again. Grateful to be free, he made his way back over to Alice, sat down next to her and lifted his pint to his lips, draining nearly half the glass in one much-needed gulp.

"Well, I thought you should have won," said Alice, giggling with caustic humour. She'd clearly enjoyed the discomfort she'd put him through, though not maliciously. She'd set him a challenge, knew he could do it if he only tried, and was overjoyed at his triumph. "See, George? Taking chances isn't so hard, is it? If you can come seventh in an Elvis Presley costume competition, just imagine what else you can do?"

"Yes, the mind boggles!" he said, a relieved smile spreading across his lips.

They both giggled then, gazing deep into each other's eyes, and for just a second the rest of the pub seemed to disappear. The rest of the town was gone. It was just the two of them, locked in a moment. It was about as close to perfect as George had ever known.

And as he sat there, gazing at this curious creature – this beautiful woman who'd somehow cast a spell on him – his heart filled with a warmth he'd never known and he felt that if they could just stay there forever, gazing at each other, smiling, lost in each other's eyes, then that would be enough for him. What could possibly spoil such a perfect feeling?

"Who's this fucking prick?"

The words came hurtling at them, bursting their gaze like a bubble, crashing them back to the pub and the sight of an irate man glowering down at them. "Well, come on Alice, who is he?"

"Oh, for God's sake, Michael," said Alice sharply. "Can't I even come out for a drink without you acting like... like... well, like this? It's not fair. I am allowed to have a life, you know."

"You had a life, Alice. You had a life, until you chose to throw it away," replied the man, his voice crackling with a mixture of anger and sadness. He was tall, with short dark hair and a sheen of stubble on his cheeks. He was slightly overweight, with a small pot-belly resting on the buckle of his belt. His face was red and tired, as if he hadn't slept in a week, and the alcohol clearly wasn't helping. He wasn't drunk, but he was not far off, and his words were tinged with a slur. He looked like at any second he might either lash out in anger, or burst into floods of tears. "So come on," he said, turning his gaze to George, "who is this prick?"

"He's just a guest from the hotel," she said dismissively. "He's in town on his own; he had no-one to hang out with, so I said I'd go to the pub with him. There's nothing going on, Michael. As usual, you're being paranoid and sticking your nose in where it's not wanted. Mr Thring," she said, turning to George, "this is my EX-husband." She over-stressed the 'ex' part, as if trying to hammer home a message. George gazed blankly at the man, looking at him but not really taking him in.

Just a guest: the words pierced George's heart like a knife. That was all he was to her. Just a guest in her parents' hotel. She'd seen him alone in the restaurant and taken pity on him. Sat with him just to pass the time, or just to be friendly, and he'd taken it for more than it was. He knew it was too good to be true. How had he got the wrong end of the stick so easily? He suddenly felt sick, the disappointment making his chest feel heavy. All the light seemed to fade out of the room. The noise became a distant hum.

Oh God, when he'd asked her out, did she only say yes out of pity? Of course she had. He'd let his brain run away with him, allowed himself to hear what he'd wanted to hear. Of course she didn't want to be here with him! This wasn't a date; she was just being polite. She'd probably entered him in that ridiculous competition just to get rid of him.

She didn't feel what he'd been feeling, nothing like it. There he was, lost in this dense cloud of emotion; daring to dream that he'd found someone who could make him happy, feel the same way about him. And it was all just in his head. Where he saw the most beautiful creature he'd ever seen, all she saw was a sad, lonely man who'd landed in her town on the wave of a nervous breakdown, dressed as Elvis bloody Presley. George suddenly felt incredibly foolish.

Alice and Michael continued to argue but George felt totally lost. Everything seemed to be going in slow motion and all he could hear was the blood rushing in his ears; his own voice cursing him for being such an idiot.

"Yeah, I'm not buying it," Michael said angrily. "That's my slag of a wife you're drinking with, mate," he said, reaching over and pushing George's shoulder. The drink was taking over. He was over-confident and looking to provoke a reaction.

George snapped out of his dream. He rose quickly to his feet, standing face to face with the man; chest puffed out in defiance, his chin raised high and his eyes tight and staring. "What did you say?"

This was quite unlike George. Had he been totally conscious of what he was doing, he might well have told himself to sit back down and just hope the big, angry man would go away without any further trouble. But he definitely wasn't feeling himself. He'd just been delivered a crushing blow, found out the girl he thought he might just be falling in... was it too quick to have fallen in love? Maybe, but he was sure that's what he was feeling. And he thought that's what she might have been feeling as well. But she wasn't. She hadn't been. His heart was shattered, crumbled into a million pieces on the floor at his feet, and the last thing he needed was this idiot causing trouble.

Out of nowhere, and for the first time in a very long time, George lost his temper. Something inside him snapped. He couldn't explain it, but it was as if after all the loneliness, disappointment and frustration he'd suddenly had enough. And he wasn't going to hold back any longer.

"I suggest you take a step back, apologise to the lady, and then get the hell out of my sight before I'm forced to teach you a lesson in manners," he said very loudly. He didn't shout; he didn't sound angry or aggressive. He spoke very clearly and calmly, and with more authority than he'd ever mustered before. The whole place descended into silence, as every head in the place swivelled to see what was going on.

The man snarled back at him, eyes wide and staring, his red, puffy face glowing in the near darkness. And then, just as quickly as George's bravery had appeared, it seemed to shrink back down inside him again. That immediate rush of blood to the head rushed straight back out and he found himself practically nose-to-nose with a very angry drunk man who, it was quite reasonable to assume, may well punch him.

Oh my God, what the hell was he doing? This wasn't him, he wasn't a fighter. He wasn't the sort of man who stood up to people in pubs, defended ladies' honour and threatened to teach angry men a lesson in manners! He was quiet George, who avoided all forms of confrontation. He was invisible George, who blended into the background and didn't like to make a fuss of himself. He was timid George, who didn't like shouting or raising his voice. He certainly didn't like threatening people. He'd never had a fight before in his life; not a proper one. He wasn't even sure what you were supposed to do in a fight.

But then, just over 48 hours ago he hadn't been the sort of person who'd run away from home – accidentally or not. He hadn't been the type of person to hang around a small town dressed up as Elvis Presley, drinking in bars with strangers. And he certainly hadn't been the type of person who'd take part in a ridiculous fancy-dress competition. It had been a time of fairly significant change for George Thring.

It was too late now, of course. There was no way he could back down. He didn't know much about fighting, or even arguing, really. But he was pretty sure it was bad form to threaten someone, shout in their face, then instantly sink back down into your chair in retreat, hoping they'd just forget what you'd said and be on their merry way. So he stood there, looking as threatening as he could and trying to hide his shaking knees.

"Yeah, well…" said the man defiantly, his mouth hanging open like his brain was trying to find the words to complete the sentence. He was staring hard at George, sizing him up, calculating his move. Then he simply spun on his heels and walked away, pushing himself through the crowd, bouncing violently off the people in his way.

George couldn't believe his luck! He dropped quickly back to his seat, grabbed for his glass and downed the rest of his drink.

"I'm so sorry, George," said Alice, with genuine sorrow in her eyes. "That was Michael, my ex. He can't seem to get past the fact that we've split up. He's not usually that bad, but when he's been drinking he's… well, you saw him."

"Oh, no problem," lied George, still grateful for his incredible turn of fortune. If all fights were as easy as that, he'd have nothing to worry about. Not that he was desperate to ever find himself in that situation again.

And then he remembered Alice's words. He was 'just a guest'. Yes, of course. And this wasn't really a date after all. He felt totally deflated again.

"That was really kind of you, though. And really brave, standing up to him like that," she said, smiling softly at him, appearing genuinely impressed.

"That? Oh no, it was nothing, really. I just told him off a little bit." He looked away from her, embarrassed at how silly he'd been. How had he let himself get so carried away, thinking this was a date, thinking there was more going on than… well, what was going on? None of it was clear any more.

It had been a confusing few days, all-in-all, what with everything that had happened. All that talk of the future; of changing his life. It had been nice for a while – exciting – dreaming like that. But what was he really doing? He looked down at his sweaty, sequined clothing. What the hell was he wearing? What was he doing here? Perhaps it would be best if he just got back in his car and drove home. He should go back to his safe life, where at least he wouldn't feel stupid; where he wouldn't make these ridiculous mistakes.

"If it's all the same to you, Alice," he said, not quite managing to look her in the eye, "I think maybe I should call it a night. It's been a long day and I'm pretty tired and…"

"Oh, okay," said Alice, looking suddenly crestfallen. At least he thought it was crestfallen, he couldn't tell. Suddenly everything had become so very confusing. "Are you sure you don't want another drink?"

"Erm, no, I think it's probably best if I just go," he replied. That wasn't strictly true. He didn't really want to leave. What he wanted was to carry on their date, to stay here drinking with Alice, smiling and laughing and chatting together. He wanted to carry on believing that someone like her could be interested in someone like him. But now that he knew the truth, it wasn't the same. This wasn't a date; it was just pity. He just wanted to get out of there as quickly as he could; get back to the safety of his room, where he could admonish himself for daring to dream and ignore the world.

******

Alice drained the last of her drink and with a glum look on both their faces they left the pub and strolled back up the hill in silence. They moved at a faster pace than before, George marching ahead forcefully as if he was late for something or simply trying to get away and Alice trying to keep up. They were further apart than before, their arms no longer brushing tantalisingly against each other, separated now by an aching chasm of awkwardness.

What had gone wrong? It had all been going really well, or so she thought. They were having fun, weren't they? Laughing and drinking, and getting along. Okay, it was a bit mean to have entered him in the contest without warning him but he'd seemed to take it in good humour. He was smiling when he came back to the table. He hadn't seemed upset.

It must have been Michael. Bloody Michael. Why couldn't he leave her alone – just accept that they were over and done with? Every time she even came close to meeting a nice guy – and there were very few decent catches that came sailing through town – he'd stalk her and ruin it.

Of course, that was it. George had seen her crazy ex, realised just how much baggage she came with and instantly gone off her. Well, she couldn't blame him, really. A drunk, threatening, abusive ex-husband turning up on your first date and threatening you would be enough to put any man off.

They approached the hotel, stopping outside the front door and nervously turning to face one another. "I'm sorry about all that business with Michael,"

123

she said, looking for some sign that she could rescue the date from disaster. "I hope it hasn't... put you off."

"Put me off?" said George. "I don't understand."

"Look, I know it can't be a very exciting prospect, getting involved with a woman who's got a crazy ex-husband practically stalking her and threatening you in pubs. But I was kind of hoping... well, I mean..." She was suddenly flustered.

"I... well, I might as well just say it..." She took a deep breath, composing herself. "I really like you, George and, well... crazy stalking ex-husbands aside, I kind of thought there might be something between us. I mean, I think you're lovely, and we were having fun before all that business, weren't we? I just... I'd hate to think one drunken idiot could have ruined that."

"*Me* not interested?" said George, confused. "I think you're just about the best person I've ever met in my life. I thought you were the one who wasn't interested in me!"

"What would make you think that?"

"Well, you said it. You said I was 'just a guest in the hotel'. That I was lonely and you were only showing me around town. You said there was nothing going on between us. You called me 'Mr Thring'."

So, that was it. God, she hadn't even realised she'd said it. Or that he'd taken it to heart. It was just an impulsive reaction.

"Oh, you are so adorable," she said, grinning widely and placing her hand on the side of George's face. "I didn't mean any of that! I was trying to protect you from Michael. I just wanted him to go away. He's so jealous, if I'd told him we were on a date he'd have given you hell. He'd have been asking questions, giving me a hard time... We'd never have got rid of him. He'd probably have wanted to fight you."

"Oh," said George.

"I'm so sorry, George. I thought you knew I was just trying to get rid of him. And you thought I was being really mean..."

"Erm... so it was definitely a date?" said George hesitantly, still not quite sure what had happened. "A proper date?"

"It still is," she said, smiling mischievously.

"Oh," gulped George, a huge, giddy grin spreading across his face. He couldn't think what else to say. What was he supposed to say? He just stood there, relieved, bemused and suddenly elated, grinning like an idiot.

"So are you going to ask me in for a drink then, or what?" giggled Alice, punching him jokingly on the arm.

"Erm, well... er, yes of course. We could go up to my room and see if there's anything in the mini-bar."

"You don't stay away from home much, do you, George?"

"Well, no, not really. Why?"

"There's no mini-bar in the room. Shows how perceptive you are."

"Oh, right," he said, unsure of what else to suggest. "Well, we could... er..."

"It's okay, you go upstairs. I'll sneak a bottle of wine up from the bar and meet you in your room in a couple of minutes."

"Can you do that?"

"It's okay," she smiled, "I know the owners."

CHAPTER 16

GEORGE raced up the creaky stairs of the hotel, partially blinded by the dark lenses of his large gold sunglasses. The wild swinging bell-bottoms of his jumpsuit nearly caught under the heel of his platform shoes with each step, threatening to send him tumbling back down.

He was excited. He felt like singing! Laughing out loud! Screaming at the top of his voice! It was a kind of reckless abandon he hadn't experienced in a very, very long time. But he wasn't really used to such emotional outbursts. Besides, it was after 10pm and he didn't want to disturb any of the other guests. So he settled for leaping two stairs at a time, chuckling quietly as he went.

When he reached the top of the stairs he felt dizzy and had to hold on to the banister for a few seconds, catching his breath and letting the burning pain in his chest subside. Tiny red and green lights twinkled in front of his eyes, his head swimming with a lack of oxygen. This childlike enthusiasm was all good in theory, but his body's lack of fitness couldn't quite keep pace with his over-eager brain.

It was the most exciting thing that had happened to George in ages. A girl was going to come up to his room. It was more years than he cared to admit since such a thing had happened. A sickeningly nervous, exhilarated feeling coursed through his body like a warm, insistent throb. He couldn't wait for her to get there. She might want to kiss him. He might even get to see her naked! He chuckled again at the thought. She might even want to see him naked…

And then he suddenly felt panicked. He wasn't entirely sure what sort of shape his body was in, from an aesthetic point of view. What if she did want to see him naked and was disappointed? He put the thought out of his head, trying not to dwell on it. "Don't panic, George," he said quietly to himself, "just take one step at a time."

He made it back to the room and looked upon the less-than-romantic setting. In a perfect world, he'd have taken her back to a penthouse suite. He would have chilled champagne waiting. Oysters, truffles, caviar… He'd have scattered the place with rose petals; written poems to romance her; had a grand piano installed so he could serenade her with her favourite song (after the required months of piano and singing lessons, of course).

He'd have done every corny, silly romantic thing he could think of to impress her and show her how much she'd come to mean to him in such a short space of time.

However, this wasn't a perfect world. It was Lower Chidbury. And the best he could offer was a cramped, dusty, slightly damp bedroom in a small hotel, with horrendous patterned wallpaper and the least comfortable bed he'd ever slept in. There wasn't even a radio, let alone a grand piano, and the reception on the telly had proved unreliable to the point of unwatchable.

George did what he could by way of tidying. He straightened out the bedclothes, but no amount of tucking and smoothing could disguise the lumps and loose springs, or the ugly brown colour. He'd like to have given the place a good wipe down, a decent hoover, and sprayed the room with a whole can of air freshener. But he had neither the time nor the cleaning apparatus at hand.

The other thing very much in need of attention was, of course, George himself. There was nothing he could do about the clothes. He was stuck in his daft, flappy costume and that was that. The sweat in his hair had thankfully dried in the cool evening breeze, but he was very much aware that he hadn't showered since the previous morning.

He hadn't dared to push his luck and even hope for any potential sexual eventualities. But he wouldn't have minded giving himself a quick splash and scrub, just in case. He didn't know that much about women but he was pretty sure that if a girl came up to your hotel room for a drink, that had to give you at least a fifty-fifty chance of getting naked together. Just thinking about it made him anxious about the state of his underpants.

And then it was too late as he heard a short, sharp knock at the door. He opened it and Alice sprung into the room, giggling. "Quick, quick," she said, ducking in behind him and closing the door, "before anyone sees me."

"You're not embarrassed to be here, are you?" said George.

"No, of course not. But it wouldn't do for people to see the girl who works in the bar sneaking into a guest's bedroom after ten. And if my Mum and Dad knew I was here…"

"I take it you don't make a habit of this, then?"

"I'm shocked you even asked, Mr Thring," she said with mock offence. "I certainly do not make a habit of it. It's only for the very special guests. Maybe one or two a month…"

George's smile dropped.

"Oh you really are too easy to wind up, George," giggled Alice. "You need to be careful or I might end up taking advantage of that."

She leaned forward, kissing him quickly on the cheek. A bashful smile spread across his lips and his face flushed pink. "I hope you like white," she said, handing him the chilled bottle of wine from one hand, holding up two glasses in the other.

They moved over to the bed and sat down, George chivalrously sitting on the largest pokey-out spring and saving her the more comfortable seat.

"So, Mr Thring," she said, pouring out two generous glasses of wine, "what next?"

"Next?" repeated George, confused. He took a sip of his wine, wincing slightly as the sharp metallic taste caught in his throat. It felt like his mouth had turned inside out and he couldn't help but cough slightly.

"Not really a wine drinker, eh?" laughed Alice, noticing his discomfort.

"No, no, it's very nice," he lied. Then, realising she wasn't convinced: "I'm not much of a drinker at all, really. But this is fine. I'm sure I can get used to it. What do mean, what next?"

"What's the next part of the adventure? You've run away from home. You came seventh in an Elvis Presley costume competition. You defended a lady's honour and narrowly escaped having to teach her drunk ex-husband a lesson out in the car park. And now you find yourself enjoying said lady's charming company over a bottle of wine."

"Yes," George agreed, "it's been quite a couple of days."

"So what's next? You can't stop now. You've got to plan the next move! Do you keep going? Will you go back and face the music? Which dead rock star will you choose to dress as tomorrow?"

"Well," George smiled, "I haven't really given it much thought. I'm not sure whether I should *keep* going because I didn't really intend to *start* going in the first place. I probably should go back and explain myself; at least call into work and apologise for my absence. But then… when I really think about doing it, that seems like the last thing I want to do. So I don't really know."

He looked solemn, then. Thoughtful. "As for dead rock stars," he continued, changing the subject and trying to lighten the mood, "I think I'll stick with Elvis for the time being. I've only just got used to walking in the shoes."

Alice laughed, patting her hand enticingly on George's knee. But his mirth hadn't quite managed to steer him from the question he didn't want to answer: "Why don't you want to go home?"

He'd dreaded it being asked; dreaded having to answer. But somehow, because it was her and because she seemed genuinely interested and sympathetic, he found the words just came tumbling out:

"I suppose I don't really want to go home," he said, looking down at the glass he was nervously fingering, "because I don't really like my life. I don't think I've ever really liked it. I know a lot of people say that. They don't like their job, or they have money problems, or they don't get along with their family. But I really don't like my whole life. I don't have any family and I don't really have any friends to speak of. I've been gone for a whole day now and I doubt whether anyone has even noticed. Sometimes I wonder whether I really even matter at all."

George couldn't quite believe what he was saying. These were feelings he'd never even really admitted to himself and here he was spilling his guts to this practical stranger. She must have thought he was a hopeless idiot.

"I'm sorry, I know that must sound terribly pathetic," he said, looking up expecting to see a face etched with pity. Instead, Alice was simply smiling that same warm, rich smile.

"It's not pathetic in the slightest," she said softly. "I think that's the bravest thing anyone has ever told me." She took his hand in hers, the sudden warmth of her touch sending a slight shiver through him.

"At least if you know you're not happy then you can do something about it.

You can go out there and find whatever it is that will make you happy. Find something that will make you love your life. What would be pathetic is if you carried on living a life that you didn't like because you were too scared not to. I nearly did that. I married Michael, and I nearly settled for what I thought I was supposed to want. Now *that* would have been pathetic."

Her eyes glistened slightly in the light, as if the very faintest of tears were forming.

"And of course you matter. You certainly matter to me. I wouldn't be here if you didn't. You should never think that, never. We're all here for a reason. Some of us just take a little longer to figure out what that reason is. And I bet lots of people have noticed you're missing. I bet you matter to a hell of a lot more people than you even know."

George smiled. It was all a little bit overwhelming. He could feel tiny tears forming in the corners of his own eyes and fought hard to hold them back. One evening in the company of this sweet, charming woman and he'd opened up more than he could ever remember. He wished he were still wearing those stupid oversized glasses so that he could hide the emotion in his eyes.

"Of course, what do I know?" said Alice. "You could just be another crazy Elvis nut with a broken down car…"

The two of them broke out laughing, both relieved at the break in the tension before an embarrassing silence descended upon them. Both of them knew what was coming. Both waited, hoping for the other to make the first move. This is it, thought George, time to be decisive. No guts, no glory. It's now or never…

He leaned forward, his heart thumping in his chest, and was overjoyed to see Alice reciprocating; leaning in, closing her eyes and tilting her head slightly to one side. George moved closer, until he could feel the faint, warm whisper of her breath against lips. Then just before their lips met she suddenly hesitated, pulling back slightly.

"Thank God," she said, her smiling face less than an inch from his, "I thought you were never going to kiss me." With that she took his face in her hands and pressed her lips firmly against his.

It was warm and gentle and absolutely perfect. Her lips were even softer than he'd imagined them. She tasted faintly of strawberries and wine. She leaned into him, her weight pushing him onto his back, and as he relaxed and went with it the weight of the glass in his hand made his wrist jerk sideways, sending the wine tumbling down onto the carpet.

"Oh God," said George, breaking away in a panic. "Oh, that's gonna leave a stain…"

"You are the oddest man," said Alice, pushing him back onto the bed and smiling down at him. With that she held up her own glass and tipped the contents out onto the floor.

"It's only wine," she giggled. And I'm sure that floor has seen far worse. "Now come here." She leaned back over, straddling George, climbing up into his lap, before pushing him back onto the bed and kissing him again.

George was actually quite surprised when he first felt her warm, soft tongue invading his mouth. It wasn't unexpected, exactly, but according to the rules that had applied to most of his previous sexual encounters he was a good three weeks ahead of schedule for 'tongues'.

First dates usually ended with an awkward, silent walk to a waiting taxi or front door. There would be a hopeful enquiry about a possible second date and, if he was lucky, maybe even a kiss on the cheek. A kiss on the lips was usually precluded until the second date, if, of course, a second date had been granted (though in his experience they often weren't). And even then it was usually a fairly cursory advance of what may or may not be granted at a later date.

A full tongue kiss was absolutely unheard of at this stage, and usually not granted until at least the third or fourth date – or, in the case of one particularly tiresome girl who he'd persisted with for far too long, a full six romantic evenings out (and even then she'd tasted like vaseline and coffee).

George would generally expect to have laid out for at least three or four meals, a trip to the cinema or zoo and possibly even flowers or chocolates to proceed to this stage. To his shame, he realised that he hadn't even bought Alice so much as a solitary drink. Perhaps, thought George, I've been dating the wrong type of woman…

But there he was, with this beguiling woman's tongue in his mouth, and, bar his own, it was possibly – no, definitely – the best tongue he'd ever had in there. He reciprocated with a sweep of her mouth with his own tongue and she didn't flinch, cry, kick, punch or bite him, so he guessed it must have been okay. He was a little out of practice but, obviously, not too rusty.

Her fingers ran circles through his hair before sliding down his face, playing softly around his neck and chin, and then scratching playfully at his exposed chest with her fingernails. George's hands remained fixed by his sides, palms flat down against the bed, scared to touch her in case he somehow overstepped the mark and ruined proceedings.

He was desperate to touch her, of course. He wanted to run his hands up the small of her back; to cup those wonderfully pert breasts; maybe even have a quick feel of her fantastic bottom. But he was worryingly out of his depth. He didn't need written permission, exactly, but this had all come somewhat out of the blue and he wasn't sure exactly to what level things were likely to progress. So for the time being it seemed prudent not to be too forward. And, in all honesty, he had to admit to feeling more than a little bit flustered.

Alice's hands continued their work at his neck and chest, before he felt the strange sensation of his collar pulling down on his shoulders. Her fingers had snaked their way inside the loose, low-cut collar of his jumpsuit and he could have sworn it felt like she was tugging at it. Like she was trying, with limited success, to remove him from his clothing.

And then it suddenly dawned on George. I think she might want to have sex! Right now. With me.

For most men this would have been welcome news. But for George it only triggered a further onset of panic. It was longer than George cared to admit since he'd last had sex. Not since Emily, in fact. He'd certainly thought about it a bit. Well, a lot actually. But he hadn't done it.

He was sure he could have done, if he'd tried. He could have found someone that would have wanted to have sex with him if he'd really put his mind to it. There were a few girls at work he might have stood a chance with – had he actually ever struck up the courage to talk to them in the first place. And there was that cute red-haired girl from the corner shop who sometimes smiled at him when he popped in for a pint of milk. Though, again, chances are he'd have to have said more than 'Hello,' 'Goodbye' and 'Oh, these bread rolls are very reasonably priced' for her to have developed romantic feelings for him.

He often got the feeling that she wanted him to say more. To offer up some crumbs of small talk. To flirt a little, or maybe even ask her out. A delicious, warm silence would spread between them and he'd find himself momentarily lost in her eyes, his mouth parted, waiting for the words. And she seemed receptive, as though she was just as eagerly awaiting those words. And in that moment he'd wonder 'Maybe I should ask her out, and maybe she'd say yes'. And maybe she would have done. But the nerves always got the better of him; his stomach readying itself for that crushing, gnawing, aching feeling of rejection. And he'd lose the words, commenting instead on the price of baked goods.

George was fairly certain he could probably have been having lots of sex over the years with a multitude of attractive, glamorous women – or at least some dumpy, homely, grateful ones – if only he'd got around to asking them.

As such, it was definitely a while since he'd been in this position. He was sure it was as simple as riding a bike; probably easier. You never really forget how to do the more simple things. But that didn't mean he couldn't mess it up, of course. And if there was one thing you couldn't afford to mess up it was this. There are several things in life that are near-impossible to either live down or recover from, and a below-average first sexual encounter with a girl was surely the hardest. George was far from the world's greatest expert on romance. Or sex. Or women. But he did know that.

******

George's sexual experience with women had been a relatively unimpressive, though not wholly disastrous, list. It read:

1)
Name: Catherine Trimble
Year: 1992
George's Age: 16

Catherine was George's classmate at school; a quiet, bookish girl who the other boys had written off as either too geeky or nerdy to fancy. But George had always recognised a distinct attractiveness beneath her long grey skirt; limp, face-covering hair; and large, dark-rimmed glasses. She was a kindred spirit; another of the 'quiet ones' and their friendship took a romantic turn one night whilst studying for a maths exam together at her parent's house.

They'd got caught up in the excitement that only solving a really difficult equation can bring, and had somehow found themselves kissing. That led to George's first proper tongue kiss (a wet, messy, heavily saliva-based affair) and the unutterably joyous feel of his first naked breast. The experience was unfairly short-lived, however, due to her pushing him away in panic at the sound of her parent's car pulling into the driveway.

Even more unfairly, it turned out to be his only sexual interaction with Catherine. A sudden growth spurt in the chest department – aided by a new pair of contact lenses and a fashion and make-up lesson from her older sister – had seen the bookish girl transform into a beautiful young woman, all in the space of one summer holiday. The other boys quickly re-evaluated their impression of her and George's hopes of a repeat performance were dashed when she took up with Gavin Johnson, football team captain and official school heartthrob.

2)
Name: Jennifer Stobbs
Year: 1995-1996
George's Age: 19-20

George met Jennifer in his second year at University. She was a wild spirit, something of an eco-nut, and always fully involved in the endeavours of at least one important cause or campaign. She was the complete opposite of George, of course, but he liked to think that's what had attracted them to each other in the first place. In reality, he was something of a project to her – another one of her causes – and she'd been attracted to the prospect of trying to fix him. He'd been attracted to the fact that she was one of the few girls who'd actually talk to him. She was also very pretty. And she had a lovely bum.

They went out for a whole year and it was she who relieved George of the wretched virginity that had blighted him for far too long, weighing albatross-like around his neck. He'd improved his kissing technique by then, thanks to excessive practice with a girl he'd met during a holiday to Spain with his aunt and uncle when he was 17 (though she doesn't make it onto the list as it was really only kissing, and considering Catherine had allowed him to touch her boobs, it was, if anything, something of a step back), but sex had thus far eluded him.

He hadn't let on to Jennifer that it was his first time, of course. Though, from the fact that proceedings had been fairly short lived, he was sure she'd probably guessed. Luckily, that disappointingly short, nervous tryst in the less-than-fragrant single bed of his student halls bedroom hadn't put her off completely. And after a few more practice goes to get it right, they'd had a pretty good run at things. They didn't have a great deal in common, but George was content with the fact that he got to see and touch a real naked girl on a regular basis.

Surprisingly, it was George who ended the relationship. Things finally broke down for him after having been dragged to one too many rallies against the plight of some poor animal facing extinction, or planned demolition of a pointless wooded area to make way for what George couldn't help but think was a very sensible and much needed road bypass.

No amount of regular sex, he'd found, could quite make up for the late nights fashioning Anti-this or -that banners out of cereal boxes, felt tip pens and stolen For Sale signs. Or the rainy afternoons standing outside embassies, wearing his hood up high over his head to avoid recognition of his embarrassed face. She'd been quite upset when he broke the news to her. But he'd had the feeling that she was more peeved at him taking away the chance to complete her project, than she was about missing out on his company and displays of sexual prowess.

3)
Name: Sarah Smith
Year: 1997-2000
George's Age: 21-24

Sarah was George's second proper girlfriend and they were together for nearly three years. They'd met during George's third year at University. She'd smiled at him from across the hall in a lecture and his heart had instantly melted. They ended up sat next to each other in the follow-up seminar group, mainly due to George having run ahead and distributed his books, bag, jacket and even one shoe on different seats around the seminar room, to give him a fair chance of collaring the seat next to whichever one she chose. They got chatting, went for a coffee afterwards and the surprise he felt at finding himself asking her out on a date was eclipsed only by the surprise of her saying yes.

The sex with Sarah was leagues ahead of what he'd experienced with Jennifer, principally because she was less bossy and less rigid and he felt more relaxed with her. She also had much bigger breasts, which George certainly didn't see as a downside. It was she who helped George to realise how much fun the whole thing could be.

They continued seeing each other after they left University and both got jobs. She embarked on a promising career as a junior solicitor at a small local firm. George started work at Eldene Associates as a Graduate Trainee, because the money was okay and he still hadn't quite figured out what he really wanted to do. When eventually she was offered a high-paid job in London and decided to move away, things came to a natural conclusion and they parted company.

George was a little sad for a while but he'd always figured it would end at some point anyway.

4)
Name: Connie Kramer
Year: 2000
George's Age: 24

Connie was George's one and only one-night-stand. They'd met at a work friend's party, back when George still used to go to such things, and they'd hit it off immediately when they were introduced. So well, in fact, that George found himself choking on his beer, coughing out a small cloud-like spatter, when she asked if he'd like to go back to her place for a coffee. Not one to forsake a golden opportunity, George actually jumped at the chance, the noticeable spring in his step propelling him onto the back seat of the earliest available taxi.

And though things had started out well enough, George soon found Connie to be more of a handful than he'd anticipated. She turned out to have a particularly voracious sexual appetite and though George did his best to keep up with the pace, he had to call proceedings to a halt more than once just to catch his breath.

And that wasn't the half of it. George had always considered himself to be quite open-minded when it came to bedroom matters, but some of the things that Connie had been keen on trying had made him literally stammer with surprise. He did his best to accommodate the less frightening proposals. He point-blank refused to try the really worrying ones. And he'd been so tired and weary by the early hours of the morning that he'd found himself cajoled into doing one thing that he really didn't enjoy and absolutely, definitely, most certainly would not be doing ever again.

He managed to sneak out when she finally gave up and fell asleep. He crept out of bed, shimmied his way out the back door and practically ran down the street, carrying his shoes in case a stray errant sound woke her up.

The next few weeks were spent with George:

- looking over his shoulder wherever he went.
- being very annoyed at the work colleague who'd introduced them (and was apparently well aware of the probable outcome).
- avoiding Connie's phone calls at all hours of the day and night.
- shivering slightly every time he saw a garden gnome.

5)
Name: Emily Grant
Year: 2001-2006
George's Age: 25-30

Emily was the love of George's life. Or so he thought.

He remembered the first day she came to work in his office: she'd looked so shy and nervous, but really sweet and charming. She had a smile so big and bright that it made George sigh a deep, loving, slightly-too-loud sigh every time he saw it. George was instantly smitten, and every time she walked past his desk he was desperate to stop her, ask her out, ask her anything just to hear that sweet golden voice. But he could never find the words.

She was slim and pretty, with delicate features and big, brown eyes that actually made his heart stop every time she breezed past and looked at him. It got to the point that George knew he'd either have to pluck up the courage to talk to her, or keep a defibrillator machine constantly on charge by the side of his desk.

He began timing his trips to the water fountain, coffee machine, photocopier, post-room and any other likely place she might go throughout the day to coincidentally bump into her as often as possible. He eventually managed to find his words, however, and the odd shared pleasantry soon turned into chit-chat.

At first they talked about nothing – the weather; the quality of the coffee in the coffee machine; whatever popular programme she'd seen on television the previous night and George pretended, somewhat unconvincingly, to have watched. Anything to keep the conversation going that little bit longer.

Over time he grew more confident and more comfortable in her presence. Their chats grew longer, until it was taking George half an hour to photocopy a single page (that didn't actually need to be copied in the first place). Or, returning to his desk with cold coffee and having to go straight back to the machine for a fresh, hot cup.

Finally, after about five weeks of innocuous chatter, and with his heart beating a painful rhythm in his chest, George plucked up the courage to ask her out.

The date went well and was followed by another, then another, and they quickly fell in love. The sex between them was better than George had ever dreamed it could be. It really did feel like they were made for each other; like they were a perfect fit and life for either one would never be quite right without the other one there to compliment them. After a few months Emily moved into George's house; they got engaged (deciding on a long engagement, so as to plan properly for the spectacular wedding she'd always dreamed about); and they started building a life.

They were together for just over four years. Four blissfully happy, couldn't-ask-for-anything-more, preparing-to-spend-the-rest-their-lives-together, glorious years. Or so George thought. Right up until the day he came home from work to find Emily teary-eyed and packing a suitcase.

It seemed that, though George had been perfectly content with his life and couldn't have wished for anything more, Emily was not quite so fulfilled. There was something missing for her – something else that she wanted – namely, to have copious amounts of sex with Graham from Asset Management. An ambition she had apparently already achieved. Every Tuesday, Friday and alternate Sundays for the previous seven months. And it was something she decided she wanted far more than her life with George.

She explained that Graham was a far more exciting person, filled with life and dreams and passion. Graham was going to show her the world; take her on adventures; give her what George never could. Graham wanted to show her all the interesting, brave, daring things that life could offer, whereas all George ever wanted to do was stay in and watch TV – an irony that George felt doubly wounded by, as he'd only ever starting watching TV to keep her happy in the first place. Of course, it was too late to argue now.

And so she left him. She took her poorly-packed suitcase and left him, sitting there on the sofa, not quite knowing what to do or say.

Unfortunately for Emily, it turned out she didn't quite get the exciting life she'd traded him in for. In fact, she didn't even get more than a few months, having fallen pregnant almost immediately after leaving him.

George and Emily hadn't had sex at all for the last few months of their relationship so he was under no illusions that the child might have turned out to be his. Emily had said she wanted to take a break from sex in order to make their forthcoming wedding night all the more special – though the truth had turned out to be something entirely different.

Unsurprisingly, Graham didn't stick around, preferring to remain a husband and father to the wife and two children he already had; the family he had promised to leave in order to be with Emily but hadn't quite got around to. He very quickly left the company, and in fact the entire town, his wife having found out about his sordid goings-on and insisting that he transfer to another branch of the business.

And so, poor Emily, far from getting to see all the magic and wonder of the world, found herself an unmarried single mother living in a pokey flat above a fish and chip shop on the high street. It should probably have made George happy to see her brought down to earth with a bump. But he was never one to delight in another's misfortune, and he just felt very sorry for her. He didn't like to see her suffer. And he certainly didn't like to think of the child having an unhappy upbringing. So he arranged with his bank manager to make generous monthly deposits into her bank account on a totally anonymous basis.

People would have said that he was mad; that he should have hated her, hated what she had done to him. But he couldn't. He had loved her at one point, with all of his heart. And though he didn't particularly like her anymore, it was hard to totally abandon the feelings he'd once felt.

He did stop eating fish and chips from that particular shop, however. Which was a real shame as their batter was easily the best in town and they were very reasonably priced.

He often wondered if she'd ever figured out where the money was coming from. Funnily enough, he'd never actually told her about his money – not the full extent of it, anyway. Somehow, because it had never really mattered to him, it had never really seemed worth mentioning. She knew that he was comfortable from some money that came after his parents had died but as he was a little touchy on the subject, she'd never pushed him for the full details.

Then, of course, a certain period of time passed, after which he could never tell her. Like when you don't immediately correct someone who gets your name wrong, thinking it more polite just to let it slide. Then you have to endure years of them calling you Bill, or Ted, or Frank, when your name is really Carl, because to correct them then would seem even more impolite.

How exactly do you drop the fact that you're actually a millionaire into the conversation, without it seeming utterly implausible, or implying that you didn't initially trust them enough to tell them the truth? *Oh, by the way darling, I have several million pounds in the bank. Could you pass the marmalade?* The thought seemed absurd, so he simply said nothing.

He often wondered whether, had she learnt the full extent of his financial well-being, she might have come running back, begging for forgiveness and the chance of reconciliation. Or maybe she wouldn't have left him in the first place – Graham's apparent abundance of life, passion and excitement not quite measuring up against all that cash. But he tried not to torture himself with all the 'what ifs'.

After that, George retreated into himself. He grew tired of the whispers that stopped when he entered a room. He was tired of telling and re-telling the most painful thing that had ever happened to him. It became easier to avoid people; to hide in his work, entrenched behind his desk. He stopped going out; preferring to stay at home, avoid the pitying eyes, just wanting to be left alone.

And so a week became a month. A month became two, then three, then six, until it was the norm to stay in on a Saturday night, hiding from the outside world. Hiding from life. Things were much easier if he didn't have to see people. It felt like all his courage and confidence had come pouring out of him that day he'd come home to find her leaving and he'd never regained it.

The notion of going out and trying to meet someone new receded further and further in his mind. He tried to picture the joy and delight of meeting someone; the excitement of embarking on a new relationship. But all he could see was the potential rejection; the nerve-shredding pain and embarrassment of being turned down. He tried to focus on all the possible happiness waiting out there for him. But all he had was the fear. And, try as he might, he just couldn't shake it loose. He couldn't take another heartbreak like that and so it was safer not even to try.

So he stayed at home and watched television and tried to convince himself he was happier, safer, better off. And before he knew it he was alone and unhappy and failing to talk to red-headed shop assistants.

But now, after just one minor breakdown; an unexpected late night cross-country drive; and quite possibly the strangest two days he'd ever experienced; he was lying on a bed, kissing a woman.

******

George felt the collar of his jumpsuit tugging at his neck again. Both of Alice's hands gripped it firmly as she managed, in one swift movement, to lift George's shoulders up off the bed, yank his top all the way down his arms and deposit him back on the bed, totally topless. Things certainly seemed to be moving at a faster pace than he'd anticipated. Lying there half naked, the signs certainly seemed to be indicating that things were getting quite sexual. But he still wasn't taking anything for granted.

All-in-all it had been slightly over six years since he'd last been anything other than fully clothed in the company of a woman – aside from the time that he'd had to see that lady doctor about a persistent bout of tummy trouble and had ended up naked from the waist down, lying on his side with his knees tucked up by his chin as she rather inexpertly inserted an exploratory finger into his bottom.

However, that was an entirely different situation altogether, on account of it not being a particularly pleasant experience (one should always hope for sexual encounters to be pleasant, at the very least) and it was as far from sexual as you could get. And, of course, the doctor had had the good sense and decorum to keep her own clothes firmly on. Which he'd thought at the time had definitely been for the best. Otherwise it might have made an embarrassing situation even more uncomfortable.

Just thinking about what might or might not be about to happen, George felt himself breaking into another sweat. The amount of fluid he must have lost in the course of that one stressful evening meant he was definitely going to need a large glass of water at some point.

Suddenly Alice broke away from their kiss, sat up in his lap and, in one swift movement, lifted her skimpy, tight top over her head, leaving her in just her jeans and bra. That was it then. George needed no clearer signal. She was definitely expecting sex. Girls don't just straddle you on a bed, kiss you and take off their tops unless things are definitely leading to sex. Do they?

They kissed and wriggled, and George revelled in the electric sensation of her skin touching his. Before he knew it, his hands found themselves unglued from the bed, gliding up and down her back, eliciting the very softest of moans from her with each breath. The speed of Alice's kisses intensified; long, deep tonguey ones interspersed with peppering his lips, face and neck with a machine-gun-fire of quick, tiny pecks.

She wriggled and moved on top of him, her breath growing harsh and ragged as she suddenly reached behind her, unfastened her bra and whipped it off, sending it fluttering down to the floor. She gripped George tightly between her thighs, rolling them both over until they were side by side, then grabbed hold of his hands and placed them quite purposefully onto her now naked breasts.

So that was it, then. They were definitely going to have sex. George needed no clearer signal. And then the panic really started.

It had been too long since he'd done this. What if he wasn't up to the job anymore? What if everything had changed since he'd last had sex and people were now doing it in a completely new, different way? He didn't want to look stupid by not knowing all the new techniques.

What if his equipment failed him? What if he was a total disappointment to her? Part of him wanted to stop this; explain that he wasn't ready, things were moving too fast. But he had her naked breasts in his hands and it would have seemed impolite to halt proceedings at this delicate stage. Besides, being with her now, experiencing this and all that promised to come, was all he wanted. He didn't want to stop; of course he didn't.

Slowly Alice trailed her hand down George's chest, slinking across his stomach, a delicious tickling tingle rippling across his skin. She halted briefly as she found the exposed waistband of his boxer shorts peeking out from under the low-cut top of his jumpsuit. She broke away from their kiss and looked at him; those deep, warm, brown eyes melting his heart all over again. He actually felt himself gulp with trepidation.

She smiled that wickedly warm, devilish smile again as her hand disappeared under the tight, blue material of his underwear.

George closed his eyes and hoped for the best.

CHAPTER 17

THURSDAY

DETECTIVE Constable Michael Keane stepped across the expansive lobby of the building's entrance and approached the grumpy, grey-haired receptionist. Her face was screwed up and miserable, as if she'd popped a boiled sweet into her mouth only to discover it was actually a ball of earwax. The sign above her head read Eldene Associates, Corporate Solutions and Strategies.

"Good morning," he said. "I'm here to see Anton Phelps."

Michael Keane had arrived at the police station precisely 45 minutes before his shift was due to start that morning, such was the level of eagerness he had for the day ahead. It was his first day as a detective; the first opportunity he had to fully demonstrate the abilities he'd strived so hard and so long to prove he possessed.

He'd done his time in uniform; walking the beat, putting up with domestics and squabbles and minor incidents. He'd had his fair share of drunken Friday night yobs loitering outside pub doorways in town; goading him, abusing him, sometimes even attacking him. He'd done the hard work; put in extra time to study; showed as much initiative, enthusiasm and sheer damned effort as he could; and it had finally paid off. He was a detective now and he was going to be the best detective this station had ever had.

Nobody, least of all himself, was surprised to see how early he'd reported for his first detective shift. Truth be told, he'd been up since 4.30am, so excited that his brain just couldn't stay asleep any longer. He'd paced around his small flat, working off some of the nervous energy. He'd gone over some of his policing textbooks, reminding himself of every possible procedural detail he might need to call into use.

He'd prepared a hearty breakfast of cereal, toast and bacon with an egg-white omelette – brain fuel that would see him through the day. Then he'd had to throw most of it away, too excited to stomach more than just a few mouthfuls.

And when he simply couldn't sit there any longer, he skipped out of his flat and ventured forth, eager to prove what an incredible police detective he was going to be.

He was somewhat disappointed, therefore, when his very first case as a detective turned out to be a minor, boring, run-of-the-mill missing person. An officer of his calibre, keen and excited, desperate to get out there and catch bad guys, was stuck trying to find some poor bloody Johnny Depresso who'd done a bunk.

He shouldn't have been given the case at all. The guy hadn't been missing long enough to warrant an investigation. At the very best, they should have sent a couple of uniforms to ask the questions, not a DC. The whole thing smelled like a new-boy initiation to Keane. A nothing case to wind up the new guy, like sending him off to find a left-handed screwdriver or a tin of striped paint.

But then, there could be more to it than met the eye. It could turn out to be a dark, intriguing murder mystery; an unexpected Mob hit; or a jealous lover who'd bumped this guy off and hidden the body. Keane allowed himself momentarily to fantasise. Maybe this guy was a secret, undercover sleeper agent. A Russian spy hidden away since the end of the cold war, suddenly re-activated and engaged in a fiendish plot to take down the government. And only Detective Michael Keane could stop him.

But, from the sound of it, that was all highly unlikely. From the initial information he'd received, the missing man sounded like a real nobody. A nine-to-five loser. A dull desk-jockey who'd most likely just topped himself. Or flipped out and run off to buy himself a Thai bride. Keane was already bored at the prospect of it.

Still, it was a case — his case — and he was going to solve it. And solve it quicker than any of his colleagues could do it. He'd have this time-waster rounded up by lunchtime and head back to the station to get himself a proper case more deserving of his investigative skills.

Anton Phelps ushered him into a glass-walled meeting room on the fourth floor of the building and sat across from him on the other side of the expansive, polished table. He was a strange-looking man, thought Keane: 21 going on 50, with a severe case of undeserved self-importance. He was tall and wiry, almost unhealthily thin, and looked like a strong wind could easily snap him in half — or at least knock him onto his arse.

He had one of those thin goatee beards, all patchy and sparse, barely sprouting out of his chin. The worst kind of schoolboy bum fluff. Keane had a sudden urge to reach across the desk and rip it from his face.

"Okay, Mr Phelps," said Keane in his best, most authoritative detective voice, "I understand you've lost a member of staff. Can you tell me why you think he might be a missing person?"

Keane pulled his notebook out of his pocket, placed it on the table in front of him, and clicked the special new biro he'd treated himself to for his first day on the job.

"Oh, he's definitely missing," replied Anton. "It's not like George to just not turn up to work and not even phone in. I've never even known him to miss a day's work. No sick days at all and he very rarely even used up all of his holiday."

"Is it not possible that he's just decided to take a bit of time off? Maybe he's gone on holiday and he just forgot to mention it?" asked Keane.

"No chance. That's not George at all. He wouldn't have the imagination."

"So, as I understand it, Mr Thring left here at 17.30 on Tuesday evening, presumably driving home. And nobody has seen or heard from him since. I take it you've tried to contact him?"

"Yes, of course," snapped Anton. "I've tried his home phone and his mobile. Just goes to voicemail, like he's got it turned off or something."

"Of course," said Keane, the urge to reach over and slap the irritating young man growing greater with every second, "I have to ask these questions."

He gave Anton a stern look, his eyes making it very clear that he didn't intend to put up with any nonsense. He paused, letting the unspoken threat hang in the air between them. "And you've contacted his next of kin?"

"Yes," said Anton. "Well, no. Well, that is, he doesn't have any. No family, no parents, no friends as far as any of us can gather. I even drove past his house, knocked on the door, but nothing. No lights on, no car in the drive, no signs of life at all."

"Okay," said Keane. "Tell me a little bit about Mr Thring."

"Well, there really isn't much to tell. I know that sounds daft, but George isn't exactly... well, very interesting. He's a nice guy, good at his job. Kind of quiet, you know?"

"Quiet," said Keane, purposely writing the word down in his notebook; gently ribbing his quarry's lack of help. "Anything else?"

"Not really. He's quiet. He always wears the same grey suit, doesn't say much during work hours. He just keeps his head down, does his work and gets on with things."

"And how long have you worked together?"

"George has worked for me for just over two years now."

That wasn't strictly true. They had worked together for that time but George didn't actually work for Anton. He was George's team leader, and technically above him, but certainly not the boss. And he'd only become team leader six months ago. Previously they'd been on exactly the same level. But it gave Anton a kick to claim that George was his employee and this policeman wouldn't be any the wiser.

"What about espionage?" Keane asked.

"George? A spy? I highly doubt it," spouted Anton, incredulous.

"Corporate espionage," smiled Keane. "What kind of work was Mr Thring in charge of? Was he privy to any high-security information? The sort of thing he might have stolen and be planning on selling to rivals or interested third parties?"

"Well, that's hardly likely," snapped Anton. "George wasn't in charge of anything. He was a number-cruncher. He analysed data; nothing sensitive, just bog-standard stuff. He wouldn't know espionage if it slapped him in the face."

"And what about friends? You say he didn't have any. He must have had some. Anybody here at work he was friendly with?"

"No, he wasn't that sociable. He certainly wasn't friendly with the rest of the guys in the team. Though it's not really that type of department. We're all very busy," he added, quickly back-tracking; not wanting to appear the leader of a disharmonious department.

"And outside of work?"

"Well, he never mentioned anybody," said Anton. "He didn't seem like the type of person who went out partying. Or even stayed in with friends. I always just assumed he was a bit... well, lonely."

"What about sex?"

"What?" gawped Anton, as if he'd suddenly been propositioned by a 20-stone biker in a tiny leather cap.

"What about Mr Thring's sex life? Was he into anything kinky? Could he just be trapped in some dominatrix's cupboard, waiting for her to decide he's not such a naughty boy after all?"

"Oh no," said Anton. "Well, I mean, I don't know, obviously. But I can't imagine George being into anything like that."

"They do say it's always the quiet ones," added Keane.

"That's true," pondered Anton. "No, I can't see it. Not George."

"Maybe he just met himself a nice girl. Or boy? Ran off to live happily ever after in the sun."

"No, can't see it. George just isn't that type. And with what we pay him, happily ever after would only last until next Thursday and then he'd have to coming running back." Anton Phelps gave a sickly, self-satisfied grin; pleased at his own joke. Keane really wanted to punch him.

"Any chance he could have had a double life? A secret wife hidden away somewhere? Maybe he was a weekend devil-worshipper, or an armed-robber. A gold-hunting archaeologist, whose latest mission to find hidden treasures has over-run a little," said Keane, starting to enjoy the silly possibilities he was coming up with.

"Well, if he did have a secret double life, he certainly never told me. But then he wouldn't have, would he?" snapped Anton, with an irritated look.

"Well," sighed Keane, "with this information, there's not really much I can do. No crime has been committed. There aren't really any suspicious circumstances." He sat back in his chair, puffed out his chest and exhaled slowly. "You say he was quiet. Kept himself to himself. Maybe he just decided to go away for a bit."

Anton's face suddenly dropped, a grey look of concern sweeping across his eyes. "I know you think this is trivial. Just another man gone off somewhere, and chances are he'll turn up in a few days. But I'm really worried, Detective Keane. This really is not like George. He wouldn't run away; he wouldn't have the gumption. I'm worried he might have had an accident. He could have run his car off the road, or banged his head and now he's walking round with amnesia..."

"Believe me," said Keane, flashing a wry smile, "that almost never happens."

"No, I know, but I am worried. Can't you look into it; make sure he's not crashed into a ditch somewhere?"

"Well," said Keane straightening himself in the chair, aware of the need to be professional and do a thorough detective's job, "there are a few areas we can look into. I'll check his personal circumstances, see what I can dig up. And I'll check the CCTV footage and road cameras; see if we can find out where his car was heading."

"Oh, thank you," said Anton.

"But," considered Keane, "if he is a missing person, there's probably not a lot I can do. Even if I do find him, there's no guarantee I'll be able to bring him back. Most runaways are exactly that for a reason. He may well want to stay lost."

"Well, anything you can do," said Anton, standing up and extending his hand to be shaken.

Keane stood slowly, looked at the bony white hand thrust in his direction and turned his nose up slightly. Instead he simply walked to the door and said, "Don't worry about seeing me out, I remember the way. I'll be in touch soon."

******

Michael Keane had always wanted to be a policeman. And not just a policeman: he wanted to be a detective. He wanted to be the man with the power; the one with the ability to solve mysteries, crack cases and catch the bad guys. He wanted to be the one who put people away, protected innocent citizens and to say, "You're nicked, Sunshine," to an array of devious, devilish-looking miscreants.

As a small child he'd spent hours in front of the television, marvelling at the analytical skill of countless TV detectives. Obviously *The Bill* had been a favourite, along with *Bergerac*, *A Touch of Frost* and *Cracker*. He'd admired the skill and intricacies of *Morse* and aspired to the same level of analytical thinking. But, in all honesty, he'd always been more greatly attracted to the hard-talking, uncompromising attitude of coppers like Regan from *The Sweeney* and the tough-as-nails Bodie and Doyle from *The Professionals*.

Some of the American cop shows were pretty good, too, though he always thought them just a bit schmaltzy and saccharine. They were overdone and unrealistic and the crimes were always far-fetched and unbelievable.

When he and his friends played cops-and-robbers in the school playground, he would always insist on taking on the role of law enforcer. And he wouldn't give his companions an easy time. When he caught up with them he'd apply the special restraint moves he'd learned from books and give them harsh penalties for their apparent wrongdoings. After a while, they stopped playing cops and robbers. Eventually they stopped asking him to play at all.

As soon as he'd finished his GCSEs he applied straight away to become a police officer and was awarded a place at the training academy. He'd achieved good grades and his teachers had been quite keen for him to stay on and study for A-levels. Possibly even go on to University. But he knew what he wanted to do, what he'd always wanted to do, and the prospect of further study just meant it would take longer to get where he wanted to be. So he headed straight into the service and never looked back.

Naturally he had excelled all through training, coming top of each class, and graduated with flying colours. Many of his mentors and training officers had found him slightly sycophantic and overly keen, but they couldn't knock his dedication.

He was over-zealous and enthusiastic, and saw the bad in people before the good. This was a concern, of course, as he was always slightly too suspicious and saw crimes and wrongdoings where there weren't any. Everyone was a potential suspect to him. Everything was black and white, right or wrong, and he had yet to learn the many different shades of grey that came with modern policing.

He was uncompromising in his attitudes towards the guilty, believing everyone should be punished for every single misdemeanour, no matter how trivial or irrelevant, and always wanted to see the maximum penalty awarded. He'd need a little reining in, but this was a guy who was destined to succeed: marked out to be a good copper and, clearly, nothing and nobody would hold him back.

A few years walking the beat had done nothing to quell his enthusiasm and he truly relished wearing the uniform, upholding the law and, wherever possible, putting the bad guys behind bars. But his real goal was never far from his mind and after years of working hard, putting in extra hours and badgering his senior officers, he'd finally been given his opportunity to play at being a detective for real. And he wasn't going to mess it up, or let anybody down.

******

After swinging by the missing man's address, to double check Anton Phelps' claims of an empty house, Keane had spoken with his neighbours to get a little background information on him. Strangely, none of them seemed to really know him at all. He was a quiet man, who kept himself to himself, and didn't seem to mix with anybody at all. None of the street's other residents had ever had more than a passing conversation with him and none could recall ever seeing any visitors entering or leaving the property.

Back at the station, he wasted no time in looking him up on the computer. Unsurprisingly, it turned up very little of interest on this George Thring. His credit record was perfect; no spiralling debts or apparent problems, no signs of any dodgy business dealings. His criminal record was totally clean as well. The man had not so much as received a parking ticket, speeding fine or even a caution in his entire life.

He'd lived at the same address in a very middle-class area of town for the last twelve years and had worked for the same company since graduating from University. He drove a run-of-the-mill, small hatchback car, which he'd had for five years and bought for cash. It was grey. Somehow that seemed perfectly apt.

As far as the computer showed, he'd never put a foot out of place; never written a bad cheque; never missed a payment for a bill. He'd never had any fun, probably. He was possibly the most boring man alive. His seemed like a life practically unlived, and maybe he'd done the right thing in doing this disappearing act. The whole case seemed to Keane far more like an unhappy man who'd had enough and simply walked out on his lot. He wasn't a master criminal or arch spy who'd set out on some evil scheme. Chances were, when he finally caught up with him, an unhappy corpse in the back of a carbon monoxide-filled car is all that would be left.

But there was something just a little bit curious about all this. Something didn't feel right about George Thring. They say it's always the quiet ones that you have to watch and Keane's policing experience had shown there to be a certain amount of truth to that. This man was too quiet, too normal. Nobody was as clean-cut as this guy's records showed him to be.

Some people do just walk out on their lives, leave their family and head off on a new adventure. They nip out for a packet of cigarettes, never to be seen again. More often than not, these were people running away from a miserable marriage; gambling debts they couldn't repay; parental responsibilities they couldn't live up to. But this Thring man didn't seem to have anything to run away from. Keane's suspicions were niggling him.

He decided the best thing to do would be to find this guy as quickly as possible, get to the bottom of the mystery slowly growing and festering in the back of his mind, then he could get on with the new job.

But how to find him? What clues were there? All he knew is that this guy had driven away from work at the end of the day, never to be seen again. So the car was the first place to look. A quick check and Keane discovered that George Thring's car had been fitted with an anti-theft tracking device, generally used to trace the location of a car had it been stolen. He logged onto the tracking system, located the car's individual signal, and a few minutes later traced the car to a small village roughly 200 miles away.

"Lower Chidbury?" he said quietly to himself. "What the hell are you doing there, George?"

He located the town on the online map, planned out a route and determined that he could make it there within a couple of hours. The usual protocol would have been to contact officers in the area and get them to check the car. They could make sure it hadn't been stolen. They could check around and see if they could find the man himself; work out why he was there and what he was doing. After all, he hadn't broken any laws, so Keane should really pass the paperwork on and get back to more pressing matters in his own town.

But the more he thought about it, the more his suspicions niggled at him. Something just didn't smell right. This guy was up to something, Keane could feel it. He couldn't figure out what it was, not without further investigation, but he knew there was something strange going on. And if anyone could get to the bottom of it, and catch this guy in the act, then newly-promoted detective Michael Keane was the man to do it.

He should really have checked with his superiors, but he reasoned they wouldn't want to be bothered with every tiny little detail. Besides, he could get up there; find this man; figure out what he was up to; either arrest him or give him a good talking to; and be back in time to clock out at the end of the day.

And if this Thring guy was up to something, and Keane were to catch him, surely it would show great initiative that he'd simply taken the ball and run with it, rather than asking his boss's permission to do his job. That was the kind of forward thinking that would see him make sergeant within two years.

So, the decision was made. He printed out the details of the missing car's location and wrote out a Post-It note explaining that he was off following up leads for a case, which he stuck to the screen of his computer. He grabbed his keys and set off for his car.

CHAPTER 18

GEORGE Thring woke at exactly 7.13am. His toes were cold and slightly numb where the sheets had ridden up in the night, leaving his extremities exposed to the bitter breeze sneaking in through the cracked window frame. He pulled his feet back under the relative warmth of the blanket and lay there, as he did every day, not wanting to move, not wanting to get up. Turning things over in his head and waiting for the evil buzz of his alarm clock.

But the alarm never sounded. And as he lay there, slowly coming round and imagining what fresh new disappointments the day might bring, he felt the same uneasiness as the day before. The feeling that something wasn't quite right.

This wasn't his bed. It was too lumpy, too soft. The itchy blankets scratched against his leg and his nose prickled in the cool air. This wasn't his room – the air was cold, not regulated as it should be by his precision-timed central heating. And it was damp; a faint musty odour clawing at his nose and throat with each breath. Everything was different. Everything was wrong.

And as the vacuum of silence grew, yawning out uninterrupted by the ever-faithful 7.15am chiming of his clock, he slowly started to remember.

The long car drive. Breaking down in the middle of nowhere. The strange little town. The hotel with the cold, dark room. The clothes he'd been forced to buy, and everyone dressing the same. One by one the images flashed through his mind, slowly building to form a hazy, washed out picture.

He remembered standing by the sea, sitting in the hotel bar. An identikit family with matching outfits. A girl with brunette hair.

He remembered eating dinner, then being in a pub. Standing in front of a crowd, sweating and feeling nervous.

Like a fogged up mirror slowly starting to clear, the events of the previous night came trickling back. But there was one thing he couldn't quite remember. Something hovering just out of focus, too unclear to make out. The images and memories swirled in his mind, just out reach.

Then George heard a sigh. At first it didn't quite register. The sound seemed far away. But as the synapses in his brain started to sparkle, and the dense fog of sleep slowly lifted, he recognised what it was.

Next he heard a yawn, then another sigh, stretching out the length of a long, contented breath. It was the most beautiful, angelic, carefree sigh he had ever heard. And it was coming from beside him in the bed.

Then the unmistakable brush of a leg against his own. Alice. And suddenly it all came rushing back.

He could feel the warmth from her lying next to him in the bed. The gentle whisper of her breath as it danced in the air. Alice. Of course. He remembered now.

He remembered eating with her, chatting and laughing. He remembered walking with her; the gentle, embarrassed grazing of hands. He remembered sitting with her, kissing her, holding her. Collapsing onto the bed together. Being naked together.

The bed shifted slightly as she rolled over. The cold morning air nipped his body as Alice delicately peeled back the blanket and silently climbed out of bed.

Still totally naked, she tiptoed across the meagre expanse of the bedroom. It was the first time he'd seen her fully naked. The previous night had been so rushed, so fervent, so explosive that he hadn't had a chance to fully take her in. And he'd been so body-conscious and unsure of himself that he'd flicked off the light at the earliest opportunity, just in case she ran out of the room screaming at the sight of his unsightly, podgy belly or... well, he didn't like to think about the other parts she might find even less appealing.

As he lay there and she slunk about the room, looking under the chair and behind the chest of drawers for a hastily-removed and far-flung pair of knickers, he took the opportunity to look at her fully.

She was perfectly formed, he thought. Not too skinny, but with barely an ounce of fat on her. Her breasts hung perfectly. Her legs were long and thin and immaculately sculpted. And that bottom! It was as beautiful, round, supple and pert as he'd imagined it to be. She was absolutely amazing.

Quickly she slipped back into her clothes, pulling up her jeans and sliding back into her tight top. Her hair was scraggly from the pillow and she hastily brushed it back with her hands, trying to neaten it as best she could. George tried to focus through the thick, foggy haze of his tired, half-closed eyes, waiting for her to turn around, readying his mouth to greet her.

But she didn't turn around. Instead, she quietly, stealthily picked up her shoes and reached for the door handle, turning it as slowly and quietly as possible.

Why doesn't she turn around? thought George.

She was leaving. The realisation hit him with a jolt. A lump caught in his throat like a stone. She was sneaking away, embarrassed, ashamed maybe. Was she wishing it hadn't happened, rueing the mistake she'd made the night before? George wished he could see her face, to see if it was etched with horror and remorse. Had she woken up, looked at George, and instantly regretted everything that had happened between them?

He felt sick; a deep ache burning in the pit of his stomach. Had it been that bad last night? Had George's performance been that terrible? He couldn't quite remember, but he didn't think so.

Admittedly, things hadn't gone quite to plan from the outset. It had taken George a few minutes to get back into the swing of things. But he'd got there in the end, only to have something of a minor technical fault, which brought proceedings to rather too abrupt a conclusion.

Far from being upset or horrified, however, Alice had just been exceptionally kind and understanding. She'd simply reassured him and when, a mere 10 minutes later, he was feeling much more relaxed and ready to try again, things had gone much better. Twice, in fact. And he was sure they'd both enjoyed it equally. She'd certainly seemed enthusiastic enough in her responses.

Now here she was, creeping out silently, escaping from a horrific mistake. He wanted to ask her why, to find out what he'd done wrong. He wanted to leap out of bed, grab her arm and spin her round like some Hollywood actor from the 1950s might have done, and demand an explanation.

But he couldn't. Better just to let her leave and retain some dignity for both of them. Allow her the escape she wanted. So he lay there silent, crushed and disappointed, watching as a harsh, thin shard of light cut into the room as the door slowly creaked open.

Then, just before she made to leave, Alice turned round suddenly to look at him. It was so quick and unexpected that George didn't have time to close his eyes and pretend he was still asleep. She saw him, their eyes catching in the early morning haze scattered across the room. He gave an embarrassed, conciliatory half-smile.

"Oh, you're awake," she said.

Here it comes, thought George. The embarrassed apology. The awkward fumbling for words. The excruciating admission that she'd made a huge mistake. He couldn't bear it. His stomach flipped over again.

And then she flashed that huge, beaming smile. She closed the door, let go of the handle and leaped back across the tiny room, landing on top of him with a thud. She kissed him quickly on the lips, running a hand through his rumpled hair and gazed lovingly down at him.

"You're leaving," he said.

"Yes, sorry. I'd love to stay longer but I've got an early shift helping mum cook the breakfasts. And I thought it was best to get out early, before the other guests wake up."

She adopted a hushed, whispered tone and said, "I don't want to get the reputation of sneaking out of guest's rooms early in the morning. If they know that sort of service is available, they'll all be wanting it." She giggled softly and kissed him again.

George laughed back, the relief washing over him like a gloriously warm, wet wave. They lay there for a few seconds, revelling in the feel of each other's bodies rising and falling together with each breath. Again that groggy, tired feeling started to cloud George's brain.

Alice kissed him quickly before jumping up and back across to the door. "See you tonight?" she called back to him, but George was already fast asleep. She smiled and closed the door quietly behind her.

******

When George woke for the second time that day, he yawned and stretched and idly scratched his balls, feeling properly rested for the first time in a very, very long time. His mouth tasted dank and heavy, and a small numb ache twitched at the base of his spine. But he smiled as he opened his heavy eyes and realised he could still smell her perfume on the pillow next to him.

Alice. If he hadn't seen her that morning; couldn't still smell the scent of her in his bed, he'd have thought she'd just been the loveliest dream he could remember. An apparition that came to him from a far-off corner of his subconscious. An angel that visited him in the night and did unrepeatable things to him with her tongue.

A smile played across his lips as he thought of her; remembered the feel of her skin against his. It had been the best night of his life – aside from the embarrassment of standing in front of a crowd, nearly getting into a fight, and the sheer, crushing heartbreak he'd momentarily felt when he thought she hadn't liked him. Other than that it had been amazing. Because he'd found her. And she'd found him. And they'd shared the night together. And he knew it was far too early to be thinking about things like love, but that's sort of what it felt like. That deep, hollow ache in the pit of his stomach that churned ever so slightly when he thought of her. The slightly dizzy sensation, as if his brain was drowning; as though he could float up out of bed at any second and simply lift off into the sky. He had a tingle in his toes, a buzzing in arms, a certain nervous tension coursing through his whole body. Altogether, George felt quite peculiar.

But could it really be love? He'd only first laid eyes on the girl just over a day ago. Love certainly seemed a bit optimistic. He couldn't ignore the fact that he definitely felt different. But love?

When he first found his way into this tiny, odd little place, with its odd little people and very strange ways, he'd certainly never expected to fall in love. He'd never expected anything. And he still wasn't sure that love was what he was experiencing. Love is a strong word, after all, and not the sort of thing that he thought he should be declaring willy-nilly before taking full account of all the contributing factors and variants. In all fairness, looking at the evidence, it could just be that he was tired and hungry.

After all, he'd usually have eaten breakfast hours before. And he'd certainly had more exercise the previous evening than the majority of his nights sat in front of the telly.

So, as a sensible person – cautious and vigilant, and keen to explore fully all possible alternatives before jumping to silly, romantic conclusions – George decided the best option would be to eliminate the various factors, as scientifically as he could, one by one. His belly rumbled again. The first test would be getting up and having something to eat.

George stretched again, sitting up in bed and surveying the small room. He checked his watch: 11.14am. He couldn't believe he'd slept so late. It was the latest he'd slept in years. Even at weekends, without his dreaded alarm clock being set, he'd wake at exactly 7.13am, cursing himself for his inability to relax and stay asleep for a few minutes longer. He certainly didn't want to be awake at

7.13am on a Sunday morning. He just couldn't help it. Ever since he was a boy.

His father had always fervently advocated the benefits of rising early; making the most of every single minute of the day; seizing opportunities while everyone else was still asleep. He'd drag young George out of bed, still kicking and grumbling, forcing him to take hold of the opportunities he was too young to realise he wanted.

Even on the last day George had spent with his parents his father had woken him at 6am, extolling the benefits of rising early. He'd said they would get to see so many more animals at the safari park if they got there first. He'd lied that the best animals only did the early shifts anyway and if you went in the afternoon you'd get stuck with the lazy animals that just slept and lay around scratching their arses. In retrospect, considering what had happened that day, an afternoon visit might well have been better advised.

But his father's ways had stuck with him, ingrained in his sub-conscious. He'd been totally unable to break the habit; waking and rising early in spite of his own hatred of it.

And now here he was, waking up practically at lunchtime. He smiled again, scratching his hand through his matted, messy hair. And, despite the uncomfortable bed springs digging into his back, he breathed in the late-morning air, rubbed the sleep out of his eyes, and gave his balls another long, slow scratch. It occurred to George that sleeping in was actually rather a nice thing to do.

But he couldn't stay there all day. He had things to do, choices to make, breakfast to find. A whole strange, exciting new world to explore.

He swung his legs round, sitting up fully, and his feet landed with a splat into the small, cold, wet patch on the carpet where the wine had spilt. It squelched up between his toes, sending a shiver right through him. He picked up his clothing from the floor, closely inspecting it. Usually he would have been horrified at the prospect of wearing the same clothes two days in a row and not having a freshly pressed, meadow-scented shirt to slip into. But he wasn't exactly inundated with options. Without his usual compliment of grey suits and white shirts on hand, he had no choice but to go with his two-day-old boxer shorts and Elvis Presley jumpsuit.

He gave the armpits a cursory sniff. Not too bad. Not as fresh as he'd have liked, but by no means an odorous disaster. The strange nylon acrylic material was clearly a lot hardier than he'd given it credit for. The same, however, could not be said about his own skin. A quick sniff at himself and it was quite clear that he was in desperate need of a shower.

George hadn't had a good wash in days. It was totally out of character for him. He was used to a strict grooming routine; used to being impeccably clean and fragrant. And now, sitting with his feet in a puddle of stale wine, a layer of dried sweat coating his skin, and a smell not unlike vinegar and sweaty socks emanating from his armpits, he realised he would have to face another of his personal fears. He was going to have to use the communal bathroom.

He was hungry and tired, and keen to get out of that room, but he really couldn't go anywhere until he'd had a shower at the very least. He looked up to the door, imagining the long corridor beyond it that led to the bathroom, and a shudder of dread quaked through him. He really, really didn't want to use a communal bathroom.

George wasn't a clean freak, exactly. He wasn't a germaphobe, terrified of all the potential bugs and diseases left behind from previous users. There were just some things that he felt should be private affairs and showering sat quite high on the top of that list. He was used to his own clean, private shower. A place unsullied by other users. The thought of the communal bathroom and all the other naked bodies that must have occupied the same space in the last few weeks made his skin crawl slightly.

But it had been quite a few days for being brave! And as he picked up the complimentary towel and cautiously opened the bedroom door, he made a mental note that when this little adventure was over he'd have to give himself rather a large pat on the back.

He cautiously made his way along the corridor, tip-toeing in order not to alert anyone else, clutching the towel tight to his chest and hoping his boxers didn't look as dirty as they felt. He made it to the door at the end of the corridor with the small brown WC sign and practically threw himself through it, slamming the door shut behind him. A small noisy extractor fan clinked, clunked and whirred into action as George pulled the light cord, illuminating the room.

It was small and grey, and though not particularly dirty in any specific way, it was far from the sparkling, shimmering porcelain beacon of sanctuary and cleanliness he was used to.

A battered-looking toilet sat in the corner of the room, shabby and tatty; a relic from the 1960s. An old white bath, the base stained black and grey, was pressed in against the wall. A showerhead, perched mid-way up the far wall, trailed down to the bath's taps by way of a worn-looking plastic tube. An old, wrinkled shower curtain printed with pictures of rather depressed-looking, yellow rubber ducks, draped down from an inexpertly-fitted and slightly wonky plastic railing.

Small dots of black mould littered the bottom of the curtain. They scattered the tops of the walls and spread out across the ceiling in elaborate, far-reaching Rorschach patterns. A deep, musty mixture of mildew, pine-fresh bleach and the sickly sweet stench of urine from the un-flushed toilet permeated the room, stabbing at George's nostrils, hanging in the air like some dense poisonous gas.

George shuddered, silently cursing the gods for putting him in this position. He just hoped to get things done as quickly as possible and consoled himself with the thought of how nice it would be to finally feel clean. He turned back to lock the door behind him and sighed. Although there was a lock in place, it was not only broken but totally unusable and clearly had been for some time. Of course, he thought.

A deep throb started pounding in his chest and he could feel his face heating up. He fiddled with the lock, sliding the tumbler back and forwards, somehow hoping that the missing piece that was supposed to hold it in place would magically re-appear. He pushed the door, hoping it might simply stay in place. He played with the handle, trying to make it inoperable, but it was no good.

He looked across the room, scanning for items; anything that he might be able to block the door with, or wedge it shut, but there was nothing. He wondered if he'd be able to climb into the bath, stand under the shower and simultaneously reach over and hold the door shut. But it was too far away.

The door was unlocked and he'd have to risk having a shower with the possibility of anyone walking in at any time. Oh God!

He tried bargaining with himself. Did he really need a shower? Couldn't he get away with it for another day? But he couldn't. He really needed to wash.

Gingerly, George stepped over to the shower. He fiddled with the taps and a thin, lacklustre spray poured from the showerhead. It volleyed in fits and spurts between arctic cold and searing heat as George finely tuned the taps, settling on a disappointing lukewarm. He glanced once more to the door, employing the only tactic left to him that might just help to avoid unwelcome visitors walking in on him. Singing.

And so, partly because he was unused to singing in the shower, partly because he was under more than normal pressure, and partly because it was the only song he could think of, he burst out with a very loud chorus of *Heartbreak Hotel*. Which, under the circumstances, seemed particularly apt.

"Since my baby left me," he almost shouted, in a flat, unmelodious monotone. He whipped off his underpants, diving into the fine, lukewarm spray, and quickly pulled the shower curtain over to cover him.

"I've found a new place to dwell..." He dipped his head under the water, almost sighing with relief as the warm spray soaked his head, washing the sticky sweat from his face.

"It's down at the end of lonely street..." He reached for the soap he'd placed carefully on the side, lathering it up in his hands.

"...at heartbreak hotel." He rubbed the soap in his face, pulling at the skin, massaging the life back into his eyes, his nose, his cheeks.

It was at this point that George suddenly realised that he actually only knew the first four lines of *Heartbreak Hotel*. And so he'd have to repeat them, again and again, until he was done. *"Since my baby left me..."*

The shower was far from ideal but it was warm and wet. As George set to work with the bar of soap, raking it back and forth across himself with lightning speed – giving greater attention to the important areas and skimming across the rest – he felt himself coming back to life. Back to normal.

His hands worked quickly, soaping, lathering and exploring all the various nooks and crannies, as he tried to set the world record for the fastest-ever shower. He didn't have any shampoo so he did the best he could with the bar of soap, coughing and spluttering, and nearly forgetting all the words to his song as the suds ran down into his mouth.

When he was satisfied that he was clean enough he rinsed off quickly, jumped out of the shower, wrapped himself in the towel and scampered out of the bathroom as quickly as he could. He practically ran down the hall, his wet feet leaving soggy footprints in the carpet as he swung the door open, darted into the room, and closed it firmly behind him. He stopped momentarily, resting his head on the door, breathing out a long sigh of relief that his nightmare shower experience was over. He was back into the relative safety of his room.

Or at least, he thought it was safe. Until he turned round to see the stern looking man sitting on his bed.

CHAPTER 19

GEORGE stood motionless, unable to speak, simply contemplating the strange man sat on the bed in his hotel room.

At first he wondered if he'd accidentally barged into the wrong room, what with all the fuss and panic of the preceding few minutes. But his room was the only door at the end of the corridor and not easily mistakable.

He wondered whether, having come up to find the room empty, the old landlady had simply assumed George to have checked out and another new guest was now entrenched in what had been his room. But Alice had assured him that the room was his for the rest of the week.

So George looked at the man, and the man looked at George. And with no solid conclusions reached, and not knowing quite how to start the conversation, George simply stood there, dumbfounded.

"Mr Thring?" announced the mystery figure, finally breaking the tension. "Hope you don't mind me letting myself in; technically we're not supposed to. But, given the choice of breaking protocol, or continuing the rather unusual conversation I found myself having with a strange-looking family all dressed as Elvis Presley, I thought I'd take the chance and hope you didn't mind.

"You don't mind, do you Mr Thring?" It was said more like an order than a question. A subtle hint of menace lingered on the words, making it clear the man didn't really care whether George minded or not.

"Erm, well…" stammered George, mildly confused and very aware that he was wearing nothing more than a towel. A single rivulet of water ran down his cheek as a thin breeze tickled his wet back, making him shudder. "Sorry, who are you?"

He was a stocky man, fit and well built, with piercing eyes and a thin, tight mouth. His hair was short and tidy. His suit was clearly new, but slightly ill-fitting, and his shoes were impeccably shiny. Although he was calm in appearance he seemed very intense, agitated almost, like a rubber band stretched until it was about to snap. He was clearly very determined about something.

"Apologies, Mr Thring. I'm Detective Constable Keane. Sussex C.I.D." He reached into the inside pocket of his suit jacket and produced a wallet, flipping it open to reveal a card emblazoned with a picture of the man's face and the words POLICE OFFICER in bold type.

Police? Standing there in just his towel, beads of water dotting his chest, George suddenly felt very ill at ease. A chill rattled through his bones. He had that strange fear that only being confronted by a police officer can unexpectedly induce.

The police, thought George. What would the police want with me?

157

Instantly he felt guilty, as if he'd done something wrong and been caught out. He felt like a naughty boy, confronted by a disgruntled teacher waiting for an explanation of his bad behaviour. Images of being arrested flashed through his mind: being put in the back of a police car; thrown into a cell with a random group of undesirables.

Oh God, what would they make of George in prison? They'd tear him apart. They'd prey on him, beat him up, steal his food, do unmentionable things to him in the showers. He'd have to find someone to bring him cigarettes in jail – that was the underground currency they used 'inside' wasn't it? A simple, quiet man like George would never be able to cope with prison life. He could feel himself starting to crumble already.

But George had done nothing wrong. Certainly nothing illegal. Nothing that would warrant a detective constable coming to confront him.

George had never broken any laws. He didn't even bend them. Not even the little ones. He'd certainly never murdered anyone, or held up a bank. He never drove above the posted speed limit, never spat in the street, never smashed windows or threw litter on the pavement. He even made sure to put his recycling in the correct bin and put it out on the right day – not technically a legal requirement, but the sort of thing that might have seen him get a fixed-penalty fine from the council if he'd disobeyed it.

Of course George hadn't broken the law. Had he?

He racked his brain, contemplating every single misdemeanour he might inadvertently have perpetrated, every accidental crime he could possibly have committed. Was it something to do with the car? Had he broached some law when he'd broken down at the side of the road. Had he accidentally hit something in the rain? An animal? A person?

Then it occurred to George that maybe the policeman wasn't here to arrest him. Maybe he'd tracked him down to break some bad news. Had a relative died? Had something happened to his house, since he'd been away? It must have been bad for them to track him all this way.

And that was another thing, how did he even know George was here in the first place? George barely even knew he was there himself.

"It's okay, Mr Thring. There's nothing to worry about," the police officer said, breaking the silence again, adopting a tone that sounded like it was supposed to be more sympathetic but lacked the necessary softness. It simply made George worry even more.

"Oh," he said quietly. "What can I do for you, detective?"

"Well, you've given a few people a bit of a fright back home, Mr Thring."

"People?" said George. "A fright?"

"Disappearing like that. Taking off into the night, not turning up for work. Most unusual. Your boss, a Mr…" he pulled a small black notebook from his jacket pocket, flicked it open and scanned the crisp white pages. "Mr Anton Phelps. He said it was very unlike you not to turn up for work. Not to call in. Suspicious even," he said, underlining something on the pad with his finger.

"Oh," replied George, "well... erm... I'm sorry if I worried anyone. I certainly didn't mean to."

So that's why he was here. Because George hadn't phoned work to tell them he wasn't coming in. It all seemed a bit much, sending a police officer to slap him on the wrists for not phoning in. It was a bit rude perhaps, and definitely in contravention of standard company policy regarding sickness and unauthorised leave. But surely not a matter for the police?

"I'm sorry, I'm confused," continued George. "You came all this way just to tell me off for not phoning in sick for work?"

"Of course not," said the detective, "that would be ridiculous. If we reprimanded everyone that did that... well, we'd never catch any of the real criminals, would we?"

He chuckled slightly, laughing at his own joke. But his eyes stayed dark and serious.

"No, your colleague, Mr Phelps, phoned us to report you as a missing person and we have to take all of these cases very seriously. The circumstances surrounding your case did seem a little... peculiar, so I decided to follow things up. Make sure that nothing bad had happened, or that you'd... well, you know."

"Right," said George.

"Of course," said Keane, standing up from the bed, "now that I can see you're okay, I guess we can consider this a closed case." Again he flashed that fake smile.

"I suppose we can," repeated George.

Keane turned away, moved past George and took hold of the door handle.

"Only," he said, stopping abruptly, releasing the handle again and turning back, "it does seem a bit suspicious." He looked closely at George, his eyes becoming thin slits as he carefully studied his prey.

"It does?" said George. "I mean, what does?"

"The sudden disappearing act," said Keane. "I mean, you don't appear ill. And Mr Phelps tells me you didn't have any holiday booked. He said you weren't really the type to take holidays, in fact."

"No," said George. "I suppose I'm not really."

"Never missed a day at work," continued Keane, circling around the point he was clearly trying to draw out. "No sick days on the record; model employee; never one to step out of line."

"Where are you... I mean, what is... sorry, what is this all about?"

"Oh, come on Mr Thring. You must admit it does seem a little odd. The man who always turns up on time, never misses a day's work, keeps himself to himself, never does anything out of the ordinary..."

George felt disheartened at hearing himself described in such a way. He wanted to protest, cry out, contradict the man. But in truth there was nothing to contradict. He really was that boring. He just hadn't realised quite how boring until now.

"This quiet, normal man all of a sudden just disappears. Leaves the office at the end of the day, gets in his car and drives off. And then nobody hears from him again. He doesn't go home, doesn't turn up for work the next day, nobody has a clue where he is."

"Erm, well I suppose so. But I don't think any of that is illegal, is it?" said George suddenly feeling empowered and forthright.

"Quite right, sir," replied the detective, seeming to enjoy the fact that George was fighting back. "Not illegal, sir. Not illegal at all. But quite suspicious, I think you'll agree."

"Well, I don't know about suspicious…"

"Out of the ordinary, then?"

"Well, yes…"

"Out of the ordinary, and, to the casual observer, certainly a bit suspicious. Added to that, not only does the man not go home after work but he turns up a few days later, hiding out at a hotel some two hundred miles away."

"I wouldn't say hiding out," protested George, now starting to wonder what exactly he was being accused of.

"No, sir?"

"Well, no, I mean it's all very simple really."

Of course, it wasn't simple at all. It was far from simple. It was the unravelling of George's mental well-being. It was a strange psychological episode that he'd endured and wasn't too keen on recounting to anyone, let alone a police officer. George was sure it wasn't technically illegal to have a mental breakdown in the car and accidentally drive two hundred miles in the wrong direction on the way home from work. But it didn't seem a good idea to tell a police detective that was what had happened.

"Simple, sir?"

"Yes, well, I just wanted to get away for a few days and so I got into the car and decided to come here… and stay at this hotel.

"Hmmm…" said the detective. "Just wanted to get away for a few days? I'm sorry, but something still just doesn't quite add up for me."

He was doing his best Columbo impression now: dancing around the words, letting George speak, waiting for him to trip up. To tell the lie he wouldn't be able to hide from. That's how they get you, isn't it? thought George. They twist what you say, sit back and wait for you to stumble, then throw it all back at you, making it look like they've caught you out.

"You see," said the detective, "for a man who never misses a day's work; never takes holidays; never does anything out of the ordinary… to suddenly decide on the spur of the moment to get away for a few days? He doesn't tell anyone he's going away. He doesn't even go home and pack a bag. He simply gets in the car and drives two hundred miles to stay in a small hotel in the middle of nowhere. It just seems a bit… suspicious."

He drew out the last word, elongating it, letting it drip from his mouth. An uncomfortable silence hung in the air between them.

"Yes, well I suppose when you look at it like that…" confessed George, still unsure as to what he was confessing. "I've just been feeling a bit... you know, tired. In all honesty – you're going to laugh at this – but, well, it was all just a bit of an accident really."

The detective didn't laugh. "An accident?"

"Yes, I mean I guess it does look a bit odd, but it was just a kind of... an accident. I sort of... ran away from home. By accident."

"You ran away from home by accident." Not a laugh, not a grin, not even a smirk. Keane's face remained stony.

"Erm, yeah," continued George, flustered now, not quite sure what he was saying any more. His mouth moving of its own accord; the small boy back again, desperate to explain himself, to convince this policeman that he hadn't been naughty and it wasn't his fault and he certainly hadn't known that he was doing anything wrong.

"I just got in the car after work," explained George, "and I went to drive home, only my mind started wandering, I guess. And I just kind of drove and drove, a bit dreamy, and the next thing I knew I woke up in the middle of the countryside."

"You fell asleep at the wheel?" blurted the detective, a look of alarm on his face.

"No, no. God no!" said George, realising he was making things worse for himself, but unable to stop talking. "No, I just kind of drove without really knowing where I was going. Then I ran out of petrol, and the car broke down, and by the time I got it towed it was too late to go home. So I found this place and stayed the night. Incidentally, how did you know I was here?"

"You have a tracking device in your car, in case of theft. I picked up the signal and followed it here," said Keane, sounding more than a little pleased with himself. "Quite easy when you know how. But that's beside the point. You say you left work on Tuesday night and ended up driving here by mistake?"

"Well, yeah."

"This is Thursday morning, Mr Thring. Two days later. Why didn't you go home yesterday?"

"Erm, well..."

George suspected there wasn't much point confessing all about his sudden existential crisis. His feelings of bewilderment, of suddenly realising how alone and inadequate his life had become. How one night away from it had made him realise how unhappy he was, how desperate he was to get away. And how, upon contemplating returning home, he'd realised he wanted nothing less in the world. About how he'd stayed in the strange little town, his temporary refuge from life, simply pondering how he'd come to be who he was and what his future could possibly hold.

This detective didn't really look the type to be sympathetic to George's recent 48-hour struggle with the meaning of life, the world and his place in it. If anything, he looked more inclined to call for the men in white coats and have George carted off to a loony bin.

"…as I say," continued George. "I just felt like I needed a break. And as I was here, I thought I might as well stay for a little while."

"But not phone work? Not call anyone and let them know you're okay? Just stay here, in this little room. In disguise."

"In disguise?"

Keane looked over at the chair in the corner of the room, the pale blue Elvis costume draped carefully over it. It was not where George had left it, discarded on the floor.

That was it. The detective had shown his ace: the little secret he'd been holding onto. Keane had obviously seen it, put two and two together and come up with 97. He'd picked it up and draped it there on full display; toying with George, waiting to reveal the incriminating evidence he thought he'd found. But incriminating of what, George still had no idea.

"Yes, well that's another long story," said George.

"Oh, do tell. I'm intrigued."

George explained how his clothing had been ruined. How he'd had to buy new clothes and this was literally all he could get.

"You know, this story gets richer and richer every second," chuckled Keane. "But I'm not buying it."

"Well, that's what happened," said George, becoming more defensive. "And correct me if I'm wrong, but none of it is actually against the law."

"Against the law, no," said Keane, narrowing his eyes again, his lips screwing up into a small, taut circle. "But it all sounds very suspicious to me. And when you've been doing this job as long as I have, you tend to focus in on suspicions. They say it's always the quiet ones you have to watch and, believe me Mr Thring, I'm watching you."

"Look, exactly what crime am I being accused of here?"

"Crime?" repeated Keane, playing his next gambit straight out of suspect interrogation 101. "I never said anything about a crime. Why are you saying crime?"

"What? No, that's not what I… you know what I…"

"Have you committed a crime, Mr Thring? Is that why you're hiding out here? Is there something you want to confess?"

"No, of course not. And I'm not hiding out, I'm…"

"What was it Mr Thring? Girlfriend threatened to leave you so you taught her a lesson?"

"What? Of course not. I don't have a…"

"Oh, I know," said Keane, his voice taking on a harsh, angered tone. "You didn't mean to do it, you were just upset. You just wanted to stop her leaving, so you hit her. You pushed her. But you were too rough. You didn't mean to be, you just couldn't help it. Next thing you knew she was dead. So you dumped the body and ran away."

"Don't be ridiculous," countered George. "That's utter…"

"Maybe it was money, eh? You've been creaming off money from work, hiding it in offshore accounts. Now you're making your getaway to live on the stolen loot?"

"Of course not, I don't even work with any…"

"Jealous husband, then? The woman you've been shagging in secret got you to top her husband. Now you're hiding out here till the heat dies down, waiting for her to come and join you?"

"This is preposterous," shouted George, getting angry. "Do you have even a single scrap of evidence to back up any of these claims? No, of course not, because none of it's true."

"Evidence? Not yet, Mr Thring. Not yet. But believe me, the evidence is there and I'll find it. You're up to something, Mr Thring. You're up to something. I don't know what it is yet, but I'll find out. And when I do, I'll have you."

"Up to something? What the hell are you talking about?"

"People don't just randomly walk out on their lives, Mr Thring. People don't just get in the car after work, drive two hundred miles and hole up in a hotel in the middle of nowhere, dressed as Elvis fucking Presley. Not unless they're up to something."

"Well I do, Detective Keane," said George. "And I'm not up to anything. At least not anything that would concern the police."

Keane stared back at him, his dark eyes pinched and intense.

"Now, I think you'd better leave," said George, pulling the door forcefully open and stepping out of the way, gesturing the detective out of the room.

"How long will you be staying in town, Mr Thring?"

"That is none of your business."

"We'll see, Mr Thring. We'll see. Just remember, I'm onto you. And I'll be watching. And when you slip up, I'll be there to put the cuffs on you."

George simply looked to the door, then back at Keane, matching the intensity of his glare.

"See you soon, Mr Thring," said Keane, and he walked out of the door. George slammed it shut behind him.

CHAPTER 20

DETECTIVE Constable Michael Keane strolled purposefully out of the hotel, almost skipping up the cracked, black path. Absolute classic, he thought, smiling deviously to himself. Interrogation 101, just like back at the Academy. If old Hawkins could see me now, the miserable tosser of an instructor, even he'd have to pat me on the back for that one. Textbook suspect-badgering. The guy had practically crumbled in front of him.

He couldn't have predicted the towel, or the fact he'd be dripping with water, but neither could he have asked for a better piece of luck. It always helps to get the suspect on edge; make them uncomfortable. You rattle their heads, trick them, trip them up. If you can get them feeling insecure and worried they forget what they've said, what they're supposed to say. Before they know it their lies aren't quite adding up. They don't ring true, and the whole house of cards comes tumbling down. And then you've got them.

Standing there dripping, shivering in the cold, feeling almost naked and exposed, this Thring character had fallen to pieces. He didn't know what he was saying, making up lies and excuses and bullshit stories. All Keane had to do was push and prod, give him enough rope and yank it back, reeling the sucker in.

None of his story had made any sense. Thring knew it, and he knew that Keane knew it too. That's why he'd backtracked so many times. That's why he'd lost his cool and become so paranoid and defensive. That's why he'd come up with such a lame story that Keane had wanted to burst out laughing at how ridiculous it sounded. At least, he would have done had he not been so insulted that this moron had actually expected him to believe it.

He'd got in the car after work and just driven and driven, lost in a merry little haze of thoughts, and simply ended up here. Bollocks, thought Keane. Nobody does that. Nobody.

And suppose that were the case, that he'd accidentally stumbled his way out of town and ended up two hundred miles away in this place, thought Keane, scanning the landscape, taking in the grey, quiet surroundings, why the hell would he want to stay? Anyone in their right mind would have got back in their car at the earliest possible opportunity and driven like mad to get the hell away from here.

No, you're up to something, George Thring, thought Keane.

None of it added up – the sudden disappearance, just getting in the car and leaving, not even going home to pack a bag or take any possessions. Then he turns up in this place, the middle of nowhere, the last place anyone would look for anyone. And in disguise as well. Dressed up as Elvis bloody Presley of all things. These were not the actions of a sane, innocent man.

But what is it? What was he up to? Keane had already made several radio inquiries on the car journey up here. Nobody else from Thring's workplace had disappeared. Neither had anybody else been reported as a missing person in the last 72 hours. Which made it less likely that he'd topped someone and done a bunk until the dust settled. Not that the absence of any solid missing person leads meant that he definitely hadn't done something like that. All that meant was that no-one had been missed yet and no bodies discovered.

And, true enough, the chances of him having embezzled millions from the company accounts seemed unlikely, due to the nature of the work he did. But again, it was not entirely impossible. It was always these quiet, innocent-looking types that turned up in the papers caught with their hands in the cookie jar, funding a secret life of hookers, speed boats and a jet-set lifestyle they couldn't afford on their own meagre incomes.

This guy was definitely guilty of something. Keane could feel it. He could smell it on him. He could see it in his panicked eyes, as he reeled and rocked, Keane landing every single sucker punch. This guy had done something, or he was planning to do something. Keane still couldn't tell what it was but he was sure as hell going to find out.

Keane climbed into his car, pulled his mobile phone from his pocket and checked for messages. Three calls from his Detective Sergeant, no doubt trying to track him down, wondering why he wasn't at his desk. Three voicemails. He knew what they'd say and he didn't particularly want to listen to them, so he slipped the phone back into his pocket.

He should have called in, let them know his whereabouts and the leads he was following up. At the very least he should let them know why he was two hundred miles away following up a simple missing person's case, and not tackling the 'new boy' dross they'd no doubt stacked up on his desk for him to trudge through.

He should be back at the station, poring through witness statements about the latest spate of muggings they'd never solve; chasing up leads on the stolen cars that had probably been chopped, re-badged and flown half-way across Europe by now. An endless stream of pointless jobs that nobody else wanted to be lumbered with.

He certainly shouldn't have gone A.W.O.L. on his first day, tracking a potential criminal halfway across the country. He'd definitely take a bit of heat for that. Bollockings from the DCI and more late shifts than he'd care for would be coming his way as a means of punishment. Not to mention an even bigger caseload of pointless rubbish, to really put him in his place.

But he could take it. Besides, once they realised what he'd achieved, they'd soon change their tune. When they saw how, on his first day, he'd tracked a bad guy all this way and used his initiative to take him down. And not just any bad guy: this George Thring was a serious nutter, he could tell. He could feel it.

Once they saw what he'd done here, they'd be more than impressed. Maybe even mark him out as potential for early promotion. His eyes glinted with pride at the thought.

If he did call in now they'd be sure to order him back, tell him to give up on his wild goose chase. Or worse, they'd realise what he was onto. They'd piece the puzzle together, like he had, realise that this Thring guy was up to something seriously bad and they'd call him back so they could send a more experienced officer to swoop in and make the arrest.

Well screw that, he thought. I'm not letting someone else take all the glory after I've done all the hard work.

He'd have to stay off the radar for a little bit longer. He'd have to stake this guy out, watch him and figure out what he was up to. He'd hang out in town, gathering evidence, stalking this Thring. Waiting until he slipped up. And then he'd pounce.

Keane rested his hands on the steering wheel, gripping it tightly as he gazed intently out to the road in front of him. "So you're just hanging around, Mr Thring?" he said to himself. "Well, two can play at that game."

But first, Keane decided that he needed to make his presence felt just a little bit more. It was only a small town but there must be some kind of police presence here. So he'd go and pay them a visit – a courtesy call to let them know that he was in town. One copper to another, just being polite. And, more importantly, to let them know that Thring was his collar, and that they'd better stay the hell out of his way when it all kicked off.

CHAPTER 21

GEORGE Thring lay on his back on the grubby brown carpet, his legs hoisted up onto the bed to try and force the blood that had drained from his head back to where it was supposed to be. He wasn't sure that he definitely would have fainted, given he'd never actually fainted before. But when he suddenly came over light-headed, a curious cold sweat chilling his brow and a thick foggy blackness creeping in at the edges of his vision, he thought it too prudent to lie down rather than fall down.

So far it had been a pretty stressful morning. He'd come within a whisper of sheer, devastating heartbreak, only to find out he was just being needlessly paranoid. He had endured an utterly horrendous shower in the least sanitary bathroom he'd ever seen. And he had just undergone some kind of bizarre interrogation from a rather crabby, accusatory policeman. By whom he was still uncertain as to exactly what he was being accused.

It was no wonder George felt safer down there on the floor, lost in a daze, his eyes fixed firmly on a curious brown stain on the dirty white ceiling as he forced himself to take long, deep breaths. He shivered slightly, dressed as he was in still just a towel, as he contemplated the meaning of it all.

It was when the detective had stormed off, looking angry yet strangely triumphant, that George had suddenly become overwhelmed and taken a bit of a turn.

The detective had seemed strangely vehement, totally convinced that George was some kind of master criminal, hiding out, evading the authorities. 'In disguise' he'd said. That was the most ridiculous part of it. As if George would have chosen that ridiculous outfit on purpose. And it wasn't much of a disguise – the garish blue material made him stand out a mile.

Was George really the main suspect in some kind of criminal investigation? It was incomprehensible. George Thring a suspect in a crime!

Even George himself couldn't imagine anyone less likely to commit a crime. He returned the money when gormless shop assistants gave him too much change. He sometimes picked up litter in the street and put it in the bin. He wouldn't even park in the mother and baby car parking spaces at the supermarket (even though he personally didn't see why simply having given birth gave someone the right to park closer to the door than anybody else) in case someone saw him and reported it.

He thought back to the conversation; what the man had actually said. He'd thrown lots of words about, mentioned various theories, some wild criminal motives. But he hadn't mentioned any particular crimes. From what he'd said, it sounded less as though the detective was investigating an actual crime and more like he was just investigating George. But that couldn't be right. Could it? Why would anybody want to investigate him?

And he'd seemed so determined, so unutterably certain that George was guilty of something. It was as if he'd set himself a challenge of arresting George for any crime he could possibly attach to him, whether he had committed it or not.

George had heard of the police pinning crimes on people in order to wrap up cases they couldn't otherwise solve. But pinning cases on people just because they thought they might be up to something? That was a new one on him.

A cool breeze whistled through the room, slapping George's still-damp skin, breaking him from his trance. His stomach grumbled an unruly, loud growl, making him feel instantly nauseated and incredibly hungry at the same time. He had to eat. And he had to eat now.

Slowly George raised his head, checking whether the wooziness had receded. He placed two fingers to his throat to assure himself that his racing pulse had returned to normal. All seemed fine so he set about getting dressed. A mere 11 minutes and 42 seconds of wriggling, jerking, shunting, twisting and squeezing himself into the tight blue jumpsuit and he was ready to leave the room.

Looking down at himself, dressed in the crumpled Elvis suit he'd worn all the previous day, and sweated in the night before, he barely recognised what he saw. This was not George Thring, at least not the same George Thring of only a few days previous. This was a man he barely recognised – and not just because of the large gold sunglasses obscuring thirty per cent of his face.

George left the room and made his way down the stairs, through the lobby and out through the front door. He was disappointed that there was no sign of Alice on the reception desk. He'd hoped to see her, if only just to reassure himself that the previous night had actually happened and hadn't been just an extension of his curious psychological meltdown.

He felt a little fuzzy just thinking about her, remembering the look on her face as they kissed. He was sure he'd see her again that evening and he couldn't wait. He left the hotel with a grin tickling his lips, almost skipping down the cracked, black path. He was so carried away with his thoughts that he barely even noticed the neatly dressed man before crashing straight into him, almost sending him tumbling to the floor.

"Look where you're going, old man..." said the stranger in a thick, syrupy accent.

George stumbled backwards, dazed and apologetic. "I'm so sorry," he offered. "I'm having a hell of a day..."

"No problem," barked the man, dismissive and uncaring. "Try not to share it around, though, eh?"

Something about the man's voice seemed odd. It was too forceful. Too posh. His clothes were impeccably neat; almost too neat. Altogether he seemed wrong somehow, not quite right. Almost like an impression of a person, or a parody. Even more fake than the dozen or so Elvis Presleys ambling their way along the street.

The man marched away briskly, disappearing through the door to the hotel. George couldn't quite tell what to make of him but his stomach rumbled loudly again, so he shrugged and turned, strolling idly down the black path.

He made his way down the hill to the small selection of shops on the high street. He hadn't paid much attention on his previous visits and was trying to figure out where and what he'd be able to eat when he noticed a suitably quaint-looking tea shop at the end of the parade. It seemed like a reasonable choice, given it was open, appeared to serve food and drink and, most importantly of all, was practically empty.

George was just about to enter when he remembered the previous night's embarrassment at finding his wallet completely empty. He crossed the road to the small bank opposite and looked closely at the cash machine on the wall outside. He was not surprised to find that it was, as Alice had predicted, completely out of order.

George peered in through the large glass window and sighed discontentedly to see the long line of people queued up at the teller's counter. His stomach grumbled even louder at the realisation his breakfast would be put off even longer.

CHAPTER 22

IT was no surprise to Major Fairview that John and Steve Clefton were still asleep when he went to wake them. Rather than being ready and prepared for the military-precision-style mission they were to undertake, the pair were still wallowing in their beds as he knocked sharply on the door. The sight of a beleaguered Steve Clefton opening the door dressed only in his boxer shorts was a far cry from the keen, regimented troops he would have hoped for.

The big man gaped a disgruntled yawn, reaching into his underwear to rearrange his testicles as the Major pushed passed him into the room. It stank of stale cigarette smoke, whisky and body odour.

"Well, it looks like you girls got a good night's sleep," said the Major.

John Clefton peered out from under the thick, itchy blanket, his eyes squinting in the bright daylight.

"I wonder, though," continued the Major. "Seeing as we've got this big job on today… perhaps you might like to get the fuck up and get fucking ready." He stared fiercely, anger tingeing his voice.

"Alright, alright," grumbled John, peeling back the covers and following his brother's lead by reaching into his briefs. "We know what the time is. Everything's ready. We were just getting up."

He looked over to the neatly packed bags by the bedroom door. "Everything's ship-shape, Bristol fashion, checked, checked and triple-checked, sah!" he said, standing abruptly and raising his hand to his temple in mock salute.

"Less of your fucking cheek," the Major retaliated. "Today is a big deal, and everything needs to run like clockwork. One single minute late and we're in the shit. And I'm not going back to jail because you pair of morons fancied a little lie in."

"You worry too much."

"It's not worry, Jonathan, it's good common sense. Now, if you want to end the day with a large sum of money in your pockets, rather than another trip away at Her Majesty's pleasure, get yourselves dressed, check the bags again, and stop dicking about. You and your dopey fucking brother can yawn and salute and scratch each other's balls as much as you like when we're out of here. Until the job's done, and we're in the clear, you do exactly as I say. Understand?"

Steve Clefton stood in the corner of the room, looking at his feet. His brother crashed back down onto the bed, sneering.

"Where have you been anyway?" he said suspiciously. "Could've sworn I heard your door going a while back. Been out and about have we? More secret phone calls?"

Major Fairview fought to hide his shock. He'd underestimated the big oaf. He hadn't realised the man had heard him leaving. He had indeed snuck out and he had been making phone calls, the nature of which he certainly didn't want the two brothers to know about. But he was sure that John was too stupid to really suspect anything. There was no way the gorilla could know that he'd secretly exited the hotel, made his way round to the getaway car and prepared a final little surprise for them.

"If you must know," he said, speaking fast and loud to try and confuse the man, "I was doing a final check of the premises, going over the plan, making sure there won't be any unhappy surprises. That's how plans are made, you see. Everything is in the details."

The man sneered, disconsolate at having been proved wrong. The Major breathed a tiny, imperceptible sigh of relief. He certainly didn't want these oafs having any idea that they were walking into a double-cross even a second before it happened. They might have been no match for his intellect, but in terms of brawn they were a formidable pair – the exact reason he'd hired them in the first place.

And he certainly didn't fancy the torrent of anger likely to be unleashed when they realised what was in store. Not before he was armed and ready to deal with them, anyway.

Of course, had the Major been as clever as he thought himself to be, he might have decided to keep a slightly closer eye on the two brothers. If he had, he would have realised that, far from languishing in their beds dead to the world, the two men had woken earlier than he had. The bags had indeed been checked and double checked, in part to ensure that everything was in place for the job to come, and partly to guarantee that their criminal leader hadn't planted any nasty surprises for them.

Such was John Clefton's desire never to go back to prison that he had developed rather a severe case of paranoia when it came to working with criminals other than his own brother. Especially when those criminals were highly dubious to start with, had a back-story more suspicious than a priest in a woman's changing room, and who kept disappearing to make secretive phone calls.

John had known they were dealing with a conman right from the start. He'd known there was something not right about the Major the very first time he'd laid eyes on him. He was a man definitely not to be trusted. A man who almost certainly was planning on depriving them of their share of the loot as soon as the job was completed. The potential rewards, however, were definitely worth the risk of working with the slimy bastard. Especially if they got in before he could and took all the money for themselves.

So he'd played along with the Major's assumption that he was an idiot. A drunk, lazy moron useful only as a blunt instrument or weapon of intimidation. It made it easier to keep an eye on the man, to work covertly to lay his own trap, when he was assumed to be too stupid to even think up a plan of his own.

So the men had got up early, checked the gear and gone over their own plan, laying the tools they'd need in place. When they heard the door at the end of the hallway creaking open slowly, and an unmistakably slight gait tiptoeing down the hall, John Clefton had followed in pursuit. He stalked the Major to the getaway car, watched him secrete a handgun in the glove compartment and then talk for ten minutes into his mobile phone.

He'd then rushed back to hotel, flung his clothes on the floor and jumped back into bed, maintaining the illusion of a knuckle-headed buffoon who hadn't a clue as to what was really going on.

And so, with both parties content that they had the upper hand on their rival, John Clefton unzipped one of the large duffel bags and pulled out his clothes.

"We're ready to go, just as soon as you are," he said.

"Good," replied the Major, reaching into one of the duffel bags and pulling out a shiny swathe of pale blue material. "Now, no peeking chaps. I need to get changed as well."

CHAPTER 23

THE lunchtime air inside the bank was thick and heavy, causing a debilitating lethargy in George. He was hot, the clawing material of his clothing sticking to him, as a single bead of sweat rolled agonisingly down his neck. His head swam and he could feel his eyelids slowly starting to close. With each in breath he grew more tired; more apathetic to the business at hand. He was standing in a queue of five people, all patiently waiting for the young teller behind the glass to deal with each of their requests. He hadn't moved forward in at least ten minutes.

The big red numbers on the digital wall clock read 12.37. Despite there being three available windows, and regardless of the apparent lunchtime rush, only one position was manned. The other staff were clearly more interested in huddling round in the office space behind the serving desk, no doubt embroiled in a highly important confab about a soap opera or the latest goings-on in some minor celebrity's love life.

George scanned the rest of the people in the queue. All of them were, of course, dressed in an assortment of Elvis Presley costumes. Some were rather impressive and fancy; others fairly shoddy and homemade. Shiny, flowing, bell-bottomed, sequined jumpsuits spread out in front of him, as if a circus had exploded and all the bits had scattered to earth and landed in front of him. He felt like he was standing in a line-up of felons wanted for crimes against fashion.

Even the old lady in front of George, holding herself up on a Zimmer frame with one lone wheel at the front and handlebars with grip-operated breaks, was doing her part with a pink jumpsuit that sagged and hung in the most unattractive places.

The only one not in a jumpsuit was a man at the front of the queue. He looked to be in his late 40s and was dressed as a 1950's era G. I. Elvis, with full khaki military costume.

George was no longer surprised by all the costumes. If there was one thing he could say about the people of Lower Chidbury, it's that they were all keen to take part. It wasn't as if just a few of the locals had dressed up to celebrate the festival; literally everybody was in costume. And, judging by the number of people in town and in the pub the previous night, quite a few visiting Elvises had also come along.

As George's mind meandered in the heat, he wondered what other strange rituals the locals might have revelled in and to what degree they embraced them. George had heard of a village, somewhere up north, where townsfolk hurled great lumps of cheese down very steep hills then duly threw themselves down after them. He'd seen pictures in the paper of these fearless cheese-chasers, cartwheeling, tumbling, bumping and falling down hills so steep that most normal people would fear to inch their way down. They clattered to the bottom, emerging bloodied and bruised, but curiously cheerful and smiling.

George could never really understand what would possess someone to risk the inevitable stretcher and broken limbs that faced some participants, all in the quest for a lump of cheese.

The tabloid newspapers were always equally enraged and enthralled by the crowds who would descend upon the small Spanish town of Pamplona for the annual Running of the Bulls. Crazy people would excitedly career down the street with half a ton of angry bull stomping along behind them. Those who escaped unscathed did so cheerfully; a tale to tell the grandchildren. Those unlucky enough to find themselves battered and beaten, or, worse still, gored and stabbed, would scream in agony though probably still relish the unique wound-shaped souvenir of their trip to the Corrida de Toros.

The whole world over, people engaged in unusual traditions. From pitching in to make world-record-breaking Paellas; to dancing around with bells on their ankles; to throwing poor donkeys off tall church steeples, tradition dictated that people threw themselves into these peculiar activities wholeheartedly. George couldn't honestly remember the last time he'd ever thrown himself wholeheartedly into anything. If ever at all.

And maybe a whole town deciding en masse to dress up as a long-dead pop singer was not the craziest. But George couldn't imagine another town anywhere where the residents would engage so fully in the activities. It was actually quite heart-warming. There was something ever so pleasant about the kind of togetherness it seemed to create. Everyone in, nobody left out.

Gradually George moved up the queue, as people came and went from the bank. The automated voice called him to window three.

Surprisingly, the young woman behind the counter was not dressed as Elvis, instead opting for traditional navy blue and white bank uniform. She was young and pretty, with long blonde hair, sparkly blue eyes and dense, black eyelashes. Her face was adorned with slightly too much make-up; her cheeks flushed pink and her lips thick with bright red lipstick.

"Hello sir, sorry about the wait," she said, slightly unconvincingly. "What can I do for you today?"

"Oh hello," George replied, "I need to withdraw some cash please. Maybe two hundred pounds. You see I arrived in town last night, and I had problems with my car. My suit got ruined, and I had to buy…"

He stopped short as the young girl rolled her eyes, breathing out heavily and noisily through her nostrils. She then looked very purposely at the crowd gathered behind George, and gazed back at him with raised eyebrows.

"Yes, well, if I could have two hundred pounds, please," he said handing over his plastic bankcard. "And if you could tell me what my balance is as well, please. I haven't really checked it for a while."

The girl scooped up the card from under the plastic security tray, scanning it through the terminal in front of her. She tapped at the keys on her keyboard and looked up at the screen. Then her face froze, her crimson lips parting as her jaw dropped and her mouth hung wide open.

She sat there looking at the screen for a few seconds, dumbfounded and silent. The machine suddenly spat out a piece of paper, breaking the girl from her trance, and she pushed it back through the slot to George.

He took the small square of paper from her and read it. It had George's name and account number printed on it. Next to the words Account Balance it said £7,419,176.78. George looked at the incomprehensible figure. There were so many digits it was more like a phone number than a bank balance. It was ludicrous. It didn't seem real. It had never seemed real to him.

Maybe it was because he'd never actually wanted it. Knowing how and why he'd come to have so much money, where it had come from and the cost of having it, he'd never wanted any of it. Not a single penny.

It had actually been quite a relief to have it held from him in trust until he came of age. For one thing, it meant that those who would gladly have squandered every penny for him had no chance to steal it away. And what would a boy of 11 want with all that money, anyway? Aside from a toy car or a bag of sweets, George hadn't really wanted anything. He certainly didn't want millions of pounds. He wanted his mum and dad.

He'd gladly have given up every single penny to have his parents back; to have had his family with him as he grew up.

Of course, had George managed to make such a magical trade and bring his parents back to life, he was in no doubt that his father would have disapproved. "I mean we're nice people, your mother and I," he could imagine him saying, "and we're very grateful, of course. But come on George, think of all the things you could have done with that money."

By the time the trust fund was released and the money was his to do with as he pleased, he found that he didn't actually want to do anything with it. He couldn't imagine spending it or getting any pleasure from it, such was the guilt and sadness attached to it. So he simply ignored it, using a little here or there for the things that he really needed but leaving the majority aside as a kind of grim reminder of what he'd rather have had instead.

It did cross his mind to give it away to charity, but every time he contemplated it he was struck with the image of his father, red-faced with anger, coughing and spluttering at the thought of having given so much money away.

"Goodness," said George, looking back up at the girl, still gawping in shock, "that's a little more than I was expecting. In that case... well, let's make it five hundred pounds."

The girl stared back at him through the thick, transparent plastic separating them, the cogs in her brain clicking slowly into place. "Yes, sir," she finally said, before tapping again on her keyboard and counting out a pile of cash on the counter in front of her.

"So," said the girl, handing over the small bundle of twenty-pound notes, her face growing suddenly more animated, "you just got into town last night?"

Clearly something about George had now caught her interest, and the other customers in the queue were not quite so important to her.

"So are you staying in town for long? My name's Kelly, by the way," she smiled, pointing at the name badge pinned to her blouse, her eyelashes fluttering like an epileptic butterfly.

"Oh, well…" George stumbled, disoriented by the girl's sudden change of attitude. "I'm not sure, Kelly. Things have been a little strange for the last few days. I'm not sure how long I'll be staying in town."

"Well, if you need someone to show you around," she said, her voice suddenly taking on a sexy, huskier quality, "I'd be happy to show you the sights. There's not a lot to see, but I know all the best places to go." She smiled at him, leaning forward, her bright blue eyes growing wider and her shirt automatically opening a little to show slightly more cleavage.

George suddenly realised that, for the second time that week, a woman was most definitely, irrefutably flirting with him. He felt embarrassed, his cheeks turning hot and pink. Then he felt guilty, as if he was in some way cheating on Alice, betraying her by flirting back. Had he been flirting back? He wasn't sure. He really wasn't very good at this at all.

"Oh… erm… that's very kind," he said as plainly as possibly, so as not to give the wrong idea, "but I think I know my way around. But thank you for your kind offer."

"Okay," smiled the bank clerk back at him. "Well, I'll see you around, I'm sure."

George stepped away from the window. There were seven people in the queue still waiting to be served; two people jabbing buttons on the paying-in machines; and a young couple, hand-in-hand, stood chatting with the G.I. Elvis as they passed each other on their way into the bank. Five people sat fidgeting on the uncomfortable-looking red sofas, patiently waiting to see the personal banker who was vacant from the small cubicle.

And, though they probably should have been annoyed at spending their lunch breaks and free time waiting in a bank, everybody actually seemed quite contented. They were smiling and chatting and all looked happy. Maybe this was what life here was like, thought George. Maybe something about this strange uniform they were all wearing brought out a different quality in them.

This was a happy little place, with happy people. A haven of friendship and sanctuary, and George felt at peace here. He felt at ease, like he'd never felt before. It was as if nothing could go wrong. Things were only going to get better for him. The last 48 hours had proved just how different his life could be and for the first time in a long time he could see a bright future ahead of him. His glass was most definitely half full. Things were going to be good.

George took a long, contented breath, fully filling his lungs. As he breathed out he felt his lips curl into a full, beaming smile, something that had become increasingly more frequent over the last few days. He felt happy, and he couldn't think of a single thing that could possibly spoil that.

"Everybody down on the ground," a deep, ragged voice suddenly screamed from somewhere behind him. "This is a fucking robbery!"

CHAPTER 24

JOHN and Steve Clefton burst in through the heavy glass doors of the bank, M16 machine guns lofted high in front of them, the barrels pointed menacingly at the gathered customers. "Everybody down on the ground," shouted Steve. "This is a fucking robbery!"

The customers froze to the spot, not moving, not making a sound. The only indication that the brothers had made any impact at all was written in the stunned look on their baffled faces. However, the confusion may not have been caused solely by the shouting and swearing. Or even the heavy-duty machine guns glistening in their leather-gloved hands. It was the rest of their appearance.

Unlike the traditional uniform of the average bank robber, neither man was wearing jeans, a bomber jacket or even a black, knitted ski-mask. Instead, both were decked out in full flowing Elvis Presley jumpsuits. John's was jet black with red and gold sequins littering the arms and legs in spiral patterns. It was a snug fit, not too tight or loose anywhere. And though he would never have admitted it to his brother, he actually quite liked the way it felt and thought he looked pretty good in it.

Steve's costume was bright red with shiny silver and black sequins, sewn in similar patterns. His was not such a good fit; his bigger, bulkier dimensions being harder to accommodate. Both the sleeves and ankles came up slightly short. The crotch rode up on him and the armpits were more than a little snug. The one realistic feature he did possess was the adequate paunch almost bursting out of the suit at the front. He found it difficult to move in the outfit, but he could walk and he could still swing his gun well enough to scare anybody that got in the way.

The outfits were both bold and bright enough to match the clothing worn by everybody else in the bank, but not so garish or detailed that they would stand out or be easily recognisable compared to all the others. Both men's look was finished off with preposterously high-quiffed jet-black wigs, and their faces were almost totally obscured by huge, bushy black stick-on sideburns and oversized, thick-rimmed gold sunglasses with heavily darkened eyepieces.

Both men were almost totally unidentifiable and it would have taken a very close look from a friend or relative to recognise them at all. Luckily, the customers in the bank were doing anything but scrutinising their facial features, preoccupied as they were by the panic suddenly gripping them and the rather large guns being waved in their direction.

"Well, fucking go on then," yelled John. "Get down on the ground!"

All at once, the customers snapped awake and duly complied. A man in his early 30s, wearing a white and blue jumpsuit, stepped away from one of the paying-in machines, raised his hands to show he had nothing in them, and dropped to his knees. The young couple, who just moments before had been enjoying a friendly chat with G.I. Elvis, looked worryingly into each other's eyes before dropping quickly to lie face down on the floor, the fingers of their trembling hands still interlocked.

The customers waiting for the personal banker slid from the uncomfortable red sofas, crawling down until they were lying on the floor. One over-eager beaver adopted a full star shape, fingers spread wildly outwards, his face flat on the ground, keen to demonstrate that he most certainly was not, and would not even think about, getting up to anything funny.

The young girl behind the counter, separated from the emerging terror by the thick, reinforced glass, sat open-mouthed and wide-eyed. Her mind should have been racing with emergency procedures, the security training she'd been given kicking in as she activated various robbery prevention protocols and leapt into action to save both her customers and the bank's money (though not necessarily in that order).

Instead of jumping to everybody's rescue, however, she instead adopted the posture of a houseplant, possibly hoping that if she just remained completely still nobody would even notice she was there.

George Thring shoved his newly-bulging wallet deep into his pocket and dropped to his knees. He moved slightly too quickly, though, and felt a blinding pain crunching in each kneecap, shooting like lightning through both thighs. It took every ounce of reserve to keep from screaming out in agony, desperate as he was to remain completely silent. He crumpled onto his front, pain searing through his legs, making sure to keep his eyes fixed on the two large, gun-toting Elvises; tracking every terrifying movement.

Two younger men from the queue assisted an old lady away from her wheely-walker, and helped her crouch into a sitting position, her knees and hip joints cracking under the strain of bending more than she had in years. They then joined the rest of the terrified queue in facedown positions on the floor of the bank's lobby.

Within seconds all but one had made the transition from customer to hostage, lying prostrate on the floor; some trembling and scared, some simply stunned and silent. The only man left standing was G.I. Elvis. His arms were crossed tight across his body in a pose of sheer defiance, his face turning redder by the second and his outrage threatening to bubble over and explode.

Major Charles Fairview strolled casually into the bank, closing the doors behind him and pinned a sign in the window. It read:

SORRY, WE ARE TEMPORARILY CLOSED DUE TO A TECHNICAL FAULT.

He too had changed out of his more distinguished attire and slipped into an almost regal pale blue jumpsuit, with gold and white stitching running up and down the legs and sleeves in an intricate pattern. A large black wig sat atop his head, a little better combed and coiffured than the brothers', and his face was equally concealed behind large sideburns and gold glasses. He pulled a stopwatch from his pocket, gazed intently at it, then stepped into the lobby of the bank.

"Good afternoon, ladies and gentleman," he said in a deep, authoritative, yet sympathetic tone. "I do apologise for the interruption but I'm afraid my associates and I have decided that we would like to rob your little bank today. All terribly exciting, isn't it?"

The customers looked on: silent, scared and intrigued.

"Now, I'm sure you'll all have noticed the rather large guns my two associates are holding. Believe me, we have absolutely no desire to shoot anybody. So, if everybody simply co-operates, allows us to do what we've come here to do and doesn't interfere, then I promise we'll have our business concluded in just a jiffy and be out of your way.

"Of course, if anybody does try and put the mockers on our little scheme, then we will have no choice but to take drastic measures. Isn't that right, chaps?" he said, looking over at his heavily-armed accomplices.

The two Cleftons signalled their agreement by very purposefully pulling back the charging handles on their machine guns and releasing them noisily to cock the weapons ready for firing.

"Now," said the Major to the man dressed in the G.I. military uniform, "I do believe my associates kindly asked everybody to get down onto the ground."

"Who the hell do you think you are?" barked G.I. Elvis loudly, spittle flying wildly from his mouth. He spoke in a southern American accent, a high-pitched twang bouncing at the end of each word.

"Oh dear," sighed the Major, clutching his forehead in his hand for a brief second, before looking back up. "I do believe we've already established everybody's roles in this little escapade. We three jolly souls are the bank robbers. You and the rest of the players present are the... well, let's just say that you're the unfortunate people in the wrong place at the wrong time. We're here to rob the bank, and your role is to get down on the fucking ground and do as you're told. I think I've already mentioned the consequences for disobedience.

"Now, if you wouldn't mind," he continued, waving his arm in a 'get down on the ground' motion, "we have a rather pressing schedule to stick to."

"Screw you!" the G. I. Elvis screamed back. "Screw you! How dare you? How dare you defile the good name of the King like this? This is the biggest insult I have ever seen. To think that you would degrade the image of Elvis Aaron Presley in this despicable manner."

A wave of sighs shuddered throughout the rest of the hostages. They all seemed to be thinking exactly the same thing: *Shut up, you prick. Just let them rob the place and leave!*

"I, for one," continued the man, growing more vehement by the second, "will not stand by while you three assholes rob this bank in the name of Elvis

Presley.

"*We* won't stand by," he said, turning and motioning to the rest of the customers. "Will we folks?"

Nobody moved. The back-up he was looking for remained firmly fixed to the ground. Clearly, the rest of the Elvis fans were far more concerned with preserving their own lives than the memory of their favourite dead singer.

The man turned back, timid and much less sure of himself, just in time to see Steve Clefton advancing on him, snarling loudly and swinging the extended barrel of his machine gun. The weapon connected hard into the man's face, smashing the left cheekbone and crunching forcefully into his nose, which exploded in a burst of thick, red liquid.

He tottered for a second, a look of confusion swimming in his eyes, before his legs crumpled beneath him and he collapsed, hitting the ground with a sickening thud. He lay there, flat out, totally still and completely unconscious.

A wave of relief washed over the other customers, who all grimaced slightly at the sound of the impact. They very happily looked the other way, keen for the robbers to conclude their business and be on their way as promised.

"Very well then," said the Major, indicating for Steve Clefton to take up position guarding the front door. "Shall we?"

John Clefton placed one half-full duffel bag down on the floor by the front door. He removed three sets of shiny, silver handcuffs and a length of rope, and carried the other empty bag over to the security door that led into the back room of the bank.

CHAPTER 25

GEORGE had often wondered how he might react in a robbery. Like most people, he had mused about how his brain would cope in such a high-stress situation. He'd often day-dreamed about finding himself in just such a spot; desperate men thrusting guns into his face, ordering him to comply with their demands.

In some of these scenarios George would play the part of negotiator, taking it upon himself, with no real training to speak of, to confront the robbers. He'd talk to them, calmly and carefully, helping them to see the error of their ways. He'd negotiate the release of the other hostages, finally convincing the robbers to give it all up as a bad job, surrender their weapons and turn themselves in to the police.

Naturally, George always had a word with the arresting officers afterwards, telling them how the robbers were just confused kids, in a terrible situation, and weren't bad guys really. He'd get their sentences reduced, and the robbers would look at George with respect and appreciation as the police cars pulled away.

More commonly, the scenario would involve George leaping to everybody's defence, taking down one robber and stealing his gun. Then he'd rely on his skill, intellect and special forces training to outwit the rest of the criminals, taking them out one by one in a hail of bullets, blood and explosions as he saved the day. Naturally he wouldn't want any thanks afterwards – he was just doing what any man would do. But, as she insisted, he always agreed to take the thankful, sexy, blonde cashier out for dinner.

Now that it was actually happening for real, however, and there were actual real men, with actual real guns, shouting at him to 'get down on the fucking ground', neither of those scenarios had played out. Instead of leaping to everybody's defence, George had found himself just stood there with a confused, stupid look on his face, not really knowing what to do.

Everybody else had done the same. They just stood there. That was another surprise. It wasn't at all like you see in the movies, with people screaming and wailing in panic; papers suddenly flying as everyone scattered and darted for safety. In fact, the customers didn't really seem scared at all. They were more baffled. It was all so unexpected that nobody really knew how to react.

When the second order came for everyone to get down on the ground, everything suddenly came rushing in at him. He found himself simply complying without question. All thoughts of acting the hero, leaping for one of the robbers' weapons and enacting a one-man vigilante reckoning disappeared from his mind as he dutifully dropped to his knees.

It wasn't fear exactly; he didn't have time think about how he felt. When men with machine guns tell you to get on the ground, you get on the ground as quickly as you can. And that's that.

But George knew he was not totally powerless. There was one thing he could do. He could keep his eyes open, study the robbers when they weren't looking, and compile a detailed description of them. They might get away with the money now, but as soon as George Thring went to the police with his observations of the robbers' appearance, they'd be lucky to get twenty miles before the law caught up to them.

Carefully, secretively, George angled his head to get a better look at the villains. He craned his neck, peering out of the corner of his eyes.

He soon realised, however, that there was one distinct flaw to this plan. All he could tell the police for sure was that the bank was being robbed by three men dressed as Elvis Presley.

In most robberies that would be enough of an observation. But considering that nearly everybody in the bank – in fact, nearly everybody in town – was dressed as Elvis Presley, it probably wouldn't be that helpful. If nothing else, it was sure to lead to a very long list of suspects.

For the most fleeting of moments George wondered if he should try jumping up, disarming the closest machine-gun-toting villain and turning the tables on them.

It didn't take long to rule this option out. It wasn't that he was afraid to get involved – although truth be told he was quietly terrified – it was more that, having weighed up all the options, it seemed far more sensible to let them get on with what they were doing and hope that nobody else got hurt.

After all, that is what the police tell you to do. And for a very good reason. For every have-a-go-hero that prevails to rapturous adulation from their fellow victims, there are probably six or seven who end up injured or shot. Or feeling the wrong end of an automatic weapon in their face – G.I. Elvis being very much a case in point.

So George lay there, face down on the floor, simply hoping for the robbery to be over as soon as possible. He looked round at the other hostages, who all seemed to be doing the same as him. He could hear a few people whispering, comforting each other. Somewhere behind him a woman was softly whimpering. The guard at the door stood firm, carefully scanning his prisoners, training his weapon on each of them in turn.

George thought of Alice and wondered whether he'd make it out of this alive. Would he ever see her again? Wouldn't that be just his luck, to finally find a woman he might just fall in love with and then get killed in a bank robbery the very next day?

CHAPTER 26

MAJOR Fairview walked across the hall of the bank, carefully stepping over the various limbs that lay in his path. He approached the serving window where the young female bank teller sat, white-faced and motionless.

"Hello… Kelly, is it?" said the Major, reading from her name badge. "Terribly sorry for all the fuss, but like I say, with a little help from you we'll hopefully be away in no time."

Kelly sat frozen to the spot, totally incapable of movement. The Major snapped his fingers several times, then knocked loudly on the glass separating them until she finally stirred, broken from her fear-induced catatonia.

"Hello," he smiled. "Now, my associate here is going to come round to the back, so that he might relieve you of all that lovely cash. Wouldn't be much of a robbery if we didn't do that, eh?" he laughed to himself. "So if you could just buzz him through, that would be great. Go on, it's okay."

Kelly reached down in front of her, pushing a button secreted beneath her desk, and an electronic buzzing sound indicated that the security door was unlocked. Steve pushed it open, making his way through to the area behind the counter.

"Now Kelly," continued the Major, "I wonder if you wouldn't be a dear and push that little silent alarm button you've got under your desk there. Go on, don't be shy. Wouldn't be terribly fair of us not to at least give the police a sporting chance of catching us, now, would it?"

Her face crinkled with even greater confusion.

"Go on. Really. Push the button."

The teller duly reached down beneath her desk and pressed the silent alarm button. The Major smiled, clicking a button on the top of his stopwatch.

John Clefton appeared behind her then, looped a length of the specialist climbing rope around her arms and midriff and secured her firmly to her chair.

The assembled bank customers remained fixed in position, face down on the floor, frozen from the threat of Steve Clefton's gun. He intermittently altered the angle of his weapon, focusing on each of them in rotation.

The Major followed John into the back of the bank where the remaining staff were crouched on the floor, whimpering and terrified. They all seem to have remembered as much of their specialist robbery prevention training as the girl tied to the chair behind the counter.

The manager was the most scared-looking: his face bright red and his eyes wide and shining. He'd made a kind of human shield out of his two junior female co-workers and was ungallantly cowering behind them, trying to mask it as a comforting, protective hug. His breathing was erratic. Short sharp bursts of air sucked in through his thin, taut lips.

The two girls were much calmer, albeit in a dazed kind of way. Their eyes were big and blank, and they stood motionless, the shock of the robbery only just outweighing the stupefaction they felt at the peculiar sight of a very posh-sounding Elvis Presley holding up the bank. Their pretty faces snapped back into action when the Major spoke.

"Hello there," he said. "Now, as I'm sure you've probably already heard, we're here to rob your little bank today, and I'd be ever so grateful for a little assistance. As I say, we're working to a fairly brisk time-frame, so no messing around, eh?"

He gave the girls a sly, reassuring wink. "Now, could you two lovelies do me a favour and step over to the side, where my friend is waiting. Let the dog see the rabbit, so to speak?" he said, pointing at the manager.

The two girls stumbled slightly to the side, despite the Manager's protestations that they should all stay together. They managed to tear themselves away from his pathetic, clawing grasp, where they were instantly handcuffed, first to each other and then to a large metal filing cabinet.

"Good afternoon to you, Sir," said the Major, addressing the bank manager who was now cowering before him, tears openly streaming down his cheeks and his arms held high in surrender. The Major again looked at his stopwatch, making a mental note of the time.

"Right then, jump up," he continued. "Take your keys out of your pocket, open up all the cash desks and then let me and my friend into your safe.

"NOW," snapped the Major, adding a harsher authority to his voice.

The manager looked up at him, teary-eyed and non-believing. It was as though he thought that if he just knelt there and did nothing then everything would be okay. Like he could shut his eyes and when he reopened them the robbers would be gone, the crisis over, and everything back to normal. He even tried it, clamping his eyes shut as tight as he could and counting to five.

Except that when he did open them up again, the Major was still there, looking down on him, joined now by his rather desperate looking, snarling accomplice. Sensing he was probably only seconds from feeling the edge of the big man's gun colliding with his face, he quickly resigned himself to doing what he was told.

The manager climbed up from his kneeling position and made his way along the row of cash desks by the counter, unlocking each one in turn. John Clefton followed on behind him, dipping his rough, fat fingers into the metal trays, clawing out big wads of mixed notes and thrusting them into the large canvas bag.

When the trays were empty, the Major motioned for the snivelling man to lead them out into a back room. John Clefton reinforced the order with a hefty shove to the man's back, nearly knocking the terrified manager off his feet. Again, the Major checked his stopwatch, calling out, "Three minutes, ten seconds," before disappearing through to the further recesses of the bank.

They stepped into a small office, barely large enough for all three men to fit inside. The room housed a simple desk, upon which stood a computer keyboard and monitor. Next to the desk, on the farthest wall, was a large, grey, oppressive looking safe. It was four feet high and three feet wide, with two keyholes mounted on protruding circular discs and a large, three-pronged locking handle. The safe was dug into the wall and above it was mounted a smaller metal box, eight inches by six inches in dimension and painted bright red.

The bank manager unlocked the red box first, revealing two separate safe keys, and removed them both. "You do realise this safe has a twenty minute timer delay? Once I unlock it, I can't actually open the safe door for twenty minutes."

"What do you think we are," growled John Clefton, "bloody idiots? D'you think we don't know what we're doin'?"

The Major calmly raised a hand to quieten his colleague, before again looking back at the ticking stopwatch in his hand.

"Never fear," he said to the manager, "we're quite aware of your restrictions. Now if you wouldn't mind unlocking the safe. Time and tide wait for no man. Not to mention the boys in blue, eh?" He smiled a sickly, toothy grin.

The manager carefully placed both keys into their respective holes, turning them simultaneously. The locks clicked and clunked loudly, the sound echoing somewhere inside the large, grey box. He left the keys in place before reaching back up into the red cabinet and turning over a small wooden egg timer, the sand beginning to tumble down from the full glass bulb at the top.

"It's... so I know when to turn the handle..." he said to the Major.

"Of course," replied the Major. "I do have a stopwatch in my hand, but whatever works for you."

The manager's sweaty face blushed even redder. "So... what now then?"

"Now we wait," said the Major. "For twenty minutes."

Just then the sound of a distant siren could be heard, gradually growing louder, getting nearer and nearer to the bank. The walls flashed blue as a police car skidded to a halt outside the building.

"Ah good," said the Major, "they're here. Right on time. Go and have a look, would you?"

John Clefton stared hard at the bank manager, leaning in slightly and closing his eyes to thin, dark slits to reinforce the menace. Then he walked off into the main hall of the bank. Major Fairview stood calmly, alternating his view between looking at the manager, glancing over to the small egg timer, the sand slowly trickling from the top bulb down into the bottom, then back to the flickering numbers on his digital stopwatch.

John Clefton appeared back in the rear of the bank again. "Police," he said to the Major. "One car parked across the street. Two old bill: one fat and useless, one young and dopey lookin'. Don't seem to know what they're up to; just having a look round, trying to clear the street. I poked my head out the door, showed 'em the gun. Fat one nearly shat himself. Shouldn't be bothering us just yet."

"Good," replied the Major. "Sixteen minutes, twelve seconds to go here. Go and prepare for stage two."

John Clefton huffed under his breath. He wasn't keen on the way the Major had started dishing out orders; talking down to him. He reassured himself with the image of how the posh git's face would change when he and his brother relieved him of all three shares of the proceeds. He actually had to stop himself from smiling as he walked back into the bank, remembering just in time to reinstate his scary face.

******

It was the longest sixteen minutes and twelve seconds of the bank manager's life, during which he re-evaluated a number of times whether or not he wanted to carry on with his, to date, fairly unimpressive, unexciting career at the bank. The Major stayed resolutely calm throughout, not speaking, just checking the time and smiling at the terrified man.

As the last grain of sand landed in the bottom of the egg timer, John Clefton walked back into the outer room. The Major looked up at the bank manager, pointed to the safe, and said, "Okay then. Let's get this show on the road."

They watched as the manager took hold of the locking wheel, turned it to the left with a great, wrenching pull, then twisted it round until the safe was fully unlocked. He pulled the wheel towards him, the heavy metal door creaking out of its housing.

Just as it started to open, John Clefton stepped forward, grabbed the manager by the shoulder and pushed him out of the way, sending him tumbling to the floor. He took over the work on the door, swinging it fully open, revealing three metal shelves all heavily stacked with bundles of various denominations of bank notes.

The two robbers stood briefly, taking in the sight. It was difficult to tell exactly how much cash was there but it was easily over two hundred thousand. They turned to each other, beaming smiles spread across their faces.

John Clefton placed the duffel bag on the floor in front of the safe and greedily started clawing money from the shelves, allowing it to fall down into the canvas receptacle. It took just a few seconds before the safe was emptied and he was tidying the bundles into the packed bag, stuffing them in to make them fit and then zipping it up.

"Excellent," said the Major. He took a pair of handcuffs from his pocket and leaned down to secure the bank manager's wrist to the handle of the filing cabinet he was now huddled in front of. "Thanks ever so much for that."

John Clefton picked up the bag and the two men strolled back through to the main hall of the bank, stepping over the hostages. The Major again checked his stopwatch. Exactly twenty-three minutes and thirty-four seconds had passed since the triggering of the alarm. In that short space of time the robbers had cleared the tills and the safe and were assembled back by the front door ready to make their escape.

"Well, ladies and gentleman," announced the Major, "that wasn't too bad, was it? Thank you all very much for your patience."

He looked at his stopwatch, and seemed to be calculating something. "Is everything ready to go?" he said to Steve and John Clefton.

Both nodded in affirmation.

"And how about our friends outside? No new additions, just yet?"

"Nobody," said Steve Clefton.

The Major walked over to the front door and peered out to the street outside. One police car was parked on the other side of the street, its blue lights still whirling and flashing. Two policemen were huddled behind the car, staring back at the bank, with bewildered looks on their faces. They seemed anxious to get things going, to formulate a plan, but too nervous to react before reinforcements arrived. But that wouldn't be too much longer.

"Good," said the Major. "Well, let's not hang around too long, eh?"

He turned back to look at the assembled hostages still gripping tight to the floor. "Okay folks," he announced, "our business here is concluded, and I'm sure you'll all be pleased to hear that we will be on our way presently. But first I'm afraid I'm going to have to ask another little favour of you all. So if you wouldn't mind standing up now, that would be just great."

Tentatively, the hostages got to their feet. G.I. Elvis remained crumpled on the floor, still completely unconscious, small, bloody bubbles intermittently inflating and popping from one nostril.

"Oh, no, not you dear," the Major shouted across to the old lady, trying her hardest to pick herself up from the floor. "You stay where you are and relax, we won't need you for this part."

The old lady smiled back, and sat back down on the floor again.

"Now let's all line up at the door, please," said the Major.

The hostages slowly stumbled forwards, egged on by the two Clefton brothers shoving them each in turn, herding them into a group by the front door.

"Now," said the Major, "when I give the word, I'm going to open this door, and I want you all to run through it as fast as you can. Is that clear?"

The assembled crowd stared back at him in stunned silence.

"Okay then," he said, taking a firm grip on the handle of the door and easing it slowly open. "On your marks… Get set…"

CHAPTER 27

THE plump, juicy doughnut sat staring at him, tantalising him, begging to be eaten. The soft golden brown flesh glinted in the dim light of the small police station. One thin rivulet of blood-red jam oozed from a wound-like hole in the side, slowly dripping down and pooling on the sugar-scattered card of the box beneath.

He knew he shouldn't eat it. He'd already had two since breakfast and it would be lunchtime soon anyway. But it looked so good. The very thought of picking it up and taking a bite, feeling the thick, sweet strawberry jam burst out and fill his mouth, had him salivating.

He shouldn't really be eating doughnuts at all, not since the doctor had ordered him onto that boring healthy-eating diet. It consisted of little more than carrots, bits of limp lettuce, and, if he was very lucky, the odd baked potato — minus butter, salt or anything that might actually make it taste good. He was supposed to be careful, thoughtful about what he ate. He was supposed to stick to sensible foods and cut out all the bad things he shouldn't be eating. Well, he was *supposed* to.

Sergeant Pete Collins had never been bothered by his weight. He'd always been big. As a child he was podgy and never really thought anything about it. His mother was the worst kind of influence, berating him for his extra heft and lack of exercise (like she was a great deal slimmer herself!), but then dishing up extra-large portions for her 'growing boy' and offering an endless supply of sugary snacks, chocolate biscuits and little treats to keep him happy. And so a podgy boy grew into a big man. Not fat exactly, but large and well built.

He'd always quite liked the extra weight. It gave him a little bit more status and confidence. And, being a police officer, it had its distinct advantages. He was never going to be particularly gifted when it came to chasing down suspects. But when he came face to face with a criminal — arresting a drug dealer or squaring up to a mugger — more often than not they'd look at his considerable stature and have second thoughts about resisting arrest or putting up a fight. He only really needed to give them a mean look and his big arms and puffed out chest would do the rest. If he could get the suspect cornered, they'd invariably give up.

Several years of walking the beat, enduring the mild physical exercise that the job required, had kept him from bloating out too much. But as he got older and more experienced, promoted up to the rank of Sergeant, and his days had become increasingly deskbound, his girth had increased. The weight had piled on and where he'd previously been bulky, he could now be more accurately described as wobbly.

But he didn't see what was so bad about being fat. He was happy, he enjoyed his life and he got to eat what he wanted. Rather that than become one of these calorie-counters, who only ate low-fat yoghurts and rice cakes.

Of course, that was all before his little heart 'scare' the previous year. It hardly came as earth-shattering news that a 20-stone man in his early 50s ought to be watching his food intake and trying to get more exercise. But when he finally felt the repercussions of all those years of unhealthy living: the shooting pains racing up his arm; his chest tight like he was being crushed; barely able to catch his breath; it all came rushing up to him like a slap in the face. Myocardial Infarction, the doctor had called it. He did, of course, mean heart attack. And Collins knew he was very lucky to be alive.

It had been a big enough shock to make him wake up. Being fat had never been a problem for him, but being unhealthy was a different matter entirely. So he tried to stick to his diet, aided by the constant nagging of his wife and daughter, but it wasn't easy. Temptation was always there, most commonly in the form of doughnuts.

He knew he was also extremely lucky still to be in a job. The usual course of action would have been to force him to take early retirement; pensioning him off on medical grounds. But he'd begged and pleaded against it. He'd had a bit of ill health, he couldn't deny that, but he certainly wasn't ready for retirement. He wasn't ready to be told he was of no use any more.

So the Chief Superintendent had pulled a few strings and had him reassigned from the main police headquarters to the smaller sub-station in Lower Chidbury. It was pretty much a caretaker's job, where all he'd have to do was sit and smile and maintain a constant presence.

It was a cushy number, to all intents and purposes. The majority of crimes reported covered fairly minor disturbances such as a shoplifting from the newsagents, graffiti sprayed on walls and the odd hanging basket being pinched. And since most of those crimes could be attributed to young Billy Jenson, the village's 12-year-old juvenile delinquent extraordinaire, there wasn't a lot to be done.

There certainly wasn't enough for two officers. Which is why he was so surprised to have been assigned a young Police Community Support Officer by the name of Tony Clamp, to work with him. He'd been told they wanted him to act as mentor; give the young officer the benefit of his twenty-three years as a serving officer. He had been quite flattered that they'd thought him to be a worthy mentor.

It transpired, however, after just two days in the young man's company, that the truth was something quite different. Apparently Tony Clamp was the nephew of the Chief of Police. He'd been given a job as a favour, but he was nowhere near being up to standard. They didn't know what else to do with him so they'd packed him off to the place he was least likely to cause any real trouble.

He was a good kid. 19 years old; not very bright but keen to learn – though not much of what he was taught ever actually seemed to stay inside his head. But his heart was in the right place. And in truth it had been nice to have the company. Collins quite liked the peace of having his own little police station but it did get terribly quiet some days.

He couldn't deny that, every now and again, he did miss his old life walking the beat, catching criminals, protecting the public. He'd always enjoyed the respect he'd had whilst wearing the uniform. But what he'd really revelled in was helping people on a daily basis, making a real difference in the world, keeping the bad guys off the street when and wherever he could.

He was well aware of what some of his former colleagues thought of his new role: laughing at him behind his back; chuckling at the pointlessness of it all. All they saw was a lazy man, sitting on his fat arse all day, drinking tea and doing little else while the real coppers did a real job.

And it did seem too pointless to him too, sometimes. But he liked his village life; the quiet restful days; the lack of stress. He liked the community feeling it gave him – how he knew everybody that lived there – and he liked the way everyone called him Sarge. He wouldn't have traded back. He was happy and that's all there was to it.

That doughnut was still looking at him. In fairness, they shouldn't have food in the station at all. "It looks unprofessional," the Chief Superintendent had rebuked him the last time he'd popped down for an unplanned inspection, "when members of the public call in to report a crime and see you two stuffing your faces."

He had to agree, it did lack a certain element of professionalism. But considering they hardly ever had anyone actually popping in to report a crime he didn't see how it really mattered.

And so, with his daily rations cut down to an amount that wouldn't keep a hamster well fed, and with very little going on throughout the day to keep him occupied, it was never very long before his thoughts turned to food. They kept an inexhaustible supply of biscuits in the kitchen – chocolate ones for special occasions – and Ted who owned the bakery down the road often popped in with any unsold cakes or pastries. Which is why they had a box of doughnuts.

He was just about to reach forward and pick it up when the front door opened and in walked a thin, very straight-looking man with immense determination etched on his face.

"Good afternoon," said the man, a very serious tone to his voice. "I'm DC Keane, just in the area for a day or two." He pulled a warrant card from his inside jacket pocket, flashing it enthusiastically at the Sergeant, confirming his credentials.

"Hello Detective Keane," returned Collins with a warm smile. "And what brings you to Lower Chidbury today?"

The smile was lost on Keane. He didn't have time for pleasantries and being friendly. "Just a professional courtesy," he said, "thought I'd pop in and let you know I was in town. I traced a suspect up here this morning. Following up a few leads, you know."

"Traced a suspect?" enquired the Sergeant. "So you're here to arrest him? And you need some help with that?"

"I certainly don't need help arresting a suspect," Keane threw back with a dismissive laugh. "I'm just keeping him under observation at the moment."

"And what exactly is he suspected of doing? It must be bad for you to follow him all this way."

"Don't worry, he's not dangerous. I've got him under control."

"I said: what did he do?" returned Collins, a little more forcefully. "If there's a dangerous criminal in my town, you have an obligation to let me know."

"Well, technically, at the moment, I'm not sure. Missing person, very suspicious, just upped and left. I tracked him down here and he's acting very strangely."

"So, he hasn't actually committed any crime? Maybe he's just here on holiday. I know it's not exactly the most exciting place," chuckled Collins, "but people do visit from time to time."

"Oh, he's up to something all right. One look at him and I could tell that. I haven't figured out what it is yet, but I will. And then I'll get him."

"Okay, well, if we can be of any assistance," said Collins dismissively.

"I'll let you know," said Keane, turning on his heel and walking out of the small police station, letting the door bang noisily behind him.

"Who was that?" asked Tony, walking through from the kitchen carrying two freshly-made mugs of tea.

"Not sure," he said. "Detective from out of town. Could be trouble."

Collins took one of the mugs from the young man and had just about raised it to his lips when the phone rang. "Get that, will you?" he said, dumping himself back down into his seat. "Honestly, it's all go today."

The young man lifted the receiver, held it to his ear for a few seconds before calling out, "It's central control. They're saying the silent alarm has been triggered in the bank. What shall I say?"

"Silent alarm?" said the sergeant, jolting upright in his chair, spilling hot tea onto his fat belly. "Give me that."

He yanked the phone from the young man's hand and pressed it against his ear. "Yes," he said. "Understood. Yes, they've probably tripped it by accident, knocked the button or messed around with the fuses. Okay, we'll pop down and check it out. No, hold off on the back-up till we've had a look. Like I say, it's probably nothing."

He put the phone down, a quizzical, worried look flashing across his face. "Right we'd better go and have a look, then," he said. He took one long swig on his tea, pulled on his jacket and headed out to the car.

They were at the bank exactly two minutes and 13 seconds later. Collins had driven down with the lights flashing and sirens blaring, not because he genuinely needed them but just for the effect it had. He hadn't used them in so long he wondered whether they actually still worked.

For fun, he skidded the car to a halt – again, more for the effect than anything else, and came to a stop on the opposite side of the street. Both men climbed out and peered across to the bank. Nothing much seemed to be going on. The street was as quiet as it usually was; a few people milling about here and there.

Nothing terribly dramatic seemed to be going on in the bank. There was a sign in the window of the front door which appeared to be hand written and Collins couldn't quite make out what it said.

"Wait here," he said to his colleague. "I'll have a look."

He stepped round to the near-side of the car, straightened his hat and adjusted his belt upwards slightly. Then he marched purposefully across to the bank. He barely made it halfway across the street, however, before the door was suddenly flung open and a stocky, angry looking man dressed in an Elvis Presley jumpsuit burst out, waving a heavy-duty machine gun in his hand.

"This is a fucking robbery," he yelled. "Don't come any closer, or I'll kill the bloody lot of them."

Collins stopped in his tracks, spinning round and nearly tripping over his feet as he raced back to the protection of the car, belly-flopping to the ground, taking cover behind the vehicle. The pedestrians in the street and, worst of all, his own young sidekick remained motionless, simply standing there gawping at the man with the gun.

"Get down," yelled Collins. "He's got a gun!"

At that everyone else seemed to catch up: instantly scattering; jumping behind parked cars; racing through shop doors; running away in panicked screams. Tony crouched down next to Collins, the bank door closing noisily as the armed man went back inside.

Collins gripped the radio attached to his shoulder, pushed the transmit button and pulled it close to his mouth.

"Hello," he said, somehow completely forgetting every protocol for reporting action back to control. "Hello, is anybody there?"

"Hello," snapped the voice on the other end of the line. "Who is this?"

"This is Sergeant Collins," he said, panic making his voice race, "requesting urgent back-up to Lower Chidbury bank. Armed robbery in progress. There's a guy in there with a big fucking gun. And hostages, as well, I think. Send police back-up. And ambulances… just in case. Please," he added, aware that he was making a mess of reporting in and wanting to seem polite at the very least.

"Okay, Sergeant," replied the voice. "I'm despatching police back-up, armed units and ambulances now. They're about 20 minutes out from your location."

"Okay, thanks," replied Collins.

This wasn't supposed to be happening. All at once his quiet little life had exploded into terror and mayhem. Men with guns. Big guns. Hostages in the bank. How many were there? Who was in there?

He looked over to his young colleague, crouched down next to him. The young man looked back at him. "What do we do now, Sarge?"

The sensible thing to do was just to sit there and wait for back-up to come.

They'd called it in and now they should hold off for the professionals. They were certainly not equipped to deal with machine-gun-wielding bank robbers. But he couldn't just sit there, doing nothing, waiting for help to come. He was here to protect these people, not just sit there cowering behind his car at the very first sign of trouble.

"You wait here," he said to the young support officer. "Keep an eye on things, make sure everyone stays down out of sight. I'm gonna go and have a closer look."

Collins took a deep breath, crawled along the car to the far edge and peered around the boot. He couldn't see anything happening; no immediate signs of danger. He got to his feet and, in a crouched position, ran to take cover behind the next car on the street.

He did this a few times, running and crouching, his stumpy legs bounding along the pavement, his fat belly bouncing up and down with each step, fearful that the gunman may have his weapon trained on him from inside the bank. He got far enough along until he could dash across the road unseen. Then he made his way back down the street, past the bakers, the chemist and the tea shop until he was standing next to the bank.

Carefully he peered round the corner, sneaking a glance in through the window. People lay in groups across the floor of the bank; none apparently harmed in any way, and – thankfully –nothing that looked like a dead body. There was no real sign of damage or destruction at all and it didn't look like the guns had even been fired. Yet.

He couldn't see clearly enough to make an accurate count but he guessed at fifteen hostages, discounting whoever was out in the back rooms. It was difficult to tell who anybody was: they were all dressed alike. Of course he recognised old Mrs Etherall, dressed in that pink costume of hers, sprawled out on the floor with her Zimmer frame collapsed next to her. Other than that, the hostages could have been anybody.

One big lump of a man was patrolling the floor, machine gun held high at his shoulder, pointing it randomly at the people lining the floor. It wasn't the man who'd waved his gun around in the street. He was nowhere to be seen. That meant there were at least two bad guys, and maybe more out the back.

It was too dangerous to try to make contact with any of the hostages, although he was desperate to tap surreptitiously on the window just to alert them to his presence; let them know that help had arrived. But he couldn't take the risk. He didn't know what the robbers had planned. It wasn't going to be a quick grab-and-dash, like most hold-ups; take as much cash as you can carry and run before the police arrived. Now that Collins was here, there was no way they would be doing that. At least not without exiting the building in a hail of bullets. And he was quite keen to avoid that.

If it were a standard hold-up, the robbers would be in there, panicking at the police presence and readying for either a protracted stay or readying to make a run for it. But that didn't seem to be the case at all. The man hadn't seemed in the slightest bit surprised to see the police turn up. He'd actively opened the door to let them know exactly what was happening. They hadn't been caught out by the silent alarm. They were expecting the police to turn up.

The man patrolling the hostages inside wasn't worried or flustered. He seemed very calm, going about his business like it was all part of the plan. They were perfectly prepared for the police to be there and that was what worried Collins most. How were they planning on getting out?

Collins peered across the road to see a man stalking his way down the hill, taking cover behind trees, cars and buildings as he went. He was very serious and determined, moving with more stealth than was strictly necessary. As the man got closer he could see that it was that idiot detective from earlier in the police station. Oh great, he thought, that's all I need.

Peering in through the window, Collins waited until the armed man was facing away from him and dashed back to the cover of his police car, just as the detective arrived

"Well, well," said the detective Keane, "looks like you've got yourself a bit of action, eh? And I bet I can guess who's behind it. Looks like you could use *my* help," he added with an obnoxious tone to his voice.

The fat sergeant struggled to catch his breath, before saying, "Hello again, detective. Everything is under control here, thank you very much. I've called for back-up, and I've inspected the bank. Full-scale hostage situation; two or more armed men. They haven't told us what they want yet so the best course of action is to secure the perimeter, which as you can see my colleague has done, and now we're waiting for back-up to arrive."

"Yeah, looks like you've got everything under control," Keane said flippantly.

"Is this your man, in there?" barked the Sarge. "If you've allowed a gang of armed criminals to come into my town and done nothing to stop them, I'll have you for this."

"Whoa, I never knew anything about a gang of robbers. I'm just following up on a suspicious missing person. Does seem rather a coincidence, though. I track this Thring guy all the way up here, and the next thing someone's knocking over the bank."

"Maybe," replied Collins. "Have you actually found him? Spoken to him?"

"Spoke to him this morning, about an hour ago. Seemed very shifty, like he was up to something. I had no idea he was into armed robberies but I'll bet he's got something to do with this. I'm gonna go and have a look," he said, turning away.

"Just you bloody well wait there," said Collins, grabbing the man's arm. "I've already had a look and there's nothing more to see. It's too dangerous. There are hostages in there and they've already warned us about getting too close. I'm not risking hostages' lives just because you want to play the big man and take charge."

"But…" replied Keane, failing to find a convincing argument.

"We can't do anything else now," said Collins. "Back-up should be here soon. I suggest we just hold the perimeter, keep an eye on things and wait for the cavalry."

"Okay," said Keane. "Not much we can do before the armed units turn up."

There was a little too much excitement in his voice for the Sergeant's liking, as if he was looking forward to it; a kid wanting to see a real-life shootout.

"I take it you've got the back covered?" said Keane.

"No back exit to the bank," Collins said confidently. "See that alleyway running down the side of the building? That's the only way round to the back. And to get down there, they'll have to come out the front, won't they? I can't imagine them trying to do that, can you?"

CHAPTER 28

WHILE Steve Clefton held guard over the hostages and the Major waited patiently for the time-lock delay on the safe to run down, John Clefton had been quietly unpacking the contents of the half-full duffel bag by the foot of the bank's front window. He neatly stacked the grey metal canisters in a row on the floor, then pulled out several packs of firecrackers. He removed them from their wrapping, primed the fuses ready for lighting, and laid them out carefully in front of the grey tins. He placed a shiny, new silver cigarette lighter on the floor next to them.

Finally, he took out the computer speakers, slotting the plug into the socket on the wall and connecting them to the MP3 player. He powered up the device, selecting a song ready to play and ramped the volume up to full.

With the hostages corralled at the front door, he and his brother took up position as the Major played sheepdog, priming the captives for release.

"On your marks… set…" said the Major. The hostages bustled, readying themselves for action. A nervous tension built up inside them. "Wait for it, wait for it…"

With that the two brothers swung into action. John bent down and collected two of the metal canisters, detaching the ring pulls in turn, as Steve swung the heavy metal machine gun into the large glass window. It shattered instantly, collapsing into great, heavy shards that smashed and crashed down onto the pavement outside.

John released the firing mechanisms on the cans in his hands, the safety clasps pinging off as he lobbed them through the hole to the street outside. They landed on the road with a tinny clank, bouncing two or three times and rolling to the side before coming to a stop. They were quickly joined by four other cans which landed near them on the road.

They sat silent and still for five whole seconds, an eternity for the two policemen outside and the few rubbernecking pedestrians, all standing with mouths agape, frozen in fear and waiting for the things to explode. Far from a loud bang, however, they each popped with a slight fizz and began to seep smoke. It started as thin and wispy at first, insignificant like cigarette smoke, but quickly grew thicker and denser, pumping out and filling the surrounding air.

Within seconds the street outside was almost completely obscured by a mixture of white and blue fog. Two cans were thrown to the back of the bank, and the inside of the building started to fill with the choking mist.

John Clefton kneeled down, pressed 'play' on the MP3 player and a lively version of Elvis Presley's *Burning Love* pumped out at an incredibly loud volume. It was a little clichéd, the Major knew, but the idea was to cause as big a distraction as possible and the resulting confusion from the loud, up-tempo music could only aid that. And he did have to smile at the ridiculous irony of it all.

Next, John grabbed the cigarette lighter. He sparked the fuses on all six sets of Chinese firecrackers, waiting for them to begin smouldering before flinging them through the smashed window. Again one set was thrown into the back of the bank, disappearing into the growing plumes of white smoke.

All the sets of crackers burst into life at the same time: banging, popping and crackling in the thick, darkened atmosphere. People screamed, inside the bank and out on the street. The smoke filled their throats and they started to cough and splutter, convulsing on the spot.

The mixture of smoke, loud music, terrifying banging and people screaming all built up into a delicious cacophony of sensory overload. People in the street jumped and ran, leaping behind cars, panicking, scattering, fearful that the robbers had opened fire and unsure where the bullets were heading. The hostages in the bank hustled and jolted, agitated and desperate to flee. Yet they stood firm, not wanting to act until instructed to do so.

As the frenzied crescendo peaked, and the gathered hostages jostled nervously, the Major threw open the front door and yelled: "GO!"

The terrified crowd remained firmly in place, hesitant, like a timid animal fearing an outstretched hand.

"GO, GO, GO!" screamed the Major, shoving the first few people hard in the back, driving them forward and out onto the street. The whole group suddenly bolted, dashing out the door after them. Screaming and shouting, still uncertain of what they were heading into, they just ran: stumbling; tumbling; running; falling; and bouncing off each other in a desperate bid to get away.

The scene outside the bank was utter chaos, as a small army of Elvis Presleys suddenly raced out in all directions, utterly unable to see where they were going, ducking down and shielding themselves as best they could from a swathe of imaginary bullets pinging and zipping past their heads.

They dived and leaped, jumping behind parked cars, clambering into shops, desperate to conceal themselves. They sprinted into the dense smoke, colliding with unsuspecting pedestrians, crashing to the ground in a tangle of flared limbs and sparkly capes.

Just then a new set of sirens came screaming down the road, red and blue flashing lights illuminating the ghostly, thick air. Police cars screeched to a halt, nearly colliding with other vehicles and only just missing the marauding crowds of fearful people running for their lives.

"Let's go," shouted the Major, as the last few stragglers stumbled out of the building. "And leave the guns."

"Leave the guns?" Exclaimed John Clefton. "Are you mad?"

"We need to blend in with the crowd," said the Major. "Carrying huge machine guns might just be a tip off, don't you think?"

John Clefton humphed and threw his weapon to the floor. It disappeared into the rapidly thickening smoke.

"Come on Steve," he called to his brother. "Let's get out of here." Then he raced ahead to the large front door.

CHAPTER 29

THE time seemed to drag on for hours as George lay on the cold floor of the bank. He was starting to wonder if they'd ever get out of there. He'd noticed the flashing lights and sirens of a police car. One of the robbers had opened the door and shouted something. And then nothing. Everything had gone quiet again. Surely there should have been a phone call, finding out how and when the robbers wanted their escape helicopter delivered.

George's legs were starting to cramp up; pins and needles buzzing in his left foot. He wasn't sure how much longer he could hold his position. And although food really should have been the last thing on his mind, those painful, gurgling hunger pangs were still rumbling deep in his stomach. In the films, didn't they always send in water and pizzas to keep the hostages going?

George hadn't heard even a single voice being broadcast over a loud hailer, reasoning with the criminals; urging them to give themselves up peacefully and come out with their hands up. Were they not trying to negotiate the safe release of the hostages at all?

How long had this been going on? How much longer would they have to endure this? George snuck a quick peak at his watch and discovered to his dismay that hours hadn't actually passed by at all. It had been a little over twenty minutes since the robbers first screamed at them all to get down on the ground. Had it really been that recent?

George risked another look around. The big man, whose costume seemed a bit on the tight side, was still stalking around the bank slowly, pointing his scary-looking machine gun at each prostrate person in turn. The posh one, who was clearly in charge, hadn't emerged yet from the rear of the bank. The third one was crouching down by the window at the front, doing something. George couldn't see what he was up to but it didn't look good. It looked like he was assembling something.

Ever so slowly, to avoid making any sound, George shifted his weight; angling his head to try and get a better view. All of a sudden the man jumped to his feet and went marching back through to the outer part of the bank. George froze, gazing hard at the floor in front of him, anxious not to let on that he'd been spying.

He could hear chatter coming from the back of the bank, followed by a long, drawn out creaking sound. Then there was the sound of soft thudding, something being dropped to the floor. And before he knew it, footsteps were coming his way again.

The two robbers emerged into the foyer, the posh-sounding one heading straight for the door while the bigger one marched right back over to the window where he'd been stationed previously. He dropped a large bag, now full and bulging, to the ground and then stood to attention as if awaiting orders.

The next thing he was aware of was being dragged to his feet by the biggest of the robbers and pushed forcefully towards the door where the rest of the victims were gathering. He ended up at the back of the jostling pack, glad not to be caught in the middle of the throng but worried about being exposed and even more worried about being closest to the two bullies with automatic weapons.

The hostages stood looking at each other, quivering and startled, all too terrified to speak; fearful of what might be coming next. Were they all going to be released? Just like that?

Or was something else coming?

The two bigger men stood facing them, their heavy guns glinting in the light, making them seem somehow even more oppressive. George suddenly pictured the scene from the end of The Great Escape, where the captured escapees are huddled together in a field before a machine gunner cuts them all down with one hellish blast.

Then the posh one announced that he wanted them to all to start running. George looked to the front of the crowd and the posh man's hand on the door handle. He looked to the clear sunny day outside. Freedom.

"On your marks... set... wait for it..."

A loud crashing sound behind him. Then frenzied activity as the two jumpsuited goons started throwing things out into the street. The crowd in front of George were buzzing; fear and anxiety mixed with exhilaration, trepidation. They hummed like a car engine ready to roar into action; desperate to move but waiting for the green light.

The air around them suddenly became thick with dense, sweet-smelling fog. George coughed, the smoke invading his throat and making his chest tight and his lungs feel heavy. All around him people began to splutter.

Crying, coughing, shrieking and yelling filled the air, lost in the thick smoke. Then a sudden booming joined the mix: a tinny guitar sound twanging loudly, followed by a rolling drumbeat.

Lord almighty, I feel my temperature rising. Higher, higher, it's burning through to my soul...

The words echoed loudly in a very distinctive voice.

Music. They were playing music now. George listened carefully, analysing the sound. It was... surely not. It was. It was Elvis bloody Presley. Oh, God save us, thought George. Either these robbers really were incredibly dedicated Elvis Presley fans or they were taking the bloody piss. George was pretty sure it was the latter.

The music seemed to grow louder as the smoke thickened. The street outside disappeared, shrouded in the heavy mist. The inside of the bank was disappearing too as small grey canisters pumped out a sickly fog; everything dissolving into a haze. That's when the banging started outside in the street, then inside too. Bullets?

George ducked down, holding his head tightly in his arms, thinking the two men had opened fire on them. But the sound wasn't right somehow. George had never actually heard gunfire, not in real life, but something about this wasn't right. It didn't seem loud enough, nor quite as destructive as George imagined it would be.

Then the posh one threw open the door and screamed, "GO, GO, GO!"

The crowd in front of George scrambled, pouring out of the door, dashing this way and that, disappearing into the smoke. Nobody could see where they were going; they just wanted to get away as fast as they could. They tripped over each other, clattering to the floor, picking themselves up and scrambling forwards.

Suddenly the smoke started flashing red and blue. High-pitched sirens cut through the deafening music and repeated popping and banging. The cavalry had arrived, albeit just too late. Or possibly, from the criminals' point of view, right on time.

George just stood there, totally disoriented, searching all around with his hands and eyes like a blind man separated from his stick. The smoke was so thick that he could no longer see the door, just two bulky figures approaching him at speed. Everyone else had exited the building together with the posh man, and his two accomplices were racing out of the bank after him.

"Here, take this," he suddenly heard someone shouting. He looked up to see who it was and a large, green canvas bag came hurtling towards him through the smoke, hitting him square in the chest. He just about caught it, the heft of the throw nearly knocking him off his feet.

"You carry the bag," the disembodied voice continued. "We'll make sure the coppers aren't waiting outside for us. You follow on behind. Let's go, let's go." The two large figures raced straight past him, disappearing into the thick smoke.

George stood there, the fat bag heavy in his hands. He was pretty sure he knew what it was but he daren't look close enough to confirm it. Knowing he had no choice but to look, he grabbed the cold metal zip, peeling it slowly back until a small hole appeared along the top of the bag. He held it close to his face so he could peer into it. Money. Bundles and cash, stuffed in, filling the bag to the brim. What?

Why had they given the bag to him? Had they mistaken him for somebody else? Or did they actually want him to follow them, carrying the bag for them? Was he still a hostage?

He looked up to where the two men had stood and found the space empty. They were running out of the building, a clearing forming in the smoke. George could just make out a thin streak of light bursting through the smoke. The front door. The two men ran through it and out into the street.

That was it, then. The robbers had escaped the building and he had somehow been left with the cash. But was he supposed to be following them?

This put him in something of a predicament. Naturally his first instinct was to surrender. He would simply hold his hands up, wait for the police to storm in and surrender the money. They'd see what a monumental mistake the robbers had made, pat George on the back for his quick thinking, thank him for his honesty and all have a good old laugh about it later.

Then he remembered what the detective had said to him earlier: "You're up to something. I don't know what it is yet, but I'll find out. And when I do, I'll have you."

But surely he wouldn't think George was involved in this. Nobody could think that George Thring was a bank robber. Could they?

The situation didn't look good. For one, he was the only person left in the bank after it had been robbed and all the hostages had been let go. Second, he was dressed exactly the same as the robbers. Third, he had no good reason for being in that town at all and he could see how it might look suspicious to anyone that didn't know he just wasn't the bank-robbing type. Fourth – the most damning fact of all – he was holding a bag of stolen money.

Finally, and most worryingly, there was an overzealous detective who had tracked him all the way here, convinced he was up to no good, and determined to arrest him for a crime – no matter what that crime was.

George had seen stories like this on the television. Innocent people, through no fault of their own, simply ended up in the wrong place at the wrong time and find themselves accused or, even worse, convicted of a crime they didn't commit. Of course George knew he was innocent but proving it may very well be a different matter entirely. His natural instinct to do the right thing and hand over the cash was quickly diminishing as a new, more urgent instinct took over: get the hell out of there.

If he just had time to think he could work out the best plan and come up with the right solution. But time was something he didn't have. The police were here, the hostages had been released, and the robbers were already making their getaway. He had literally seconds to decide what to do.

Realising he'd already wasted more time than he could afford, George zipped up the bag, grabbed it tightly under one arm, and followed the robbers out of the bank.

CHAPTER 30

JOHN Clefton emerged from the bank first, followed by his brother lumbering slowly behind. The smoke canisters had worked better than any of them had expected. They were almost too good, in fact, as the smoke was so thick he could barely see where he was supposed to be going. The police hadn't managed to find their way through the smoke, so at least they wouldn't have to fight their way out. They just had to run for it. But that was proving trickier than expected.

There was supposed to be an alleyway here, running adjacent to the bank. It was their getaway route. It would lead them directly to the back of the bank and the waiting car. But try as he might, John Clefton just couldn't see it anywhere. He'd been turned around so many times in the fog, tripping over fleeing hostages and scanning the area for potential dangers that he'd got himself quite lost.

He could still hear the music playing from inside the bank and headed towards it. If he could get back to the building, find the wall at the front, then he should be able to make his way along it until he came to the gap. But was it on the right or left hand side of the building?

Suddenly he heard a voice from behind. "Come on, you idiots. This way!"

That posh, grating voice could only belong to one man. But hadn't he left the bank after them? How had he got all the way over there already? God, this fucking smoke.

Grabbing his brother by the sleeve, John Clefton made his way over to where the voice was coming from, pulling the bigger man along behind him. They made it into the alleyway, following the smaller, wiry man down the passage. The smoke thinned out more and more as they picked up pace and ran round to the back of the building

The red Mondeo was waiting for them and the three men piled in. John Clefton climbed in behind the wheel and Major Fairview jumped into the front passenger side.

"What kept you?" asked the Major tersely.

"This bloody smoke," coughed John. "Couldn't see a bloody thing."

"Yes, well that was rather the point."

Steve Clefton landed heavily in the rear passenger seat, slamming the door shut behind him.

"Everybody here?" said the Major. "Jolly good. Shall we go then?"

The engine revved hard as the car pulled away in a screech of tyres, snaking its way out onto the road that cut across the back of the town. Soon the smoke, sirens and urgent policemen were just a distant memory in the rear view mirror.

CHAPTER 31

THE smoke wasn't letting up any. All George could do was to follow in the path of the two large men, the smoke parting in big ripples as they moved through it. He made it out through the front door, stalking cautiously behind, not wanting to get too close. The cold air hit him as he made it onto the street. The flashing lights and screeching sirens spun him around. He turned this way and that, straining to see, lost in the thick atmosphere. He could barely see his hand in front of him and he momentarily lost sight of the two men.

Then he heard someone calling. Sudden movement. A path opened up again in the smoke. He followed along, finding himself in a narrow alleyway he hadn't previously seen that ran adjacent to the bank.

The two men marched on ahead, the smoke thinning out slightly as they progressed further from the bank. George could see them more clearly. They must have ditched their weapons, as they were no longer carrying those big machine guns. But they were still every bit as scary.

Still not sure if the robbers were expecting him to follow on, George slowed down to a creeping walk. They certainly weren't waiting for him. They ran on ahead, not looking back, and as they neared the end of the alleyway they ran around the corner and disappeared.

George looked back over his shoulder to make sure the police weren't following behind. That would really compound the situation. There'd be no pleading innocence if he were caught escaping along with the armed robbers, actually carrying the stolen loot. There wouldn't be a court in the land that would believe he'd been handed the money by mistake. He couldn't go back now, he had to keep moving forwards.

As he neared the end of the alley, he pressed himself up against the wall of the bank, peering round the corner. He could see all three of them now, the two larger men having caught up with the smaller one. They climbed into a big, red saloon car, revved the engine loudly and raced off, tyres screeching and small stones hurtling out from under the wheels.

Well, that was one problem taken care of. Now all George had to do was get the hell out of there without being arrested.

He looked down at the heavy bag gripped tightly in his pale hand, and his head started to swim. The bank wall did a good job of holding him upright as his legs started to quiver and the blackness crept in from the edges of his vision.

"Not now," George, he told himself. "There's no time for this. Pull yourself together. You need to get out of here."

With that he straightened up and took a long deep breath. With his heart still thumping in his chest, he tightened his grip on the bag and snuck out from the alley.

He found himself on a much smaller road, which seemed to trail round the back of town. Tall brown wooden fences lined the street, hiding the rear entrances to the shops, as the road snaked down towards the sea. In the other direction it curved up the hill and out of sight. On the other side of the road lay a dense wood, dark and eerie, with tall trees shooting up out of the cold, muddy ground.

George ran across the road, darting into the woods, immersing himself in the trees. His feet squelched in the soft mud and the tall heels of his white boots made it difficult to walk. He moved as quickly as he could, surging further and further into the trees, wobbling and stumbling on his unsteady footing. He ran and he ran, his heart beating wildly and his breath coming in short, ragged gasps.

Soon he was far enough away that the sirens were a distant blur and he could barely see the buildings through the dense trees. He looked up to the sky, red and blue flashing smoke still pouring up into the ether. There was no sign of anybody following him so he collapsed down onto the trunk of a fallen-down tree, breathing hard and sweating profusely.

The green canvas bag was still tucked tightly under his arm. It wasn't too heavy, but it was fat and bulky where the cash had been hastily shoved in. He dropped it to the floor at his feet and again pulled the zip open, this time all the way. It was the most cash he'd ever seen at one time before. It was a complete mix of notes – 10s, 20s and 50s – some collected into neat little stacks, some shoved in randomly, crumpled and wrinkled. It must have been thousands, tens of thousands, maybe more. George suddenly felt very uneasy again.

Of course it would have been better to drop it in the bank, leave the money and just run. Somehow, though, without even thinking, he'd just taken it with him. He couldn't explain why. It was the panic. He knew he had to get away and he'd just run, not really thinking about the fact that he was, in effect, the one actually stealing the money.

How could this week get any stranger? On Tuesday night all he'd done was leave work, get into his car and attempt to drive home. By Thursday afternoon, he was hiding out in the woods, dressed as Elvis Presley, after having – to all intents and purposes – just robbed a bank. This was not good.

He was hot and clammy. His face was bright red with sweat trickling down his neck. His heart beat fast, banging heavily in his chest, and he felt a little woozy. A sudden whoosh of nausea pulsed through him and he lurched sideways, bending over the tree trunk and throwing up. A few dry heaves later, and he sat back up, feeling a little better.

He looked back down at the money and a strange cold calm washed over him. "Right, that's it George," he said to himself, "that's the panicking done. Now pull yourself together. You need to get out of this mess."

He certainly couldn't stay there. It wouldn't be long before the police realised the robbers were gone, along with the money, and they'd soon have people out checking the surrounding areas, looking for any traces of how they'd escaped.

He needed to get back to the safety of the hotel.

The simple facts were that nobody had seen him leave the bank with the bag. Nobody knew he had it. Everyone had been disoriented when they ran out of the building. Even the robbers had become so confused they'd accidentally given their haul to him and then run off without it.

If he could get back to the hotel he could grab his keys, get in his car and drive away from this whole mess as quickly as possible. But first he had to do something with this bag.

His first thought was just to leave it. He'd be rid of it then and it would be someone else's problem. He could walk up the hill through the trees, find his way back to the hotel and it would seem like he'd just been out for a stroll.

But if the police found the bag, would they be able to do tests on it. Could they check for DNA or fingerprints, or something? They might be able to prove that he'd held the bag; small particles of his sweat or a stray hair caught up in the porous fibres of the material. And then they'd want to know why he'd been holding the bag.

And it wouldn't be long before the robbers realised that they didn't have the money. What if they came back, looking for it? They might realise what had happened and track him down. If he didn't have the bag and they got angry, there was no telling what they might do to him. If he knew where the money was; then at least he'd have some kind of bargaining chip.

But what to do with it? He couldn't very well go marching up the street with it clutched under his arm, hoping the police wouldn't spot him. He thought about burying it, but the ground was damp and muddy. There was no way he could dig a hole deep enough to conceal the bag without a spade at least.

Perhaps he could climb a tree, leave the bag suspended on a sturdy limb? But George had never been very good at climbing trees, and he didn't fancy his chances now.

Time was running out. He couldn't stay there much longer, the police would be scanning the area. What to do, what to do?

He picked up the bag, eyeing it furiously, taking out his frustrations on this stupid inanimate object that could very well see him sent to prison. Most people would have been wondering how they could keep it for themselves, make off with the money and plan an extravagant life abroad. Not him, he just wanted rid of the damn thing. His anger bubbling over, he stood up, lofting the bag high over his head and he threw it down with all his force against the fallen tree trunk.

It landed with a strange, hollow clunking sound. That was odd. George kicked the wood where the bag had impacted. Clunk again. He raced round to the far end of the tree to find that the end of the trunk had rotted away, leaving it hollow.

There was just enough room for the bag, so George stuffed it in, covering the end with twigs, branches, leaves and mud for camouflage. He looked around and only then did he notice the fact that he'd stumbled into a small, circular clearing, with the fallen tree almost smack in the middle. Carefully eyeing up the terrain, he picked out a few landmarks so he could remember his way back there, and plotted a safe course up the hill through the trees.

He took a deep, calming breath and set off, wobbling through the mud on his heeled boots. With a bit of luck, he might just get out of this yet.

CHAPTER 32

THE stolen red car raced away, the streets thankfully clear of cars and pedestrians. They made their way out of the town and into the quiet maze of small roads taking them out into the countryside. The police would never catch them now; as far as they knew, the robbers were all still inside the bank. They wouldn't make a move until the smoke had dissipated enough that they could see clearly, and it would take at least 10 minutes for that to happen.

It would be twice as long again before they'd rounded up all the fleeing, terrified Elvis Presleys, each one a potential suspect. Once they figured out that they only had the hostages in custody and the actual robbers had escaped, there would be no way to tell which direction they'd gone in. To all intents and purposes, they'd have disappeared in a cloud of smoke. Again, the Major smiled to himself at the irony of making it all so comically literal.

The three men laughed and cheered, quickly discarding the uncomfortable wigs, stick-on side sideburns and heavy, dark sunglasses.

"That was bloody brilliant," barked John Clefton, totally elated. "Did you see that bank manager's face? Totally shit himself."

"Yes, he was something of a coward, wasn't he?" replied the Major, relaxing and joining in the fun.

"Yeah, and did you see that fucker when I hit him with my gun?" chuckled Steve from the backseat. "He definitely didn't see that coming."

"Yes, credit where credit's due," said the Major, "you both did very well. A perfect robbery, carried out perfectly. And not a bad bit of planning, if I do say so myself."

"How much d'you reckon we got away with?" said Steve Clefton, a giddy childish exuberance in his voice.

"Well, I don't know," replied the Major. "What do you think John, at least two hundred? Not bad for an afternoon's work, eh chaps? Here, throw me the bag, let me see all that lovely money."

"What d'ya mean, throw you the bag?" returned Steve, confused.

"The bag. Pass it forwards, so I can see how much we got away with."

"How can I give you the bag? You've got the bag."

"Oh, don't be facetious, man. Pass me the bloody bag."

"I ain't got the bag. You've got it. You carried it out of the bank."

"Well, how could I have the bag? I left the bank before you did. It was your job to carry the bag," the Major barked, becoming more and more agitated with each second.

"But I threw it to you," said Steve Clefton.

"No you didn't."

"Yes, I did. I threw it to you so you could carry it, in case me and John had to take out any coppers on the way out of the bank. You were gonna follow on behind us."

"What? I left the bank before you did, you fucking numbskull. How could you throw me the bag if I'd already left the bank?"

"Well, I threw it to *someone*," Steve said resolutely, as if that would help his case.

"So, let me get this straight," the Major screeched, fury flashing in his eyes, "no-one has the bag. Nobody in this car has the fucking bag, with all the fucking money in it. We've just pulled off the perfect bank job, except for one small detail: we forgot to the take the fucking money with us?"

"Erm..." stuttered Steve Clefton.

"Two jobs I gave you. Two fucking jobs. Look scary and carry the fucking bag. Two simple jobs, and you managed to fuck that up?" His received pronunciation slipped as his anger rose, a more earthy tone slipping into his voice.

The car continued to hurtle and weave its way around the tight bends of the country road, the driver still in full getaway mode.

"Might I make a small suggestion?" said the Major, turning to John. "Do you want to stop the fucking car? Only, I don't know about you two dickheads, but I can't help but feel we're missing the point slightly."

John Clefton slowed the car, pulling into a small verge at the side of the road. All three men sat silently for a moment, facing forwards, not wanting to look at each other.

The Major sighed heavily, calming himself. "Okay," he said, breaking the silence, slicing through the tension. "Well, we're just going to have to go back."

"No way," said John. "It's too risky."

"Risky or not, we have no choice," replied the Major. "I'm not leaving with nothing. All that work, all that planning... I'm not leaving with nothing."

"But the police?" countered John. "We'll be nabbed within minutes."

"Well, not necessarily," said the Major. "It's a risk, I grant you. But no-one can identify us, can they? That was the point: we all looked the same and we looked exactly like everyone else in there. No-one in the bank can tell it was us."

"That's one big fucking risk, though."

"Yes, but a necessary one. Thanks to this big lug, someone has our money. And I'm willing to bet that they still have it. Who's going to hand over all that cash to the police? No, if they've managed to get it out of the bank, they've still got it. All we have to do is head back into town, keep a low profile, and keep our eyes open for anyone with a guilty enough conscience."

"It could be anyone, though," said John.

"Not really," offered Steve, his voice low and slightly hesitant.

The Major looked at him with disgust, like a disappointed parent whose drunken teenager had just thrown up in their car.

"Why not?" asked John.

"Because I thought it was him, didn't I?" he said, pointing at the Major.

"Yeah, but it wasn't," replied his brother, stating the obvious.

"No, but it looked like him, didn't it? Same height, same build. He had the same clothes on. Blue, like his are."

The Major's eyes lit up. "Well, there you go," he said, suddenly less angry, "we've already got a tip. We know whom to look for... kind of. We just need to be discreet, if you two morons can manage that. Keep your mouths shut, let me do all the talking and we'll find the man who has our money."

The major smiled, a wicked glint sparkling in his eyes. "And then you two can very politely convince him to give it back."

"Cheeky bastard," said Steve Clefton. "I'll bloody kill him."

"Okay," said the Major, sliding the gold sunglasses back onto his face. "Looks like we'll have to keep these awful clothes on for a while. Turn the car around and get us back to town."

CHAPTER 33

THE smoke had all but vanished. Just the remnants of haze lingered in the air outside the bank. Keane could barely believe what he'd just witnessed. Out of nowhere the street had filled with horrible noxious fumes and they'd all been sent sprawling, fearful that it was some kind of poisonous gas attack. It had taken literally seconds before the whole street was a blank wall of sickly white and blue smoke.

Then the music had started. Elvis bloody Presley – no doubt someone's idea of a sick joke – before they randomly started opening fire. Or at least that's what it had sounded like. For one terrifying second, as people ran from the building, tripping and stumbling, crashing into each other and screaming as they tumbled to the floor, Keane thought he was witnessing some horrific bloodbath.

Firecrackers. It had been no more than cheap market-stall firecrackers, banging and spluttering; the mere illusion of gunfire. But it had been enough to confuse everybody and have them leaping for cover.

The fat cop was the first to drop, diving down behind the car. He lay there, clutching his head between his elbows, knees tucked up to his chest like a baby. His young apprentice had just stood there, dumbfounded, staring blankly at the ensuing carnage. Keane had had to grab his arm and forcibly pulled him down to the ground as he himself dived for cover. If those had been real bullets, a stray shot would have rattled right through him before his slow brain had time to register it.

Keane couldn't believe the audacity of it. Create this impenetrable confusion, let the hostages out and then escape out the back while nobody was looking. A simple collection of cheap tricks and standard misdirection was all it had taken to baffle the local police forces. And he shamefully had to admit that he'd been just as bamboozled.

It had all been done with exacting precision, escaping just as reinforcements arrived, adding even more chaos and mayhem to the scene.

"Oh, you're a clever one, George Thring," Keane muttered to himself under his breath.

It had taken a good ten minutes for the smoke to dissipate sufficiently before the armed response unit felt confident enough to make a move on the building. When they finally made it through the front door, all they found were a collection of startled but unharmed bank workers. One young girl was tied to a chair, two were handcuffed to a filing cabinet and the manager was on his knees, coughing and wheezing and in floods of tears.

An American man, dressed up like a soldier, with a cracked and bloodied face, was just coming round from unconsciousness. And an old lady, dressed in an obscenely bright pink outfit was sprawled on the floor, desperately trying to right herself like a tortoise trapped on its back.

By the time they'd realised the robbers had made a clean getaway with the money, there was little chance they'd be able to track them easily. A series of roadblocks were in the process of being set up with instructions issued to surrounding police forces to be on the lookout. Of course, they couldn't really relay exactly what to look out for, as they didn't know themselves. They had no idea of the make, model or colour of the getaway car or even whether they'd escaped in a car at all.

As far as a description of the robbers themselves, there was very little to go on there either. All of the hostages had eventually been rounded up and taken back to the small police station for questioning. When asked to describe the robbers, the only thing that they could all say for certain was that they had been dressed as Elvis Presley.

Well, how was that supposed to help? Aside from himself, the other police officers and the bank staff, everybody else on the scene – in the whole town – was dressed as Elvis bloody Presley. It could have been any of them. Or none of them.

Everybody had to be treated as both suspect and victim, even those whose identities could be verified by the local plod as being highly unlikely to be involved. Everybody could be lying, or telling the truth, or both. There was no way to tell before the forensics teams got in there to search for clues, and everyone that had been caught fleeing the bank had been thoroughly interrogated. It was a logistical nightmare that was sure to slow the investigation down by hours, if not days.

Keane could feel the trail going icy cold as he stood there. The robbers would be miles away by now, holed-up somewhere quiet, counting the proceeds of the job and waiting for the heat to die down. The police would make a big show of things, send out appeals on the local telly and radio, but Keane could see this as what it was: a pointless bloody chicken chase.

Very clever indeed. But not clever enough. Thring had let his guard down. He'd obviously forgotten that he'd been tracked up here. Either that or he'd been incredibly bold and thought he could pull off a job like this even with the police already suspicious of his story. If Keane had doubted for a second that Thring was up to no good, he was absolutely convinced of it now.

Keane knew exactly what had transpired here. And he knew who the guilty party was. Most importantly, there was no way he was going to share this golden nugget of information with the local police. This was his lead, his suspect, and he wasn't going to share the arrest with anyone. Keane was going to take this villain down on his own, and capture the rest of his gang, whoever they were.

Cracking an armed robbery case and bringing in the suspect on his first day in the job – that would do very nicely, indeed. That would really prove his mettle; mark him out as what he already knew he was and what everybody else would soon come to realise. He was Michael Keane: first-rate detective; master bad-guy catcher; force to be reckoned with. Criminals beware; colleagues take note; and ladies, slip your knickers off in preparation.

And he'd feared his first day was going to consist of nothing more than chasing after a boring missing person.

CHAPTER 34

THE heavy black door swung hard in the wind, crashing shut as George raced into the hotel and clattered up the stairs. His heart was racing, sweat pouring down his face. He sprang into the small room, closed the door quickly behind him and leaned back against it, breathing hard.

His keys. Where were his car keys? He looked all around the room but couldn't see them. He needed his keys. He had to get to his car; get out of here; run away as far as he could before the police caught up with him.

He dashed around the small room, scanning the bed, the chest of drawers, the top of the TV. No sign of them. If he didn't get out of here soon, it would be too late. Every inch of him screamed to get the hell out of there. Where were his damned keys?

Then he had a sudden thought: Alice. What about Alice?

If he ran away now, he might never see her again. But if he stayed, he'd probably end up in prison, or murdered. Or worse.

But perhaps he shouldn't run. After all, he hadn't actually robbed the bank. That was the most important fact. He was innocent. And if he ran away now he'd just be making himself look guilty. Surely the best thing to do would be to stay and face the truth.

Then there was that detective. He'd seemed so convinced that George had been up to something. And he was more than capable of putting two and two together and coming up with six hundred and ninety-four. There'd be no convincing him that George had just been an innocent bystander. He really seemed to have it in for George and that couldn't be good.

Not to mention the actual robbers. They'd be less than pleased to find out they'd made their escape without actually taking the stolen money with them. They hadn't seemed like a particularly nice group when George had first encountered them, standing there armed with machine guns. If they figured out that George was in possession of their stolen loot, what might they do to him?

George really didn't want to stick around and find out. But he didn't want to leave Alice and risk losing her for good.

A sharp knock rapped on the door. George froze.

This was it. The police had found him. They must have seen him running, or caught him on camera, and they'd tracked him here.

What to do? What to do? He should run, make a break for it. The police would never believe he hadn't been involved in the robbery. His story was far too ludicrous. Even he could see that. "The robbers just gave me the money and ran off, honest guv." They'd laugh him straight into a jail cell.

George was going to spend the next 10 years in prison for a crime he didn't commit. He'd end up sharing a cell with some great hulking brute called Bubba, who'd take a shine to him and make him do all sorts of unenviable things that he couldn't even bring himself to imagine. Unless he could figure out a way to get out of there.

He'd never make it out through the door with the police in the way. And the hallway was far too narrow. They'd be blocking the whole exit.

He looked over to the window. It was big enough for him to fit through, but the drop was too great. He could try jumping, but chances were that he'd break both ankles on landing. And then there would be no running anywhere. George's heart thumped painfully in his chest.

The door rattled again as another round of knocks cracked against the wood. Time was running out. Whatever George was going to do, he had to do it now. He clambered onto the bed, and opened the window.

"George," said a voice from outside the door. A woman's voice.

"George, are you okay?" It was Alice. It wasn't the police after all.

"George, can you let me in please, I'm worried."

George leapt down off the bed and opened the door. Alice, looking shocked and worried, stood before him. He grabbed her arm, pulled her into the room and slammed the door behind her.

"George, what's going on? What's happening?"

"Erm… well…" George could barely speak.

"There are alarms going off in town, police cars and sirens everywhere. Someone said the bank had been robbed."

"Erm… well…"

"I saw you running up the stairs. Are you all right? I thought you might have been caught up in it. I thought you might be hurt."

"Erm… well…" He still couldn't get a sentence out, didn't know what to say or where to start.

"For God's sake, George," said Alice, frustration tinting her voice, "what the hell is going on?"

George took a deep breath and managed to calm himself enough to recount the full story. He told her how he'd been waiting in the bank, and was suddenly set upon by armed robbers. How he'd found himself in possession of the money. How he'd ended up out on the street, confused and panicking, and then just ran, not knowing what else to do.

Alice stood there wide-eyed. "So they just gave you the money?"

"Yes. It was dark and smoky. They must have thought I was one of them and handed me the bag. I couldn't see where I was so I just followed them out. They drove off and I was left there."

"Oh my God! And where were the police?"

"I don't know; I didn't hang around to find out. I was outside the bank, dressed exactly the same as all the robbers, carrying the stolen money. I just panicked. I ran away."

"So where's the money now?"

"I hid it. I didn't know what else to do. Then I came back here."

Alice sat down on the bed. "I can't believe it," she said. "Were you scared?"

"I suppose so. I'm not sure. It all happened so quickly."

"Did anybody see you leaving?"

"I don't think so. It was so smoky I could barely see where I was going myself, until I got round to the back of the bank. Then I just ran into the woods. I tracked my way back up the hill through the trees. I managed to sneak back in whilst nobody was looking."

"Okay," said Alice, drumming her fingers against her chin, her eyes busy as she thought. "Did anyone see you leave the hotel?"

"Well, one man, but it was very quick and I was dressed like this, so he might not recognise me."

"And would anybody have recognised you in the bank?"

"No, I don't think so. Everybody was dressed the same, we all looked alike."

"Okay, so as far as anyone is concerned, you haven't left your room all day. If you haven't left your room, you can't have been involved in a robbery."

Alice stood up, her gaze fixed on the door as a plan formulated in her head. "I can say that we spent the night together. I left you sleeping and went to work. I have to say that, people saw me serving in the breakfast room. But I can say that I popped back a few times to see you. At least that's a partial alibi."

"Are you sure? I thought you didn't want your parents to know that you stayed here last night."

"Bigger picture, George. I can take care of Mum and Dad, if it means helping you stay out of jail."

"Yes, sorry. Of course. Thank you. Do you think it will work?"

"I don't know, but it's the best plan I can come up with at the moment. First of all, though, we'll have to do something about that." She pointed to George's boots. They were caked with mud where he'd tracked his way through the sodden woods. The mud had spread half way up his legs, soiling the bell-bottoms of his Elvis suit.

"We can't really claim that you've spent all morning indoors if your clothes are covered in mud. Take those off, and I'll throw them in the washing machine."

"Yes, of course," said George. He quickly peeled off his jumpsuit, and handed it along with the boots to Alice.

"Right, you stay here and I'll take care of these. Don't go anywhere until I get back."

"No problem."

Alice was just about to leave the room, when George stopped her. "There is one other small thing that I should probably mention. Erm... a detective came to see me this morning."

"A detective," said Alice. "You didn't think to mention this before? What did he want?"

"Well, he followed me up here from home. He told me I was a missing person, on account of the fact that I just upped and left without telling anyone, and he was in charge of tracking me down."

"Okay," said Alice. "That doesn't sound too bad."

"Well, no. It's just that he… well, he seemed to think that something was up. More to the point, that I was up to something. He kept saying it was really suspicious that I just disappeared, without telling anybody. And that it wasn't the actions of a sane or innocent man. He said he thought… no, he *knew* that I was guilty of something, and that as soon as he figured out what it was, he was going to get me."

"Get you?"

"Get me."

"God, George, you're not making this easy, are you?"

"Erm… do you think that's bad then? Do you think he might think I had something to do with the robbery?"

"A detective tracks you down and tells you he's suspicious that you're up to something. And then a couple of hours later the bank gets robbed. I'd say he might just see it as a possibility."

"Yeah. That's probably quite bad then."

"Yes, George. I think that is probably quite bad."

Alice looked down at the armful of muddy clothes in her hands. "One thing at a time, though, eh? You stay here. I'll go and take care of these. And when I come back we'll think it all through properly."

"Thank you Alice."

Alice reached for the door, but this time stopped herself. She turned to George and with a slight glint of unease in her eyes, said, "I'm sorry George, but I have to ask. You didn't have anything to do with the robbery, did you?"

"No Alice, I promise. I'm not a criminal, it really did happen exactly the way I said."

"Okay, George. I'm sorry, but you understand I had to ask. Now, you wait here till I come back."

Alice opened the door and had stepped halfway out when George stopped her a second time.

"Yes, George."

"Erm… I don't suppose you could rustle me up a sandwich or something? It's just that… well, the whole reason I went out in the first place was to get some lunch. And I'm still really hungry."

Alice slowly raised a disconcerted eyebrow. "I'll see what I can do," she said, and left the room.

CHAPTER 35

GEORGE collapsed back onto the bed, beads of sweat still tingling on his scarlet neck, dressed only in his shabby boxer shorts. He felt much calmer, his breathing slower and more relaxed, and his heart beating just slightly faster than normal. He sighed one long, heavy sigh and stared again at the dirty brown mark on the ceiling.

It was all going to be all right. Alice was going to help him. All he had to do was stay here, let the panic die down, and it would all go away. He'd done nothing wrong. The police had no real reason to suspect him and if he just stayed cool things would be fine.

George closed his eyes and breathed deeply, a warm wave of calm washing over him.

A loud knocking shook the door again. Alice must have forgotten something. George sprang up quickly and pulled the door open.

Only it wasn't Alice. It was a rather angry-looking, red-faced detective.

"Mr Thring," said Detective Constable Keane. "I'm surprised to see you here. I thought you'd be miles away by now."

George's calm evaporated instantly, fizzing into the air like a pocket of steam.

George looked panicked. He knew he looked panicked. He could feel it etched on his face: the muscles tense, skin tight, his eyes wide. He tried to not look panicked, to keep his cool, inject an air of nonchalance into his expression, but he knew it wasn't working. And the more he tried not to, the more panicked he looked.

"Erm… detective… er, nice to see you again. Well, no… not nice, exactly… not that it's not nice, of course…" He couldn't speak now, didn't know what to say. Every red-hot syllable that fell from his lips felt like an admission of guilt. He could feel himself crumbling, dissolving into a puddle on the floor.

"I've got a few more questions for you, Mr Thring," said Keane pushing past him into the room, leaving the door wide open.

Standing there in just his pants, George felt a sudden urge to slam it shut quickly, in case anybody walked past and saw him. But the alternative of being trapped in a room with this angry policeman seemed far more terrifying so he left it open.

He turned to face Keane. "What can I do for you?" he asked, as calmly as he could manage.

"I wonder, Mr Thring," said Keane, "whether you've noticed all the commotion going on down at the bottom of the hill?"

"Commotion?" replied George, trying to sound as vague and unaware as he could. "Erm… well, I heard some sirens, yes. Has something happened?"

"Don't give me that, Thring?" barked Keane. "You know full well the bank's just been robbed."

"Robbed?" said George, trying his hardest to sound bewildered.

"You know it's been robbed, Thring, because you just bloody robbed it, didn't you?"

"What? I have no idea what…"

"Come off it, Thring, it's written all over your face. The thing I don't get is how you thought you were gonna get away with it. In fact, more to the point, what the hell are you still doing here?"

Keane was, in fact, as surprised to see George as George had been to see him. When he'd marched up the road and barged into the hotel, he'd expected to find George's room empty and abandoned. He'd figured the guy would have fled the scene along with his accomplices and made off in a series of getaway cars. Keane was simply following up his own secret lead, intent on turning over the hideaway of the key suspect that only he knew about. He was here to strip the room clean; scour it for clues; find some tangible piece of evidence linking the man to the robbery.

The last thing he expected was to find the guy still there. Lounging about in his pants, for God's sake, as if nothing had happened. Arrogant bastard. To not only go ahead with the robbery, knowing a detective had tracked him down and figured out what he was up to, but to hang around afterwards goading him; practically fucking mocking him! Oh, he was going to love taking this fucker down.

"Robbery?" said George. "What are you talking about? I haven't even left my room since you were last here."

Keane's eyes scanned the room, searching for a clue, anything that would betray George's story. Nothing obvious stood out. No major inconsistencies. Except…

"Where's your disguise, George?"

"Disguise?"

"That ridiculous Elvis suit you had. The one you were using to conceal your identity?"

"Conceal my…"

"What did you do? Rob the bank, dispose of the evidence, then head back up here hoping to blend back into the crowd?"

"No, of course not. I had nothing to do with any robbery and I've been nowhere near the bank today," he lied, managing to draw a bit of courage up from within himself. "I didn't even know there had been a robbery until you told me."

Keane sneered, squinting his eyes, staring hard at George's pink, blushing face.

"My clothes, if you really need to know, are being washed," continued George. "I met a girl last night, and we spent the night together. She works here at the hotel. She offered to wash them for me while I waited up here."

"Oh, it gets better," laughed Keane. "Something of a Lothario as well now, are we? As well as a bank robber."

"I am not a bank…"

"Where's the getaway car?" Keane said, cutting him off.

"What getaway car?"

"Where are the other two? Your accomplices? The victims inside the bank said there were two others."

The questions were coming thick and fast, Keane bombarding him with words, trying to force him off-kilter.

"I don't know what you're…"

"Clever plan, George. I have to give you that. Confuse the police; have them looking one way; make them think they're under attack. Get them really rattled. Then you sneak out the back way just as the reinforcements show up."

"Detective, I really don't know what you're…"

"Don't give me that, George," shouted Keane with a sudden burst of rage, slamming his hand angrily down onto the chest of drawers. He'd seen that on countless detective shows, and it always seemed to really unsettle the suspect. "Do you think I'm stupid?"

"No, of course not," replied George, trying his best to conceal the fact that he really thought quite the opposite.

"As I was saying, it was a clever plan," he said, suddenly sounding very calm again. "And you might just have got away with fooling these local yokel coppers. But you forgot about one thing, didn't you?"

"Oh?"

"Me. You didn't count on me tracking you down here, figuring out what you were up to. Not many coppers would have found you. They'd have written you off as a simple missing person, filed a report and got back to work. But I knew there was something not right about you, George. I could smell it."

"Smell?"

"Your little disappearing act didn't fool me one bit. It was obvious what was really going on. That's why I followed you out here George. And I have to say you've got balls, too. Either that or you're just incredibly arrogant. Going ahead with the robbery, even though you knew I was onto you?

"Right… again, I really think you've got the wrong end of the stick, here," said George.

Just then Alice appeared in the open doorway, holding a sandwich and a glass of milk. "Is everything alright, George?"

Alice. Thank God for Alice.

"Erm… Alice… yes… this is Detective… er… Keane. The policeman I was telling you about. Apparently there's been a robbery at the bank. He seems to think I might have been involved for some reason."

"Robbery? Involved?" said Alice, managing to stay just the right side of overacting. She placed the food and drink on the chest of drawers, using the distraction to take a quick breath and compose herself. "Well, that's crazy."

"Is it?" barked Keane, spinning around and addressing Alice. "And who are you, exactly?"

"I'm Alice," she said, defensively. "I work here at the hotel."

"And how do you know Mr Thring?"

"He's my boyfriend."

Boyfriend. The word shot across the room like a cartoon arrow, exploding as it hit George and showering him with an instant warmth. He was her boyfriend. His skin tingled as he thought it. And that must mean that she was his girlfriend. He couldn't help but break out into an instant beaming smile that covered half of his face.

Alice shot him a look as if to say: "Focus, George. One thing at a time!" He dropped his eyes to the floor, trying to look serious and concentrate on the gravity of the situation. But he couldn't help being pleased at the revelation that he was now somebody's boyfriend. He instantly pledged to himself that, if he managed to stay out of prison, he was going to be the best boyfriend ever. And if he did go to prison he'd write at least one letter every day.

"And how long have you known Mr Thring?"

"We met a couple of days ago. We went out on a date last night, we spent the night together, and I can categorically tell you that George hasn't left this room all day. Well, other than to have a shower..." She could feel herself stumbling, conscious of every single word. "Which means he couldn't possibly have been involved in a bank robbery."

"You can categorically tell me that he hasn't left the room all day? How?"

"I've been here with him." She could feel that she said it too fast, too assuredly.

"Oh, really?" replied Keane. "You weren't here earlier, when I first spoke with Mr Thring. And you weren't here just now, either."

Damn, she was making a mess of it. "Well no, not the whole time," she backtracked. "I had to go and serve in the kitchen. But I've been back up every 15 or 20 minutes to see him. I think I would have noticed if he'd nipped out quickly to rob a bank." Did that sound convincing? She couldn't tell.

"How well do you know Mr Thring?" continued Keane. "You said you only met him a few days ago."

"That's right. But I think I know him well enough."

"Did he tell you why he was here in town?"

"Yes. He's here for a short break, to get away from things."

"And did he tell you that he just upped and left, without a word to anyone. Didn't even pack a bag. Just vanished after work one night. Didn't tell anybody where he was going."

"So what?" replied Alice.

"And that didn't seem a little odd to you? It seemed very suspicious to me. Almost as if he didn't want anyone to know where he was going."

"People go away all the time. He's a grown man, if he didn't feel the need to tell people…"

"Sorry, but I'm not buying it. People don't just disappear. Not unless they don't want people to know where they've gone. And in my experience, that's generally because they don't want people to know what they're doing. Which all adds up to…"

"I'm sorry," interrupted Alice, "but where are you going with all this?"

George stood quietly, happy to let Alice take over.

"Quite simple, Miss," replied Keane, in a well-practiced tone of condescension. "Your boyfriend here skips town unexpectedly, and without explanation. I smell a rat, so I track him down here to the middle of nowhere. I find him hiding out, dressed in disguise, with no reasonable explanation as to why he's here or what he's doing. And then, less than an hour later, the bank down the road is robbed. It doesn't take a genius to realise that Mr Thring is looking pretty guilty."

"Oh come on, that's all circumstantial," she snapped. Was that the right word? She thought it was. They used it in courtroom dramas all the time on telly. It certainly sounded quite impressive, anyway.

"Besides," she continued, "if you're going to interrogate George, shouldn't you be doing it in a police station, with a tape recorder, and witnesses?"

The policeman's eyes flickered. She'd caught him out and they both knew it.

"And another thing," she pronounced, landing the final blow, "are you even allowed to question George? Shouldn't the local police be here to do that? Do they even know you're here?"

"This isn't an interrogation," Keane laughed, in defence, "just a friendly little chat. Isn't that right, George?"

"Well, I wouldn't call it friendly, exactly, I'd…"

Keane cut in again. "Anyway, I have work to do, leads to follow up. Don't go too far, George, I'll be back for another conversation before long. And don't forget, I've got my eye on you."

Keane struck Alice a menacing glare, vexed at having to admit defeat.

"Word of advice, Miss," he said. "Think carefully about who you choose to associate with. People aren't always what they seem."

He reached into his pocket and pulled out a small white business card. He flashed it in front of her face before slapping it forcefully down onto the top of the television. "Here's my mobile number. Give me a call when you've come to your senses."

With that he swept past her and out of the room, slamming the door shut behind him.

George slumped back down on the bed and sat there looking up at Alice. "So, what do we do now?" he said.

"I don't know George," she replied, crossing the room and sitting down next to him. "I don't know."

They both simply sat there, in silent contemplation.

"Oh," said George suddenly, pointing at the sandwich on top of the chest of drawers. "Is that for me?"

CHAPTER 36

JOHN Clefton pulled up outside the hotel. The Mondeo's engine hummed in the relative quiet as it sat stationary in the street. At the bottom of the hill an ominous thin fog still lingered, working its way slowly into the ether. Red and blue lights flashed, the sirens having been silenced, and people jostled and rushed like scuttling insects.

"Right," said Major Fairview, "you two idiots go and get rid of this car. The place is already swarming with police and the last thing we need is to be caught in possession of a stolen vehicle. Take it somewhere quiet and dump it. Clean it for prints and... acquire something else. Something fast, in case we need to run."

"The car's fine," replied John Clefton. "It has clean plates, no-one'll know it's nicked."

"Yes, but I think it prudent not taking any chances. Somebody might have seen it leaving town or parked near the bank. No point in taking unnecessary risks."

"Unnecessary risks? Like stealing another car?" snorted John.

"No, that's a *necessary* risk. Just make sure you don't get caught. And for God's sake be discreet."

"Fine, we'll sort another motor. And what are you gonna do?" he added with a suspicious tone.

"Don't worry about that, just get the car sorted and meet me back here. I'll sort out the rooms. And have a look round to see if I can spot the swine with our money. Now get out of here before the police see you."

The Major climbed out of the car and watched it disappear down the road before reaching into his pocket and retrieving his mobile phone.

"What the hell are you calling me for?" snapped the voice on the other end.

"Just a quick progress report," replied the Major with an over-exaggerated chirpiness. "Thought I'd let you know how we're getting along."

"The only progress that you should be reporting is that the job went off without a hitch, and that you're on the way to the rendezvous. In fact, you shouldn't be calling me at all, you should already be at the handover, waiting for me."

"Yes..." said the Major. "Well, I'm afraid there's been a tiny hitch..."

"Hitch? What fucking hitch?"

"Nothing to worry about, exactly. Nobody's been arrested, or anything like that."

"What happened? Did those idiots do something? They've not got carried away and plugged someone, have they?"

"No, no, nothing like that," chirruped the Major with an unconvincing false laugh. "We've just had a bit of a problem with the... proceeds."

"Proceeds?" grumbled the voice.

"Yes, we've er... we've temporarily mislaid the money."

"You fucking what?"

"Yes, it's the darndest thing, really. We've lost the money."

"Lost the money? How did you lose the..."

"But it's okay," interrupted the Major, "because we know where it is. Or at least we think we do."

"Oh, well that's all right then. Are you fucking joking?"

"Sadly no," said the Major, releasing a crestfallen sigh. "But don't worry. We'll get it back. We're just slightly delayed for the time being. We'll have to stick around in town for a while. I've sent the brothers off on an errand while I formulate a new plan. I'll be in touch when we're ready to move again."

The voice on the other end of the line remained silent for a few moments, before returning with a much calmer timbre. "Charlie," it said, soft and quiet, "find that money and bring it to me. Or if you don't..."

"Yes, yes," cut in the Major, "I know the drill. You'll do unspeakably violent things to me."

"That's only the start, Charlie. And believe me, you don't wanna know what'll be coming next. Get me my money!" The phone went dead.

Major Fairview rolled his eyes at the phone and slipped it back into his pocket. He went to straighten his tie before realising he was still in full Elvis costume and sighed. He took a pensive gaze about him, exhaled heavily and strode down the path to the hotel.

"Ah, my good woman," he said to the old lady standing behind the counter as the door shut sharply behind him. "You're looking as ravishing as ever."

She giggled like a girl, instantly won over by the flattery. "Major," she said. "I thought you'd checked out and left us already. That's what it says in the book."

"Ah yes, well I did check out earlier and I was due to be on my way. However, my plans have been delayed slightly, so my associates and I thought we might stay on in your charming little town for an extra few days."

"You sticking around to watch all the Elvis impersonators? There are still a few good shows going on for the rest of the week, you know."

"Quite!" replied the Major. "My friends and I are terribly big Elvis fans and as our plans have changed we thought how jolly it might be to hang around and take in a couple of the shows. Do you think it might be possible to accommodate us? You haven't let out our rooms already, have you?"

"Well, normally you'd be out of luck. This is our busiest week of the year, you know? But I think I can help," she said, scouring the pages of the guestbook in front of her. "We've had a few people check out after that nasty bit of business earlier, you see."

"Nasty business?" said the Major.

"Yes, some dreadful brutes have robbed the bank. Did you not know? Seems to have scared a few people away... So if I just jiggle a few things about here and there... Yes, I can give you back the same two rooms."

"Marvellous! Well, it'll take more than a few brutes to scare me off," he chuckled.

The old lady plucked two keys from the board behind her and placed them in the Major's hand.

"My dear lady, thank you ever so much," he said. "Now, if you'll excuse me, I think I might take a quick stroll into town. There's one Elvis in particular that I'm very keen to see."

******

John and Steve Clefton drove 20 minutes to the nearest town and abandoned the Mondeo in the car park of a small supermarket. It would be a few days before anybody noticed it parked there.

They waited until an elderly man pulled up in a relatively new-looking silver Vauxhall Astra. It wasn't the fastest of cars but it was quick and manoeuvrable and would blend fairly well into the background. The blue disabled badge in the windscreen was also a bonus; it would make them less conspicuous and meant they could park anywhere.

They watched as the man limped his way slowly to the entrance of the shop. He wouldn't be back too quickly, which gave them time.

Steve Clefton hadn't picked up many useful skills in prison, or in fact at any point in his life, but breaking into cars was something he could do better than anyone else he knew. He was an idiot savant of grand theft auto. Armed with just a thin sliver of metal and a screwdriver, it took him less than 30 seconds to gain entry to the vehicle, disable the alarm and turn the engine over.

John Clefton quickly unscrewed the license plates from their previous stolen vehicle, swapped them onto the Astra, and the men pulled away in their new car, all in under three minutes.

It wasn't the most elegant solution to the problem. It wouldn't be too long before the man noticed his car was missing. And once he'd reported it stolen it would go onto the police hot list within just a few hours. Swapping the plates would give them a bit of a head start, but it was still risky. However, chances were that a pensioner's missing car wouldn't be too high on the local police force's list of things to track down. Especially as they were currently trying to catch a group of bank robbers.

"I don't like any of this, you know?" said John Clefton. "There was nothing wrong with that car. We put legit plates on it, nobody saw it; there's no way the cops would be onto it."

"No," replied Steve, truffling about in the glove compartment and delightedly retrieving a bag of Werther's Originals. "But the Major is right. There's no point taking chances."

"No, I don't like it. I don't like him. I knew there was something screwy about this job. I just knew something was gonna go wrong. You gonna give me one of them sweets, or what?"

"Don't worry, the Major will know what to do. All we gotta do is find that fucker with our money, take it back and leg it."

"You put too much faith in that la-di-dah fake Major, you know. As far as you know, there probably is no fucker with the money. It's just Major..." He stopped dead, his face dropping with the sudden realisation. "That BASTARD!"

"What?" replied Steve.

"Fucker! He's the fucker!" shouted John, punching the steering wheel and nearly veering off the road.

"What?"

"The Major! There is no other man. You must have given the bag to the Major. Don't you get it?"

"Get what, John?" Steve replied, totally flummoxed.

"There was nothing wrong with that car. He just wanted us out of the way. I can't believe you've been so stupid!"

"*Me* stupid? What are you on about?"

"He's got the money. The Major's got the money!"

"No, he can't have. I accidentally handed it to someone else."

"He made the whole thing up, you idiot. You *did* hand him the bag at the bank. He's stashed it somewhere then pretended you never gave it to him."

"Well if he's got the money, why did he send us off to get a new car?"

"Because he wanted us out the way, of course! He's got the money and he's sent us off on a wild goose chase so he can go running in the other direction with all the cash."

"No! Really? Do you think so?"

"Of course that's what he's done. That sneaky fucker. I knew he was gonna try and take all the money for himself."

"But that's what we were gonna do," said Steve.

"Exactly."

"So what do we do now, John?"

"He can't have got too far. Not yet. He would have thought we'd take longer getting a new car and he'll have to go back to wherever he's stashed the money. With a bit of luck we might just be able to catch up with him."

"Fucker!" said Steve Clefton.

"Fucker!" said John Clefton, forcing his foot down hard on the accelerator and speeding off around the bend.

CHAPTER 37

GEORGE sat on the edge of the bed, staring blankly at the wall in front of him. He'd been looking at the same patch of discoloured wallpaper for roughly three hours, since Alice had been called back downstairs to work in the kitchen. The odd passing car growled past the front of the building, which groaned and creaked like an old man's knees. Otherwise, the room was silent. And George was left alone with his thoughts, tumbling and clanking around inside his head.

His mind raced with worry and his imagination ran wild. He pictured himself in an interrogation room, trying to explain to an angry policeman how it had all been a terrible misunderstanding. He had visions of himself in court; a grimacing judge handing down a sentence and being led away along a dank, dark corridor.

The temperature had dropped in the room. The sun was falling in the sky, replaced by a thick, murky dusk as early evening set in. A cool breeze trickled in through a gap in the window frame, tickling his bare skin. The walls weren't exactly closing in but it was a very small room, which seemed to be growing smaller with every passing minute. It was too small to get up and walk around, so he had to just sit there, waiting and thinking. He felt like he was trapped in the very prison cell he was so desperate to avoid.

He couldn't stay in that room any longer. He had to get out.

He picked up the freshly-laundered, pale blue jumpsuit that Alice had delivered back to him and stared at it. He'd resisted putting back on until now. He hadn't wanted to wear it, partly as it seemed like something of a bad omen considering what had happened the last time he'd worn it. And partly because the damn thing was so difficult to get into. But he was cold, and he had to leave the room, and he didn't have anything else to wear.

When she'd brought his clothes back up, Alice had made him promise not to leave the room. Not until she'd finished her shift, and they could figure out their next move. He'd agreed with her, in principle, that it was far wiser for him to stay put. He'd agreed with her logic that he couldn't get into any more trouble if he didn't leave the room. But in practice it was more difficult to sit still and do nothing than he'd expected. He was claustrophobic. He was bored. And the longer he stayed inside the room the more he worried about what might be going on outside it.

What was that detective up to, and to what ridiculous conclusions was he leaping? Where were the real robbers? What had they done when they realised that they didn't have the stolen money? Was there any way that they would know that George had it? Were they on their way to his room right now?

The thoughts went spinning round and round in George's head until he felt dizzy. He had to get out of that room. He couldn't just sit there wondering and worrying.

Surely it wouldn't hurt to leave the room for a few minutes. Just long enough that he could see what was going on; reassure himself that he was in no immediate danger. Just to put his mind at ease. He couldn't screw things up too much just by popping down to the hotel bar and taking a quick look around.

He unfolded the jumpsuit, wishing he was holding one of his boring grey suits. How nice it would have been to slip into those grey slacks and white shirt, and just pretend that none of this had ever happened.

But then, if none of it had ever happened he'd never have met Alice. He thought of her. He pictured her twinkling eyes, and he smiled. Then he thought of that man, shoving a bag of money into his hands and running off, clutching a machine gun. The smile tumbled from his face again.

Once more George twisted and convulsed, squeezing himself into the tricky blue suit. He pulled on the freshly-cleaned white boots and slid on the large gold sunglasses.

Slowly George opened the bedroom door, peeking around the edge to make sure the hall was empty. He stepped out of the room and descended the long, dark staircase hesitantly, glancing all around for signs of impending danger. The air was thin and quiet, an eerie silence jangling his nerves. He flinched at the sound of his own feet making every floorboard creak. He tried to walk as lightly as possible but that just seemed to make the sounds louder and more piercing, so he made his way briskly along the narrow corridor, past the unmanned reception desk and into the small bar.

The old man, Alice's father, was stood behind the bar, that ridiculous dark wig still adorning his head and a stony grimace weighting his face. There was no sign of Alice. She must have been in the kitchen, probably preparing for dinner. The place was almost empty save for a young man sitting at one of the tables, dressed as Elvis of course, nursing the last quarter of a pint and fastidiously scribbling away into a small notebook. George wondered what he was writing about.

The only other occupant, seated at his regular seat at the end of the bar, was Les.

"Thring," the man cried out upon seeing George in the doorway. "Thring, how are you? Come and sit yourself down."

The young man in the corner looked up to see what had broken his concentration, rolled his eyes in disapproval and returned to his scribbling.

"I was worried about you, Thring," said Les, "after you staggered out of here yesterday. Three sheets to the wind, eh?" He laughed, leaning forward and slapping George on the arm.

George winced, not sure whether he really liked being slapped.

"Oh, no need to worry," he said. "Just needed a little lie down, you know. Clear my head."

"Yeah, I'll bet you did. Preparing for your hot date, eh?" laughed Les.

George's eyes sprung wide and he turned to look at the man behind the bar.

A jolt of terror shot through him, like a bucket of freezing water thrown over his head. The old man glared at him: the same blankly disapproving expression weighing down the loose, wrinkled skin of his face.

Was he angry? George couldn't tell. When he came to the bar he hadn't even considered the possibility that he'd have to face Alice's father like this. It hadn't even occurred to him that people would know they'd been on a date. Oh God, did they know she'd spent the night in his room? George's face burst out in a scarlet glow, his heart thumping in his chest.

But the old man just stared, not saying a word, not moving. Was he totally passive? Was the man even breathing?

Suddenly he moved, reaching up for a pint glass. He filled it with the same beer that George had been drinking the previous day and placed it on the bar in front of him. Then, without a single word or flicker of expression in his gruff, weathered face, he simply turned and walked out through the door at the back of the bar.

"Don't worry about him," said Les, gauging George's embarrassment. "I think that's his way of saying he likes you."

"Oh," said George, trying to force a smile before picking up the glass and taking a long gulp.

"Either that or he's poisoned your pint," laughed Les.

George coughed and spluttered, nearly spitting the beer out over the bar.

"Ha! Just pulling your leg mate."

George had to work even harder to fix a grin on his face, and raised the glass again to take another long sip.

"So, you and Alice, eh?" said Les. "Sorry, but you didn't think something like that would stay quiet for long in a town this small, did you? Stranger swoops into town and sweeps the prettiest girl off her feet. Its had a few tongues wagging today."

"Erm, well, yes," replied George, hesitantly. He still wasn't entirely certain what the official story was, or what he was allowed to admit to. But the news of he and Alice seemed to be unequivocally out.

"Well, for the record, you must have done something right last night. Don't think I've ever seen the girl so happy. Real spring in her step."

"Oh?"

"And don't worry too much about her old man. He might look a bit fierce but he's a good man really. And if Alice is happy, he'll be happy."

"Oh, good," said George, relaxing slightly as he took another draw on the glass. The beer was cold and refreshing and he could feel his stress ebbing away as he drank.

"So, what have you been up to today, Thring? Anything exciting?"

"No!" said George, slightly too forcefully.

Les seemed surprised at this sudden forthrightness.

"Um, no," he continued, trying to sound more laid-back. "I've just been in my room all day. Just kind of... hanging out."

"Really? Well, there was a man in here earlier. Asking questions about you. Said he was a police detective."

"Oh?" said George, his spine straightening with tension, his face muscles instantly going taut. "What did you... tell him?"

"What could I tell him? I don't know anything about you. Apart from your unusual name. And the fact that you're not the world's most gifted drinker, no offence."

"None taken."

"Besides, I don't have a great deal of time for policemen, as you can imagine. And even less time for those who go around discussing other people's business. So I said I didn't know you and sent him on his way."

"Oh good."

"Seemed to have a pretty low opinion of you, though. Said you were up to something, and you're not to be trusted. You're a dark horse, Thring, I must say. First you're telling me about your little accidental running away and then you're being pursued by detectives. You're not on the run are you? Here, you didn't have anything to do with that robbery today?"

"What? No!"

Damn, again he'd said it too quickly, too forcefully. He sounded flustered, guilty. Calm, George. Just keep calm. "Erm... I mean, no."

"It's all right, Thring," chuckled Les, again slapping him playfully on the arm, "I'm only messing about. Somehow I don't really have you down as the machine-gun-wielding, bank robber type. Nasty business though, eh? You didn't get caught up in it at all?"

"No, no," said George.

Keep calm. Stick to the story.

"No, like I say, I've just been up in my room all day. Bit tired you know... Just relaxing... Chilling out..."

Was he saying too much? Overdoing it? He picked up the glass again, taking another long sip, just to stop himself from talking.

The door of the bar creaked open and in strolled another Elvis fan. He was wearing a pale blue jumpsuit – almost exactly the same as George's.

The man looked George up and down several times, a quizzical expression furrowing his brow, before breaking out in a strange, satisfied smile. "Nice clothes," he said.

George recognized the voice instantly. It was the well-dressed man that he had nearly bumped into earlier in the day, as he'd left the hotel and walked into town. George froze again. This was the man who could ruin it all. He'd seen George leave the hotel. He could tear a great hole in his alibi.

"Oh... er... thanks," replied George.

"Almost exactly the same as mine," the man said.

"Erm... yes... I guess they are..." said George.

"Well, I commend you on your impeccable taste," he said.

He hadn't recognised George. Or, at least, he hadn't seemed to.

Alice's father appeared behind the bar again. The man ordered a large neat scotch, then sat at a table in the corner of the room.

Alice's father poured another pint each for George and Les, and George secretly let out a huge sigh of relief. It was still too early to celebrate, but things seemed fine so far. Of course, he'd only made it as far as the hotel bar but nothing had gone terribly wrong. There was no sign of that annoying detective; no police of any kind. Nothing particular seemed to be out of the ordinary. And, best of all, there were no signs of those thuggish bank robbers. George couldn't help but let a small contented smile briefly creep across his lips.

He looked up to see Alice's father grimacing back at him and the smile shattered and fell from his face. He picked up his fresh pint and took another long draw. At least the beer was helping.

CHAPTER 38

DETECTIVE Constable Keane had spent an infuriating four hours hanging on the sidelines of the official investigation, looking for clues or anything that would help him get a handle on exactly what had gone on here. It was frustrating knowing he already had the main suspect in his sights but couldn't arrest him. If he had his way, he'd have dragged George Thring into an interrogation room and piled on the pressure.

He was a devious one, that Thring, sticking to that lame story about coming there for a holiday; acting all timid and confused. Who did he think he was fooling? Keane knew he could break him. Given enough time and pressure he'd get a full confession out of him. The guy would crack, just like any criminal.

But he couldn't risk just hauling him in. For one thing, that ridiculous local Sergeant he'd spoken with earlier would never submit to Keane requisitioning his station to question the suspect. And there was enough local plod on the scene now, all trying to take charge of the situation; all with their own agendas. There was no way any of them would allow Keane access to the case; not without wanting to claim the collar for themselves. And there was no way Keane was letting that happen.

Even more frustratingly, he knew he had to first build a case. He hated to admit it, but the woman who had interrupted his earlier interrogation had made a fair point. His evidence was all circumstantial.

He couldn't prove Thring had been at the scene. No-one had even seen him leave the hotel. There was no sign of the money, or the guns, or anything else that would link him with the robbery. Keane wouldn't be able to do a thorough search of the room without a warrant and there was little chance of getting one before Thring cleared away everything even remotely dodgy.

So far he had no real evidence linking the man to the crime and if he carried on as he was doing, the CPS would likely refuse to prosecute under fear that Thring could sue for harassment. Either that or that some smarmy lawyer with too many plaques on his wall would get the case thrown out of court because the arresting officer hadn't carefully dotted all the is and crossed all the ts before so much as asking a question. What is the world coming to, thought Keane, when you can't just lock up the bad guys any more?

He knew Thring was guilty, but rather annoyingly he was going to have to prove it before he arrested him.

So Keane had spent the last few hours skirting the edges of the local plod's investigation. He couldn't get too involved because he was miles away from his own patch. The local coppers wouldn't take too kindly to him stepping on their toes and interfering with their enquiries, especially when he swooped in at the last minute and made the arrest for himself.

Secondly, the local force seemed totally clueless as to what had really happened. Keane was still the only one who knew anything about Thring. It was his secret lead; something that he didn't fancy sharing with anyone. He hadn't tracked a bank robber all this way, watched him and figured out his plan, only for someone else to get the credit for the arrest. Keane knew he had to be a bit sneaky and stay under the radar.

He couldn't officially question any of the witnesses or the hostages from the bank. But simply hanging around close enough to listen in on conversations, and chatting incognito to the rubberneckers loitering around the crime scene, had revealed that nobody could identify the robbers at all. Not even one of them. The only conclusive description seemed to be that there were three robbers, all wearing the same Elvis costumes as everyone else in the ridiculous town.

The men's faces had been pretty well obscured by dark glasses and large stick-on sideburns. They'd spoken with Sussex mockney accents, but so did half of the people in town – when they weren't adopting that annoying mumbling southern drawl, in an attempt to sound like Elvis Presley as well as look like him. The leader had apparently spoken in a slightly posher voice but it had seemed disingenuous enough, so that there was some debate over whether it had been the man's real voice or simply put on to fool the hostages and bank staff.

When the doors had opened, smoke pouring out into the street, and what they thought was gunfire started crackling all around them, everybody had simply ducked and run for safety. It was no surprise that nobody saw what happened to the robbers, or in which direction they ran. They had effectively disappeared into thick, smoky air.

It wasn't until the mist had cleared that people had taken note of the small alleyway to the side of the bank. And, because the back-up forces had taken so long to arrive, the two local officers had been stationed at the front of the bank with nobody covering the rear. The robbers must have run down the alley to where a getaway car would have been parked, and made their escape before anybody knew what was going on.

The road at the back of the bank led out of town in two directions, each route dividing into a myriad of tight, twisting country roads. Tracking them within five minutes of the job would have been tricky enough. By the time anyone had cottoned on to the fact that the robbers had fled by car and were not still in the bank firing pot-shots at them, the trail was long cold.

The whole thing had been so well planned; the key to its success being the total ineptitude of the local police. The robbers had managed to get in and out, in broad daylight, with nobody able to describe much about their appearance or which direction they had run off in.

Two sources had alluded to one quite interesting piece of information, however. Apparently, the lead robber, the man calling the shots, had been dressed in blue. Not exactly the link that was going to break the case – at least not for the local detectives bumbling about and scratching their heads.

But there was one particular man that detective Keane knew, sitting in a hotel room, dressed in blue and pleading his innocence. A coincidence? Not likely.

CHAPTER 39

"WHAT'S he doing now?" asked Sergeant Pete Collins of his hapless support officer.

"Still walking about, all suspicious-like," replied the young man. "He's having a good old look around, talking to people. Should I go and tell him to clear off?"

"No, no. I think we'll leave him for now. Just keep an eye on him; see what he gets up to. If he does anything strange, be sure and let me know."

Sergeant Collins was well aware that Detective Keane had been hanging around the crime scene. The idiot seemed to be under the impression that nobody had noticed him sneaking around, peering through the window of the bank, examining the evidence from not-so-afar. And he'd been less-than-inconspicuous in his supposedly casual interrogation of various eye-witnesses.

Of course it hadn't taken long for a number of the town's residents to ask the Sergeant who the strange, creepy man questioning them had been. Either the guy just didn't understand the concept of a small town, where everybody knew everybody else, and a stranger – no matter how inconspicuous they thought they were being – stood out like a whole handful of sore thumbs. Or he really wasn't as clever as he thought he was. Collins suspected it was a bit of both.

He'd been watching Keane sidling about, furtively listening in on conversations. He'd seen him watching the other police officers, stalking them almost; spying on what they were doing and smirking to himself. He seemed terribly pleased with himself, like he knew something that nobody else did.

Collins hadn't liked Keane from the second he'd met him. He was arrogant and rude, and over-enthusiastic to the point of aggressive. Collins had seen his type many times before. Newly-qualified detectives who thought they knew it all. It was as if stepping out of the uniform, into the bog-standard cheap, ill-fitting suit most of them chose to adopt, somehow robbed them of the capacity to act like a decent human being.

Thankfully, he'd also been around to see plenty of them fall flat on their faces; their over-zealous determination to prove their worth as a detective proving a far greater stumbling block than any criminal could. Just one look at Keane was enough to see he was following the exact same trajectory.

He'd rolled into town, making bizarre allegations about this man he'd followed up here. It had sounded a bit off to Collins when he first heard it and he'd assumed it would all just blow over. But now all this had happened. Perhaps there was something to the claims after all. It did seem too big a coincidence to ignore.

Collins was sure Keane would be making all the same assumptions as himself, with a handful of other ludicrous theories thrown in for good measure as well. One thing was for sure, though, this man that Keane had been chasing was someone Collins would definitely have to talk with. And he'd have to be careful to make sure he did it without Keane finding out.

All in good time, though. There was still a hell of a mess to be dealt with.

Collins was no longer in charge of the investigation. A team of detectives had whirled in like a twister from the big town up the road and demanded to take over. A few years back that sort of thing would have upset him. He'd have been every bit as eager as Detective Keane to solve the case himself and take all the credit. He'd have been seething, determined, desperate to get to the truth before anyone else.

But time, and age, and ill health had taught him the benefits of taking a back seat in these matters. So he held back and watched the furore of excitement as witnesses and hostages were rounded up and questioned.

The men in the cheap suits flashed their warrant cards excitedly, and said things like, "And where exactly were you at the time the robbery took place?" They stomped around, looking very important, but seemed just as clueless as everyone else.

Thin wisps of smoke still hung in the air. Collins could taste it in the back of his throat. It made him think of the robbers: how they'd vanished so quickly and how with each passing second they were getting further and further away. If they were going to be found then decisive action needed to be taken. Collins was damned if he was going to let these thugs get away.

But the sight of Keane skulking about, hiding information, trying to get one up on the rest of the officers investigating the case was what really worried him. At times like these you needed everyone working together. Information was key to catching crooks and everyone had to share what they knew for the benefit of the case.

Keane jumping in and trampling on the other detectives leads or – more importantly – hiding his own leads in order to take the credit, was exactly the kind of thing that would hold up the investigation and allow the robbers to get further and further away.

Collins had seen exactly this kind of deluded one-upmanship between officers lead to the destruction of several solid cases over the years. And he was damned if he was going to allow this jumped-up little copper from out of town to screw this one up. These villains had come into his town; threatened people; hurt people; and stolen money from the people he knew and spoke with on a daily basis.

They'd harmed the people that he was paid to protect; the people that came to him when they had problems. Worst of all, they'd done it so damned well that he'd been left to stand there with his hat in his hand looking like a bloody fool.

He was also aware, however, that there was no way Keane would be straight with him about what he knew. He had his secrets and he was likely to want to keep them that way. So for the time being, Collins would have to resort to exactly the kind of behaviour he hated. Spying on another officer.

His stomach growled a deep, rumbling gurgle. It had been hours since he'd eaten and he was starving. The image of that plump juicy doughnut flashed through his mind, glistening with sugar, rivulets of jam aching to be licked off. Perhaps, he thought, there was just time for a quick bite to eat before ploughing on with his investigations.

"Tony," he called out to his support officer. "Get the car. There's a few things I need to take care of back at the station."

"But what about this detective Keane? Don't you want me to keep an eye him?"

"Oh, don't worry about that," said Collins. "I'm pretty sure I know where he's heading. And we might just be able to get there first."

CHAPTER 40

NEITHER John or Steve Clefton had actually expected to see the Major as they raced into the hotel bar, red-faced and panting, nearly falling over each other as they clattered noisily through the door. So it was a bit of a shock to see him perched at a table in the far corner, sipping a glass of scotch.

They crossed the room briskly, anger and agitation burning in their faces, and threw themselves down onto the two stools opposite him. The stools were so low that both men's knuckles almost brushed against the ground as they sat. A brief flash of a smile shot across the Major's lips as he noticed it.

"Chaps," said the Major. "How did you get on with your little bit of business?"

"Never mind that," barked John, trying to keep his voice as low and quiet as possible. "What have you been up to?"

"Yeah, what you been up to?" echoed his brother.

"You must think we're stupid," continued John, not allowing the Major to reply. "Sending us off, getting us out the way, so you can head back here and pocket all the…"

He stopped suddenly, taking a slow, cautious look around to make sure that nobody was listening. Two men at the bar were deep in conversation, not paying them any attention. A quiet man sat at another table, scribbling silently in a notebook.

"Pocket all the money for yourself," he whispered.

The Major closed his eyes, pinched the bridge of his nose between finger and thumb, and exhaled a long, exasperated sigh. He then straightened himself up, tugging gently on each cuff in turn, and looked down at the two men.

"My dear boys, of course I don't think you're stupid," he said, raising one eyebrow into a high, tight arc. "But do you really think if I had perpetrated some kind of devilish double-cross that I would be sitting here waiting for you to get back?"

The two men looked at each other, doubt furrowing their brows.

"I can assure you that I do not have the money. None of us do. Thanks to brain of Britain here," he said pointing at Steve.

The two men sat back, a look of solemn realisation slowly drawing across their faces. It was true: if the Major had taken all the money for himself there's no way he would have hung around waiting for the brothers to catch up with him and literally tear his arms off. He'd be as far away as possible.

It could be a double bluff, of course. And if the Major hadn't double-crossed them yet, John Clefton knew it was only a matter of time before he did. But at least they had him in sight now. And John intended to keep it that way.

"So, I take it we have a replacement vehicle?" the Major continued.

"Yes we do. Though I still think there was nothing wrong with the other motor," said John. "So what *have* you been up to?"

"Well, for starters I've managed to secure our rooms for a few more nights. Base of operations until we catch up with our little friend. And I've also been doing a little detective work."

"And?" grumped John.

"I had a little wander around town. Spoke to a few people. The town is swarming with police. Thankfully they're as clueless as we'd hoped. Our little ruse seems to have worked, and they don't look to have a great deal of leads yet. And I believe I may have found our man."

The two men sat staring, silent and stupefied.

The Major rolled his eyes again, then nodded in the direction of the bar. "Look familiar?"

John and Steve glanced round, staring at the two men sat there. One of them was wearing a very distinctive pale blue jumpsuit.

It took Steve Clefton a few seconds to realise exactly what he was looking at. Neither he nor John had noticed the man as they entered the bar, so intent were they on confronting the Major. But now that he looked again, there was definitely something familiar. He was sure he'd seen that clothing before.

Suddenly his eyes widened, his jaw dropped, and he involuntarily spluttered a single word: "Fucker!"

John, who'd already realised what the Major was alluding to, quickly clamped his hand over his brother's mouth, spun him round in his chair and tried to pretend nothing had happened. It didn't work. The bar fell silent as the other occupants all looked round to see the source of the outburst.

"Tourettes," the Major deftly announced to the room. "Poor boy's a sufferer. Never know what filth is going to come spilling forth from one minute to the next. Terrible, really."

He adopted a very sombre, sympathetic look.

"Isn't that right, Steven" the Major said, kicking him under the table.

"Er… yeah," he said, adding, "Tits! Shit!" for effect.

The men at the bar gave them a quizzical look and the man with the notepad tutted, before all three looked away.

"Nice work," whispered the Major. "Could you two be any more conspicuous at all?"

"So, what the hell's going on?" asked John. "That's the guy?"

"I believe so," replied the Major. "I've been watching him for a while. Listening in on the conversation. I'm pretty sure that's our man."

All three turned for a surreptitious look, then turned back again, eyes narrowed with suspicion.

"That suit is almost identical to mine. And he's a pretty similar height and build to me. You said the man you gave the money to was wearing the same clothes as me, Steven. Do you think that could be him?"

"Yeah. Well, it was pretty smoky in there, but it definitely looks like him. Well, like you. I think. I mean it might be," replied Steve.

"And you just followed him in here?" asked John.

"Didn't have to. I came in here to wait for you two and he was sitting at the bar."

"So how do you know it's our guy?"

"For one thing, the clothing. Secondly, he looks a little bit shifty. And thirdly… well, let's just say I have a pretty good reason to suspect him."

"What reason?"

"Never you mind, Jonathon. We all have our little secrets."

"Okay, if that's him, why don't we go over there and beat our money out of him?" urged John.

"As much as I'd like to agree with you, I'm not sure that assaulting a man in public and demanding the return of the money we stole from the bank earlier in the day would necessarily be our best tactic," said the Major. "Considering all the police that are camped out at the bottom of the hill. I'd say it might just look a tad suspicious."

John humphed and slumped down on his stool. "So what do we do then?"

"Simple," said the Major. "We wait. And we watch. We need to be clever about this. We don't know anything about this man. More importantly, we don't know where the money is. So for now we just sit tight. I'll watch him and see what he does, where he goes, whom he talks to. If he has the money, it's only a matter of time before he leads us to it."

"Time's running out," said John. "We can't afford to hang around, not with all these coppers about."

"Believe me, I don't want to be here any more than you do. I'd quite happily take our friend off to a dark room and beat him until he tells us where our money is. But it's too risky. We have to be smart, and we have to stay inconspicuous. So for now we watch, and we wait."

"Yeah, well, while you're watching him, just remember that I'll be watching you," sneered John with a menacing tone.

"I'm sure you will," replied the Major. "Now, go and get yourselves a couple of drinks before you look even more out of place. This is a bar, after all."

CHAPTER 41

WATER tumbled from the taps, thudding noisily against the base of the steel basin, slowly filling the sink. The sound was almost therapeutic, momentarily blocking out everything else. For a few seconds at least, Alice felt calm again. She plunged her hands into the hot, soapy water, the bubbles tickling her forearms, as she breathed in a lungful of lemon detergent scent.

For that brief second, it was like she was back in her old life. That simple life, where all she had to worry about was washing dishes, preparing a few meals for the hotel guests and just plodding along in her mundane routine. So much had changed in the last 48 hours.

She thought of George, sitting there in his underpants in the hotel room, a mixture of fear and bafflement filling his eyes. Then she thought of those eyes – those sad eyes – and how they'd looked the previous night. How they'd made her tummy tumble, and how just gazing into them had made her feel like giggling. She couldn't remember the last time she'd felt like giggling. She couldn't remember the last time she'd felt very much of anything.

There she was, getting along quite nicely in her simple little life, saving for the future. Planning her adventures, dreaming about all the wonderful things out there waiting for her. Then out of nowhere, this poor lost soul comes wandering into her life. This drowned kitten of a man, desperately in need of help and love. A man who had made her smile more in one night than she had smiled for the whole of the previous year.

Stood there at the sink, scrubbing an awkward spot of congealed ketchup from a dirty plate, she found herself suddenly laughing, just thinking about him and how he made her feel.

Could she really be in love? So soon? After only just meeting this man?

She wasn't sure. She thought she'd been in love with Michael. She'd even married the poor guy before realising that it wasn't love she felt for him; more a kind of respect and friendship. She'd wanted to love him. Tried to love him. It would have made life so much easier if she could have loved him. But try as she might, even after all those years together it just never came.

Now, after such a short space of time she found herself giggling at a sink full of dirty dishes; thinking of George; worrying about him; equally as eager to race upstairs, rip his clothes off and jump into bed with him. If it wasn't love, it was the closest she'd ever come to it.

He made her happy, she knew that much. And she could see that, no matter what, he was the kind of man who'd want nothing more than to keep on making her happy.

There was one slight problem, of course. He was lead suspect in an armed robbery that had just taken place. And without even really think about it, Alice had lied to a policeman to provide him with an alibi. How had that happened?

She thought of all the times she'd read about these women in the papers, who stood by their criminal husbands no matter what. They always claimed they were nice guys underneath – when you really got to know them – despite their killing sprees or violent behaviour. She'd berated these idiot women for being duped by such thugs. She found herself shouting at the TV during crime dramas and soap operas: "Why can't you see what he's really like? How stupid are you?"

Was she one of these women now? Was she just being stupid? How had she got herself involved in this?

But George wasn't a bank robber. Of course he wasn't. Just one look into those deep, sad eyes could tell you that he didn't have a cruel bone in his body. He wasn't capable of hurting people. He was honest, and nice, and caring. He wasn't a thief, or a bank robber.

Or had she just been taken in, like those other deluded women?

She should walk away from George, thank him for a very nice evening but tell him that she didn't have room for this kind of drama in her life at the moment. She should be sensible; tell him to leave town and leave her alone.

But the thought of never seeing him again seemed somehow too horrible to bear. She imagined telling him that things couldn't work out between them and suddenly felt empty, as though her insides had been scooped out. She didn't want to never see him again! He was her knight in shining armour – albeit a rather down-in-the-dumps knight, less shiny and more dullish-grey. But he was her knight and she wanted him to rescue her, take her away from all this and whisk her off to a new, happy life. Isn't that what all girls want?

And the worst part, of course, the thing she really didn't want to admit to herself, was that it was the most exciting thing that had happened to her in years. Maybe ever.

She knew her life was missing a bit of drama and things didn't get much more dramatic than finding yourself involved with a bank robber. Even if he wasn't really a bank robber – just a hapless soul mistaken for one.

Part of her wanted to run upstairs, grab George and make a run for it. Two fugitives, setting out on the open road, no idea how far they'd get before the law caught up with them. How much more exciting could it get? Now that really would be an adventure.

But it would never work. George didn't really seem the 'life on the run' type. He was more the 'cup of cocoa and a good book before bed' type. And the more Alice thought about it, the more she realised that's what she really wanted. A happy peaceful life with a kind, caring man.

With just a little bit of adventure thrown in for good measure.

She lifted the plate and placed it onto the drying rack. There was more washing up to be done, but it could wait. The restaurant was empty and she could sneak away for a few minutes at least. She had to see George. Somehow she knew that if she just looked into his eyes, placed a hand on his face and kissed his lips, then everything would be all right again.

Alice dried her hands and ran out of the kitchen, leaping two stairs at a time as she raced to see George. She knocked loudly on the door before flinging it open, surging into the room, ready to be taken into his strong arms. But he wasn't there.

Instead she found an empty, slightly draughty room, with no George and not even so much as a note to say where he was.

"Oh for God's sake, George," she said to herself, loud and agitated. "Where the bloody hell have you gone now?"

CHAPTER 42

THE air in the bar was thick like soup. George drained the last of his beer and a warm glow enveloped him, his eyelids growing heavy again. Soft murmurs of hushed voices trickled quietly in the corner of the room. Les continued to speak in a deep, gruff voice but George could not concentrate on what he was saying. He was now simply replying out of kindness with nods of his head and affirmatory hmms.

He should go back to his room. His brain was already feeling fuzzy and he needed to keep his concentration. He was convinced now that the police were not huddled outside the hotel, preparing to burst in and drag him away to a cold, dank cell. But there were still dangers out there. That detective was surely still lurking and George didn't know whether any of the other police officers in town had made any connection to him yet.

And then there were the robbers. George had done well to evade them so far but there was every chance they could have figured out what had really happened to the money. And then they'd be back to find him. God knew where they were right then. Hopefully still miles away, George thought.

Les's voice suddenly broke through the dense fog swirling around George's head, offering another drink. He certainly shouldn't have another, he knew that much. He had to get back to his room. How long had he even been sat there? Alice might be looking for him. He needed to go.

He stood up and for the briefest moment wasn't entirely certain that his legs would hold his weight. He clutched tightly at the edge of the bar, steadying himself, waiting for the whooshing sound in his ears to subside and his eyes to regain focus. Les looked at him quizzically. George made his excuses and quickly stepped out of the bar.

He made his way slowly up the stairs, looking all around for signs of Alice. He was desperate to see her, but equally keen to make it back to the room before she found out that he'd left it. Holding tight to the banister, he dragged himself up the narrow staircase, transferring his hands to the wall at the top, carefully guiding himself along the corridor, through the door and into the relative safety of his room.

He collapsed down onto the bed, the springs squeaking loudly as he lay back and allowed his eyes to slide closed, deciding that perhaps the best course of action was just to have a very quick nap.

Barely had his head hit the pillow, however, before he heard a short, sharp rap on the door. It must be Alice, he thought, back from her shift in the kitchen. George clambered up and opened the door. And for the second time that day he was taken quite by surprise.

Instead of the pretty brunette girl with the cute bum, the doorframe was amply filled by three men all dressed in bright, flowing jumpsuits. At the front was the abrupt, posh man. Standing behind him were two great hulking brutes, with dark angry faces and more muscles than seemed necessary. He'd seen them just moments before down in the hotel bar. From their demeanour, George thought they looked like two gorillas corralled into submission by a circus ringmaster.

The bank robbers. It had to be. They'd found him, tracked him back to his room. George suddenly felt very scared indeed.

Without so much as a word, the smaller man pushed past George into the room. The bigger men closed ranks, forcing George to step back and then followed him in, closing the door behind them. The room suddenly became much smaller. The air seemed to drain away as if sucked from the room. Looking up at the two gorillas, George's head swam in a woozy swirl, his heart beating faster in his chest.

He twisted round to find the other man perched on the end of the bed.

"Good afternoon, sir," he said calmly, the upper-class accent trickling from his lips like syrup. "I don't believe we've met. Not officially, anyway."

"No," replied George. "I don't think we have. Is there… something I can help you with?"

"Hmmm," said the man. "I certainly hope so. For your sake, anyway."

A large, heavy hand connected with the back of George's head, smacking him heavily from behind and forcing him forwards until he too was sitting on the bed.

"I shan't bother with formal introductions," said the posh man.

He picked up George's wallet from the chest of drawers, eagerly pawing through the contents, pulling out George's bank card and driving licence.

"You don't know us, and it's probably better for you if things stay that way. But we certainly know you, Mr Thring," he said, reading the name from the licence. "We know everything about you."

"You do?" stumbled George.

"Oh yes. For example, we know where you live." He flashed the driver's license at him. "We know when you were born. We know you have a membership at Blockbuster video store and a loyalty card for Tesco."

"Um…"

"We know you're not from around these parts; just visiting. We know you have rather an unusual taste in clothing," he said, looking George up and down.

"Well, I…" said George.

"And we also know that you were at the bank today," said the man, suddenly sounding more serious. "We know you found yourself in a small bit of bother. And we also know that you found yourself in the possession of something that doesn't really belong to you. Didn't you?"

George sat there, mouth agape, a blank look of terror spread across his face.

"It's our property," continued the man, smiling calmly, "and we'd very much like to have it back. So much so that I'd dread to think what might happen to you if we don't get it back."

The larger of the two men – the one that George had immediately and secretly decided was probably the least intelligent of the three – grabbed George by the shoulder and threw him up against the closed door. A fat, meaty hand thrust up to grab him by the throat.

George's head slammed back hard into the door. He struggled to break free of the man's grip but the gorilla was far too strong.

"Where is the bag, Mr Thring?" the posh man said, still very calm.

"I... I don't know... What bag?" George coughed, struggling to breathe, let alone speak.

"Come now, Mr Thring. You and I both know that you left the bank with a bag. A large green duffel bag. It belongs to us and we want it back. Where is it?"

"I don't know... I don't have any bag."

The posh man nodded at the large man holding George. His fingers tightened, gripping George's throat like a vice, slowly closing in like a constrictor toying with its prey. The man's eyes twinkled with delight, the corners of his mouth stretching into the slightest of smiles. George would have commended the man on finding work that he seemed to truly enjoy – such a rare thing nowadays – had that work not involved strangling him.

"The bag, Mr Thring. I have all day to sit here asking you, but I fear you don't have quite so long to answer."

The man's grip tightened further. George could feel his airways being forced closed; heat rising in his face; panic growing in his chest. He could barely speak, just managing to rasp: "I... don't... know... what..."

The large man glared at him, pushing his face closer to George's. His eyes were burning with rage. George lashed out, trying to punch him, swinging his arms wildly as they simply ricocheted off the man's hefty bulk. He didn't flinch, move or relinquish his grip in the slightest.

"The bag, Mr Thring?" repeated the posh man, annoyance tingeing his voice now. "Where is it?"

George's arms grew tired, his legs so weak that he could barely hold his own weight any longer. Thick black fog crept in at the edge of his vision. He felt so light-headed, so tired. He could feel himself losing consciousness; starting to fall backwards.

Everything went silent and from far off George could swear he heard the sound of the ocean; waves sweeping in and flowing out. A strange sort of cold calm washed over him, like a cool ocean breeze tickling his skin. An image of Alice flashed into his mind. Her smiling face. Her pretty, smiling face. God he loved that face.

Everything turned black and George's head filled with silence, interrupted only by a dull, insistent, electronic bleeping.

"Shit!" said the posh man. "Shit... let him go. Let him go before you fucking kill him."

The large man did as he was told, huffing under his breath like a child ordered to stop playing with its favourite toy as he released his grip.

A sudden great wash of cold air shot down George's throat like a tidal wave, filling his lungs as he fell to the floor. He coughed and spluttered, bright light shattering the blackness, stinging his eyes as he clutched at his burning throat.

Lying face down on the dirty, brown carpet, George looked up to see the posh man reach into his pocket and retrieve a small mobile phone. His eyes rolled as he looked at the caller display before answering.

"Yes," he said, agitated. "I'm rather in the middle of something here, can this…"

His eyes narrowed as he listened intently, his expression changing as he turned his head and looked down at George. "Really? Yes… yes, it could be. Hmm… really? Yes, very interesting. Okay."

He disconnected the call, a curious smile playing across his lips as he slid it back into his pocket. The big man looked at him, eyes like a playful puppy, keen to hear the order to start torturing George again. But it didn't come. Instead the posh man crossed the room and whispered something to the other thug. He nodded, smiled a disgusting ogreish grin, and promptly left the room.

"It seems a new piece of information has come to light, Mr Thring. Please, help our new friend up off the floor," the posh man said to his associate.

The big man grabbed George by the collar, picked him up and threw him down onto the bed.

"There's something that needs my urgent attention so I'm afraid I shall have to leave you for the time being. But I would like to continue this conversation. Do you think you could meet me again, say in one hour, down in the hotel bar? Should give you a bit of time to think about where our property is."

George sat stunned, panting slightly, his hand still gripping his aching neck.

"Oh, and if you were thinking of simply running away, I'd really advise against that," he said, waving George's wallet in the air. "We know who you are and we know where you live. If I don't see you in one hour, it could end up very badly for you. Very badly indeed. For you and… others."

The last word rolled off the man's lips with a devilish flick. The two men left the room, and George fell back onto the bed.

******

"Where's John run off to?" asked Steve Clefton, as he and the Major hurried down the stairs. "Who was that on the phone?"

"Never you mind who was on the phone," replied the Major.

"Who was on the phone?" growled Steve, grabbing the Major by the arm and spinning him round.

The two men stood still on the landing, glaring at each other. Steve Clefton breathed angrily; a grimace scrawled across his face; a red tinge flushing on his neck.

The Major had pushed him quite enough for one day and he didn't need the big lug getting angry now. Especially not without his brother in tow to keep him in line.

The Major could control the pair well enough with words the majority of the time, but Steve especially was prone to bouts of aggression and extreme physical violence. The Major had underestimated him in the past; seen just how dangerous the man could be when his frustrations were unleashed.

A simple game of cards not going quite his way had been enough to see the big lug unleashing his frustrations on four fellow prison inmates. A collection of broken jaws, cracked ribs, black eyes, snapped fingers, broken noses and bruised testicles were dished out evenly between them before five prison guards brought the man under control. And by that point he'd pretty much calmed his outburst of rage and was willing to go reasonably quietly – although not before throwing one guard down the cold, sharp, metal stairs, just out of badness.

Major Fairview certainly didn't want to contend with one of those meltdowns now. It seemed prudent to relent and hopefully quell the potential violence he could see growing in the man's eyes.

"That was an associate of mine, calling to give me some information," said the Major, smiling. "Something that could be very interesting in dealing with our forgetful friend in there."

"What information?"

"It seems that Mr Thring has a girlfriend. I've sent your brother to have a word with her."

The grimace slid from the big man's face, replaced by a look of bafflement.

"He's going to grab her. Tie her up."

The man's face remained still. The lights were on but the owners were at a party down the road.

"We can use her as leverage," said the Major, raising his eyebrows and slowing his words into a patronising monotone. "Then we can get him to tell us where the money is…"

"Oh..."

"Honestly," the Major muttered under his breath, pulling himself free of the big man's grasp and turning to walk down the stairs. "It's like working with a shaved bloody ape."

The large man grimaced.

"Right, come on," he said to Steve. "We need to find your brother. But first we need to get changed."

CHAPTER 43

THE ageing wooden boards creaked disconcertingly underfoot as Sergeant Collins pulled his tired, heavy frame slowly up the narrow staircase. He was getting old and stairs were no longer his friends.

There was a time he'd have raced up them in a spurt, leaping two, three at a time; kicking down doors, barely even out of breath; and dragging villains away to the cold, miserable cells where they belonged. Now, in the later years of his life, and with the daily threat of his heart condition – not to mention the four or five extra stones he was carrying on account of now being more inclined to tackle a box of fondant fancies than an organised crime gang – he had to settle for a somewhat more sedate style of policing.

He wheezed slightly, clinging onto the banister to help pull himself up the treacherous wooden mountain. Only halfway up the stairs and already out of puff.

His tongue instinctively located a small cluster of runaway sugar granules, left over from his earlier doughnut, hidden in the corner of his mouth. The resulting micro-sugar-rush gave him just enough of a boost to conquer the last seven stairs.

Standing at the top, feeling slightly dizzy and pausing to catch his breath, he faked flicking through his police notebook, looking for essential information. He maintained the illusion just long enough to compose himself before knocking on the door, without losing face in front of his young apprentice.

In all honesty, the boy was so clueless he wouldn't have noticed if his fellow officer was having a full-blown heart attack. But Collins was the senior officer there and he had to try and keep up appearances, if only for his own sense of pride.

The two police officers approached the door and knocked. Nothing. Collins waited a few seconds before rapping again, this time harder and with more authority.

"Mr Thring?" he called out. "Could you open the door please? It's the police. We'd like a word with you."

Collins could hear footsteps inside the room, pacing with agitation. He was just about to repeat his request in the harsh, threatening voice he so rarely got to use anymore, when the door creaked open, revealing a rather sheepish, worried looking man.

"Mr Thring?" said Collins.

"Er... yes. Yes, that's me..." replied the man in a thin, quiet voice.

The man didn't look quite right. Something had clearly upset him. He was as white as a ghost, and looked frightened; petrified even. There were red marks on his neck, as if he'd been in a fight. He appeared to be on the verge of tears.

"Is everything all right, Mr Thring?" Collins said.

The man seemed to rally, quickly straightening himself up, clearing his throat.

"Erm… oh yes," he said. "Yes, sorry, I've just been having a nap. He ran his fingers through his straggly hair and gaped his mouth wide, pretending to yawn.

"Asleep?" said Collins, not buying a word of it.

"Yes… too much beer last night. You just woke me up actually. Been in bed all day. Terrible hangover."

"But you're fully clothed."

A sudden realisation flashed across the man's face, his gaze darting down to take in the fact that he was in fact wearing clothes.

"Oh… er, yes… well… I guess I must have been really, er… wasted."

You're no actor, thought Collins. No Oscar for you.

"Do you mind if we come in, Mr Thring? We'd just like to ask you a few questions, if that's okay?"

"Questions? Erm… okay… yeah, that's fine. Come in. What do you want to know?"

He was trying to sound nonchalant now; too obedient; too happy to help. Maybe Keane had been right about him after all.

Sergeant Collins stepped into the tiny room. Given how small it was, and how full it had suddenly become with his less-than-modest frame now occupying a good third of the floor space, he instructed his young colleague to wait outside in the hall and keep his eyes open. There wasn't much point in telling him what to keep an eye out for, as Collins was sure he'd be daydreaming within seconds of being on his own.

"So, what brings you to our peaceful little town, Mr Thring?" said Collins, shutting the door firmly behind him.

"Oh, you know… just fancied a little break away. Little holiday."

"Is that right? Just fancied a little holiday. Elvis fan, I suppose," he said, pointing to the man's clothing.

"Oh yes. Yes, of course. Elvis fan. Yes, that's why I'm here."

"For the festival?"

"For the festival."

"Hmmm…" said Collins, thoughtfully. This man was about as much an Elvis fan as Collins was an anorexic.

"And you arrived when?"

"Erm… two nights ago."

"Two nights ago. And how are you finding our little town?"

"It's very nice."

"You've done a bit of sightseeing? Been for a tour of the place?"

"Erm, yes. I had a little walk round… Sorry, what was it you wanted?"

They were double-edged questions, as Collins deliberately edged his way around the conversation; carefully observing each answer, each reaction, building up to the critical blow.

"Only," he continued, "I had a bit of a strange visit this morning. From a Detective Keane. He was very insistent that I should 'keep an eye on you.'" Collins made quote marks in the air with his fingers.

The man's ghostly face turned an even paler shade of white at the detective's name. That was it. That was the reaction Collins had expected.

"Keep an... eye on me?" the man said softly.

"Yes, he seems to think that you're up to something. His words, not mine. Told me all about how you disappeared after work one night, told nobody where you were going, and just vanished. People back home are quite worried about you, apparently, so he tracked you down and found you here."

"People? Worried?"

"So I'm told."

"Well, it's not exactly a crime, though," said the man, the slightest hint of guilt tingeing his voice. "I don't believe it's against the law to go away and not tell people. I just fancied a break away, so that's what I did. I came here... for the Elvis festival."

Collins scanned the room pensively. Nothing looked particularly out of place. A slightly unmade bed. A wallet sat discarded on the floor.

"Of course not," said Collins, suddenly lightening his tone, smiling and turning on the friendliness. "Between you and me, I didn't much like Detective Keane. Bit rude, I thought. Somewhat over-eager."

The man's face brightened over the shared common ground, exactly as Collins had expected. Keep him on his toes, thought Collins, make him wonder where I'm going next:

"So, where were you today at around 1pm, Mr Thring?"

Immediately the man looked rattled again. "I... er... I told you, I was here. I've been in bed all day..."

"With a hangover," Collins cut in. "Really? You haven't been out all day?"

"No."

"You didn't pop into town at all?"

"No."

"You didn't go to the... bank?" He drew the last word out slightly, letting it land with greater impact.

Both men knew the question had been coming, but Thring somehow still looked surprised that it had been asked. "No, I told you, I've been here all day. In bed. With a hangover. I didn't have anything to do with the robbery."

"Robbery," said Collins, his voice bouncing slightly with enjoyment. He'd been hoping for this chance. "Who said anything about a robbery? I never mentioned a robbery. Why do you say robbery?"

It was literally the oldest trick in the police handbook. The one they all loved using. And this man had fallen for it hook, line and sinker. He was physically squirming now, his bogus story disintegrating in front of his own eyes.

"Come to think of it, how would you even know about the robbery? If you've been in bed all day with a hangover, I mean."

"Erm... well... well, I heard the sirens. They woke me up earlier. And I... er... I guess I must have heard someone talking about it... in the street..."

"Hmmm," said Collins. "You have to admit, it does all seem a bit suspicious. This morning a detective comes and tells me that he's tracked down this mystery man to my town. Tells me to keep an eye on him and that he's up to something. Then just a few hours later three men rob the bank in town. Let me ask you a question, Mr Thring: if you were me, who would your finger be pointing at?"

The man seemed to shrink before him. But not in the way he'd seen so many others shrink, with the sudden realisation they'd been caught out and there was no point in arguing any longer. He didn't look guilty; he just looked defeated.

He slumped down onto the bed, sitting with his head bowed, collecting his thoughts. Then he looked up.

"I can see how it might look," said the man very calmly and confidently, "but I've done nothing wrong. I'm nothing, a nobody. I have a boring job in the marketing department of a boring company that I really don't care about. I have a boring life. I live in a boring house, in a boring town. I don't ever really do... anything."

He looked so down-trodden; so broken.

"I guess, if I'm honest," he continued, "I've hated my life for some time now. And I suppose... I suppose it all just got a bit too much for me. I got into my car after work on Tuesday night and I drove home. Except I never quite made it home. I just drove and drove, and before I knew it I'd ended up here. And I don't know why. I've been trying to figure that one out myself.

"So, not exactly normal behaviour, I'll give you that. But not a crime either.

"The reason I didn't tell anyone where I was going is because... I didn't know that I was going anywhere until I'd got here. I know it sounds stupid, and I may be the only person that's ever done it, but I guess I ran away... by accident.

"And I ended up here, in this funny little town, dressed in this daft get-up because my clothes got ruined and this was the only thing I could buy. And I met a girl, and we had a nice time and for the first time in my life I think I actually felt really... happy.

"And then I wake up this morning and I have policemen hounding me because I dared to leave home without telling people – people who couldn't even give a damn about me, by the way. And then you turn up here accusing me of... what are you actually accusing me of?"

His tone changed then, a look of righteousness glowing in his eyes. Slowly but surely the fight was coming back to him.

"I'm not a fucking bank robber. I'm just a man. I'm just a sad, lonely, boring man who hasn't done anything wrong and who would very much like to be left alone now, please. So, unless you have any plans to arrest me, or take me to the police station for questioning, then I'd really rather you left now. I've watched my fair share of television and I'm pretty sure you need some kind of warrant, or evidence or just cause or something.

"So, unless you have any of those things, perhaps you and Detective Keane can go and work on your conspiracy theories somewhere else. Or better yet, try and catch actual criminals and just leave me to get on with my life."

Sergeant Collins stood speechless for a second. He couldn't figure this guy out. Only a few minutes earlier, Collins had rattled his cage and he'd broken. He was out for the count, ready to give up, practically climbing into the back of the police car without question. Then out of nowhere he was giving the warrant speech, fighting back with an unexpected vigour.

"I'd say you have been watching a few too many detective shows, haven't you Mr Thring?" said Collins in retaliation. "It's not all about warrants, I can assure you. But don't worry, I didn't come here to arrest anybody. I just popped in for a friendly chat."

He smiled his best, biggest, friendliest smile. Thring did not reciprocate.

"But you're right, there are criminals out there and I really should get out and round them up."

He stepped back to the door and gripped the handle.

"Sorry to disturb you, Mr Thring. Needless to say, there's quite a big police investigation going on in town at the moment and one of my colleagues will likely be back to take a statement. Probably best not to leave just yet. In case you get another one of your disappearing moods."

He reached into his pocket and pulled out a small white rectangular piece of card. Handing it to Thring he said, "Here's my number. Please call me if there's anything you think of, or remember. Or anything else you'd like to discuss."

He smiled again, then stepped through the door, turning back just long enough to say, "I'll see you soon, Mr Thring." He pulled the door closed behind him.

******

George Thring hadn't been at all what he'd expected. He certainly didn't seem like the average bank robber. Maybe he really was just a lonely man trying to escape from his life.

Collins still wasn't sure that he followed Keane's logic that the man was up to something. But there was definitely something going on. Something that Collins couldn't quite put his finger on.

"Well?" said the young policeman, as Collins re-joined him at the top of the stairs. "Aren't we going to arrest him?"

"Not yet, son. Not yet," said Collins, still thinking hard. "Let's just keep an eye on him for now, eh?"

CHAPTER 44

"YOU'RE sure this is her?" said Major Fairview, peering through the open doorway into the kitchen. The brunette woman stood at the sink, washing dishes and muttering under her breath.

"Yes, I'm sure," grunted John Clefton. "There can't be too many young, brunette chicks that work here, can there?"

The Major eyed him, unconvinced.

"Besides, she's spent the last five minutes muttering to herself. And by the sounds of things she's not too happy with a fella named George. Or with the mess he's got her into."

The woman did sound annoyed. The water in the sink splashed noisily as she scrubbed the dishes with venom. "One simple thing, George," she huffed to herself. "Stay in the bloody room. How hard can that be?"

"Hmm," said the Major. "Sounds like our woman."

"That's what I said!" John Clefton grunted with greater annoyance.

"Right, John, you head back to your room," said the Major. "Get changed out of those clothes then stand outside the door looking scary. Steve, you follow me. And let me do the talking, by which I mean literally say nothing. And try not to look too menacing. We don't want to scare the poor thing. Not just yet, anyway."

John Clefton disappeared down the hallway as his brother prepared to follow on behind the Major.

"Try smiling, will you? Or the closest approximation your mouth will allow," ordered the Major.

Steve Clefton grimaced. The Major pushed past him and breezed into the kitchen.

"Alice?" said the Major, approaching the woman at the sink. His voice was low and sympathetic.

She spun round, startled, water splashing onto the floor between them, narrowly missing the Major's shoes. She eyed him with suspicion.

"Mrs Alice Corby?"

"Y... er... yes?" she mumbled.

"Hello Alice," said the Major, reaching into his pocket and pulling out a very realistic-looking police warrant card. "I'm Detective Inspector Fairview."

It was amazing what you could buy for £200 if you knew the right people – or, more accurately, the wrong people. The warrant card was unlikely to fool a professional, of course, or stand up under close scrutiny, but it was good enough to trick those who didn't really know what they were looking for.

Emblazoned with the correct official logos, titles and a shiny, smiley picture of the Major, it had worked handsomely in the past, allowing him access to secret locations he'd normally have trouble entering – and subsequently stealing from. It had enabled him to travel free on all forms of public transport, the officials buying his story that he was undercover and secretly trailing a known, dangerous convict.

On many occasions the fake I.D. had even seen him abscond from shops, bars and nightclubs with the contents of the till. The owners had been left dumbfounded when Detective Inspector Fairview told them that all the notes in their till were counterfeit and had to be removed, but reassured that they could file a claim for compensation by popping into the local station and asking for him personally the following morning.

One quick flash under the woman's nose and she was instantly convinced. Strangely, though, she didn't immediately drop her guard like most others would. It was as if she'd been expecting the encounter and she seemed to harden slightly.

"What can I do for you, Detective?" she said sternly.

"It's about a friend of yours, Alice. A Mr Thring?"

"George? What about him?"

"It's bad news, I'm afraid. My colleagues and I are investigating the robbery that took place earlier today. We've been interviewing people in town to find out if anybody saw anything at all. We've been talking to people in the hotel and we were going to ask Mr Thring some questions when… well, he simply ran off."

"Ran off?" said Alice, quietly.

"Yes, I think we must have given him the willies because he jumped up from his seat in the bar and bolted. He's holed himself up in a room upstairs and he's asking for you. Says he won't come out until he's spoken to you."

A look of panic flashed across the woman's face. But again, she didn't seem surprised.

"I've got one of my men standing guard outside the door. We wondered if you might come and talk to him for us. Let him know he's not in any kind of trouble. Unless he's the one who robbed the bank, of course."

With that the Major let out a blast of over-enthusiastic laughter. He turned to Steve Clefton, who joined in with a menacing raspy chuckle.

"I mean, you don't think he could have had anything to do with the robbery, do you?" continued the Major.

The woman's face had turned sheer white, her eyes wide and staring. "What? No… what… George? No, of course not. I've already told the other detective that George has been in his room all day!" she said in sheer defiance.

"Other detective?" the Major blurted in shock.

What other detective? This was not good news. There was another detective already sniffing around this bloody Thring character. What did they know? Had he been seen leaving the bank? Clearly the sooner they got the money and got the hell away from this place the better.

"The other detective that was harassing George earlier," the woman continued. "That'll be what spooked him. You lot badgering him, insinuating that he had something to do with this robbery."

It was the Major's turn to stare blankly, trying to ascertain just what had been going on.

"Well," continued the woman, picking up a tea towel from the side and drying her hands. "You'd better show me where he is so that I can talk some sense into him. And once George has answered your questions, I've got half a mind to file a claim of harassment against you lot."

The Major marched out of the kitchen, Alice following, with Steve Clefton stomping along behind. They made their way up the stairs, down the narrow corridor and came to a stop outside a hotel room door where John Clefton stood.

"He's still in there, constable?" the Major said to John Clefton.

The big man looked back at him with confusion. The Major had taken a risk proceeding with the plan without filling the two brothers in on the details, simply hoping they'd have enough sense to improvise along with it. Luckily for him, after a few seconds of blank, open-mouthed staring, and a wide-eyed look of appeal from the Major, John Clefton finally said, "Erm... er... oh yeah. Yeah, he's still inside."

"Good," said the Major, relieved.

Turning to Alice, he continued, "Now, we don't believe the door is locked but he was threatening to jump out of a window. Which is why we didn't want to run in there 'all guns blazing' so to speak."

"But..." said the woman in a confused tone, "this isn't George's room? Why would he have gone in here?"

"That is a good question," replied the Major. "We simply approached him to ask some questions and he bolted. We chased after him and he ran in here. We assumed it must have been his room..."

"Oh George," said the woman under her breath.

"I wonder, perhaps, whether you could head in and try and reason with him?" said the Major.

"Of course," she replied.

The woman stepped up to the door, breathed deeply and turned the handle. Slowly she opened it, the hinges creaking and squealing as she peered through the widening gap.

"George?" she said. "Are you okay, George?"

She slowly pushed the door open, putting one foot inside – only to find the room completely unoccupied. "George? George are you in here?"

She stepped fully inside, looking around into every corner of the room, before turning back: "Hey," she said. "What's going on? There's nobody in here."

She looked up just in time to see Steve Clefton's hand rise and clamp firmly around her mouth. He almost picked her up from the floor by her face as he pushed her back into the room. She tried to kick and punch, and wrestle him off, but he was too strong. Every lash she threw at him merely bounced off his arms and chest.

He marched her over to the bed, pushing her backwards until she was lying on it, and held her firmly in place with a knee on her waist and that giant hand clamped firmly over her mouth.

The other men strolled into the room, closing the door behind them. The Major walked over to the bed, leaning down so that his mouth was just inches from her ear, and said, "Now then, Alice. Where is our money?"

CHAPTER 45

HOT blood pumped in George's veins. It whooshed loudly in his ears. His face was hot; a burning red ember. He felt slightly faint but utterly exhilarated. Out of nowhere a sudden anger had come over him, groaning in the pit of his stomach then bubbling up and spilling out as he'd unleashed his frustrations at that policeman.

He hadn't fallen to pieces, like he'd thought he might. He'd stayed calm. He'd stayed strong and resilient and told him where to bloody well go. Or something like that. It was all a bit of a blur now.

He wasn't sure where that little speech had come from and in hindsight he'd probably been a bit too candid. All that stuff about his boring house and his boring life; it had just flowed out before he really knew what he was saying.

He'd pulled the cork from a bottle he'd kept stoppered up tight for so long. He wasn't just fighting off the policeman with the information; for the first time George had finally admitted to himself just how unhappy he'd really been.

Ever since he'd wound up in this strange little town, George had felt a real change come over him. It was fair to say that in the space of just a few short days, his life had become somewhat more dramatic. Things had happened that he could never even have dreamed of. He behaved and reacted like he'd never have thought possible, almost like some*one*, some*thing* had taken control of his body and was making him do things he'd never have been able to do before.

Just two nights previously, George would have been alone in his quiet little house, reading a book or watching some anodyne, pointless, uninspiring dross on the television, wishing for something exciting to happen. Now he was sitting in a grotty hotel bedroom, miles from home and a possible fugitive from the police – he was still unsure as to his actual criminal status, given that the police had so far been very circumspect in their accusations.

He'd been beaten and threatened by villainous thugs, bent on extracting from him the stolen loot that he'd been unfortunate enough to find himself in possession of. He'd been forced to traipse through the mud and dirt, after stashing the money in the woods, fearful for his very life.

He'd been hounded by detectives and policemen, desperate to arrest him for a crime – any crime – whether he'd committed it or not.

He'd met a girl, and fallen in love. There was no use in pretending any more, or affecting even a modicum of nonchalance; it was definitely love. And he'd fallen head-first into it like a muddy puddle.

Something exciting had happened all right. Something altogether far too exciting.

George looked down at the policeman's card in his hand, screwed it up and threw it down on top of the television next to the one Keane had left earlier that day. He sat down on the bed, then instantly stood up. He paced the tiny room, heading two full steps in one direction before having to turn round in the cramped environment and pace two steps back. He sat back down on the bed again.

The robbers had found him. This was bad.

They knew he had the money. This was even worse.

George looked at his watch. It had been 32 minutes since the robbers had left, giving him an hour to report back to them. That bloody policeman had taken up too much of his time with his ridiculous questions. George hadn't had time to think things through and now he had just 28 minutes before he needed to be down in the bar.

They wanted the money. That was the main thing. They wanted their money, and George had it.

Perhaps if he just gave it to them they would leave him alone and be on their way. Would he have time to race down to the woods, get the money and bring it back here before he was supposed the meet them? He didn't think so.

And even if he did, the place was still crawling with police. It was unlikely that he'd manage to leave the hotel, make it to the woods, get the money and race back without at least one person seeing him.

Besides which, George was certain that Keane was still lurking somewhere, ready to pounce if he stepped even slightly out of line. Being caught in possession of a large bag of stolen money would certainly not have helped his case with the over-eager detective.

Really, George should have gone straight to the police. He should have told Sergeant Collins everything he knew about the robbery. He should have explained how he'd accidentally ended up with money; how it had never been his intention to run but he didn't know what else to do. He should have told him how he'd just been threatened by the real criminals and led the police straight to the money.

But somehow George wasn't confident that the police would believe his reasonable, rational explanation. The evidence against him was more than slightly compelling and if he confessed to even having been in the bank he was sure he'd end up behind bars.

What if George simply ignored the robbers? He could hide up here in his room, ignore their threats and hope they'd eventually just get bored and go away. If there's one thing you've become good at over the years George, he thought to himself, it's hiding from the truth. But then, look where that's got you.

And the chances of the robbers simply giving up and leaving was pretty slim. Besides which, they now knew George's home address. And though he wasn't sure exactly what the man had meant, his threat of bad things happening to him and other people had seemed rather ominous.

Like it or not, George would have to go and meet them.

More than anything, George wanted to run and find Alice. She'd know what to do. But then that was also the last thing he wanted to do.

He'd only met the girl a few brief days before. And despite all the odds, somehow she had found him attractive. Even more incredible, they had really hit it off and had rather inexplicably started a romance.

Since then, George had managed to get himself in a fight with her ex-husband; had sweated almost to the point of collapse in preparation for their first sexual encounter; had managed to become involved in a bank robbery; and had all but fallen apart in front of her no less than three times. George was acutely aware that he was not presenting the most confident, manly, accomplished impression of himself.

Now, sitting on the bed in the tiny room, he felt a strange new sense of confidence surging through him as if a light had been switched on in a long dark building. He needed to take charge. He wanted Alice to know that he was a capable man. A man who could take charge of a situation and be brave when it was called for.

He wanted her to know that he was the type of man who could take care of her, not some blithering, blubbering idiot who'd come running to her for help whenever something went wrong. He had to prove that he could be more than meek, mild-mannered and humble.

More than anything, he knew that this was his mess and something that he needed to sort out for himself. It wasn't fair to involve Alice any more than he already had.

Just a few days before all this nonsense, his natural fight-or-flight instinct would have seen him running to his car and driving away as fast as the legal speed limit would allow. But now, with so much at stake, and with George feeling more out of his depth than ever before, he knew that simply wasn't an option.

For the first time in his life, George had something to fight for.

He jumped up from the bed again, enthusiasm propelling him quite literally into action. This is it, George, he thought to himself. This is your moment to shine.

All he needed was to come up with a brilliant plan. There had to be a way to see the robbers brought to justice; George's name cleared of any wrongdoing; the money returned to its rightful owners; and the girl he loved positively swooning at his heroism.

You can do this, George, he thought. You're a clever man. You're resourceful.

George stood, full of optimism. He stared at a dark, damp patch on the wall in front of him, tapping his forefinger intently against his lips as he carefully slotted all the relevant pieces of information together in his mind. He thought and thought, patiently waiting for the solution to materialise.

He tapped his finger more intently. He thought and he thought.

He tapped again. He thought again.

He tapped and thought, and tapped and thought.

His mind remained a blank.

George slumped back down onto the bed, resting his weary head in his hands. He now had only 16 minutes before he needed to be downstairs in the bar. Clearly this was going to be harder than he'd anticipated.

CHAPTER 46

THE rope dug tightly into Alice's wrists. It was thick and hard and brightly coloured; some kind of professional climbing rope, like the type seen looped around the torsos of mountain climbers. She tried to move her hands, testing the knot's integrity, but it was tied so tightly that it chaffed roughly, pinching at her skin with each slight movement.

The big man had picked her up, almost with no effort at all, and thrown her down onto the bed. She'd been instantly terrified, unsure as to what he was planning, and obviously fearing the worst.

She'd wanted to scream; to shout out loud, alert someone – anyone – to what was happening. But somehow she just couldn't. She opened her mouth but no noise followed. It wasn't at all like you see in horror films where the heroine comes within fifty feet of trouble and unleashes a loud, blood-curdling scream. Here she was, in real, imminent, terrifying danger, and she couldn't even squeak as loudly as a mouse.

He'd flipped her over then, pulling her hands hard behind her back, as the other huge brute had slipped the rope around her wrists and tied them tight. Then she'd been thrown back into the corner of the bed, fear preventing her from moving or speaking, as the three men stared back at her with eyes dark like thunderclouds.

How could she have been so stupid? Looking up at them now, it was so obvious that these were no policemen. The man's identity card had looked real enough and maybe it was the hindsight of all that had happened in the last three minutes but she couldn't believe she'd ever fallen for the whole policeman bit.

The two bigger men were hardened and thuggish and looked like they had no more than a handful of brain cells between them. The larger of the two had a ruddy, angry face and big, rough hands like cement blocks. She half expected to see jets of steam shooting out of his nostrils, like a snorting cartoon bull. The other one's face was strewn with stubble and tiny scars, where he'd clearly seen more than the odd scrap or two. He had dark, shaggy hair, and his eyes were all menace and fury.

These two had clearly spent far more time eluding the police than serving alongside them.

Alice guessed the third man must have been the leader. He certainly seemed to be doing most of the talking and was about as slippery a human being as she'd ever encountered. He was like a giant slug, slithering and squirming his way around the room. He was very well dressed: in a suit and tie, with incredibly shiny shoes. But something about him was wrong. He looked artificial.

"Now believe me, Alice – can I call you Alice?" he said. "We have absolutely no interest in hurting you or harming you in any way."

That voice wasn't fooling her for a second. The exaggerated plummy tones, the over-enthusiastic rolling of the R's – this man was no more upper-class than she was. He was clearly a liar, and – quite aside from the fact that he and his friends had tricked her, grabbed her, tied her up and were holding her captive – she could tell that he was definitely not to be trusted.

He did, however, seem strangely genuine in his assertions that he wouldn't hurt her. Alice had no doubts that, should he have allowed them to, the man's thuggish accomplices could have inflicted a very great deal of pain on her without any real qualms whatsoever. But this strange, conniving fake detective had control over them and was stopping them from hurting her.

The posh man came close to her. His lip curled into a crooked, lop-sided smile and a deceptive glint twinkled in his eye as he spoke.

"Now Alice, as you've no doubt already deduced, we're not really officers of the law."

Deduced? Officers of the law? Who the hell speaks like that, thought Alice. This guy was working far too hard on his false persona.

"And, as you now know that, I'm guessing that you've probably figured out who we really are," he continued.

Alice sat silent, her face stony and uncooperative.

"We are... oh, what's the word for it?"

"Bank robbers," barked John Clefton from the back of the room.

"Hmmm, quite," said the Major, raising an eyebrow. "I suppose that is technically an adequate description. I prefer to think of us in slightly more romantic terms. Financial liberators... master criminals..."

He looked disapprovingly at his two accomplices.

"Though in this case, I suppose bank robbers is probably most apt. These two aren't exactly what you'd call the romantic type," he said, coughing out a smarmy chuckle.

"But allow me to introduce myself. My name is Major Charles Fairview. I won't go through the whole back story, but needless to say that yes, we are the devilish fiends that robbed your town's bank today."

Alice sat silent.

"Unfortunately, there was one minor hiccup in an otherwise flawless, carefully constructed, well-thought-out plan, in that my colleague here decided for reasons best known to himself, to give our hard earned – well, hard stolen – money to your boyfriend."

The big man at the back of the room sneered and grunted.

"So you robbed the bank and you managed to get away without actually taking any of the

ice. "Not exactly *master* criminals."

"Quite," said the Major, grimacing at his two cohorts. "And that is something that we are most keen to rectify."

"And where exactly do I fit into all of this?" she said.

Alice did, of course, know exactly where she fitted in. But it seemed more sensible to at least feign ignorance of the situation. She didn't know how much they knew about her, or about George, so it made sense to stay on the back foot for the time being. Mostly, though, she just felt like being bloody-minded.

She realised that it probably was not particularly wise to antagonise three men who were known to use violence, menaces and machine guns to get what they wanted. Not to mention the fact that they were currently holding her hostage and tied up with climbing rope. But there was something so insufferable about the Major that she couldn't help but want to wind him up.

"You can think of yourself as incentive," the Major said. "Your boyfriend has our money. We want it back. And you are the incentive he needs to make sure he gives it to us instead of doing something stupid."

Alice grimaced with a look of derision as the Major reached into his pocket and pulled out a mobile phone. He clicked a few buttons, pointed it at Alice and said, "Look as scared as you can."

Alice raised an eyebrow and flashed her most disapproving face as the Major snapped a picture of her.

"Hmm, not quite the Mona Lisa," he said examining the picture, "but it'll do."

"I have no idea what you're talking about, you know," said Alice in a less-than-convincing voice. "George doesn't have your money. He's been in bed all day with a hangover. He hasn't been anywhere near the bank."

"Please, my dear, credit us with some intelligence. Well, me at least," said the Major, rolling his eyes in the direction of the other men. "We know he has the money. And if he has any sense, he'll do exactly as I say and give it back."

Alice shifted on the bed.

"I don't want to hurt you, Alice, I really don't. But I'm afraid I can't say the same for my two friends here. They've already missed their dinner and they get terribly angry when they haven't been fed," he laughed. "There's only so long that I can appeal to their better natures – what little they have, that is."

"You won't get away with this, you know," said Alice. "I happen to know the local police sergeant personally and he's not going to stand for you coming into our town, robbing the place, taking people hostage. It's only a matter of time before he catches up with you. The best thing you could do is to let me go right now, get in your car and drive away as fast as you can."

The Major chuckled to himself.

"Oh yes, I believe I've seen your sergeant. Tubby fellow. Very scary," he said with a mock look of fear on his face. "He certainly stamped his authority when he allowed us to rob the bank and get away practically unchallenged. He looked highly formidable diving for cover and stumbling behind a car when he thought these two had opened fire on him. Quaking in our boots, weren't we chaps?"

The two men laughed a heavy, derogatory chuckle.

"Yeah, well, you didn't get any money, did you?" said Alice.

"Not yet, said the Major, a darker tone playing in his voice as a look of real annoyance flashed in his eyes. "Not yet."

Alice tried her hardest to remain nonchalant. She didn't want to give in to the feelings of terror that were slowly growing inside of her. She wanted to appear staunch and resilient; not give away even the slightest hint that they were getting to her. But the thought of these two thugs being let loose on her was more frightening than she wanted to admit to herself.

"Now," said the Major, looking at his watch, "you'll have to excuse me, but I'm afraid I have a rather pressing appointment."

He turned to the smaller of the two men and said, "You stay here and keep an eye on our guest."

He then picked up a large, shiny swathe of material and threw it to the other. "Here," he said. "Put this on."

"Ah, not again," complained the man, looking disdainfully at the outfit.

The Major picked up a second outfit, and moments later the two men had transformed into second rate Elvis impersonators. Alice had to hold back from laughing at the ill-fitting costumes, the larger man looking like a giant, cranky baby.

The Major crossed the room and placed a hand on the doorknob.

"Alice, we'll be back presently. Hopefully with the news that this whole sorry mess has been resolved. You just sit tight and... enjoy the sparkling conversation."

He coughed out another smarmy chuckle then he and the other man left the room.

Alice looked at her remaining captor. He gazed back at her with a simple, blank stare.

"Oh George," she whispered to herself, "I really hope you're worth all of this."

CHAPTER 47

A THICK fog of stale beer and crisp fat filled the air of the bar as George walked in through the door. Small particles of dust hung like a curtain, sparkling and twinkling, dancing gently as loose beams of light illuminated their ethereal form. The place was empty. No grumpy old barman, no Les in his usual seat. No customers at all.

George had been hoping to find Alice serving behind the bar but there was no sign of her. Where was she anyway? She should have been back to see him by now.

George approached the bar, peering behind the counter to check that the place really was empty. An ominous silence filled the room. He crossed it and sat at the small round table in the corner, facing the door.

The open collar of his outfit hung loose, exposing far too much of his pale, bony chest and he became acutely aware of just how he looked. A pale blue Elvis Presley jumpsuit would hardly have been his first choice of outfit for an occasion like this. It wouldn't have been his first, second or even tenth choice for pretty much any outing. But then, he wasn't sure what he would have worn, given the option to change. What is the appropriate attire for a showdown with armed robbers?

He tried pulling the collar together, urging it to stay in place. But it flopped languidly open, revealing three wiry chest hairs that sat, embarrassed, above the start of a meagre paunch. The pink, swollen curve of his stomach seemed to smile up at him.

Unsure of whether or not the dark glasses covering half his face made him look more, or less, ridiculous, he opted to leave them on in the hope they might offer some small modicum of menace.

"Mr Thring," said the Major loudly as he walked in through the door of the bar. "How good of you to meet me here."

He crossed the room, smiling sycophantically as he perched on the stool opposite George. The larger of his two accomplices lurked at the back of the room, standing guard over the doorway, gazing around furtively and visibly bristling with aggression.

George remained still and silent, hiding behind the large gold rims of his plastic sunglasses.

"Terribly sorry to have to dash off like that, George – can I call you George?" said the Major.

George said nothing.

"Good. Now, where were we?" The Major stared up into the corner of the ceiling, theatrically tapping his lips with his forefinger and pretending to think.

"Oh yes, that's right… our money."

George opened his mouth to speak, but the Major instantly cut him off.

"Now, before we get into that old nonsense – 'I haven't got the money,' 'yes you have,' 'no I haven't,' 'yes you have' – allow me to show you something."

He reached into his pocket, pulled out a mobile phone and clicked several buttons. He turned it round and held it up so that George could see the screen.

George's mouth fell open. An icy chill ran the length of his spine. A heavy knot throbbed deep in his stomach, and he suddenly thought he might be sick. He pulled the giant glasses from his face and looked closer. It was a picture of Alice.

His Alice. Tied up and hunched back on a bed. George's heart pounded in his chest, the blood whooshed in his ears again.

He grabbed the phone from the man's hand, pulling it closer to his eyes and inspecting it. The look on Alice's face was one more of defiance than terror. And if he wasn't mistaken, George could have sworn he saw more than a subtle flash of annoyance.

"That's… what… how?" George stumbled.

"Yes," chuckled the Major with a menacing grin, "I thought that might get your attention."

"Where is she? What have you done with her?"

"Don't worry George, Alice is perfectly safe. She's upstairs right now with one of my colleagues. And if you do exactly as I say, she'll stay that way."

"And what if I don't?" George blurted. The words took him more by surprise than anyone else. He genuinely didn't know where they had come from, or what had prompted him to say them.

Perhaps he *had* been watching too much television. He'd never been in a situation like this before and had absolutely no idea how to react. What exactly are the protocols for this kind of thing? What are you supposed to say when someone shows you a picture of the woman you love tied up and held prisoner?

As an unfortunate consequence George found himself falling back on his limited cultural references of similar situations, blurting out random reactions like a bit-part actor in a bad TV crime drama.

What if I don't? Could he have said anything more stupid? He would have apologised for uttering such an obviously pointless question and put the whole thing down to nerves, but he suspected it might harm his position of power in the equation. So he sat, stony-faced, and tried to ignore their looks of derision.

"I should have thought that was perfectly obvious," chuckled the Major. "But if I must spell it out… Give us our money, Mr Thring, and you and Alice will go unharmed. I promise you that.

"Don't cooperate," he continued, in a far more sinister tone, "and after the brothers here have beaten you, cut off any loose body parts and buried you alive in a shallow grave, I'll leave them in a room alone with Alice. For as long as it takes.

"I daren't even imagine what kind of horrible things they'll think up," he said, screwing up his face and raising his hand to his mouth, pretending to hold back the bile from rising, "but it won't be pleasant. I promise you that as well."

George's mouth turned desert-dry, his face flashing deathly pale. It was all he could do to remain upright in his seat, not lurch forward and throw up all over the tiny table separating them. He suddenly wished he'd kept the sunglasses on. He was sure the man could see the terror in his eyes.

"The situation is very simple, George," the Major continued. "You have our money. We have your girlfriend. I think the best course of action would be to see those two things returned to their rightful owners as expediently as possible. Agreed?"

George nodded solemnly, afraid to speak in case a tell-tale crackle sparked in his voice, betraying his nerves.

"Good. Now, where is the money?"

A part of George wanted to tell them exactly where the money was. Let them go and get it and be on their way. He didn't care about foiling their plan; depriving them of the proceeds that were not rightfully theirs. He didn't care about seeing them punished for their crime; brought to justice and made to pay.

He didn't even care about standing up for himself, using this misadventure as the opportunity finally to assert himself and prove that he was capable of doing something more than floundering through life agreeing to people and doing as he was told.

He just wanted Alice back. And he wanted these people – Major Fairview, the Thug Brothers, Detective Keane, Sergeant Collins – out of his life for good. And surely the quickest way to achieve that would be to give them their damn money and hope they just slipped away.

But he also knew that giving them the location of the money was the worst thing he could do.

Aside from the fact that there was clearly something very suspicious about this Major Fairview – the odd way he would deviate, just momentarily, from his posh accent into something darker and more earthy – George had seen first-hand what these men were really like. They were armed robbers; kidnappers; brutal thugs. The image of that poor American man's nose exploding as it collided with the butt of the machine gun ran through George's mind, and the hollow thud which reverberated around the bank as his stunned body collapsed to the ground echoed in George's memory.

These were not men to be messed with, and definitely not to be trusted. If he did give them the location, there was no way he could rely on them to honour their promise of releasing Alice unharmed.

The fact that George was still walking around freely meant two very important things: 1) The money was George's leverage: they were desperate to get their hands on it and desperate to make sure that George gave it only to them rather than handing it over to the police or even keeping it for himself. 2) With all the police still present in town, the robbers were clearly wary of trying to force George's hand too aggressively. That's why they had taken Alice, to threaten him indirectly.

As long as George was the only one who knew where the money was, that would keep Alice safe and buy him some time.

George took a deep calming breath, straightened himself in his seat, then picked up the large golden sunglasses and placed them back on his face. From somewhere deep down inside himself, in a place he hadn't been for many years, he drew up his very last reserves of courage.

"Yes, I have your money," he said. "But you can't have it back."

CHAPTER 48

"WHAT did you say?" Major Fairview's face flashed with a mixture of confusion, exasperation and rage.

"I said you can't have your money back," George replied, "at least, not yet anyway. The money is safe. It's hidden in a place not too far from here. Somewhere that nobody will think to look for it."

The Major went to speak but George held up a hand to indicate that he didn't want to be interrupted.

"Believe me," he said, "I want nothing more than to give you your money, send you on your way, and never have to see your faces again. I only have your money in the first place because that idiot shoved it into my hands. And I didn't want to hang around and wait for the police to arrest me."

"So you'll get your money back," he continued. "Just, not yet."

"Remember we have your girlfriend, George," snapped the Major. "You'll go and get our money now, or I swear to God she'll…"

"No!" shouted George, slamming his hand down onto the table so hard that the glasses hanging behind the bar shook and tinkled with the impact. It was so hard, in fact, that George felt a blinding, searing pain explode in his palm, surge out to the tips of his fingers and shoot up through his wrist. It took all of his strength not to cry out in agony, as he winced and ground his teeth hard together.

He was thankful that he'd thought to replace the dark glasses on his face as they concealed the tell-tale specks of tears welling up in his eyes.

"You listen to me," George said, summoning as much authority in his voice as he could. "This place is crawling with police. Now, I'm no criminal mastermind, but I can't help but think that a man strolling down the street with a duffel bag full of stolen money is likely to draw more than a little attention."

George was on a roll now. He felt powerful and in command. Little rushes of adrenaline surged through his blood; moistened his palm; made his skin tingle.

"I'm in no hurry to get arrested. And the fact that you three are cowering here in this hotel tells me that you aren't either. So, assuming you don't want the police taking possession of the money, or coming here and arresting us all, you'll have to wait until I can get the money safely."

The Major bristled with annoyance, appearing to contemplate George's words. He raised no objections.

"Very well, Mr Thring. What do you suggest?"

"I'll get you the money and we'll make the exchange. But we have to lie low for the time being. I'll have the cash for you tomorrow. And you give Alice back to me. And if you've hurt so much as one hair on her head, I'll…"

"You'll what?" shouted the large man at the back of the room.

George had got so deeply into his role that he'd almost forgotten the thug was there. It stopped him in his tracks. He realised he'd got carried away with himself again, spouting insults and threats and slipping into bad cop drama clichés.

If you harm a hair on her head... Calm down, George. Keep cool.

The adrenaline shuddered through his veins. He took a deep breath and composed himself.

"Just have her there," he said.

George couldn't bear the thought of leaving Alice alone with these men overnight. He wanted to attack them, launch himself at them, fight them until he could force them to release her. He wanted to pick up the small table, smash it into the Major's head and throw it across the room at the other one. He wanted to stand up like a man and force the men to deal on his terms.

But that was just the adrenaline talking. George was also acutely aware of his own physical restrictions. Besides being literally half the size of the man guarding the door, George had never been in a fight in his life. He'd never even been particularly aggressive towards anyone.

One time he'd come running out of his house early on a Saturday morning, anger surging through him, all ready to admonish a man for letting his dog crap on his lawn. Somehow George had ended up apologising to the man, patting the dog on the head, and clearing up the mess himself.

George wouldn't even know where to start when it came to fighting these men. Where do you stand? How do you stand? Do you all do stretches first to avoid pulling muscles and injuring yourselves?

He still hadn't even been able to lift his throbbing hand from the table in case he'd done some serious lasting damage to it. He hadn't wanted to shatter the illusion of appearing calm by howling in agony at a broken wrist.

George knew that the only chance he had of successfully rescuing Alice was if he forced the men to make the exchange on his terms. The time to be a hero would come, but for now George would have to leave Alice with them. He knew they wouldn't hurt her so long as George still had the money.

Besides which, he needed time to plan things. He couldn't just jump straight into being heroic, he needed to work up it. Heroism is a far trickier business than people give you credit for, he thought.

"Very well, Mr Thring," said the Major, "you make a fairly good point. There are a few too many police officers in the vicinity at present. And I suppose it wouldn't really do to be caught acting too criminally in their presence. Tomorrow it is, then. Meet us in the small car park at the back of the hotel at 6am. I trust that will allow you adequate time to retrieve the money from wherever you have it hidden."

"No," said George firmly.

"No?" said the Major, surprised.

Once again George shocked himself with his sternness. And he was aware that he was really pushing his luck in disagreeing with the Major. But he had to do things his way. If George simply gave in to the man's every demand he'd lose every bit of power in the exchange. He knew he had to force the upper hand if he and Alice were going to walk away from this, and to do that he couldn't allow the Major to dictate proceedings.

It was also extremely unwise to allow the Major to determine the meeting place. He would have no idea of what he was walking into and, most importantly, what hidden dangers might be awaiting him. Meeting in a quiet car park at the back of a building before the rest of the town was up and out of their Elvis Presley pyjamas? How stupid did he think George was?

"No," George said again, "if you want your money then we do it my way."

He cleared his throat, shifting slightly in his chair, trying hard not to show his nervousness. His throat was dry and tight. "An empty car park at 6am? I think we'll meet somewhere a little bit more public, if you don't mind."

"Might I remind you that we have your girlfriend, George? I'd hate it if something bad were to happen to her, like... oh I don't know... falling down and breaking all of her fingers."

"If you hurt her..."

"It doesn't need to be like this, George. We're both intelligent men. Just do as I say, stop all this messing around, and I promise you she won't be harmed."

George sat quietly for a second, again thankful for the dark glasses hiding the uncertainty that was surely flashing across his eyes. He took a deep steadying breath and said resolutely, "No. If you want your money we do it my way. We meet tomorrow night, somewhere a lot more public with plenty of people around."

The Major's jaw clenched, his eyes narrowing to thin slits, as for the first time George felt as though he'd managed to seriously annoy him. He seemed to think for a second before saying, "Fine. And exactly where do you have in mind?"

George was instantly stunned. He'd been concentrating so hard on keeping his cool and forcing the Major to accede to his plan, that he hadn't actually given much thought to what his plan was going to be.

"Erm..." he said. "I... er..." Silence.

A heavy air hung between them. In the background the large man grunted with annoyance. Instinctively George looked over in his direction. His eyes fell upon a poster fixed to the wall right next to the man's large, shaven head.

"There," said George pointing at the poster.

"Oh dear God," said the Major turning in his chair to look. The poster read:

THE RED LION, LOWER CHIDBURY
PRESENTS
OUR WORLD FAMOUS
ELVIS IMPERSONATOR KARAOKE TALENT CONTEST
FRIDAY NIGHT
8 TILL LATE

"Very well, Mr Thring," said the Major, standing from his seat. "We'll see you tomorrow at 8pm. Don't forget the money."

The two men left the room. George waited a few moments until he was certain that they had gone before pulling the dark glasses from his face, slumping back in his seat and exhaling heavily.

What on earth had he got himself into? Was he really going to be able to pull this off and rescue Alice?

George jumped up and made to leave, just as Les walked in through the door.

"Hello Thring," he said. "Fancy seeing you here. You joining me for a drink?"

"Oh no, thanks," said George, "I have to get back to my room."

Less looked at him quizzically, then gazed round at the empty bar.

"Where is everyone?" he said. "What are you doing down here in an empty bar?" Then noticing George's pallid expression, he said, "Hey, are you all right, Thring? You're as white as a ghost."

For a second George considered confessing everything. Les was a knowledgeable man, after all. He was familiar with the criminal element. He'd been to prison. He might be able to help in some way.

But then, as friendly as he seemed, how did George know whether or not he could be trusted. After all, he was familiar with the criminal element. He'd been to prison.

George had only known him for a few days and had no idea how he might react. He might be appalled and go straight to the police. He might see an opportunity to get rich himself and try and get George to hand the stolen money over to him instead.

At that moment, the only thing in his favour – the only thing keeping Alice alive – was the fact that only he and three other men knew that he had the money from the robbery. George couldn't be sure what danger he might be putting Alice in if he let anyone else in on his secret. So for the time being he would have to do this all alone.

"Oh no, I'm fine thanks," he said to Les. "Just a bit tired. Think I could do with a lie down."

George didn't wait for a reply. He dashed out through the door, made his way quickly up the stairs and rushed into his room shutting the door firmly behind him. He perched on the end of the bed, seeking out the familiar brown stain on the wall and resumed his despondent gazing.

His mind raced with terrifying, horrible images. Thoughts of what they might be doing to Alice. He again entertained notions of heroism – tracking them down, sneaking into their room stealth-like, striking with brutal force and rescuing her. Then he remembered the very good reasons why that plan was unlikely to succeed.

He felt nauseous thinking of Alice tied up, helpless, having to spend the night in the company of those thugs. But there was nothing he could do. He'd bought himself some time and that was the main thing. Now he could sit there all night, examine all the angles and explore every possibility. He'd think up a genius plan to catch these criminals and get his Alice back safe and sound.

He gripped his chin between thumb and forefinger, stared straight ahead at the wall and thought hard.

Minutes later George was lying flat on his back, snoring loudly; lost in a dense, distant sleep.

CHAPTER 49

THE light outside the window had long since died away, leaving behind a cool, dark night sky. A distant golden streetlight haze hummed in the air outside as a gentle breeze rustled the leaves on the trees. Red and blue flashing lights scarred the black of the sky; the beams floating up from the bottom of the hill and bouncing off the buildings outside. The mad chatter and hurried footsteps that had previously filled the air had died away, faded like a scattered mist, and an eerie quiet filled the town.

Alice couldn't be sure exactly what time it was or how long she had been in the room. A soft chinking of cutlery on plates, mixed with a soft murmur like bees buzzing in a hive, throbbed somewhere beneath her, rising up through the floor. Dinner service was in full swing in the dining room.

No doubt Mum would be cursing her name for ditching her shift, leaving her to cook the food and tend to the scattering of customers. She'd manage, of course. Dinner service was never busy. Though she'd be annoyed nonetheless.

But would anyone actually be missing her? Probably not enough to send out a search party. Not yet, at least.

The ropes on her wrists seemed to dig in more with each passing second, cutting off the blood to her hands and making them numb. A wave of pin-prick stings rippled and buzzed along on her fingertips. Her legs were stiff and sore where they'd been sitting for so long in one position and a dull ache throbbed in the small of her back. Thankfully they'd chosen not to gag her as well; she had no tatty rag stuffed in her mouth to keep her quiet. She was thankful for that small mercy at least.

The big man sat in the chair opposite her, yawning his own dissatisfaction at the situation. He didn't seem concerned about the throng of police that had been swarming around outside for the past few hours. Alice had expected him to be more desperate somehow; concerned about the possibility that the good guys could be seconds from beating down the door and dragging him off. But he just seemed bored and annoyed at having been detained, like he'd been forced to work late and wanted to get home for his dinner.

Either this guy was one very cool, collected customer, thought Alice, or he was a bit... well... simple.

Since the two of them had been left alone together not a single word had been said. It had felt like hours; the cool early evening air and virtual silence seeming to freeze time, drag seconds on for minutes, turn minutes into hours. In truth it had probably not been more than half an hour.

Alice wondered what the men were doing. She assumed they'd gone to confront George. That's certainly what the Major had alluded to and presumably why he'd taken that picture of her. Evidence of his captive.

She wondered whether George would be okay. Would they hurt him? Had they already hurt him? Maybe they'd try and take him captive too and force him to turn over the money.

Would he go to pieces when he saw that picture and give them the money outright? Maybe help was already on its way.

Or what if they couldn't find him? What if he'd already taken off? Grabbed the money, jumped into his car and disappeared.

After all, what did she really know about George? He'd seemed nice, genuine and loving. She'd assumed her feelings for him were reciprocated. But a stressful situation like this could well have changed everything. Maybe he didn't like her as much as she thought. Maybe he was already back at home, watching EastEnders, glad to be away from this whole sorry mess.

Suddenly the door swung open. A dissatisfied looking Major stormed into the room, his face like thunder, flanked by the third man. He marched over to the window, gazing out into the night, seeming to settle himself before turning around and addressing Alice.

"Hello Alice. I trust my colleague here has been taking good care of you."

"Aside from the lack of cucumber sandwiches and being held here against my will, I have no real complaints," she snorted.

"Hmm," said the Major, "very droll. Well, I hope you're comfortable, because it seems you'll be in our company for a little while longer."

Alice went to speak but her own incredulity was cut short by that of her previously silent companion.

"What?" he said. "How long? What happened to the money? Where's the money?"

The Major raised an eyebrow.

"I decided," he lied, "that we should put off the trade until tomorrow. There are still too many police hanging about. We need to keep out of sight for the time being. We can't risk moving too early."

"We've already been here far too long as it is," replied the man. "I don't like it. We should get out now. Find this Thring guy, force him to hand over the cash and get the hell out of here as quick as we can."

"And we will. But we have to wait until the right time. Need I remind you that it's your brother's fault that we're in this mess in the first place?"

"Well, when then?" barked the man angrily. "When do we get the money?"

"Tomorrow night. Don't worry, I have a plan."

"And what if this Thring has already taken off with the money?"

"Oh, I think there's very little chance of that," said the Major, turning back to Alice again. "Is there?"

Alice sighed to herself. She honestly didn't know.

CHAPTER 50

FRIDAY

GEORGE woke with a start. He sat bolt upright in bed, scratching his head and looking around. It took him a second to realise where he was, his sleep-fogged brain and his half-shut eyes failing to make sense of his surroundings.

Then it all came flooding back in an instant. Alice. The robbery. The money.

George glanced at his watch. 10.23am. He felt an instant chill of panic wash over him.

He hadn't meant to sleep this late. He hadn't meant to sleep at all. He was supposed to have spent the whole evening thinking over his situation, trying to mastermind a devilishly clever plan. Instead he'd passed out and was now no further on than when he'd left the bar.

"Brilliant, George," he sighed to himself. "What the hell am I going to do now?"

His mouth stretched wide with a yawn as he scratched a hand through his hair, trying to flatten down the most erratic sleep-starched peaks. His belly rumbled loudly: a deep gurgling, monstrous sound. He hadn't thought to eat the previous evening, such was his frantic mood and desperation. Now he was absolutely ravenous, a dark hunger aching in the pit of his stomach.

The sandwich that Alice had brought him was the only thing he'd eaten all the previous day and the limited sustenance he'd derived from that had long since worn off. He felt weak and slightly queasy, his head swimming from the lack of energy. He had to eat.

One of those epic fried breakfasts would go down a treat, he thought to himself. But was it really the done thing to sit and eat your way through a full meal, gorging yourself on sausages, bacon and fried eggs – not to mention toast, he'd have plenty of toast – when your girlfriend was being held captive?

It seemed slightly disloyal, and more than a little unfair. And he really should be using that time to work on devising his master rescue plan.

But then, he reasoned, surely his mind would function far more effectively if he were fully fed and firing on all cylinders. Taking on a hearty breakfast would only help him to think more clearly; get the cogs turning quicker.

Besides which, the breakfast was included in the price of the room, so it really only made sense to take advantage of it.

George stood, his mind made up and his stomach rumbling in anticipation of the food to come, when a sharp tapping sounded on the door.

George froze. He looked at the door, almost as if he'd be able to see through it if he stared hard enough.

Who is it now? The robbers again? That infernal detective? Had the police finally come for him?

Cautiously he reached out and gripped the door handle. He twisted slowly, pulling it open, his mind racing with all the horrible scenarios he'd spent the past twelve hours fearing. Then he let out a confused, garbled murmur.

Before him stood not a gang of dangerous thugs, an overly enthusiastic detective or a squadron of armed police, but a very meek, supplicant looking Anton Phelps.

"Hello George," he said in a quiet voice. "How are you?"

"Anton?" said George, still not entirely believing what he saw before him. "What are you... when... what are you doing here?"

"I could ask you the same thing," he said, forcing a laugh and attempting to sound friendly.

All of the man's usual cockiness was gone; his confidence drained from him and replaced with a mild, almost embarrassed demeanour. He seemed smaller somehow. He looked to George like a scared, apologetic boy who had knocked on his door to confess to smashing a window with his football.

George still struggled to find the words. Of all the people he supposed might be knocking on his door that morning, Anton was possibly the last. It occurred to George how strange it was that he'd thought it more likely he'd be carted off to prison – or even a shallow grave – than that a work colleague had come looking for him. It made him feel suddenly rather sad.

George stared at Anton. Anton stared back at George. A long, uncomfortable silence grew between them, like a balloon inflating close to the point of popping. Finally Anton broke it.

"Can I come in?" he said.

George looked back into the room: the messy bed standing proud; a heavy smell of dust and stale sweat filling the small confines. His stomach rumbled and gurgled loudly again as a stab of hunger throbbed deep inside him.

"No," said George, surprising both of them with the force and defiance with which it was delivered.

"No?" replied Anton.

"No. But I am quite hungry. Why we don't we go and have some breakfast?"

The two men made their way downstairs to the dining room, walking in near silence, and found a table in the middle. The old lady, Alice's mother, still dressed in her homemade Presley jumpsuit, brought over two cups of strong, tar-like coffee and took their order.

When she was gone, Anton said, with a look of pure bemusement on his face, "What is this place, George? And what's with your outfit? Does everyone around here dress like that?"

"It's a... long story," replied George firmly.

Silence hung between them again, the two men eyeing each other cautiously.

The old lady arrived at their table, placing two plates of fried food down in front of them. The plates were so heavy with food that they landed on the table with an audible thunk. Two fat sausages sat centred amid slices of crispy bacon, oil-drenched mushrooms, fried bread, beans, black pudding, tomatoes and runny-yolked eggs. A perfect circle of grease ringed the outer edge of the plate, a tiny oil rainbow glinting in the early morning light.

Anton physically winced as he took in the greasy plateful. George's belly rumbled loudly as he picked up his knife and fork and enthusiastically started eating.

Finally, with a mouthful of bacon, George spoke. "What are you doing here, Anton?"

"Well, when you didn't show up for work the other day we were all… worried about you."

Worried. The word hung unnaturally between them.

"We?" asked George.

"Yes, me, Clive… Louise. It's not like you, not coming in to work. I don't think I've ever known you to take even one day off sick."

Worried. They were worried about him? George had certainly not expected that. He'd honestly believed they'd barely even have noticed he was missing. But now they were worried about him?

"You didn't call," continued Anton. "You didn't email. We thought something might have happened to you."

Something certainly had happened to him. A lot more than he was prepared to share with Anton.

"Yes, sorry," said George, taking a large bite of sausage. "I suppose I should have phoned. I just needed a bit of time away and I thought I'd take some."

George was actually slightly amazed at himself. It was totally out of character to act with such blatant insubordination. Anton was technically still his boss, and it was unacceptable behaviour to simply take off without giving the standard week's notice and filing an official holiday form with Human Resources. But with a large bag of stolen money hidden in the woods, his girlfriend held captive by armed thugs and an overzealous detective harassing him, office protocol really was the last of George's worries.

He'd expected Anton to raise this; to rebuke him for flouting the correct procedures. If George or anyone in the team ever stepped even halfway out of line in the office, Anton always took the greatest deal of pleasure in pointing it out to them. A strange, self-satisfied grin would spread eagerly across his face as he quoted company policy, threatened to escalate the incident to management and told them that not just he but the company expected more from them as an employee.

Strangely, none of that came. There was no cocky grin, just a very straight, calm face.

"Okay, George," said Anton in a low, quiet voice; the practiced neutral tone of someone trained to deal with difficult situations. "I can understand that. We all need a bit of time off every now and then. And you deserve to take time off. So you came here and dressed like…"

George looked down at his clothes, stuffing another forkful of food greedily into his mouth, purposefully ignoring the observation.

"But that's not like you, George. So naturally we worried."

This time he leaned his head to one side, widening his eyes. It was presumably designed to infer some degree of concern, but it actually just made him look a bit simple. George suddenly felt an overwhelming urge to reach over and slap the stupid look off his face. But he forced it down with another bite of sausage.

"How did you find me here?" George said.

"Well, when you didn't turn up for work we knew there must have been something wrong. I went round to your house to find you, but there was no-one at home and your car was gone. That's when I called the police and spoke with a detective…"

"Keane?" interrupted George. "That was down to you?"

"Keane, yes. That was his name. He called me yesterday and told me that he'd found you here. He said that you were acting… strangely. So I thought I'd come here and see if…"

"What? See if I was off my rocker? See if I was having a nervous breakdown?"

It wouldn't have been totally off the mark. It was what George had thought himself only a few days before. But he resented Anton thinking it. It was one thing thinking you've gone mad yourself but another thing entirely to have somebody else suggest it.

"No, of course not. I just thought I'd see if I could find out what was happening. If I could help, maybe?"

"Help with what?"

"Like I say, George, it's not like you to just take off and not tell anyone. I was concerned that you might be…"

"You do think I'm crazy," said George indignantly.

"Not crazy, George. I never said that. But maybe you're suffering with… stress. It's nothing to be ashamed of; it affects more people than you'd think."

"Stressed?" said George. "Stressed? I'm not stressed."

He was, of course, incredibly stressed, but not for the reasons that Anton thought.

"Okay, but you must admit that it's not normal behaviour to just take off; to not turn up for work without so much as a phone call. Not to mention a bit unprofessional."

Was that it? Was that the real reason he was there? Despite the caring, sharing act, this strange little man had driven all this way to rebuke George for not following company procedure. Did he intend to frogmarch him back to the office to face a disciplinary?

George looked up from his plate, blowing out a long, exasperated sigh.

"Do you know what, Anton? Maybe I should have called to say I wasn't coming in. Maybe I shouldn't have just taken time off without asking. But I just... don't care. To be honest, I genuinely didn't think anyone would even notice I was gone."

"Oh George, that's not true. You're a very valued member of the team."

George could practically hear the man's skin creaking as he forced a sickly, rictus grin onto his face.

Valued member of the team? George had never felt particularly valued and wouldn't say he'd been treated as such. And as far as being part of the team? There was about as much team spirit between the four of them as between a pack of dogs fighting over a steak – George, of course, being the mutt that gave up early and went off in search of a quiet place to sleep.

"What are you doing here?" George said again, piercing another hunk of sausage with his fork. "And don't give me any of this worried shit. What are you really doing here?"

George was nearly as shocked at having sworn as Anton appeared to be. Maybe he really was having a nervous breakdown. He definitely had to agree that he was acting out of character. In fact, since he'd left work on Tuesday night, he hadn't really acted *in* character at all. Whatever it was, though, it was very liberating.

"Well, okay... yes," said Anton, looking slightly embarrassed, "there is slightly more to it."

George just looked at him, chewing loudly, raising his eyebrows as an indication for the man to get to the point.

"We've... er... well, we've been having trouble running the daily reports..." he said sheepishly.

George burst out laughing, nearly spitting a mouthful of food across the table.

"Are you telling me you've driven all the way here because you couldn't run the daily reports?" He laughed again. "I'm not the only one in the building that knows how to use the system. Clive or Louise should have been able to do it. Or you, for that matter."

"Well, we tried. Several times. But we just couldn't get the figures to look right. I've got Linda bloody Cardigan breathing down my neck, threatening to go to the MD if I don't get her the figures by Monday."

George shook his head. It was farcical. The reports that were the bane of his life. The thing he got more grief for than thanks. They were what had brought this man to come and find him. He wasn't a valued member of the team at all. They just needed him to do something they couldn't manage themselves.

"So, when were you thinking of coming back George? If we left now, we could be back in the office by lunch. Plenty of time to get the reports sorted, and then you could take the rest of the day off. Have a nice long weekend. How does that sound?"

"I'm still eating," said George nonchalantly.

"Well no, yes, of course. We can leave after you've finished your breakfast."

"No," said George flatly.

"No?"

"No. I'm not going back with you today. I have things to do, and I'm not leaving until they're done."

"Oh, okay. Erm... well, Monday then? You'll be back in on Monday, won't you?"

Something still didn't add up. There was something else in the man's eyes betraying a very different kind of concern.

"As gratified as I am that I appear to have suddenly become so indispensable," said George, "I'm just not buying it. You wouldn't come all this way and beg me to come back over the reports. Even if Linda was going mad, you'd just pass the buck and lay the blame square at my feet. You wouldn't come here and tell me how valued I am. There's another reason you're here, isn't there?"

Anton's face screwed up into that of a petulant child caught out in a lie.

"Well, it doesn't exactly look too good for me, does it? One of my staff goes totally tonto, races off into the middle of nowhere and is found days later dressed up like... what the hell is that costume, anyway?"

"Elvis Presley," George said, openly stunned at the young man's lack of cultural references. "You don't know who Elvis Presley is?"

"Well, whatever. Anyway, one of my staff has a breakdown and I didn't even notice the warning signs? Doesn't exactly signal great managerial potential, does it? What are senior management gonna think?"

"So, the real reason finally comes out," said George with a knowing smile. "You're not concerned about me at all, you're just worried about your own place on the ladder."

"Hey, you may not care about your career, George, but I do. I've already made team leader and by the end of the year I intend to be Junior Deputy Manager. After that the sky's the limit. But not with people like you dragging me down. You may not have any ambition, but I do. I want to get somewhere in life, not end up some sad, lonely, boring old man like..."

He suddenly stopped and looked down at the table.

"Like me?" said George, the insult hurting more than he'd have expected. Not because he was worried about what the inconsequential young man thought of him, but because he couldn't disagree with him. He wouldn't want Anton to end up like him either. It was no kind of life, not really. And he wouldn't have wished it on anyone – no matter how much of an insufferable idiot they were.

"I don't blame you, Anton," he continued. "I wouldn't want to end up like me either. Or at least not how I was."

"You... what?"

"Why do you think I'm here? Why do you think I bunked off work without calling, drove all the way out here and have spent the past few days dressed like this and not really knowing what I was going to do next?"

"I... I don't understand."

"I'll share a little secret with you, Anton," said George, furtively peering around the room for comic effect and then beckoning the man to lean in closer. "I *am* having a nervous breakdown."

The young man stared back, incredulous.

"At least, I thought I was. I left work on Tuesday night, got into the car and without realising I drove over 200 miles. I had no idea what I was doing, or where I was going, until my car ran out of petrol and I ended up here. I thought I was going totally crackers."

He threw a loud, maniacal laugh out into Anton's face.

"But then, since I've been here, taking some time to myself and just sort of… thinking… I realised it wasn't a breakdown at all. It was an awakening. Believe it or not, I had no idea how sad and pathetic I'd become. Seriously. But then, I mean, you don't really, do you? You just live your life, trundling from one day to the next, just sort of… being. And then it hit me, just like that, what an awful life I was living."

Anton looked back at him, with no idea what to say.

"So I don't blame you for not wanting to end up like me. Because I don't bloody well want it either."

"What are you saying, George?"

"What am I saying? I'm saying I don't want any of it anymore. The reports, the spreadsheets, the meetings, the inane conversations about cost benefits analysis… None of it matters. Seriously, none of it matters at all. If you want to make your life about that stuff then go ahead. But I don't want any of it."

"Now you are sounding crazy, George," said Anton defensively. "What are you going to do exactly? Sit around in a grotty hotel all day, dressed in stupid clothes? How long is that going to last? You have to have a job and there are far worse ones out there."

George sighed heavily.

"I don't doubt that. But it's not about what I'm going to do, it's about what I'm *not* going to do. What I've decided I can't do anymore."

"I really think you're overreacting, George. You're not thinking clearly. Why don't you come back with me? Come back to work. We'll put this down as a holiday. I'll say the request form was mislaid. Clerical error. You could take next week off, too. Get your head straight, recharge your batteries. You can even stay here, if you like. Finish whatever it is you're doing here."

George put down his fork, sighing heavily and pinching the bridge of his nose between thumb and forefinger.

"You're just not getting it, are you? I'm not coming back. I can't go back to that…"

He was going to say 'that version of myself', but Anton already thought he was crazy enough and he was conscious of trying not to come over too new-age. Instead he settled for 'shithole'. It was not strictly fair – George had always considered the offices and working conditions to be very reasonable, if a little lifeless – but the word held enough resonance to give his argument adequate weight and dissuade Anton from continuing with his pleas.

A look of panic stretched over Anton's face, his mouth opening and closing silently as he seemed to be searching for the right words.

"I'll give you a pay rise," he finally blurted.

The words shot out like bullets and George found himself actually recoiling with surprise. He'd expected Anton to get defensive. He hadn't anticipated this.

"What?" he said.

"And a promotion," continued Anton. "How does Senior Analyst sound?"

"What?" repeated George.

"And we could move the desks around if you want, make it a bit more cosy."

He was scrabbling around now, desperately throwing out ideas as they came to him.

"I mean, I can't actually promise on the last two, I'd need to get it signed off by management. But I can definitely do the pay rise."

George suddenly had a vision of himself sitting at his desk, typing away as he always did, with Clive huffing and ranting to one side of him, and Louise squawking on her phone and surreptitiously sneering at everyone around her to the other side. His heart sank at the thought of it; the utter dread of spending even one more minute living that life. There was no way that he could go back to that. Not now that so much had happened to him. He finally knew that he could never go back to that life.

"I'm sorry Anton. I really appreciate the offer of a pay rise, but I'm not coming back."

"You know, George, I didn't have to do things this way," said Anton petulantly, suddenly changing tactics. "You should be glad I'm even letting you keep your job. By rights I should report you to HR and have them take out legal proceedings against you for breaking the terms of your contract."

George just smiled at him. "You do what you feel you have to, Anton."

"Oh please come back. You have to George, you have to," said Anton in a final burst of pleading. "What about me? What do you think they'll do to me?"

"Oh, I'm sure you'll be all right," George said, standing up from the table. "With a bit of luck, we're all going to be all right."

Anton looked up at him with a quizzical expression, but it was too late. George was already marching towards the door with a determined stride.

CHAPTER 51

DETECTIVE Constable Michael Keane twisted and stretched in the driver's seat of his car. A dull ache throbbed in the small of his back. A sharper, more insistent pain screeched in the right side of his neck where it had been pressed up against the driver's side window for the past six or so hours.

His mouth was dry and filled with the grubby taste of morning. He cupped his hands to catch his breath and grimaced as he sniffed.

He hadn't actually intended to spend the night sleeping in his car. He would have preferred to stay in one of the local B&Bs but the whole town was fully booked with ridiculously-dressed, overly-enthusiastic Elvis fans and there were no free rooms.

He had, naturally, tried pulling rank; flashing his warrant card and demanding the use of a room in which to conduct his official police investigation into the robbery. He'd been given fairly short shrift by the first three hotel managers he'd tried this tactic with, however. And when they'd called his bluff he'd felt pretty stupid having no real recourse to force them into providing him with a room.

The whole town was clearly very serious about this odd festival, and somehow the nutcases dressed in shiny, sparkly romper suits, who swivelled their hips in the street and seemed capable of endless "uh-huh-huhs", were apparently more deserving of a decent night's sleep than a hardworking police officer on a mission to catch a dangerous, violent criminal.

Try as he might, Keane could not see the appeal of it. He remembered having seen Elvis Presley on the TV when he was a child. His dad had been something of a fan – not a crazy, costume-wearing, quiff-sporting, hip-gyrating nut-case like the crowd that had invaded this town. He just had a few records, a couple of books on the shelf and, now that Keane thought of it, some kind of commemorative ashtray. But he'd never shown even the slightest inclination to dance in the street, sing-a-long Elvis-style or attend strange festivals and conventions.

Keane didn't even mind the music, not really. It wasn't his sort of thing, exactly. He wasn't much of a music fan at all. But it was fairly inoffensive and Keane could appreciate that the man had a certain appeal; a substantial level of talent. Certainly more than most of the Saturday night talent show hopefuls that seemed to be in no short supply. But what was it about the man that caused people to go so over the top?

He glanced out of the fogged-up windscreen to the sequin-littered, multi-coloured passers-by who twinkled in the early morning sun. He yawned loudly, shook his head to wake himself up and stretched as best as he could in the meagre confines of the car.

He should really have driven home. It was after 10am and he should have been at the station over an hour ago. It was bound not to have gone unnoticed and Keane's new DCI would be less than impressed at his tardiness.

Keane reached for his mobile phone. He really should call the station and check in. He should give them a full and detailed progress report and let them know what he'd been working on for the past 24 hours. But then that would mean admitting he was working on a case that he was not, strictly speaking, supposed to be working on. Technically, this was still just a standard missing person's case, and he should have filed it, forgotten it and moved onto to other more serious matters.

If he called in now and reported what he was doing, there was every chance the commanding officer would blow his lid, order Keane to hand over his leads to the local force, and head back home for the bollocking that was awaiting him. There was no excuse for him simply disappearing, travelling all this way and not reporting in. There was certainly no excuse for doing it on his first day as a DC.

The only way to vindicate himself, and get out of this without the instant return to uniform that likely awaited him, was to come back with the goods: George Thring arrested, confessing and the return of the stolen money.

Besides, Keane had worked too hard to give up now. He was on the verge of cracking his first major case. And if they thought he was going to hand over an arrest like this to that fat, useless bumpkin Collins, they had another think coming.

Keane had told Collins too much already. He'd practically handed him the suspect on a plate. He'd have been worried that the small town cop might try and arrest Thring for himself, had he not already displayed his ineptitude in his handling of the robbery. The man didn't have the gumption to do proper police work; arrest proper criminals. Another very good reason for Keane to stay put; he didn't trust a single man on the local force to do a proper job and put Thring behind bars.

As long as George Thring was still in town it was Keane's duty to hang around and keep an eye on him. He was sure to slip up at some point.

Keane yawned again. He massaged his stiff shoulders, twisting his head from side to side, hearing the gravel-crunch clicking of the bones in his neck. He opened the driver's door and stepped out into the cool morning air. There was no harm, he reasoned, in continuing his surveillance from inside the hotel, rather than sitting parked outside it. Perhaps with a spot of breakfast to keep him going.

He made his way into the hotel and walked through to the dining room, sitting hidden at a table in the corner. He ordered a bacon sandwich and a cup of coffee. The aged waitress brought it over and Keane was actually shocked at the size of it.

The sandwich was constructed from two of the thickest slices of white bread he had ever seen and contained nearly a full pack of bacon. Great rivulets of grease mixed with lashings of butter and ran down the sides, pooling in tiny, shiny puddles on the plate. Keane could practically feel the heart attack just looking at it. He picked it up and made to take a bite when his attention was suddenly caught by the appearance of two men entering the room.

George Thring strolled purposefully through the door, still wearing that same ridiculous blue costume. He was followed closely by a lanky, weaselly looking man with a thin goatee beard.

It was George's boss, Anton Phelps. The man who had originally called Keane to investigate the case. What the hell was he doing here?

Neither man noticed Keane and he instinctively slumped down slightly in his chair, arranging the faux-leather-bound menu, the tomato-shaped ketchup bottle, and assorted condiments, into a huddle in front of him.

Thring and Phelps sat at a table in the middle of the room. It was too far away for Keane to hear what they were talking about. He would have to rely instead on his self-taught – and if he said so himself, highly accurate – lip reading skills. The main problem with that, of course, was that Thring's boss was sat with his back to Keane and doing most of the talking.

Thring simply sat there stuffing food into his face like a man who hadn't eaten in days. When he did speak his mouth was either obscured by a fork, or full of food, so the few words that Keane did manage to pick up made absolutely no sense whatsoever.

Despite not being able to tell what they were saying, this was clearly a very important development. What exactly was this guy's boss doing here? Keane mused. How was he involved? Was he here to collect the money, or maybe organise some kind of escape plan? Maybe Thring was organising another job and he'd called for reinforcements.

But if Phelps was involved somehow, why the hell had he called Keane in to investigate? None of it made sense.

When Keane had phoned with a progress report, Phelps had seemed shocked to learn that he'd tracked Thring to somewhere so far away. And when he'd first met the man, he'd seemed genuinely perturbed, worried for Thring's safety.

It was, of course, possible that he'd driven to talk with Thring. To make sure he was okay, and maybe persuade him to return home. But people don't really do that. If there was one universal truth that Keane would swear to it's that the world is full of bastards and nobody really cares about anybody else. Love thy neighbour? More like trick thy neighbour into thinking you give a shit about them, then look for a way to abuse and exploit them.

Keane had been on the job way too long. He'd seen the horrible things that people do to each other. He knew that people were fundamentally self-centred and he couldn't believe anyone would drive all this way just to check on an errant employee.

Besides which, Anton Phelps had not struck Keane as the loving, sharing, caring type. He was a childish, selfish, stab-you-in-the-back prick if ever he had met one. So what was he doing here?

It was more and more strange behaviour. And it all backed up Keane's theory that George Thring was definitely up to something. If he'd had any doubts about that, any thoughts of giving this up as a bad job, that maybe somehow he'd made a mistake about Thring, they were well and truly gone now. He was going to nail this bastard no matter what it took.

On the other side of the room George Thring stood from the table, shared a few words with his boss and walked out of the dining room. Keane observed as the young man slumped in his chair, burying his head in his hands. He was clearly upset about something.

He sat there for a few moments longer before calling the old lady over and paying the bill. He then let out a long, audible, depressed sigh, stood from the table and trudged dejectedly out of the room.

What did he say to you? thought Keane. Why are you so upset? There was only one way to find out.

CHAPTER 52

UNSURPRISINGLY, Alice hadn't slept. Not even for a single second. She'd lain there all night, every minute feeling like an hour, hoping that her body and brain would succumb to tiredness and she'd fall into a slumber. She craved the escape. She hungered for release, however short it may be. But sleep didn't come to her.

Aside from the increasing pain in her wrists; the coarse ropes seeming to grow tighter and tighter and the numbness in her hands turning into a continuous, throbbing ache, her mind had been racing all night. Her thoughts beating away at her like an insistent metronome, tick-tick-ticking.

She'd lain motionless for hours with her eyes clamped shut, affecting the illusion of sleep. She might not have been able to escape these idiots, but at least she didn't have to look at them. Unfortunately, she couldn't do anything about having to listen to them.

For the first few hours she'd endured the brothers grumbling about being stuck there in town, moaning about their hunger, planning what they would do with their share of the money when they finally got their hands on it. And then more grumbling.

Eventually they fell asleep, one on the second bed and one on the floor with his back pressed up against the door to keep people from getting in. And maybe also to ensure that none of them could get out.

Alice spent the next few hours listening to the two men snoring; producing loud, grating, guttural noises, like two wallowing hippopotamuses. They growled, snored, grunted, moaned, coughed and farted in a gruesome symphony of bodily noises, subconsciously trying to outdo each other in both volume and foulness.

But it was all just a surreal backdrop as Alice's mind whirred and spun, racing from thought to thought.

How had she managed to end up in this situation? Just a few days ago her life had been so simple. Boring? Yes. Depressing? Definitely. But simple, nonetheless.

Two days ago the worst thing that was likely to happen was that a customer on table four might complain that his eggs weren't runny enough. Now she was in very real danger of injury or death at the hands of three maniacs.

Yet, as she lay there, and the thoughts tumbled in her head like odd socks in a washing machine, she found herself less concerned with her own safety and more worried about George.

What was he up to now? Where was he? Had these men hurt him? Or worse?

And though she felt bad for thinking it, she couldn't help but wonder if he was out there doing something that would just make this whole mess even worse. Not meaning to, of course, but still…

He was such a curious soul, not at all the kind of man Alice would ever have pictured herself with. As long as she could remember, Alice had always been drawn to the type of men who could possibly be best described as dickheads.

She loved that excess of confidence that some men seemed to exude. She liked the arrogance, the way some men can walk into a room and just be so sure of themselves. It was a totally primal thing, she knew. A deep-seated human instinct. The female of the species subconsciously seeking out the protector and provider – the partner most likely to prove the best mate. It was the sort of thing that stirred loins and got the blood pumping.

The trouble, of course, was that once you peeled back that top layer, and the initial exciting, loin-stirring passion had dwindled, you invariably found yourself left with a selfish, inconsiderate man-child. Definitely not the sort you dream about settling down with.

Alice's ex-husband was a prime example. Michael had very little going for him, when she stepped back and really thought about it. He was handsome enough, though nothing particularly special. He had a pretty average body – not overweight and flabby, but neither toned, tanned or rippling with muscles.

He was not stupid, but hardly an academic. He was not exactly what you would call cultured – his idea of humour being limited to Mr Bean and those shows where people film their family members falling into ponds. Not forgetting, of course, his incomprehensible assertion that there was little point in reading a book when you could always wait for the film to come out.

He was a kind man, in his own way, but not terribly sensitive. And he didn't have a single romantic bone in his body.

On paper Michael was hardly the greatest catch. But what he lacked in all those other departments, he had always more than made up for in swagger.

Michael had more than his fair share of confidence and there was just something about the way that he walked into a room, the way he held himself, all cocksure and arrogant, that just made her tingle. At least it had.

He had been the most exciting man she'd ever met and somehow his confidence seemed to rub off on her. When they first started dating he'd made her feel like they could do anything, go anywhere, be anybody they wanted to be. With him the world seemed like an endless list of possibilities.

They'd rushed into a hasty marriage, bought a house and within just a few short months the truth about Michael shone through like the dull metal of a cheap ring when the gold plating starts to wear away.

He had confidence all right, but no ambition to go with it. He was too happy settling for an average life – everything that Alice wanted to avoid.

He had a good income from his own business, an affordable mortgage on a medium-sized house and a nice, not-too-flashy car. He had enough money to live a more-than-comfortable life, with two weeks in Spain each year and enough left over to save for the future and the inevitable bigger house they'd need to upgrade to when Alice gave up work and took up her new role as baby-making factory.

And for many people that would have been enough. It should have been enough for Alice and she felt bad that it wasn't. But she wanted more from life. She wanted to do things, see the world, explore who she was and who she could be. And if none of it ever happened, then that was fine as well, but at least she wanted to dream. She wanted to know that exciting things were still a possibility before settling down and surrounding herself with nappies.

With Michael, Alice knew that she'd never really want for anything. Except, of course, all of the things that she really wanted. It was like the whole rest of her life had been planned out for her before she'd even had the chance to think about what plans she had for herself. And so she'd walked away, not knowing where she was going, but certain of where she didn't want to be.

Aside from Michael there had been only a few other men. She'd had two brief relationships (fun at the time but never likely to last); a solitary one night stand which she'd found both incredibly thrilling and utterly regrettable in equal measure; and a few passing fancies that had never really come to anything.

But all of these men had shared one common factor: that cocky, arrogant, unquantifiable 'dickhead' quality. Alice always cursed herself for her own poor taste and swore solemnly that next time things would be different. But one cocky swagger later; one flash, arrogant smile from an over-confident idiot; and she'd get that trembling, heart-fluttering feeling as the pattern repeated.

Now, somehow, things really had changed and she'd found George. He couldn't be any more different from her usual type if he'd tried.

Where her previous men were overbearing and full of themselves, George was meek, shy and retiring. He wasn't full of cheap talk. He wasn't undeservingly impressed with himself. He was thoughtful and genuine.

Most importantly, George was not self-centred and uncaring. He was considerate, kind, generous and Alice got the very real feeling that he would do literally anything for her.

Alice would never have imagined herself with a man like George. But when she first saw him: rain-soaked, muddy and looking for help, she just felt so drawn to him. She'd never given much credit to the idea of soul mates, or of there being one person out there that she was meant to be with, but when he walked through that door she had an overwhelming sense that they were supposed to be together somehow. And she couldn't say why exactly, but she got that same heart-racing tingle.

The funny thing was, having thought she'd found a much more stable, dependable, normal man, her life had become a great deal more chaotic in only a few hours. Something exciting had definitely happened. Whether or not that was a good thing was still to be decided. But one thing Alice was sure of: as long as she knew George Thring her life would certainly not be boring.

A short, sharp squeaking sound suddenly stunned Alice back into awareness. On the other side of the room the Major shuffled in his chair, making the aged wooden joints creak and scrape.

He had barely made a sound all night. At first Alice had assumed that he had been asleep as well. But when she had surreptitiously half opened her eyes to see what was happening in the room, the Major had been sitting bolt upright in the chair opposite. At points he gazed intently at his glowing mobile phone, click-clicking as he typed on the keypad, sneaking furtive glances at his two companions.

At other points he sat staring thoughtfully out of the window. At one time she saw him fiddling with a large green duffel bag on the floor. He seemed to be looking for something as the bag rustled and the zip slid noisily open and closed. Alice had tried craning her neck to look but she couldn't see what he was doing.

The larger man, Steve, grumbled loudly, shuffling about against the door as he slowly awoke. He yawned and stretched his arms and legs wide as a low guttural sound echoed from deep within his gut. He opened his eyes and looked around.

"So," said the Major, "the monster awakes."

Steve Clefton looked over in the Major's direction, seemed suddenly to gauge where he was and replied with a terse, "Fuck off."

Alice opened her eyes then, deciding that she had feigned sleep for long enough. Seconds later, Steve gave the leg of his brother's bed a hefty, angry kick, and John Clefton woke up with an even more discontented expression.

"Oh Christ," he said looking around the room, "I nearly forgot..."

"How did we all sleep, children?" trilled the Major in a smarmy, sarcastic voice.

"I'm starving," said Steve Clefton.

"I wanna get out of here," said John.

"Hmmm, not exactly the question I asked, chaps," said the Major. "How about you Alice?"

"I can't help but agree with your friend there," she said. "Both of them, actually. You know, we do a good breakfast here. Why don't I nip downstairs and make you all one?"

"Very droll Alice, very droll. I see a night in our company hasn't dulled your rapier wit. But don't worry about the latter. All things being well, we'll have you out of here and back downstairs making bacon sandwiches in no time. Speaking of which, we really should get the kids fed. They're an absolute nightmare when they're hungry."

John Clefton flashed an angry glance at the Major. He opened his mouth as if to protest, then thought better of it.

"Why don't you two head downstairs and get some breakfast," said the Major. "We've got about eight hours to hang around and I don't want to spend all day listening to your stomachs rumbling. Besides, it's all included in the price of the room, so it's daft not to."

"I thought we were gonna do a runner without paying the bill?" reasoned Steve Clefton.

The Major sighed and shook his head. "That's entirely beside the point."

The brothers stood and made to leave the room. "And see if you can't snaffle a couple of bacon sandwiches and some coffee for our guest," said the Major. "We can't have her accusing us of being terrible hosts."

Alice slumped back onto the bed and closed her eyes again. This was going to be a very long eight hours.

CHAPTER 53

KEANE drained the last mouthful of strong, sludge-like coffee and shivered as a caffeine rush tingled through his entire body. He felt slightly light-headed as he stood up from the table and followed Anton Phelps from the dining room with a quickened pace.

"Mr Phelps," he called out.

The man spun round, his eyes dark and heavy with worry.

"I'm surprised to see you here," said Keane.

"Oh," said the man, startled. "Detective... Keane, isn't it? Thank you for the information about where George is. I've just seen him, actually. Thought I should head up here and see what was going on. You know, as George's boss."

"Right," said Keane, making no attempt to hide the scepticism in his voice. "And that's standard behaviour is it? Company policy? Travelling several hundred miles to confront an errant employee who's bunked off for a few days."

"Erm, well... no, I suppose not. But this is a special case. As I said to you before, George isn't the type to just not show up without a word. We were all worried. That's why I called you. When you phoned and told me where he was... well, it seemed crazy. So I thought I'd come and talk to George, find out if something was wrong."

"And is there?"

"What?"

"Something wrong?"

"Well, it's hard to say, really. He's definitely not acting like himself. He seems... different. I've never known him to be so... belligerent. If you ask me it's some kind of mid-life crisis or something."

"Really?" said Keane. "You think he seems unhinged?"

"Oh, I don't know about that. Stressed, more like."

"Hmm, and they say stress can make you do some pretty funny things, don't they?"

"I suppose so. Sorry... what exactly are you getting at?" said Anton.

"I take it you know the town's bank was robbed yesterday? Three men held the place up with machine guns. Took pot shots at the police and made off with over two hundred grand in cash."

Okay, so they hadn't technically fired at the police, but at the time it had seemed like real gunshots and there was no need to downplay the drama of the situation with something as trivial as facts.

"Oh dear, that's terrible," said Anton. "But... I'm sorry, what does that have to do with me? Or with George?"

"You said it yourself. He's unhinged. Acting strangely. Suffering from stress.

315

How did you phrase it? Mid-life crisis."

"Well, I'm not sure I said…"

Keane cut him off. "He's not himself. He disappears from work, turns up here… in disguise, I might add. And the very next day the bank has been robbed. Coincidence?"

"Are you saying you think George robbed the bank? With a machine gun?"

"I don't think," said Keane, drawing out his response with an extra-long pause. "I *know* he did it."

Anton Phelps looked utterly shocked. Then a smile spread rapidly across his face before he burst out in a thunderous roar of laughter. He bent double, clutching his sides and gasping for breath.

It went on for so long that Keane flipped from initial embarrassment to deep, ragged anger.

"This is no laughing matter, Mr Phelps," he said.

Anton straightened himself up, wiping the trickling tears from his scrunched-up red face. He fought hard to control his breathing between intermittent bursts of tittering; small aftershocks from the initial belly laugh.

"I'm sorry, I don't mean… it's just the thought of George… as an armed robber! I'm sorry, but you've really got the wrong end of the stick with that one. I mean there's no way…"

"People can be capable of far worse things than you could ever imagine," said Keane with a sharp tone.

"Well, yes, but I mean…"

"What exactly are you doing here, Mr Phelps?"

"I'm sorry," said Anton, the smile dropping instantly from his face as he saw the serious look in the detective's eyes. "I told you, I came here as I was concerned for one of my employees. Jesus, you're not suggesting I had something to do with this now, are you?"

"Seems like quite a coincidence," said Keane.

In all honesty, Keane did feel as though he was aiming quite wide of the mark. But since he'd come this far with his line of questioning, it seemed worth pursuing. If all else fails, rattle the bastards and see what falls out of them, he thought.

Was it really possible that such a weak, weasel-like specimen as this could be part of, or even the brains behind, an armed robbery? He had to admit it was pretty unlikely.

Could Keane have been wrong about Thring all along? It was possible, but he'd been so sure. He'd spoken to him; seen that scared look on him. From the moment he'd set eyes on Thring he could tell there was something not right there. He was hiding something. There was some secret that he didn't want anyone to know about. Keane could practically smell it on him.

As for his protestations that he'd been in bed with a hangover at the time of the robbery? He must have thought Keane had corned beef for brains.

And his girlfriend's alibi? That held about as much water as a string vest.

No, Thring had been there at the bank all right. Keane just had to find the proof.

He still wasn't sure of Thring's role in it: whether he was behind the whole thing; just an accomplice; or, a middle man. He was definitely closer to the brains end of the scale, not the brawn.

But then, Anton Phelps' reaction had been so extreme. Keane knew that Thring was up to something; he could feel it in his gut. But that laughter wasn't fake. Phelps found the idea of his employee being involved in the robbery so utterly hilarious.

It was true that some criminals created whole other lives for themselves to hide behind. Paedophiles hiding out as schoolteachers; serial killers masquerading as family men; librarians with a side-line in burglary. And for every single one of them there was always some gormless, duped fool ready to exclaim: "I can't believe it. They just didn't seem the type."

But is that what was really going on with Thring?

"Yes, well that's all it is Detective Keane," said Anton Phelps. "A coincidence. I called you because we were all worried about George. The fact that he's ended up here, dressed in that... costume... well, there's clearly something not quite right. But he hasn't suddenly become a bank robber. And now you're questioning me? Am I a bank robber as well, now?"

"Listen," said Keane, stepping onto the back foot, suddenly very cautious of the legal implications of being too free and easy with his accusations. "I just said it was a coincidence. Your friend cracks up, does a runner from home and winds up getting too deep into something. He can't get out of it and he just keeps getting deeper and deeper. It happens more often than you'd think."

"Maybe so, but not George. Not him. Now if you don't mind, I have to get back and take a bollocking off my boss."

Anton Phelps sighed wearily, turned around and stormed off with the look of a man who had to go and tell a little girl her hamster had died.

Keane glowered at him. He waited for him to leave, then followed to the front door of the hotel. As he passed the bottom of the stairs, he narrowly avoided being squashed by two large, thuggish-looking men in ill-fitting jumpsuits with giant quiffed wigs perched atop their heads. They looked angry and, had they not been dressed in such ridiculous clothing, they would have been scary.

They came charging down the stairs with such speed and recklessness that Keane was tempted to pull them up and give them a warning. Then he smiled at the thought of calling the two over and telling them off for running in the hall.

Leave them for someone else to worry about, he thought to himself. I've got real criminals to catch.

CHAPTER 54

A CHILL breeze whistled through the gap in the window, making George shudder as he perched on the edge of the bed. The sun had sunk below the roofline of the buildings across the street, leaving behind a thick, grey early evening sky.

George looked at the piercing red display on the digital clock: 18.57. He had just over an hour until he was supposed to meet the robbers. That gave him just enough time to get to the pub, assess the venue, lay the foundations of his admittedly flimsy plan and wait for the Major and his henchmen to arrive.

After George had left Anton, he had returned straight to his room and had been sitting on the bed ever since. Thinking. He had again tried pacing the inadequate floor space, without any success. He had lain down on the bed; laid on the floor; sat on the bed; knelt on the floor; looked repeatedly out of the window; and then, sat on the bed again. All the time thinking. All the time planning.

Of course, planning a rescue and foiling a group of bank robbers was not something George had a great deal of experience in, so he didn't really know where to start. How does one go about planning a rescue, exactly?

During the course of his sedate life the only planning that was usually required involved deciding what to cook for dinner, what movie to rent from the video shop, or, anticipating the best and least busy time to visit the supermarket – though much of the stress of that had recently been reduced when he'd started using their home delivery service. He didn't mind admitting that he was more than a little out of his depth when it came to planning the safe return of a damsel in distress from a group of ruthless, armed thugs.

As such, the planning had not gone terribly well. He'd thought about what they might do on television. How the hero would always have one ace up his sleeve; a daring manoeuvre that no-one would suspect until it was too late. George had neither an ace up his sleeve nor a daring manoeuvre.

And hadn't he been told recently that he watched too many cop shows? Those things were hardly accurate, and George was dealing with a real life emergency.

In the end, and after much pondering, pacing and gazing out of the window, George had the semblance of a plan. It was fairly simplistic and had no guarantee of actually working. But it was all he had and time was running out. It had to work.

George stood and looked into the small brown wooden-framed mirror on the wall. The face staring back was barely recognisable to him, like a distant memory of himself. The same greying eyebrows were there, the salt and pepper hair and the slightly crooked nose. The same tired eyes with heavy, black bags hammocked beneath them. The same jagged wrinkles lining his forehead; years of worry and stress tattooed across his brow. But the man behind the face was irrevocably changed: a thousand years grown in just a few days.

George's cheeks were stung red from the earlier impact of Steve Clefton's hand. His bottom lip sported a thick, dried-blood tear in the centre. A small blue-green bruise bloomed at the corner of his left eye and the ghost-like remnants of four white finger-shaped marks tinged his throat where the big man had half-throttled him.

He thought of Alice. Would she still find him attractive looking like this? Would she think it sweet and endearing? Or would she now see him as weak and pathetic, a beaten man unable to protect even himself, let alone her?

He'd left her alone with those thugs for more than 24 hours. Perhaps she hated him already. She might never forgive him for bringing all this trouble to her door. The newly-formed relationship that he was fighting so hard to protect may already have been dead for hours.

He just had to hope that, should they get out of this alive, somehow she would see a way to give him a second chance.

George pulled up the large starch-stiff collar of his jumpsuit and slipped the heavy gold sunglasses onto his face.

"Now or never, George," he said to himself in the mirror. "Now or never."

He took a deep, calming breath, his heart pounding jungle drums in his chest, and picked up his mobile phone. He pressed the power button to turn it on, watching the small screen burst into colour and slowly power up. He then picked up a small piece of card from the top of the television and typed a number into the phone's keypad.

He took another deep breath as he held the phone up to his ear.

A distant voice on the end said, "Hello?"

"Hello," replied George. "I think I might need your help."

******

George marched down the stairs, out the front door and strode purposefully along the street, his eyes fixed firmly to the three or four feet of pavement directly in front of him. He tried to remain as inconspicuous as possible. He didn't want to be delayed in any way.

The street was already buzzing with activity; Elvises of all shape, size, age and description gently meandering down the hill towards the town. George blended easily into the crowd, marked out only by his fast pace and determined stride.

He made his way quickly along the pavement, crossing the street and arriving at the pub. It was already busy as he stepped through the door. Families, couples and groups of people sat at tables arranged around the small stage area in the corner.

George's mind immediately flashed back to the horror of a few nights earlier, when he'd stood on that stage, sweating and nervous, staring out into a sea of unsympathetic faces. He instinctively blushed red as a shudder of embarrassment shook through him.

The stage had been changed since his last visit. Whereas previously it had been basic and bland, perfunctory in its elevation and little more, for tonight they had made a real effort to enliven it. Now it was decorated with shiny bunting and cut-out gold and silver stars which twinkled with glitter. A large red curtain had been erected at the back, forming a small space behind from which performers could enter onto the stage. It too was adorned with shiny gold stars and looked like a homemade wizard's cape from a child's fancy dress box.

George scanned the room, assessing the faces in the assembled crowd. No Major Fairview. No thugs. No Alice. They hadn't pre-empted the meeting and turned up early to set their own trap. At least, George didn't think so. He sighed a long breath of relief.

Slowly George walked around the pub, pretending to look for a friend while furtively registering points of interest; potential locations for an ambush; possible hiding areas; and, of course, the most opportune escape routes.

There was the main door at the front, which seemed to have a fairly steady stream of comers and goers. George decided that it would be in too-frequent use to make for a speedy getaway.

A door at the side of the stage opened onto a narrow corridor, which led through to the Ladies and Gents toilets. This was equally as useless for an escape route, however. Were George able to grab Alice and make a dash for it, they'd have to squeeze their way past the seven or eight caterwauling Elvises, shimmying and gyrating and literally filling the corridor as they warmed up for their impending performances.

And even if they did manage to make it past and into the Gents, the only exit available was a shoebox-sized window that George would be lucky to squeeze an arm through, let alone the meagre paunch of his belly.

George was much too polite, and altogether too scared, to poke his head round the door of the Ladies toilets to check the possible routes for absconding. But he reasoned that it probably offered no better option.

He walked back through the pub and out a door on the opposite side of the room following a sign that said 'Beer Garden/Smoking Area'. It was not so much of a garden, however, consisting of a narrow grey alleyway that ran the length of the building and smelled predominantly of garbage, urine and cigarette smoke.

At one end of the alley sat a dilapidated wooden picnic table. At the other was a high brick wall with a wooden gate cut into an arch. It could have worked as an escape route had it not been blocked by a large metal halogen heater.

Honestly, thought George, have these people never heard of emergency exits? What if there was a fire? Or worse yet, a group of ruthless villains bent on beating and torturing you?

George immediately regretted picking the pub as his meeting point. He cursed himself for diving at the first place he thought of rather than taking his time to decide. Dejected, he walked back into the building and scanned the room again.

There may not have been much in the way of escape routes but at least the place was nice and busy. The Major and his thugs would not risk anything too dramatic or dangerous with such a large crowd there to watch. He'd seen the way they left the bank after the robbery, hiding their faces and sneaking away down a quiet alley. They were desperate not to be noticed, and they'd be even less keen to draw attention to themselves now. At least that gave George a little bit of breathing space.

George went to the bar and bought a pint of lager. There was one empty table in the corner of the room and George dashed over to it quickly, just managing to outpace an overweight couple in matching red and gold Elvis outfits. They shot him daggers then humped away, muttering and breathing heavily.

The crowds continued to build: people entering through the door every other minute, until the place was heaving. The people hummed with enthusiasm; familiar music blasted out of the speakers on the stage. It grew louder and louder, the buzzing chatter bubbling up, filling the room until George could barely hear the sound of his own terrified thoughts.

Finally the door opened and the Major's familiar face loomed into view. George wasn't sure whether the music actually stopped and the people ceased their cacophony of garbled speech, but as his eyes met the Major's everything seemed to fall deathly silent.

George's heart thrummed and a nervous sheen of moisture twinkled on his forehead. Instinctively he reached out for the glass in front of him, brought it to his lips and took a large, nerve-settling gulp. Then he nearly choked as the cold liquid hit the back of his throat. He coughed and spluttered, nearly falling sideways off his seat as he spat the cold, amber liquid into his own lap.

He shuffled in his seat, desperately trying to regain his composure and frantically wiping at the tell-tale wet spots on his trousers.

The Major crossed the floor of the pub, followed closely by Steve Clefton, John Clefton and, with her forearm clamped tightly in the grip of John's large hand, a rather annoyed looking Alice.

George looked up from his frenetic lap stroking to see all of them standing before him, his eyes burning red from the coughing fit and his chin still wet with beer.

"Hello Mr Thring," said the Major with a smirk, "you appear to have had something of a mishap."

George opened his mouth to speak, his brain searching for a likely riposte when he glanced up and locked eyes with Alice.

She looked tired. George wasn't surprised; he knew she probably hadn't slept at all. He suddenly felt ashamed, embarrassed at his own selfish sleep. Then he thought of that large breakfast he'd greedily devoured. He wondered whether she had even eaten.

He smiled up at her, not sure whether to stand. She smiled back, slightly uneasy, but that unmistakeable twinkle shone in her eyes. It made George's heart beat even faster.

"Are you okay, Alice?" he said. "Did they treat you… okay?"

"I'm fine, George," she said with a smile. "A bit tired, but I'm fine. Are you okay?"

"I'm fine," he said, the two of them momentarily losing themselves in each other's eyes, as if everyone else had simply floated away.

"Yes, yes," interrupted the Major. "We're all fine. You're fine, she's fine, I'm fine. We're all just dandy. Now, shall we?" he said, beckoning to the empty seats.

John Clefton tightened his grip on Alice's arm, pushing her down into one of the chairs. The three men sat down, staring intently at George.

"So George," said the Major. "Here we all are."

"Yes," replied George, forcing a serious edge to his voice, "here we are."

He went to speak again but quickly realised that he didn't know what else to say, so he closed his mouth and sat back in his chair, squinting his eyes and folding his arms.

"So?" said the Major.

"So?" said George, gauging that the man was waiting for him to say something else but not quite sure what.

A tense silence grew between them, almost drowning out the crowd and the loud music. The Major raised an eyebrow and sighed heavily.

"I believe there was supposed to be some kind of trade taking place? We've brought something for you," he said, indicating Alice with a nod of his head. "Have you brought something for us?"

"Eh?"

"The money, George," said the Major, a hint of deep irritation creeping into his voice. "Where is my fucking money?"

"Don't worry, you'll get your money."

"Hmm… yes, you say that, yet still… I can't actually see it anywhere."

"Don't worry, it's safe. We just have to go and get it."

"Get it? Get it?" barked the Major with incredulous rage. "No George, that is not what we agreed. You were to bring the money here. We bring the girl, you bring the money. That's how an exchange works. We've held up our end of the bargain, and I can't help but feel a little disappointed that you haven't done the same."

"Look," snapped George, his frustrations bubbling over. "I said you'd get your money and you will."

"I think you're forgetting who's in charge here, George."

The Major nodded at John Clefton. The man strengthened his grip on Alice's arm, squeezing. Her eyes creased with pain and she let out a soft whimper, her body buckling slightly.

George flinched, his stomach turning with the sight of Alice in pain. A deep urge to jump over the table and force the man to let go of her burned inside him.

"Don't make the mistake of thinking you're safe because you're in a crowd," said the Major. "Bad things happen in crowds. People get trampled in crowds. People get hurt."

He reached into his inside jacket pocket, pulling his hand back out just far enough to reveal the matt black, metallic handle of what looked unmistakeably like a gun.

"People get shot in crowds," he said, menace shining in his eyes.

"I said you'd get your money. There's no need for anyone to get hurt. It's in a safe place, we just have to go and get it."

"No George, that was not the deal."

"Look, I couldn't go and get it earlier. There were still too many police around. I couldn't take the risk. But it'll be easier now."

The Major slid the pistol back into his pocket and sighed.

"The police are gone, and this crowd will help us to move around," continued George. "We can go and get it now, it's not far. Alice stays here and I'll take you three to the money. Then you can all piss off out of our lives for good."

"No."

To George's surprise it was not the Major that raised the objection, or the two brothers, but Alice.

"I'm not letting you go off with these three on your own," she said. "There's no telling what they'll do. Probably put a bullet in the back of your head as soon as they have their cash."

"Erm… Alice, I…"

George wasn't exactly sure what to say. He was more than a little perplexed. This was his gambit to secure her safety – remove her from danger and put himself solely in the firing line. He genuinely didn't care what happened to him so long as he knew that she was safe. But Alice was the one blocking his efforts.

"No, I won't allow it," she said. "If you're going with them, we're both going."

"I have to say," interjected the Major with a sly, mocking grin, "I'm rather inclined to agree with the young lady on this. After all, what kind of kidnappers would we be if we just handed over the hostage without even a sniff of the ransom money? We'd be the laughing stock back at the Kidnappers Club."

"Wait… but…" said George, totally flummoxed.

The Major gently patted the pocket containing the gun.

"Fine, I'll take you to the money," said George. "We'll all go together. But as soon as you have it, you disappear and you let us both go."

"Nothing would give me greater pleasure, Mr Thring. Now, I would offer to buy everybody a drink, but what do you say we just press on instead and conclude our… transaction?"

Damn, thought George. Things were coming apart before they'd even started. There was no way he could take them to the money. Go marching out into the dark woods with three armed men and simply hope they'd let them go at the end? It certainly wasn't the best idea.

He needed to think. He needed to act. He needed to do something and do it quickly.

He barely had time to think before he did it. If he had, he might have reconsidered. He might have weighed up the options, reasoned that it would be either the bravest thing he'd ever done, or the stupidest. But before the synapses in his brain even had time to fire off the very start of a thought, a burst of adrenaline shot through him, forcing him into action.

He jolted up from his chair, picking up his half full pint and threw it full force into the face of John Clefton. The glass smashed into his forehead with a solid thunk and he released his grip on Alice's arm as his hands went to his injured head and he tumbled backwards. He let out a low, surprised moan as he crashed back onto the floor behind him.

The Major barely had time to register what was happening before George gripped the edge of the table with his fingers and tipped it forwards. The opposite side of the heavy tabletop crashed down into the laps of the Major and Steve Clefton, bouncing off their thighs and making them squeal in agony.

George used the falling momentum of the table to push it forwards and it caught the two men, pushing them back until they too fell to the floor, shocked and flailing.

People all around stopped and turned to see what was happening. They stood staring, stunned and open-mouthed as George took Alice's hand in his.

"This way," he said.

Alice seemed the most shocked of them all and George had to pull her up out of her chair, practically dragging her along behind him. The crowd bristled and swarmed as George pushed his way past people, attempting to make a path to the door.

He pushed this way, shoved that way, inching his way through the crowd, gripping Alice's hand tightly and pulling her through the throng of people.

A few well-meaning Elvis fans stepped forward to help the Major and the Cleftons to their feet. The rest seemed to have put the altercation down to no more than an accident or overzealous hi-jinks, and had already turned their backs on the chaos and continued with their previous activity.

George glanced back to see the Major glaring at him, deep red vengeance burning in his eyes. John Clefton, still slightly dazed, looked twice as enraged. Thick white spurts of spittle flew from his mouth as he roared and clambered to his feet.

George redoubled his efforts to traverse the crowd, but with uncooperative drinkers blocking the way, tutting and moaning as he tried to squeeze past, it was proving more difficult than anticipated. And with a steady stream of customers queuing up at the door, even if they made it through they'd still have problems actually getting outside.

Another glance back. The three men were on their feet now and attempting to work their way through the crowd towards him.

George glanced at the door leading through to the toilets. The window in the Gents was way too small, but there was a chance the Ladies might be bigger. He had to risk it.

Changing direction, George pulled Alice and headed back into the crowd, this time working his way towards the back of the room. With plenty of pushes and shoves, and more than a few swear words thrown back in his direction, they finally made it through the people to the door.

But just as George was about to push through, a large hand jutted out from the crowd, taking a firm hold on Alice's other arm. John Clefton yanked her hard and she stopped dead. One further tug and she was pulled the other way. George lost his grip on her hand and he could only stare back in horror as she disappeared into the sea of bodies.

He called out in vain, shouting her name, but the music was too loud. A small group turned to see what he was shouting about, grimaced disapprovingly then turned back again.

George tried to push his way back through the crowd but it was hopeless. There were too many people and they weren't for moving.

Alice was completely out of sight in seconds. George tried desperately to spot her, peering through the tiniest spaces between the bodies, rising up on tip toes to gaze over their heads. But he was too short and the gaps were too small.

With every second she was moving further away from him. He couldn't allow them to get away. They'd be angry now – even angrier than before – and there was no telling what they might do to Alice. He needed to find them now.

Looking around in panic he suddenly glimpsed the small stage. If he could get up there he might just be able to see over the crowd and spot which direction they were heading in.

George pushed and pulled his way through the people. He shoved and barged with a new sense of urgency.

He finally made the stage, tripping head first onto it and nearly taking a less-than-pleased-looking woman in a bright pink leather jacket with him. He scrambled to his feet, peering over the crowd, trying to pick up any trace of Alice or the three men.

Just as he thought he'd caught sight of the back of Alice's head, he was suddenly blinded by a brilliant, bright white spotlight shining directly into his eyes. The whole place fell silent as the music cut out and people turned to see what the light was pointing at.

George winced, raising a hand to shield the light from his eyes. A dull thudding sound echoed through the building as the DJ tapped his finger against his microphone and announced: "Okay folks. Well, we weren't due to start the show just yet, but it looks like our first performer is keen to kick things off."

Performer? What? George spun round, expecting to see a bad tempered Elvis standing behind him on the stage.

But there was nobody there. George looked over at the DJ standing behind his booth, signalling an enthusiastic thumbs up and waiting for George to reciprocate.

He looked up at the spotlight, then back around at the stage. He was the only person on it.

Then George noticed the microphone stand in front of him and the realisation hit him like a bucket of freezing water. The DJ was talking about him.

He looked out at the sea of expectant faces. They were all waiting for him to perform.

George squinted. Scanned the crowd. Still desperate to find any trace of Alice.

And then he saw her. Standing with the three men at the far end of the room. They'd stopped to see what was happening, and were now turned round and staring back at him.

Alice looked on in horror. John Clefton smiled back at George and made a cutting motion across his throat. Major Fairview slowly raised his hands and started clapping, seemingly excited about the performance to come.

The small TV monitor at the edge of the stage flickered, before turning brilliant blue. It was so bright that it made George's eyes hurt. The words *The Wonder of You* flashed up in white writing then disappeared, replaced with the first line of the song.

Someone at the back of the room chirruped with an excited whoop. George gazed blankly into the thick darkness, still blinded by the brilliant glow of the spotlight. He could hardly see any people. He couldn't see the eyes staring back at him. But he could hear them. A soft murmuring, breathing, chairs scraping against the floor, glasses chinking and clattering onto wooden tables. Somehow it made it worse being unable to see them but knowing that they were out there.

Music started to play. A melody George was pleased to actually recognise. His heart thumped in his chest. Sweat ran in achingly ticklish rivulets down his spine. The heat from the spotlight radiated over him, making him feel slightly faint.

He looked again to Alice and the men. They weren't moving. Weren't heading out the door. So long as George stayed on the stage, they were stood there watching him. It wasn't a great plan, but if he could stay there just a little bit longer it might give him time to think up a new strategy.

But in order to stay on the stage, he was going to have to sing.

He couldn't do this. He wasn't a performer. He'd never sung in front of people before. Every fibre of his being told him to run, to get the hell off that stage and not look back.

But his feet didn't move. He just stood there, staring out into the darkness in front of him. His eyes skipped back and forth from the microphone to the small TV.

Maybe he could do this after all. He was up on the stage. Nobody had thrown anything at him. All he had to do was sing.

It was as easy as that. All he had to do was open his mouth and sing. Of course he could do that. And who cared if he was any good or not? It didn't matter. All that mattered was that he did it.

The music built up, getting louder and faster. He reached forward and took the microphone in his hand. Without thinking he automatically raised it to his mouth. A small flutter of premature applause erupted as the audience bristled with anticipation.

He knew from the tune that the opening line was coming up any second. The words lingered menacingly on the screen.

This was it. Was he really going to do this? Sing in front of a crowd?

He could barely believe he had found himself in this position. But here he was: microphone inches from his lips; music counting down; a crowd watching and waiting.

It was too close now. There was no way for him to back out. And, strangely, he didn't want to get out of it. He wanted to try. He was going to give it a go. What did he have to lose?

His heart beast faster. His face burned red. His mouth was dry and his knees shook with a tremendous wobble. But somehow, from deep within him, a strange surge of confidence rushed through him.

It was only a song after all. What was the worst that could happen? He'd sing and people would either like it or they wouldn't. What did it matter?

The microphone seemed lighter in his hand. The first word on screen began to slowly change from bright white to garish yellow.

It was all going to be fine. He opened his mouth, his mind fixed on the word on the screen. His tongue rose as he prepared to sing and…

His stomach gurgled. A deep, watery, guttural murmur. He snapped forwards. His body bent double and he let loose a violent, thick, putrid spurt of yellow sick.

It splashed down onto his shoes. It landed in a thick, sticky pool on the floor. One retch followed by another, his sides aching, the muscles stretching and contorting with each painful hurl.

George looked up to see the crowd stunned and open-mouthed before his wobbling legs gave way, and he dropped to the ground, landing knees-first into the sickly, sticky mess.

A woman at the back of the pub shrieked. The crowd fell silent then erupted into a mixture of sympathy, panic and disgust. Chairs scraped noisily on the floor as people jumped to their feet, stumbling back, lurching away in an embarrassed stampede.

George gazed up from his kneeling position, wiping the thick, sour-tasting mess from his chin. The spotlight cut out and for the first time he was able to clearly see the faces of the people in the crowd, reeling with horror and twisted in disgust.

They had all managed to edge back a few feet, mindful to evacuate the splatter zone. In the background the music still played, the words on the screen turning from white to yellow in time with the music. The DJ clambered for his own microphone, dropping it to the floor with a terrible clunking thud.

George tried to stand and his foot slipped in the pool of sickly yellow liquid. He lurched from side to side, flailing wildly, wobbling and keening as he fought to remain upright.

The crowd grumbled loudly, disappointed and disgusted. George could hear a strange wave of concern floating through the room, mixed with the audible retching of a few unfortunate souls suffering from their own sickly reaction to George's vomiting. The whole thing was tinged with a cruel echo of drunken laughter.

George steadied himself as the DJ finally found his microphone, ceased the music from the karaoke machine.

"Well, folks," he said, "it looks like we've had something of an accident. Don't worry, we'll get everything cleaned up and have the show back on track in no time. And to keep you all in the mood, here's another classic track from you know who."

The sound system cranked back into action and people turned away from the stage – show over, nothing to see here. They were all now suddenly so disinterested that barely a single soul would have noticed the giant hand of John Clefton once again reaching out from the crowd. His chunky, calloused fingers closed tight around the high starched collar of George's jumpsuit and he pulled him down from the stage.

"Poor lad," said John with mock compassion, "let's get you some fresh air."

George just about managed to stay on his feet as the big man jerked, yanked and pulled him through the crowd and out the front door of the pub. They stumbled out into the fresh air, none of the other patrons seeming to notice that the puking singer was being manhandled along the street, or perhaps not caring enough to intervene.

John Clefton guided George across the road and down the narrow alleyway that lay alongside the bank. Major Fairview, Steve Clefton and Alice were waiting there for them.

"Bravo!" cheered the Major jokingly. "Terrific performance, George. I particularly enjoyed the bit where you vomited all over the front row. Inspired."

George looked at Alice, shamefaced, the acid tang of fresh sick stinging the back of his throat. "I'm sorry Alice, I… I was just trying to…"

"I know George," she said, smiling back. "It was my fault. If I hadn't let this big ape grab me… I thought you were very brave though. Standing up to these thugs."

John Clefton raised a hand to his head, rubbing the circular red mark and grimaced as if remembering the painful collision of the pint glass. He stepped forward, his arm raising from his side as he moved, throwing his fist hard into the side of George's face.

A sudden red-hot, burning sensation smacked the skin and crunched the bones. The force of the impact literally lifted George off his feet and he flew back, landing painfully on his bottom.

Alice squeaked a sympathetic yelp and tried to rush to George's aid on the floor. Steve Clefton held a firm grip on her arm, immobilising her so that she could only look down at the crumpled man, stunned and groaning on the ground.

The pain surged through George's face. A blinding white light burned in his eyes. He felt dizzy; didn't know where he was. He didn't even know that he was lying on the floor until the haze cleared and his eyes regained focus. He looked up to the see the Major standing over him.

The Major reached into his pocket, this time pulling the revolver fully out and pointing it at George. A tiny twinkle of moonlight reflected on the rectangular shaft. The muzzle gaped black and fearsome, growing wider with each second.

"Now then, George," said the Major, "what say we dispense with all this carry on and you take us to where you've hidden the money?"

CHAPTER 55

THEY walked in near silence; George pushed up to the front of the group to lead the way; the barrel of the Major's gun pressed firmly into George's back, pushing him forwards and deterring him from any further outbursts of bravery.

John and Steve Clefton held the rear. John's big hand still gripped a firm, pincer-like hold on Alice's elbow. George was desperate to speak to Alice, to make sure she was all right.

He wanted to hold her, to feel her warm body against him, and to tell her everything was going to be all right. He wanted her to tell him things would be okay. But they were kept deliberately apart. In truth, his jaw ached so greatly from the punch that he wasn't sure how intelligible a sound he'd be able to produce anyway. So he just plodded on.

The group moved quickly and quietly up the narrow path and out into the street at the other end. When the coast was clear they dashed across the road, disappearing between the trees into the darkness of the woods.

George was acutely aware of just how bad an idea it was to be heading into the woods – the remote, dark, expansive woods. If there was a better location for a group of gun-wielding criminals to murder him and Alice and then sneak away unnoticed, George couldn't think of it.

They trudged through the woods, the large heels on George's boots once again getting caught in the thick, sticky mud underfoot. It made him wobble, tottering about wildly, every step a potential tumble or broken ankle.

The two Clefton brothers grumbled continuously, asking "How much further?" and "When are we gonna get there?" like two petulant children on a long car journey.

Alice remained quiet throughout, walking along in stealthy silence. The Major's gun held a steady, imposing presence in the small of George's back.

After five minutes of continuous walking, as the party trudged deeper into the undergrowth, the Major said, "We seem to have been walking for rather a while now. I do hope this isn't another one of your tiresome delaying tactics. Because I warn you, my patience has well and truly worn out."

"It's just a little further," said George.

In truth, George had realised a good three minutes previously that he actually had no idea where he was or in which direction he was leading them. It had seemed a lot more straightforward before, when he could actually see where he was going. And the last time he'd entered the woods, he'd been concentrating far more on evading the police than on looking at his surroundings.

He had run across the road from the back of the bank, headed in a straight line and just ran. Somehow he'd ended up in a large clearing. He'd made note of

331

several landmarks, and he'd been sure that he could find it again during the day. But in the darkness, without so much as a torch to light the way, everything looked exactly the same. And with all the tottering and teetering on his ridiculous shoes, he wasn't even certain that he was walking in a straight line.

So for the past few minutes he'd simply been leading the group further into the woods hoping that something would look familiar. But nothing did. So now he was essentially wandering aimlessly in the hope that he might simply stumble on the place where he'd left the money.

"How much further?" said the Major, jabbing the gun harder into George. "It's just…"

George stopped abruptly, causing the whole group to bump into one another, nearly toppling over like giant dominos. He gazed around in every direction, hoping for some familiar landmark, anything that would show him where to go.

Sensing that George was stalling, the Major sucked in a deep breath, preparing to unload a furious torrent of abuse, when he was interrupted by a tinny, electronic sound trilling in his jacket. A look of deep annoyance flashed across his face as he reached into his pocket and retrieved a mobile phone.

"Yes," he said, answering the phone with a bark. "Yes… yes, I'm dealing with it now. Yes. Imminently."

He rolled his eyes and sighed loudly as the voice on the other end spoke.

"Yes," said the Major finally. "I'll call when we're en route for the rendezvous. I don't foresee any further problems."

As he spoke he looked directly at George and raised the gun to his face. He hung up the phone, placed it back in his pocket and said very calmly, "Now, Mr Thring, you have precisely three seconds to tell me where the money is."

George scanned the area around him, his eyes frantically searching in the dark for any slight sign that he recognised.

"One," said the Major loudly, an icy chill to his voice.

George started to panic, his heart thumping in his chest. He looked at Alice, her face etched with fear.

"Two," said the Major.

Thick beads of sweat rolled down the sides of George's neck, stinging slightly in the cool night air. His head swam and he ran a hand through his hair, gripping his head and silently urging himself to "Think, George, think."

"Two and a half," said the Major, practically shouting.

He pulled back the slider on top of the pistol, loading the chamber and arming the gun. This was it. Time was up.

Everything seemed to go into slow motion as George scanned the landscape one last time. Nothing. Nothing. Nothing.

Then, as the trees rustled a ghostly echo, a cloud shifted in the sky above, releasing a single shaft of moonlight that pierced the darkness and shone down, illuminating the clearing that George had been searching for.

"There," yelled George. "Over there. The money's over there."

He pointed and they all looked over in the direction of the now visible clearing in the trees.

"Fucking hell," said Steve Clefton. "That was lucky."

The Major lowered his gun and George exhaled heavily, only just managing to calm his wobbling knees and stay on his feet.

Without saying a word, John Clefton grabbed George's collar and pulled him round in the direction of the clearing. He pushed him forwards, and George led the pack onwards again. They all trudged after him, the loose, wet mud squelching loudly underfoot.

The clouds in the sky moved further away and the clearing remained illuminated as the five mud-splattered strollers made their way through the trees. As they got closer George picked up the pace, racing over to the fallen-down tree and reaching it to the hollow area in the end. He pulled out the dark green duffel bag and threw it down at the Major's feet.

"There," said George, defiance bubbling in his chest. "There's your bloody money."

"Check it," said the Major to Steve Clefton.

He bent and unzipped it, reaching in and pulling out a large handful of crumpled bank notes.

"Yeah, looks like it's all here," he said.

The Major looked down at the bag, cash bursting out like foam escaping a torn cushion, and smiled a sickly thin smile.

"Well, Mr Thring," he said, "it would appear that our business is concluded. We have what we came for and so do you."

He motioned to John Clefton who released his grip on Alice's elbow. He gave her a hard shove in the back, sending her tottering into George's arms.

George caught her, hugging her tight to help keep her upright. She found her balance and gripped back tighter, nuzzling her face deep into the cleft between George's shoulder and neck. He felt her tremble slightly, just for a second, as her body betrayed just how frightened she really was. Then she straightened up, lifted her head, looked George in the eyes and kissed him.

"Are you okay?" George said, breaking away from her. "They didn't hurt you?"

"What, these big girls?" she chuckled. "No chance. Unless you count assault by deadly odours."

"Hmm... yes," said the Major, "there's that sparkling sense of humour again. Anyway, getting back to business, I suppose we really ought to wrap things up."

He raised his gun again, pointing it directly at George's head.

"What?" said George, the grim reality suddenly dawning on him. "You said you'd let us go."

"Hmm? Oh yes, I did, didn't I? What can I say, George? Perhaps you should be a bit more selective about who you trust. Think of this as a lesson for life. What little of it you have left, anyway."

George gulped. It was far louder than he'd expected, a deep, throaty sound that reverberated through the air, echoing off trees like something from a cartoon.

"You're going to kill us?" he said.

Of course he'd known it was a possibility. A likelihood even. Somehow, though, now that it was actually about to happen, it still managed to take him by surprise.

"Well, I don't really see what other choice I have, old boy," said the Major. "I mean you've seen our faces. We wouldn't want you calling the police and telling on us, now, would we?"

George stared blankly. Alice's cold, small hand found his and squeezed tightly.

"I suppose we could make you swear, Scout's honour, not to report us…" continued the Major, "but somehow I don't see you sticking to it. So I'm afraid I do need to guarantee your silence and… well, the easiest way to do that is…"

He let the last word trail off, giving his gun a slight shake to emphasize the point.

"We won't tell anyone. We won't. The police already think I was involved, so they're the last people I want to see. I just want this whole nightmare over with."

"Don't trust him," grunted John Clefton.

"No," said Major Fairview, "on this occasion I'm rather inclined to agree with you."

George instinctively moved in front of Alice, shielding her from the Major's aim. She gripped him tightly, her hands shaking as she pressed her forehead against his back. George stared at the gun, his legs wobbling, time slowing to a blank silent expanse.

Then, from somewhere in the distance came a sharp cracking sound like a twig breaking; the rustle of leaves and trampling of footsteps; as a large, dark figure came hurtling out of the woods.

The Major only just had time to turn his head as the plump, round figure of Sergeant Collins came thundering towards him. He moved surprisingly quickly for a man of his girth and he dashed up behind the Major, raised an extendable metal baton and brought it down hard on the Major's arm. Fairview let out an agonised howl as his hand sprung open and the gun dropped to the floor. He looked round, startled, as Collins swung the baton again, thumping him hard across his shoulders, forcing another loud cry as he dropped to his knees.

John Clefton, momentarily stunned with surprise, suddenly lurched forwards – arms outstretched like a B-movie zombie – trying to clutch at Collins. The policeman simply took one step to the side, pulling the baton back behind his body before swinging it forwards into the big man's face. It crashed into him with a crunching squelch, the man's nose exploding with a thick, scarlet splatter.

Steve Clefton barely had a chance to move as Collins dashed towards him, swinging the baton low and catching him just below both knees. His mouth and eyes widened with silent shock and he tumbled forwards, appearing to fall in slow motion before crashing to the ground like a felled tree.

With the three men prostrate and moaning on the floor, Sergeant Collins casually folded his baton, strolled over to where the Major had dropped his gun and picked it up. The plump policeman stood valiant, gun in one hand, baton in the other, illuminated by a single beam of silver moonlight. He would have looked every bit the conquering hero were it not for the pudge of large belly overhanging his belt and the purple red tinge spreading across his face as he coughed and wheezed, fighting to catch his breath.

"Pete?" said Alice, completely stunned. Her mouth moved to say more but she couldn't find the words.

"Hello Alice," said Collins. "Are you two okay?"

She went to speak again but all she could manage was, "Pete?"

"Well, Mr Thring," said Sergeant Collins, "looks like I turned up just at the right time, eh? Good job you came to your senses and called me."

"You called Pete?" asked Alice.

"Yes," said George. "I figured I'd have to bring these three here to get the money at some point. Of course, the original plan was to leave you somewhere safe. I thought it made sense to have some back-up in place for when I got here."

"Yes, Mr Thring gave me a call and told me all about what really happened during that robbery," said Collins. "Told me about these three and how they were holding you hostage to get the money back. Well, we can't have that, now, can we?"

"So you and George planned this?"

"Well, sort of," said George. "It didn't happen exactly like I thought it would."

Alice looked at George, her eyes widening slightly and, despite the dark of the woods, he could have sworn he saw her pupils dilate just a little bit more.

"Come on then, you lot," said Sergeant Collins, kicking the Major's leg. "Up on your feet."

The Major stood, clutching his aching arm to his side, wincing slightly from the pain.

"You too," said Collins to the brothers. "Over there."

John and Steve Clefton clambered begrudgingly to their feet, their eyes wide and lost, still reeling, still trying to understand what had happened; how this plump old policeman had got the better of them.

Sticky, wet, black mud covered Steve Clefton's front, where he'd belly-flopped to the ground. He looked like something from a cartoon: a hideous, lumbering swamp monster. His brother's face was a flash of scarlet, his nose flattened and skewed. Blood covered his mouth and chin and seeped slowly down his neck.

With the shiny black pistol held firmly in front of him, Collins corralled the robbers and lined them up in front of a tree. He bent down to the duffel bag, inspected its contents, then zipped it up and hauled it towards him, resting it at his feet.

"Right then, lads," he said, "I've got a lovely warm cell back at the station with your names on it."

The two brothers grizzled and whined, appearing to simply accept the inevitable. The Major remained quiet, shifting his weight back on his heels and, so slowly that even the keenest observer would have struggled to notice, took the tiniest of steps backwards. He knew that there were too many of them for one policeman to control successfully. When the time came, he'd let the brothers trundle off to a cell and make a dash for it into the darkness of the woods.

If the cop had any sense he'd keep the gun aimed squarely at the Cleftons, so there would be no-one to chase after the Major. He took another tiny step backwards.

With the Major and the two brothers successfully subdued, George blew out an audible relieved sigh. The plan had worked. They were safe. He gave Alice's hand a triumphant squeeze.

"So," he said, "what do we do now? Is back up on the way?"

"Back up?" said Collins. "No. No back up, I'm afraid."

"Oh," said George, slightly confused. "Will you not need back up? I mean, can you get them all back to the station on your own?"

"Well... no, not exactly," said Collins.

"Oh... I, erm..." said George not quite understanding.

George looked at the robbers. He looked at Alice. Then he looked back to Collins. It was then that George noticed that Collins' arm had swung round and the gun was once again pointing firmly in his direction.

CHAPTER 56

GEORGE froze with a mixture of fear and confusion. He stared at the gun in the policeman's hand; the small, round muzzle winking in the moonlight.

The policeman's eyes darkened. His jaw clenched. "Change of plan," he said.

"I don't understand…" said George. "What… what are you…?"

"I'm sorry, Mr Thring, but there's a lot of money in that bag" said Collins. "More money than a police officer like me is going to see in a lifetime."

"What's going on Pete?" demanded Alice. "What the hell are you doing?"

"I'm not as young as I used to be," said Collins. "Haven't got the energy for it any more. Tell the truth, I've been thinking about jacking it all in for a while now and taking early retirement. Of course, if I go too soon my pension won't be worth all that much."

"What are you talking about Pete? What's going on?" said Alice, a desperate insistence in her voice.

"And then you phone me and tell me about this big bag of money hidden in the woods. And I couldn't help thinking… well, that would make for a very nice retirement fund."

He stopped talking, momentarily lost in thought. A deep, aching silence hung between the group as they looked round at each other then back at the policeman.

"So, I've decided that I'm going to keep the money for myself," said Collins.

"What?" said George. "But…"

The Major, who had momentarily halted his silent retreat, clapped his hands loudly and threw out a haughty chuckle.

"Bravo," he said. "Well, isn't that a turn up for the books, eh?"

"Cheeky bloody pig!" said John Clefton.

"How do you expect to get away with this, Pete?" said Alice. "You can't just take the money and think we won't tell the police what you've done."

"Well, no, I'm afraid you do make a very good point there," said Collins.

Alice went to speak again but George stopped her with a gentle squeeze of the hand. "Go on then," he said, "how are you going to explain it all away?"

"Well, I'll probably have to improvise some of the finer points. But I'm thinking something like this: You call me and tell me you have info on the robbery. You know who did it and where the money is stashed. These three clowns have got Alice and they're holding her hostage until you hand it over. You ask me to meet you here in the woods, where you promise to turn over the cash to me. Only, when I arrive the robbers have already caught up with you. They're angry that there's no sign of the loot and they kill you both. Very tragic.

"With no time to wait for back up, I march in and get the upper hand on the robbers. I manage to get the gun away from them and have to shoot them as well. Absolutely no choice, your honour, it was them or me. Sadly there's no sign of the money. And more importantly, no witnesses to say otherwise."

"So where is the money?"

"Somebody else came and took it? You tried to double-cross these three and hid it somewhere else – nobody ever found it. Doesn't matter, really."

"You can't expect to get away with this? What about evidence, forensics…"

"Someone really has been watching too many TV shows, haven't they, Mr Thring? What do you think this is, CSI Chidbury?"

"But…" said George, not quite knowing how to finish the sentence.

"There will be an investigation, of course. A few procedural discrepancies to iron out. I mean, you can't just kill three people without at least a bit of a slap on the wrist, even if you are a police officer. But I'm afraid it'll be my word against yours. And your word won't be very loud, will it?"

"They'll suspend me, of course. Brush round the edges of an inquiry, then pack me off on early retirement to try and keep things quiet. Which plays quite nicely into my hands, wouldn't you say?"

"You can't seriously be planning on killing us, Pete," said Alice. "You can't. Your Marjory would have a fit if she knew you were doing this."

"You leave her out of this, Alice," barked Collins. "Now, I'm not gonna pretend I'm going to enjoy this, but it's the way it has to be."

"No it doesn't," said George, desperation crackling in his throat. "We won't tell anyone. You can keep the money…"

"No he can't," shouted Steve Clefton.

"You stay out of this," shouted George.

The large man went to move towards George. Collins trained the gun on him and he stopped.

"You can take the money," continued George. "We'll say the robbers stashed it and we couldn't find it. We won't tell anyone. We'll help you get these three back to a cell, then Alice and I will leave town. You'll never see or hear from either of us ever again. We won't say a word."

"And what about them?" said Collins, pointing the gun at the Major and his men. "Do you think they'll stay quiet?"

"Well… no, but who's going to believe them? They're dishonest criminals. No offence," he added, turning to the Major.

"Oh, none taken dear boy," he said, recommencing his ultra-slow retreat.

Collins paused for a second, thinking carefully before saying: "No, I'm sorry Mr Thring. I'd like to believe you, I really would. But I can't take the chance."

"But you can't kill us, Pete," said Alice, incredulous. "I mean… you just can't."

"Believe me, Alice, I take absolutely no pleasure in it. I mean, I remember you when you were just a kid, for God's sake. So it's not easy for me. It's just that… well, I really want that money."

"But you're talking about murder, Pete. You're not a murderer."

"Well, the way I see it is this lot were going to kill you anyway as soon as you gave them the money. So it's not as if you *weren't* going to die. It's just a different person pulling the trigger. And this way at least I get the cash."

"Oh, well that's all right, then," she smirked.

Sergeant Collins' face folded into a darker expression. He tightened his grip on the gun. Everything fell quiet save for the fat man's ragged wheezes punching through the silence, keeping their own macabre rhythm.

George gripped Alice's hand tightly.

Collins wheezed and coughed, the gun pointing hard at George.

Wheeze. Cough. Wheeze. Cough.

His face was growing redder by the second. Great rivulets of sweat tumbling down his cheeks.

Wheeze. Cough. Wheeze. Cough.

His outstretched arm started to shake slightly, the elbow nearly buckling under the weight of the heavy gun.

Wheeze. Cough. Wheeze. Cough.

This is it, thought George, turning to look at Alice, determined that the last thing he saw in this world would be something good.

Wheeze. Cough. Wheeze. Cough.

Suddenly Collins' free hand darted up to his chest, clutching tightly. The wheezing stopped. His eyes went wide. A stunned expression spread across his red face. He let out a low, anguished groan. And he collapsed, hitting the ground with a loud, squelching thud.

Silence.

George, Alice, John, Steve and the Major looked on in surprise. The assembled crowd turned to look at each other, then back at the fallen man.

Finally the Major punctuated the silence, shouting, "Get the gun, you idiots."

Steve Clefton lurched forward, dropping to the floor and reaching for Collins' lifeless body.

"Run," yelled George, pulling hard on Alice's hand, dragging her along behind him as he burst into action and darted for the edge of the clearing. Alice followed on behind, both of their feet padding and squelching in the soft, sticky mud.

"Stop them!" cried the Major.

John Clefton jumped into action, darting forward, his arms outstretched and reaching for Alice. One foot slurped noisily upwards while the other remained firmly planted in the mud. He toppled forward, coughing out a confused grunt as he fell face first into a sticky brown puddle.

Steve Clefton scrabbled around next to him, finally prising the gun from the dead policeman's hand.

"They're getting away, you idiots," screamed the Major.

George and Alice ran.

Steve Clefton looked up, raised the gun and aimed it. A mighty bang exploded through the woods as he let off one shot, just as George and Alice cleared the tree line. The bullet shattered the bark of a tree just inches from George's head as they disappeared into the woods.

"Shit!" shouted Steve Clefton. He aimed the gun again, but the pair were gone.

The Major walked over to Collin's lifeless body and looked down at it.

"Nice try," he said to the corpse as he bent down and picked up the duffel bag. He turned to look at John and Steve, who stared back up at him like two startled rabbits.

"Well?" he said, "what are you waiting for? Get after them."

The two men slipped and squelched, finally clambering to their feet.

"What about the money?" asked John.

"I'll take care of the money," said the Major. "You need to worry about catching those two before they find another policeman. One who's slightly less dead than this one."

"Do you seriously think I'm gonna trust you with all that cash?" laughed John.

"Why can't we just take the bag and make a run for it?" said Steve Clefton.

"Because," said the Major, "unless you've forgotten, they've seen our faces. And thanks to this one," he pointed at Steve, "they know our names as well. As soon as they get back to town and alert the police we'll be lucky to get five miles."

"They'll probably try and do us for this one's death as well," he said, kicking Collins' lifeless plump belly.

The two men gazed back at the Major, sense finally seeming to prevail.

"Fine," barked John, "but you follow on close behind with that bag."

"Of course," said the Major.

"You so much as think of disappearing and I stop thinking about killing them and focus on killing you instead. Do you understand?"

"Well said," replied the Major. "Now… time is ticking. And they're getting away."

"Come on Steve," said John. The two men ran off into the darkness.

The Major picked up the heavy green duffel bag, sighed heavily, kicked the dead policeman one last time and followed on behind.

CHAPTER 57

GEORGE and Alice ran. It was pitch black in the woods, the moon again shrouded behind the dense clouds, and George could barely see more than a foot in front of him. The ground was loose and sodden under foot. Despite this, George managed a reasonable pace for a man un-used to walking, let alone running, in high-heeled boots.

George's chest burned with a deep, dry acidic pain, as if his lungs were actually on fire. His legs ached; his calf muscles screaming and seizing with every step. His ankles jarred and stung, threatening to turn and snap each time the dangerously tall shoes collided with the ground.

Sweat bubbled on his forehead and ran a tiny river down his spine. He breathed hard, with sharp ragged gasps. A sedentary life of sitting behind a desk and slouching on a sofa had seen his once admirable levels of fitness dwindle. As such, he was utterly unprepared and physically lacking for the eventuality of running through the woods to evade the onslaught of desperate, armed gunmen. He made a mental note that, should he get out of this alive, he really ought to look into joining a gym.

If his body had its own way it would have given up already, collapsing into a shivering, gasping heap on the floor and accepting its fate. But George dug deep and somehow he managed to run on through the pain. There was no way he was going to give up now. For the first time in a long time he had something to live for. Something to fight for. He could see a future for himself. He wasn't sure what that future would hold, or whether it would be good or bad, but he knew it was out there. He couldn't give up now.

More importantly there was Alice. He had to protect her. He'd got her into this mess, and it was up to him to get her out of it. He had to get her to safety. And so he ignored the pain and carried on running.

From somewhere behind them they heard twigs snapping and heavy, muddy footsteps tramping on the ground. "Come back here," an angry voice snarled.

What a stupid request, thought George. If there was one thing in the world that he was definitely not going to do it was head back in the direction of the men trying to kill him with guns.

A shot rang out, the loud thunderclap snapping and echoing through the dense trees. Twigs snapped behind them; sharp, jagged sounds reverberating in the darkness. Footsteps thumped in the mud, increasing in speed. They were gaining.

George just ran, a determination he had never before experienced driving him on, powering his aching legs and burning chest. Eventually they neared the light at the edge of the trees, bursting out of the darkness onto the quiet street.

George nearly tumbled over as his feet hit firmer ground, and Alice had to hold him upright.

They paused briefly, looking this way and that, as if hoping for a sign: THIS WAY TO SAFETY. All they saw was an empty street.

"What now?" asked Alice.

George looked back into the dense black of the woods. He could hear the footsteps getting closer. He could almost feel the brothers bearing down on them.

Another shot sounded. Closer this time, and much louder. The ground by George's feet exploded with a cloud of dust where the bullet hit.

"Keep running," shouted George.

He grasped Alice's hand and pulled her behind him as they crossed the road, turned right and ran up the hill, disappearing around the bend in the road. George glanced back with every other step, gauging how far ahead they were.

"This way," said Alice suddenly, pulling into a slim alleyway. "They won't know to follow us through here."

George followed as they ran down the alley, traversing a series of narrow pathways, crossing through a dimly-lit courtyard and heading out into the main high street. It was teeming with people and the pair quickly disappeared into the crowd, moving slowly up the hill, back towards the hotel.

"If we can make it back to the hotel, we can get to my car and get the hell out of here," said George, in between desperate, gasping breaths. "As soon as we're far enough away I'll call the police."

"What if someone sees us?" asked Alice.

"We should be able to get in and out unseen. Everyone will be at the contest so the place should be empty, shouldn't it?"

"What about that detective? The one that was stalking you."

"I don't know. But let's not hang around and find out, eh?"

"But where are we going to go?" said Alice, stopping and pulling George back to face her. The crowd swarmed around them as they stood looking at each other, breathing hard.

"I don't know. I don't care as long as we're together. I mean... I'm only assuming but... well, do you want to come with me?"

Alice gave a wry smile. "Of course I do. But where?"

"I don't know. I think we'll have to figure it out as we go. But first we need to get out of here."

They made it through the crowd, ran up the hill and crashed through the door of the hotel. The place was deserted. Not a person in sight. An eerie quiet flooding the long hallways.

George and Alice ran past the small reception desk. Past the door to the bar. George had one foot on the bottom stair when he heard a gruff voice calling out behind him.

"Thring?"

The pair froze, not wanting to turn around, not wanting to see who was there.

"Thring?" said the voice again. "Is that you?"

Slowly George turned round to see the figure of Les stood in the doorway to the bar.

"I thought that was you. And Alice too. Hello Alice."

Alice turned as well. Both stood facing him, panting and gasping for breath. Les scanned them up and down, noticing the sweat in their hair, the mud caking their shoes and legs. He saw the haggard, fearful look in their eyes.

"Christ on a bike, what the hell's happened to you two?"

Still fighting for breath, George managed, "Oh… nothing really. We… er… we… er…"

"We thought we'd go for a romantic walk," Alice cut in. "Moonlit night and all that. But we got a bit lost in the woods and ended up covered in mud." She forced a small laugh.

"Must have been a pretty brisk walk," said Les. "You're both out of breath."

"Oh yes, I suppose we are. Not as fit as we used to be." She laughed again.

They went to turn towards the stairs again but Les carried on talking.

"I would have thought you'd be off down the pub tonight, for the big show. Just about everyone else from town'll be there. Even your Mum and Dad have gone."

"Oh yes," replied Alice. "We thought we'd just have a quiet one, really. I take it you didn't fancy it?"

"No, didn't really feel like it tonight. Besides, like I say, practically the whole town's there. So I thought I'd stop on here and enjoy a bit of peace and quiet."

"Good idea," said George, slowly turning on his heel, trying to kill the conversation and retreat.

"You know your Dad's been looking for you, Alice. He was ranting and raving about you missing a shift in the restaurant. You know how he gets. I hope this one isn't leading you astray."

"Oh really? Thanks for letting me know Les. Must have been a mix up on the rota. I'll speak to Dad later."

"Hmm, well, so long as you're okay?"

"Oh yes, fine thanks."

"Good, well come in and have a drink with me."

"Oh, thanks Les, but we really should go and get cleaned up."

"Come on. Come in for one drink."

"No, really, we should get upstairs," said George.

They smiled, turned and George once again managed to place one foot on the bottom step before Les stopped them once again.

"Really," he said, his voice low and stern. "I insist."

The pair turned back to see Les with a dark, serious look on his face. In his hand he held a small, black pistol.

"Oh, for God's sake," said George.

CHAPTER 58

"WHAT the hell?" said Alice. "What are you doing Les?"

"Just get in there," said Les, pointing the gun in the direction of the vacant bar.

"What has happened to everyone tonight?" said Alice.

"Move," barked Les, grabbing George roughly by the arm and pushing him towards the open door.

George and Alice trudged mournfully into the room and stood in front of the bar. George breathed out a heavy sigh, frustration rising in his chest. If one more person pointed a gun at him tonight he was really going to start getting annoyed.

Les followed in after them, taking up position on his usual stool at the end of the bar. He rested the butt of the gun on the edge of the bar, the barrel pointing ominously at George. He then pulled a mobile phone from his pocket, pressed a series of buttons and held it up to his ear.

"Hello," he said, his voice gruff and full of anger. "They're here. I suggest you get back here now."

He didn't wait for a response from the person on the other end, he just hung up and placed the phone back in his pocket.

"The bank robbers?" asked George, slotting the pieces together in his head. "You're working for them?"

"Working for them?" replied Les with a deep, gravelly laugh. "Sorry son: they're actually working for me."

"What?" said Alice. "The robbery. In the bank. You were behind that?"

"That's right, Alice," he said. "All my idea, I'm afraid."

"But... why?"

"Well, I would have thought that was pretty obvious. I wanted the money."

"Well... I...." said Alice, stunned.

"Great little plan, as it goes," continued Les, sounding pleased with himself. "Do you know how much money goes through that bank during Elvis week? Thousands. Hundreds of thousands. All these people shipped in from literally all over the world, handing over their hard-earned cash on hotels, drinks, novelty bloody Elvis key rings, watches... an endless supply of tat. The bank actually call in extra reserves of cash to meet the demand, did you know that?

"All that money in that tiny bank, with next to no security and a manager that would fall down if you blew on him. I mean it's practically asking to be stolen. Add in the fact that the security cameras don't work; there's a direct-access escape route down the side of the building; and, the local police are incapable of making an arrest without calling for back up that takes at least 20 minutes to arrive…

"Well, when you happen to know all of these things, a disreputable brain like mine can't help but think about ways to relieve the bank of that money."

"So you planned a robbery?" said Alice, indignant.

"Couldn't help it really, what with my criminal background. Something like that is just too tempting. If anyone is to blame, you really have to point the finger at the justice system for failing to properly rehabilitate me."

"I can't believe you robbed the bank. And all this time you've been sitting there drinking… My Dad's your best friend. I call you Uncle Les, for God's sake! Well, you think you know someone," said Alice, a grim look of disappointment etched on her face.

"Technically, I haven't robbed anything. And you won't find a scrap of evidence that says I did. I merely saw an opportunity and presented it to a… colleague. For a finder's fee, of course.

"I put a plan together, they carried out the job. It was a pretty bloody good plan, too. Nothing could go wrong. And then came Thring," said Les, turning to George, shaking his head with disappointment.

George sighed. It seemed a bit unfair.

"And then came Thring, to fuck everything up," said Les. "They would have been long gone by now, Thring. I'd be sitting on fifty grand, Alice wouldn't have spent all night tied up at gunpoint, and you wouldn't have a gun pointing at your chest right now. But for some reason, you thought you'd be a hero and run off with the money."

"Well, it wasn't quite as simple as that…" George protested.

"Regardless, things have ended up in a right old mess. And as usual it's down to me to clean it up."

"No pun intended?" chuckled George.

"What?" barked Les, angrily.

"Clean things up. You know, because of your OCD?"

Les grimaced at George. Alice grimaced at George. George looked at his shoes. This was clearly not the time for joviality.

"So what happens now?" asked Alice.

"Now we are going to wait here," said Les. "As you've no doubt gathered, my associates are on their way here now with the money. When they get here, I take my cut and then I leave. Whatever happens after that is between you and them."

George sighed heavily and sat down at one of the tables. He'd had rather too much of standing to attention with a gun pointed at him, so he thought he might as well take a load off. Alice sat down next to him.

"You do realise they'll kill us?" said George.

Les shrugged. "I expect so, yes."

"And you're okay with that? I thought we were… you know…"

"Friends?" said Les. "Hey, listen, you're a nice guy, Thring. And in different circumstances, yeah, I suppose we might have been friends. But this is just the way it has to be. If only you hadn't run off with that money."

"They're going to *kill* us, Les," interrupted Alice. "*Kill.* You can't just sit there and let it happen. You're my Dad's friend, for God's sake."

Les dropped his eyes to look at the carpet, suddenly seeming rather shamefaced.

"I'm sorry Alice, I really am," he said. "I honestly wish things could be different. But you got yourselves into this, meddling with things that didn't concern you. There's nothing I can do about it now."

Alice stared at him, dumbfounded.

A silence grew between them, none of the three knowing what to say or where to look. Then the silence was broken by the sound of the heavy front door opening. Angry sounding footsteps clumped in through hall then the door crashed noisily shut again.

"Ah, there you are. George, Alice, you really must stop running off like that," said the Major, strolling casually into the room and smiling his sickly, condescending grin. "You're going to make me think you don't like me."

John and Steve Clefton blundered in after him, panting and sweating, mud caking their legs, arms, stomachs, backs and faces.

"You lot took your bloody time," said Les.

"Yes, sorry old boy," replied the Major. "We had to deal with a minor incident involving a now dead policeman."

"What? You killed a copper?"

"Didn't need to. He did it for us."

Les paused for a second, thinking. "The fat one or the idiot?"

"Hmm... well, he was definitely on the plump side. Not sure how much of an idiot he was. Depends on what you compare him to," chuckled the Major, looking over at the two brothers.

"Sounds like Collins. Shame. Well, can't be helped. I take it you've got the money."

"Right here," said the Major raising the bag.

"Very good, Charlie. Now, how about you open it up and show me what's inside. Make sure it's actually cash and not just a bag full of mud and leaves."

"Honestly," sighed the Major, "there's so much distrust in the air today."

He bent down, unzipped the bag and pulled out a large handful of bank notes.

"You know, I'm going to get hurt feelings if people don't stop questioning my honesty," he said with a wry smile.

He pushed the money back into the bag, slid his own pistol in after it and zipped it up again.

"Turn it in Charlie," said Les. "I shared a cell with you for two years and I never heard a single honest word come out of your mouth.

"You clowns probably think he's really a Major, don't you?" he said to the two brothers. "Don't believe a word of it. He's more likely to have served chips in McDonalds than served time in the army."

The two brothers looked at each other with confusion, then a sudden realisation flashed in their eyes.

"Now, let's just get this shit sorted out before people come back," said Les.

"You know he was planning on robbing you," blurted Alice suddenly, a last desperate gambit. "I saw him last night on his phone, texting someone. He thought I was asleep, but I was watching him."

The room fell silent. Les, John, Steve and the Major all eyed each other cautiously, before turning their gaze back to Alice. Then all four men burst out in uproarious laughter.

"Well, of course I was," said the Major, still chuckling heartily.

"Of course he was," said Les, leaning on the side of the bar and coughing out a rich, mucus-filled chuckle.

"I'm sorry my dear," said the Major, "but if you thought that little revelation was likely to unsettle our merry little band, then I'm afraid you're quite mistaken."

"What... but..." said Alice.

"We *are* criminals," said the Major, still laughing softly. "I mean, that's what we do."

The two Clefton brothers nodded and grunted. Les shrugged his shoulders and gave a 'caught me guv' sort of look.

"I was going to try and pinch all the money for myself. Of course I was. These two apes were going to try and steal it from me too. Probably put a bullet in the back of my head as well, if the two guns hidden in the getaway car are anything to go by."

The smiles dropped from John and Steve Clefton's face. The Major gave them a small wink.

"And I have no doubt that this old coot had something similar planned for us as well," said the Major indicating Les. "It's all part of the profession I'm afraid. I don't think I've ever done a job when at least someone didn't try to rip everyone else off. There's no such thing as honour amongst thieves."

"So none of you are upset that you were all planning to rip each other off?" said Alice, dumbfounded. She looked around the room and all four men shrugged.

"Goes with the territory," said Les. "Like the man says, we are thieves. It stands to reason we'd try and steal from each other as well. It's not just normal people we nick from."

Alice opened her mouth to speak, then a look of resignation flashed across her face and she closed it again.

"Anyway," said the Major, looking at his watch, "time and tide, and all that. We should really press on."

Once again Les raised the gun and George gulped loudly as the barrel swung to point in his direction.

This was it. It was actually going to happen. There was no way George could talk his way out of this one. No quick thinking, or last ditched attempts at a clever plan, were going to help. There was no way out of it. Nowhere to run.

These men were going to kill him. As simple as that. It sounded so unreal, like something that only ever happened in movies. This sort of thing didn't happen to real people. It wasn't supposed to. They were going to *kill* him.

George's mind flooded with images, snapshots of himself doing things he'd never done; things he'd never even thought of doing. He saw himself and Alice walking along a sun-drenched beach in some exotic country. He saw the two of them curled up on his sofa at home, watching television. He saw himself marching into work and quitting his job. He saw Alice smiling, laughing.

The images flashed quicker and quicker, running through his mind in a rapid whirr. Pictures of them eating out in restaurants; watching plays in the theatre; drinking and laughing in pubs; walking in the countryside.

As his mind wandered through the fog of possibilities, it felt like the dreamy state he'd experienced just a few days previously. The very thing that had seen him accidentally leave his entire life behind and end up in this strange town. But it was different somehow. More urgent.

He wasn't wallowing in memories of the dull life he inhabited, or regrets at the things he felt he could or should be doing. The images he saw were more vivid; more colourful. These weren't wild, imagined possibilities; they were the things he knew he was supposed to experience. This was the life he was supposed to have; the one waiting for him. And he couldn't let that go. He wouldn't. It was his future for the taking and he was damn well going to take it.

Besides which, he really, really wanted to avoid getting shot, either fatally or otherwise. From what he'd seen of it on television, it looked rather painful and never seemed to end well.

With a snap George woke from his reverie with a new determination. If they were going to get out of this, George would have to move fast. It was time for one more act of bravery.

Without a word, George jumped to his feet, gripping the edge of the table with his hand as he moved. Using his forward momentum he spun the table round, throwing it forwards. It crashed hard into the Major's legs with a dull thwack, eliciting a shrill squeal from the man as he crumpled to the ground for the second time that night.

Continuing his sudden forward movement, George curled his shoulder round, putting all his weight behind it and barged hard into a very surprised looking Les. The old man was instantly thrown into the side of the bar, the shock of the attack loosening his grip on the gun in his hand. It flew up into the air, arcing high and spinning wildly before crashing down behind the bar, out of everybody's reach.

The high wooden stool sprang out from beneath Les and the old man crashed down hard, landing on top of the Major. With no time to spare, George launched himself at the two brothers who stood just inside the doorway.

George had read that in situations such as these, where one was required simultaneously to tackle multiple combatants, the best tactic for success was to aim for the biggest, meanest looking party first. The school of thought being that the biggest member of the pack would be surprised by this, assuming that one would go for the smaller, weaker members first. This would in turn put the wind up the smaller of the group, who would naturally assume that by tackling the toughest opponent first, the attacker was supremely confident and more than a match for the entire party.

The problem was that there was very little difference in the size of the two brothers, both being hulking brutes who more than outclassed George in both size and bulk. There was little to choose between them in terms of meanness either, both being grim, gruff-looking monsters that would scare even the hardiest of opponents. Finally, there was no way to determine which man possessed the superior fighting ability – though it was obvious that they again both outmatched George.

So, with little criteria to separate the two men, George went on gut instinct and threw himself at Steve Clefton, pulling his arm well back, clenching his fist tight and launching it hard at the man's face.

The punch landed square on the intended target, the line of his knuckles colliding with the space between the man's cheek and jawbone with a gut-wrenching, bone-cracking crunch. A loud, agonised, howl filled the room and George was probably the most surprised to realise that the noise was actually coming from him.

His hand simply stopped dead as it came into contact with the big man's face. It was like punching a solid block of steel and it felt as if every single bone in George's hand, fingers and wrist had shattered all at once. Instantly George pulled the wreck of his battered, throbbing hand back, clutching it tight to his body.

Steve Clefton had not been moved by so much as a millimetre, and stood looking down at George. John Clefton let out a loud, menacing chuckle as his brother slowly pulled back his own hand, aimed it squarely at George's head and fired it forwards.

Whether it was shock, fear or the sudden realisation that he was inexorably beaten, George wasn't sure, but he was suddenly completely unable to move. All he could do was look up at the impending juggernaut of a fist as it barrelled towards his head.

Everything suddenly moved in slow motion. George could do nothing but watch as the balled-up hand grew closer.

The impact was far more effective than his own punch had been, landing smack on his temple. Pain exploded in his cheek. A brilliant light flashed in front of his eyes. His feet lost contact with the ground and he felt himself suddenly flying backwards.

Another explosion of pain erupted in George's back as he clattered into a table behind him, knocking chairs sideways as he came to rest on the floor by the far wall. A shrill high-pitched ringing sounded in his ears and a foggy sensation clouded his head as he struggled to remain conscious. His brain felt like it was bouncing around in his skull, like a ball rattling inside a whistle.

He raised his broken hand to his face, cradling his throbbing eye, which had swollen instantly. He tried lifting himself up onto his elbows, fighting back the overwhelming urge to close his eyes and simply pass out. He knew he couldn't. They still had Alice. She was still the most important thing. At least if they were hurting him then they weren't hurting her.

He looked up just in time to see Steve Clefton advancing on him again. He swung his leg forward and the heavy, boot kicked hard into George's stomach.

Another blast of pain shot through him, as all the air in George's lungs flooded out in one single, sudden burst. He coughed and wheezed, fighting for breath as the big man kicked him again and again.

"Stop," screamed Alice.

She tried to get at the man, to jump on his back, do anything she could to halt him, but John Clefton grabbed hold of her.

Another hard kick. George's ribs cracked and ached, his back twisting in an agonising jolt as the man's foot pounded him; the hard round toe of his shoe digging into George's sides; the heel stamping down onto his broken, battered body.

Kick after kick landed on George's legs, ribs, stomach and back. He lay there like a rag doll, motionless and unable even to moan. Steve Clefton paused and George looked up through one half-opened eye to see a heavy foot raised high, poised in position to be brought down hard directly into George's face.

"Leave him alone," screamed Alice, her voice desperate and panicked.

"That's enough," yelled the Major. "Don't kill him in here, for God's sake. Look at the mess you're making. Have you never heard of forensic evidence?"

The big man moaned with disappointment, lowering his foot to the ground and giving George one final sharp dig in the ribs before stepping away.

Alice rushed over and knelt down next to George. His face was a swollen, purpling, bloody mess and Alice couldn't help but suck in a sharp intake of breath as she saw the extent of the damage.

"Bloody hell, George," she said, stroking his hair, tears sparkling in the corners of her eyes. "What did you do that for?"

"I was saving the day," wheezed George, flashing a bloodstained grin. "Don't worry, I've got them exactly where I want them."

He chuckled softly then instantly grimaced as a surge of searing pain jolted through his ribs.

"For God's sake, we're wasting time," said the Major. "Get these two out of here and take them somewhere a bit more... discreet."

"There's a car park out back," said Les, stepping around behind the bar and retrieving the dropped pistol. "That's your best bet. We can take care of these two – *quietly* – split the cash, pick up a couple of cars and get the hell out of here."

"A splendid idea," said the Major, bending down and picking up the duffel bag.

A large hand gripped the collar of George's jumpsuit, lifting him up off the ground. His arms and legs swayed lifeless, his head bowed and resolute.

"Come on then," said Steve Clefton. "Let's get this over with."

CHAPTER 59

GEORGE'S feet scraped noisily along the ground as Steve Clefton dragged him out of the bar and into the corridor. Various degrees of different kinds of pain surged throughout his entire body and he struggled hard to remain conscious. He hung limp and lifeless as the big man pulled him this way and that.

He was secretly quite glad to have Steve Clefton carrying him, as he was holding the majority of George's body weight. Left to his own devices, George wasn't certain that he'd be able to stand up straight without falling down. Or, at the very least, swaying wildly like a drunk.

Steve Clefton pulled him across the corridor, through the deserted, dark kitchen and towards a back door at the far corner. John Clefton followed closely behind, keeping a firm grip on Alice's elbow, pulling her along at the side of him. The Major came next, carrying the heavy duffel bag in his hand, and Les followed at the rear, his pistol gripped at waist height and ready for use.

A faint whiff of bacon grease and chip fat wafted into George's nostrils, making him feel suddenly very hungry. He hadn't eaten since breakfast and a sharp stabbing pang of hunger radiated in his stomach. He knew he shouldn't really have been thinking of food at such a perilous juncture, but it's funny how the brain works. And at least it gave him a minor diversion from thinking about his impending death.

"I suppose a final meal is out of the question," he half-joked, looking up at the big man.

"Nice try, Thring," called Les from the back of the group. "Bit peckish myself, as it goes, but I've got somewhere to be. And so have you."

"Yeah," agreed John Clefton, "in a big fucking hole in the ground."

"Speaking of which," said the Major, stopping where he was, "what exactly are we going to do with the bodies?"

Everyone stopped and looked at each other, contemplating the question. George felt a chill race through him. He didn't like the idea of being described as a body. Especially as he was still, technically, not yet dead.

"Good point," said Les. "Best not to just leave them lying around here. Just in case the Old Bill come sniffing around before we've got away. Better take them back out into the woods and bury them. And this time, maybe don't let them get away."

"So should we kill them now or not?" said Steve Clefton sounding like a sullen teenager.

He released his grip on George's collar in an act of frustration, letting him fall to a heap on the ground.

"Well, I ain't carrying two dead bodies through the woods," huffed John

Clefton. He scanned George up and down with a derisory look. "I mean, they're not exactly big, but dead bodies can be tricky to lug around."

"Quite right," agreed the Major. "I mean, why strain yourself? Save yourself a bit of work. Get them to walk out into the woods and kill them there. Then all you have to do is bury them. Tell you what, I'll hang on here with the cash while you two pop off and take care of things. Les can go along and supervise."

"Like fuck you will," said John. "Don't think I'm leaving you alone with that money again. We all go together."

"Oh, let's just kill 'em now," said Steve, growing more impatient with every second. "They must have a big freezer we can dump 'em in, or summin'."

"Hmmm, good idea," said the Major, "bury them under the frozen peas. Alice, you don't happen to have one of those industrial-sized freezers about the place, do you?"

Alice stood aghast for a second before spitting out: "Are you taking the piss? I mean, excuse me for being obstructive, but I'm not gonna stand here and help you plan out the best way to dispose of our bodies."

"No, fair point," said the Major. "That was a touch insensitive, wasn't it? Forget I asked. Les, you know the lay of the land, any giant freezers?"

"No chance," said Les. "Hotel of this size, all they have is a small chest freezer out the back. Doubt very much if you'll fit them both in there."

He looked over at Alice, suddenly realising his own insensitivity. "Sorry Alice," he said.

The group fell silent, all contemplating the various options, before Steve Clefton sighed heavily and said, "Are we fuckin' killing 'em or what?"

"Okay, okay, well it looks as though the woods is still our best bet," concluded the Major. "Let's hold off from the actual killing for the time being. We'll throw them in the car and drive out somewhere a bit more remote. Then we can get George and Alice to stroll out to somewhere ultra-quiet and do the deed there. All agreed?"

Les, John, Steve and the Major all shrugged and gave each other affirmatory nods.

"Fine by me," said George, looking up from his crumpled position on the floor.

Steve Clefton bent and renewed his grip on George's collar, yanking him back up to his feet. With the group ready to move again, he pulled the back door slowly open and poked his head outside.

The space outside the back door was not so much a car park as a small strip of wasteland at the side of the building. The rough gravel ground was pockmarked with dents and potholes and was in serious need of repair. Ten metres from the door stood a battered, wooden fence that lined the edge of the ground.

It was dark in the car park, lit only by thin beams of moonlight that pierced the cloudy sky, bouncing and twinkling on the roofs and windows of the five cars parked up against the side wall of the hotel. Beyond the cars was pitch black. A dense, dark void like existence had simply come to a stop. An eerie silence hung outside, broken only by the sound of a cold wind catching the edge of fallen leaves and blowing them unseen across the ground.

Steve Clefton stepped carefully across the threshold of the door, searching for the ground in the dark with his foot. When he was certain it was secure, he moved out fully, dragging George along behind him. The Major stepped out next, followed by John Clefton, Alice and then Les. The group stood, staring out into the blackness. A faint rustling sound echoed in the distance.

"Which car is yours?" asked Les.

"That one at the end," replied John Clefton.

"Good. Let's get these two in the boot and get the bloody hell out of here. This place gives me the creeps."

Steve Clefton took another careful step forward and a loud electrical clicking noise sounded high up on the wall behind him. The group all instinctively looked up to see the source of the noise as a brilliant bright light burst out, illuminating the whole car park.

Everyone except for George raised their hands to their faces, shielding their eyes from the halogen glow beaming out from the hotel's motion-detecting security light. George would have raised his hands as well, except that his arms were barely functional and he couldn't lift them, so he had to settle for squinting his one good eye tight shut. The other was already swollen closed and was managing well enough on its own.

"What the fuck?" cried Steve Clefton.

"Jesus fucking…" said John Clefton.

"That's a bit bloody bright," agreed the Major.

The rustling out in the car park grew louder. The group turned back to the space outside the hotel. Slowly their eyes adjusted to the light and their sight returned. All six looked out into the now-illuminated car park. They all gasped with surprise. All of them except for George Thring, who was not surprised at all.

Standing before them, beyond the parked cars, in the space that had previously been nothing but darkness, stood a small army of Elvis Presleys.

Tall Elvises, short Elvises, white, black and even Chinese Elvises. There were men, women, old Elvises and young, and one worryingly fat-looking Elvis. They stood huddled in a large group, completely blocking the exit to the car park. They were dressed in a vast array of costumes – red, gold, blue, black – shiny, sparkling material flapping and shimmering in the breeze. There must have been at least forty of them. And they all looked angry.

One of the Elvises held a baseball bat in his hand, swinging it slowly back and forth next to his leg. Another wore an elaborately decorated gold knuckle duster on his hand, the letters K, I, N and G spelt out across his fingers in a heavy, embossed font. A man at the opposite end of the crowd, dressed in a bright red jumpsuit with sparkly gold trim, shifted his weight back and forth from his left to right foot, repeatedly throwing a balled up fist into his other hand.

Right at the front of the crowd, two paces ahead of the rest, stood a tall man dressed in a smartly ironed, khaki, 1950s G.I. Elvis costume. Both of his eyes were swollen and purpled, and a wide, white bandage stretched across his nose and cheeks.

Next to him stood Detective Constable Michael Keane.

CHAPTER 60

DETECTIVE Constable Michael Keane had spent a second frustrating day in Lower Chidbury, keeping tabs on George Thring whilst also trying to gain ground in his investigations.

The former of the exercises had proven significantly easier, due to Thring having not left his hotel room all day. Keane had bribed two teenagers he'd caught hanging around in a small car park behind the hotel to keep an eye on Thring and to call him immediately if the man moved. Of course, he couldn't guarantee that the fifteen pounds he'd given them would mean they would actually do what he'd asked. But the promise to turn a blind eye to the joint he'd caught them smoking seemed to be incentive enough for them not to mess him around.

He was playing fast and loose with his responsibilities to uphold the law, of course, and under normal circumstances he would have dragged them down to the station and seen them awarded a caution at the very least. But he had bigger criminals on the hook, and he couldn't afford to let himself be distracted with petty offences. Far better to use it to his advantage and have them work for him instead.

It had given him a few hours to head into town and dig around a bit more. He'd started by surreptitiously questioning the bank manager and several of his staff, ensuring at all times he was not seen by the other detectives. They would not have looked too kindly on his interfering in the case and would likely have marched him out of town, or worse still, contacted his bosses back home. And it was still too early to come clean about what he was really doing.

As such, he'd phoned the station early that morning, put on his best croaky voice and pretended to be coming down with something or other. Again, it was far from ideal pulling a sicky in the first week of his new job. But once he had Thring under arrest, and his bosses were praising his ingenuity, it would quickly be forgotten.

Naturally Keane didn't tell the witnesses he was questioning that he was part of the local police force, but he didn't tell them that he wasn't either. He just gave them a quick flash of his warrant card, and if they chose to believe that he was part of the official investigation then that was up to them. It was perhaps a little less honest than official protocol called for, but again this was a unique situation, and bending the odd rule was all just a part of getting the result.

Of course none of the staff had witnessed anything useful, aside from having seen a group of men dressed as Elvis Presley. And the town was hardly short of a few of those. So, not much to go on.

They were all in agreement that there had been three robbers: two with big machine guns and a third that seemed to be giving out the orders. When asked if it was possible that a fourth member might have been involved, keeping a low profile and hiding in the background, none of them were sure. It was possible, of course – everyone was dressed the same after all – but none could be certain.

The manager proved to be the least helpful of them all. He had apparently spent the whole time looking at his shoes. Or that's the way it seemed, if his rambling, incomplete, wildly contradictory descriptions of the assailants were anything to go by. One had been short, apparently, and two were tall. Or were two of them short? One was definitely skinny and dressed in green. Or was it blue?

One of them was posh, he was sure of that, and the other two spoke with Russian accents. Or maybe Greek. One of them had a limp. One of them might have been missing a finger on one hand.

All three were definitely white males. Although, thinking about it, one of them might have been black. It was too hard to tell under the giant sunglasses and big fake sideburns. Keane had sighed as the man's ridiculous speculations formed the most unlikely set of photo-fits in his head.

The most promising lead came from a girl called Kelly, who had been working on the counter at the time of the robbery. She distinctly remembered having served a George Thring – she'd definitely accessed his account – although she was sketchy about exactly what had made him stand out in her mind.

She didn't think it likely that he had been involved in the robbery. Again she seemed strangely certain of the fact, but wouldn't say why. She hadn't seen him leave the bank, or what had happened to him afterwards, but it had been so confusing at the end that she hadn't seen where anybody had run to.

The most important revelation, of course, was her claim she had definitely served him, and that put him at the scene of the crime. Which certainly contradicted Thring's claims of having been in the hotel all day.

Thring had been at the bank when the robbery had taken place. Nobody had seen him leave, and nobody had seen him after. He wasn't with the other hostages in the aftermath, which meant he'd run away in the opposite direction. And there was only one reason that he would have done that.

Keane had known that Thring was involved from the very moment he laid eyes on him, and now the pieces of the puzzle were starting fall into place. Unfortunately, he still needed more evidence. One witness statement placed him at the scene, but it wouldn't be enough. He needed more physical proof.

Naturally, Keane had asked to view the CCTV footage, hoping to catch a glimpse of Thring in the bank – or better yet, taking part in the robbery. When he was told that there was none because the cameras didn't work and the manager hadn't quite got around to getting them fixed, he lost his patience and stormed out of the bank, muttering under his breath.

From there, Keane worked his way around all the local businesses, asking owners and staff what they had witnessed. For most of them everything had gone by in a flash. Nobody had seen anyone out of the ordinary entering the bank. The first they'd known anything was wrong was when the police car screeched up outside. There had followed a good twenty minutes of waiting, worrying and speculation, and then all hell had let loose.

Some thought there'd been an explosion in the bank, glass shattering loudly and smoke billowing out into the street. Then some maniacs started shooting up the place. People dived, ducked, ran and scattered in a mad flurry, blind and bumping into each other. So, nobody had seen anything.

A few claimed to have seen the robbers exiting, firing their guns wildly into the skies, whooping and shouting, fury burning in their eyes. Of course this was nonsense. Keane had been there and hadn't seen anything like that at all. Sadly, for every five reasonable, rational witnesses who could be relied upon to give a calm, accurate, evenly assessed recollection of events, there was always one nutbag who wanted to make life a bit more exciting for themselves and reported back a wildly adventurous, outlandish, totally fictitious report. They remembered what they wanted to remember, and wanted a good story to tell their mates.

Most importantly, nobody else had seen or spoken to George Thring. Plenty said they had seen a man matching his description. But as his description matched half the people in town, it was somewhat less than conclusive.

Keane worked his way around town, casually approaching people, flashing his warrant card and asking questions. He spoke to a young woman who'd watched the action play out from the street outside. He questioned an old lady who'd been present in the bank during the robbery and who'd been forced to abandon her Zimmer frame and lie down on the floor. He spoke to an American man who'd been assaulted during the incident, a machine gun having apparently been used to squash his nose into his face.

He caught up with a man in the pub, who also claimed to have been in the bank throughout the robbery. He gave the same description of the robbers as the bank staff, and said that he had no idea what had happened to them after the event. When the robbers had pushed everyone out into the street, and he heard the loud bangs sounding, he thought, quite reasonably, that he was about to be shot. He'd done exactly what everyone else did: he'd scrambled wildly, pushing people out of the way as he ducked for cover and heaved himself behind a parked car.

He seemed slightly crestfallen that he'd reacted in such a way, as though he'd been hoping the hero within would suddenly come bursting out and foil the whole evil plan. At the very least, he'd like to have acted slightly more bravely, maybe have saved a small child or shielded a vulnerable woman from a bullet. A sad resignation sparked in his eyes, as if he'd learned something about himself he'd rather not have known. Keane had seen that look before. Most people, he knew, are just as scared as everybody else. And there's nothing wrong with that. It's a bloody scary world, after all. It's just that we like to think we're a bit braver than we really are.

Throughout the rest of the day Keane traversed the high street, calling into shops, cafés, pubs and anywhere else people were assembled, asking questions and making observations. He managed to build up a good picture of what had happened; who'd been where at what time and how events had played out.

When he'd run out of people to talk to, alleyways to look down and streets, cars and buildings to inspect, he headed back up to Thring's hotel. True to his word, he paid the young lads what he'd promised, made them turn out their pockets once more to prove they had no further illicit substances, and sent them on their way with a warning.

They informed him that Thring must have remained inside the hotel as, aside from a creepy looking family all dressed in matching costumes, not a single other person had stepped outside the hotel all day.

Content that Thring had been adequately 'surveilled', Keane climbed back into his car and continued his own stakeout. The air in the car, thick with a mixture of his own sweat and the pine-fresh fragrance from the air freshener, caught in his throat. His back ached in the hard seat, his legs felt cramped in the foot well, and he felt dirty. He hadn't had a shower in two days, and he could literally feel the grime building up on his skin.

Worst of all, he was hungry. He'd been so busy chasing up leads that he'd completely forgotten about eating. Or drinking. If he was going to make it through another night in the car he was going to need food. And lots of it. Washed down with about a gallon of coffee.

Just as he was preparing to climb out of the car and go in search of something to eat, his mobile phone started to rattle and vibrate in his pocket. He fished it out, staring blankly at the screen, which burst out in a bright green glow that lit up the whole interior of the car.

He didn't recognise the number and hesitated a second before answering it.

"Hello," said the quiet, hesitant voice on the other end. "I think I might need your help."

******

"Mr Thring," said Keane, "I wasn't expecting to hear from you."

The other end of the line went quiet, as if the man were carefully contemplating his next words, wondering if he'd made the right decision in calling.

"Have you decided to come to your senses, Mr Thring? Are you ready to tell me the truth about what you're really doing here, and what really happened in the bank yesterday?"

"I've already told you," said Thring, "I'm here on holiday and I had nothing to do with that robbery."

"Well, I know you weren't really in the hotel all day yesterday, George. I have an eyewitness who clearly remembers seeing you in the bank just before it was robbed. A cashier called Kelly. She remembers serving you."

Again silence on the other end of the line. More contemplation. Then a long sigh.

"Okay, yes. Look, I had nothing to do with that robbery, but yes, I was in the bank."

"Now we're getting somewhere," said Keane. "And I suppose you just happened to be an innocent bystander?"

"Yes."

"Wrong man in the wrong place at the wrong time?"

"Yes."

"Pull the other one."

Another loud sigh came whooshing down the line.

"Look, whether you believe me or not, I didn't do it. But I know who did and I know where the money is. I can help you catch them."

"And why should I believe you?" asked Keane.

"Well… because…" More silence. More thinking. "Look, this would be a hell of a lot easier if you just believed me and went along with things."

"I bet it would."

"Oh, for God's sake, do you have to be so bloody obstinate?"

"Fine," said Keane. "What exactly is your plan? I'm guessing you have some kind of a plan cooked up?"

"Just be at my hotel at 8.30pm. I'm on my way to meet them now, and then I'll bring them to you. I'll make sure they have the money on them, and everything you need to arrest them."

"And how exactly are you going to do that?"

"Just leave that up to me."

"I'm afraid I can't do that, Mr Thring."

"Well, that's tough, because that's the only way I'm doing this."

"Really?" said Keane. "And what if I just come to your hotel now and arrest you?"

"Because if you do, I'll tell you nothing. You won't catch the bank robbers, you won't get the money back, and you won't have enough to charge me for anything other than going on holiday without telling my boss."

"You were seen in the bank during a robbery."

"As a customer," retorted Thring. "That's circumstantial, and you know it."

What had happened to this man? Where was the cringing weakling Keane had been questioning only the previous day? The one who'd practically crumbled at the most elementary levels of interrogation.

"We'll see about that?" Keane challenged back.

"Look there's too much at stake for this crap. Just be at the hotel. I'll bring them to you."

"And how do I know this isn't a trick to get me out of the way while you skip town?"

"If I wanted to skip town I'd have done it already. Look, just trust me okay? There's too much at stake. Just tell me you'll be there at 8.30pm."

There was agitation in the man's voice; a real panic. Keane couldn't be sure what Thring was up to but he was scared of more than the simple prospect of being arrested.

Keane thought about it, weighing up the options. He should really have marched up to Thring's room, kicked the door in and dragged him away for questioning. That was what his gut told him. And he had to admit he'd get more than a little satisfaction from throwing the cuffs on him and wiping the smile off his face. But he couldn't help but feel a certain sense of curiosity.

"Fine," he said into the phone, "I'll be there."

He was going to let this one play out for a while, hoping that Thring was genuine in his promise to deliver the crooks. Or at the very least, he'd give him enough rope to hang himself.

"Good," said Thring. "See you then. Oh, and you might want to bring some back up. I suspect they'll probably be armed."

The line went dead. The light in the hotel room flipped off. A few moments later the front door opened and George Thring stepped out into the cold air, hurried along the cracked black path and set off down the hill into town.

Keane allowed the man to wander just out of sight before climbing out of his car and following stealthily behind. He would keep his promise to meet at the hotel later but there was no way he was letting Thring out of his sight. He was going to keep close to the man, find out where he went and whom he was meeting. And then he'd make the arrest on his own terms.

******

George Thring walked hurriedly down the hill towards town, side-stepping revellers and excited Elvis fans, making his way to the pub at the end of the road. Detective Keane kept his distance, making sure the man was always in his line of sight, but holding back just far enough so that he would be totally unaware of Keane's presence behind him.

Keane paused and watched as the man entered the pub. Then he raced down the hill and peered in through a window, watching as Thring made his way around the interior. He seemed to be searching the place; looking for something or someone. Finally he went to the bar, bought a drink and then raced to a table in the corner, much to the annoyance of two fat people, who had tried to outpace him to the seats and then waddled off in demonstrable annoyance.

When a group of noisy Elvis fans barrelled down the hill and walked into the pub, Keane took the opportunity to insinuate himself amongst them and enter the pub unseen. He then moved deftly through the crowd, hiding at the back of the room where he could remain hidden but with a perfect vantage point.

A few moments later three men and a woman entered the pub and approached Thring. There seemed to be something familiar about the men, but Keane wasn't sure what. He definitely recognised the woman though. It was Alice, the woman who'd defended Thring the previous day. The one he claimed to have been in a relationship with.

Something about the way one of the men pushed her down into the seat didn't seem right. It was as if she was there against her will. The group spoke for a few moments, hostility bubbling between them. Again Keane wished he could have been closer, so that he could hear what was being said. Despite this, Keane could clearly read their body language and it was evident this wasn't a friendly conversation.

"What's going on here, Thring?" Keane said to himself.

Slowly the pieces were starting to line up. Keane guessed that these were the robbers. They had to be. But why the animosity? Had Thring tried to rip them off and they'd caught up with him? Thring had said he knew where the money was. Had he tried to double-cross the rest of the team and things had gone wrong?

And what about the woman? She was clearly here under duress. But why? Thring had spoken about there being too much at stake. Perhaps the other robbers had threatened her to force Thring to give them their cut.

Just as Keane was trying to make sense of it all, Thring suddenly bolted up from his chair, attacking the other men. The people in front of them reacted, darting one way then another. Small ripples of activity flowed back through the crowd as people moved, jostled, rankled, completely obscuring Keane's view.

He tried to push his way through but the crowd was far too tightly packed, and he completely lost sight of Thring and the other men. Keane pushed and shoved, but the crowd shoved back, and he couldn't make his way through.

Suddenly the loud music in the pub stopped and bright lights burst out onto a small stage at the edge of the room. Keane stood dumbfounded as he watched Thring – now standing on the stage – look around, bewildered. He then approached a microphone, looking as though he was about to speak or sing, before vomiting all over the front row of the audience.

A large hand then emerged from the crowd, grabbed hold of Thring and pulled him away.

By the time Keane had managed to make his way through the crowd and out onto the street, Thring was nowhere to be seen. Keane ran round to the back of the pub. He searched down alleyways. Ran halfway back up the hill. But the group had simply vanished.

Things would appear not to have gone as Thring had planned them. Unless vomiting onto a group of strangers had been deliberate. But Keane thought not. He had to assume that whatever Thring had intended to do, something had gone wrong. And now Keane had lost sight of not only his main lead and suspect, but also the whole gang.

As Keane traced his way back down to the bar, hoping to pick up some sign of where the group might have gone, he again felt that nagging sensation that he should follow protocol, or at the very least try and make his way back there from the wildly undisciplined path he'd found himself on. He should call the station, report everything back to his superiors and organise a proper search for the criminals.

Things had got out of hand, and he ought to call for help.

But he was too far into this now. He'd broken pretty much every available rule, and would be facing some pretty serious charges himself. And by going along with Thring's plan, he had potentially endangered the safety of those involved and any innocent bystanders that might be harmed by them. Judging by the man who'd had his face half-flattened during the robbery, these guys were not averse to violence. Anyone standing in their way would be in danger, and Keane would be partly responsible.

He had to take care of this himself. The only way he'd be able to talk his way out of breaking protocol so grievously was to come back with a big arrest. Hopefully that would be enough to distract from his actions. More importantly, he couldn't allow these dangerous men to be loose on the streets. He had to stop them now.

The one small problem, of course, was that he had no idea where they had gone, or even in which direction they were moving. There was no sense in randomly heading off one way, simply hoping to pick up their trail. He had to think.

The only thing he could fall back on was Thring's original plan to meet back at the hotel. There was no way of knowing whether the man would be able to steer the rest of the group back there, as per the original arrangement. But Keane was out of options. He would have to head there, keep to the original meeting, and hope that somehow Thring would be able to get the robbers there as planned.

Decision made, Keane was all set to track back up the hill to the hotel when a second problem dawned on him. Thring had quite astutely suggested that the men would probably be armed. Given that they were armed robbers, and had been seen with what one witness had described as 'fuck off big machine guns', Keane knew he couldn't take any risks. He certainly didn't fancy going in there alone, but then he still had the same problem with regards to calling for back up. Until he knew for sure that the criminals were in place, and the arrest could go down as planned, if he called in support he'd be putting his whole career on the line.

Scanning the streets, looking for inspiration, Keane's gaze was drawn back to the pub. Happy, singing enthusiasts were still marching up and down the street, heading into and out of the pub. A small group of Elvises stood smoking out the front in the street. Most looked like the idiots they were, but several of the crowd were big and looked like they might be able to handle themselves. Right at the front of the crowd stood a man with a large white bandage spread across his face. A man that Keane knew, having interviewed him earlier in the day, had something of a score to settle.

It was incredibly unorthodox, but Keane suddenly wondered whether there was another form of back up he could call upon. He'd come this far, he reasoned. What would another broken rule matter? He crossed the street and approached the men.

"Excuse me guys," he said, reaching into his pocket and flashing his warrant card. "How do you fancy giving me a quick hand with something?"

CHAPTER 61

"WHAT the hell…?" said Les, looking out at a shimmering, sparkling army of Elvis Presleys.

"That's him," cried G.I. Elvis, pointing an accusatory finger at Steve Clefton. "That's the son-of-a-bitch that broke my nose!"

Steve Clefton let out a low, mean growl, like a dog trying to ward off attackers. The crowd bristled and fidgeted, anger flowing through them like a wave. They were a vengeful force, waiting for the command to attack.

Detective Keane spoke next. "Hello Mr Thring," he said. "Everything all right?"

George raised his head, squinting up at Keane through his one good eye.

"Hello Detective," he said. "Glad you could make it."

Alice looked at George with surprise. Les looked at him with a mixture of shock, rage and disgust. John Clefton kicked him hard in the back of the leg.

"This little welcoming party is down to you, I take it," said the Major.

"Afraid so," coughed George, wincing with the fresh new pain throbbing in his leg.

"Well, aren't you just full of surprises."

Instinctively, Les threw his arm up, pointing his gun at the crowd, moving it rapidly from person to person as if trying to decide who the biggest threat was. Panic shook his hand.

"What the fuck?" he said again.

"Now," said Keane with the forceful crowd-control voice he'd learned at the training academy, "let's all just calm down, shall we? There's no need for any of that. As you can see, you're more than outnumbered. Why not just put the gun down, give yourselves up and nobody needs to get hurt."

"Fuck off," shouted John Clefton. Not the most eloquent rebuke, but to the point nonetheless.

"You can't get away," said Keane. "You'll never get past us. Just give yourselves up."

Silence descended as the two groups stared each other down, weighing up the options. Feet fidgeted, fists clenched, hard deep breaths were sucked in and spat out.

Steve Clefton looked back towards his brother. John Clefton looked to the Major, then to Les. Nobody spoke. Nobody wanted to make the first move.

"Oh, fuck this," said Steve Clefton, finally breaking the deadlock.

He looked out at the assembled Elvises and let out a loud, deep, ragged growl. He released his grip on George's collar and launched himself forwards, running hard at the crowd.

George, suddenly in full control of his own weight, wobbled and swayed then tumbled to a messy heap on the cold ground. He grunted and moaned, the impact sending shockwaves of pain through his battered legs, back and chest.

John Clefton reacted quickly, letting go of Alice's arm and dashing off after his brother. Alice tried to move to George's side, but Les reached out, throwing an arm around her front, gripping her shoulder, and pulled her hard against him.

He twisted her round in front of him, using her as a shield. He stepped to his side, aiming to press his back up against the closed door as extra protection, but found it had been opened again, and that the Major had dashed through it into the building.

"Come back here, you coward," yelled Les, but the Major was already gone.

The two brothers thundered forwards like angry bulls charging at the crowd. A few Elvises broke off at the edges, panic overcoming them as they stumbled and ran, retreating from the danger. Most held their ground.

The baseball bat-wielding Elvis raised his weapon, gripping it hard in both hands, ready to swing. Knuckle-duster Elvis puffed out his chest, raising both fists in front of him like a boxer. G.I. Elvis bent his knees slightly, twisting his body sideways, crunching his hands into balls, preparing to fight.

"Stop," yelled Keane in desperation, holding up his flimsy laminated warrant card. "Police."

The two men continued running.

"Stop," he barked, panic pinching his vocal chords.

The two men continued running.

"Fucking well stop, will you!"

It was no good. The brothers came barrelling across the small car park in great strides, their arms raised high. George looked up from his crumpled position on the ground as they reached the assembled masses.

Steve Clefton piled in first, throwing his heavy fists forward. His right hand crashed hard into the side of Knuckle Duster Elvis's head, throwing him off balance and forcing him to stumble backwards into the crowd behind him.

John arrived half a second later, mimicking his brother and throwing a fist into the face of Detective Keane. The punch landed hard, lifting the policeman off his feet and sent him tumbling onto his arse on the floor.

A slightly pudgy man with greying hair, dressed in black leather jeans and jacket, stepped into the gap, reaching forwards and grabbing John by the collar with both hands. As soon as he had a grip on him, however, his face suddenly flashed with panic and confusion, as though he hadn't quite expected to get as far as he had and wasn't quite sure what to do with the man now that he had him. John Clefton dispatched him with a quick, brutal head-butt, which smashed the man's nose with a crunching spurt of crimson. His eyes rolled straight back in his head and he gurgled softly as he crumpled to the floor.

The next man behind him in the queue, dressed in a blue and silver jumpsuit, actually managed to land a punch on John Clefton's chin. It cracked into his already battered, bloodied nose, stunning him slightly. The man swung immediately forwards with his other hand, attempting to follow up with a sharp left hook, but the punch missed and John retaliated with a swift kick to his stomach.

Steve Clefton pulled back his other hand, preparing to throw it towards Knuckle Duster Elvis's chest but was thrown off guard as Baseball Bat Elvis swung his weapon, bringing it clattering into Steve's left shoulder. The blow was powerful, the man having put all his weight behind it, but it barely put Steve Clefton off his stride. He simply jolted back half a pace, mildly stunned, before turning his attention on the new attacker and throwing a punch his way.

The man was quick, and ducked just in time to see the big, angry fist go flying over the top of his head. Gripping the baseball bat in both hands, he jabbed it forwards, thumping Steve Clefton hard in the stomach.

Steve grunted and wheezed, momentarily winded and slightly off balance, fighting to stay on his feet. Immediately, Baseball Bat Elvis popped back up, raised his weapon high and snapped it down, the tip hurtling towards Steve Clefton's head.

The large man gazed up, shocked and unable to move, waiting for the impact. But seconds before it hit another hand shot out and caught the bat, plucking it out of the air and yanking it forcefully from the man's hand. John Clefton then threw it back in Baseball Bat Elvis's direction, butting it straight into his chin, which cracked loudly as the man fell back into the crowd.

Straightening up, Steve reached forward, grabbing G.I. Elvis by the throat and squeezing hard. The man wheezed noisily, his face turning instantly red as his hands flew up, scrabbling at his attacker's fingers, trying desperately to peel them away.

John Clefton turned to his right, raising the bat and seeking out his next opponent. Catching sight of a tall man in a Jailhouse Rock costume, he swung the bat hard, aiming to bring it down square on the man's impressively quiffed hair. Unfortunately, Jailhouse was too quick, side-stepping out of the way as the bat whistled inches from his face. The momentum pulled John slightly off side, and with his body spun round to the right, his face was left open to the retaliatory punch the man launched in his direction.

The knuckles landed squarely, glancing off John Clefton's brick-like cheekbone, causing as much damage to the hand as it did to his face, but it was enough to stop him. He staggered backwards slightly and looked up just in time to see the worryingly overweight Elvis bundling out of the crowd and running straight at him.

Big Fat Elvis took two hard steps and launched himself, belly first, thundering into John Clefton with staggering force, knocking him straight to the ground. The fat man came tumbling after and the two crashed to the cold stone floor with a heavy thud. John Clefton lay there, dazed and wheezing, crushed and pinned under nearly thirty stones of wriggling Elvis Presley.

With his face turning blue, and blackness slowly seeping in at the edges of his vision, G.I. Elvis continued scrabbling at Steve Clefton's fingers. It was no good, though, the big man's grip held firm. G.I. Elvis could feel himself slipping away, the dull thud of his own heartbeat booming in his ears, drowning out the noise of the desperate melee all around him.

Seeing the panic in the man's face, Detective Keane roused himself and leapt to his rescue, jumping onto Steve Clefton's back. He wrapped his arms around the man's neck, digging his knees into his sides and tried to pull him off. But Steve was just too strong, and the policeman simply hung there like he was clinging to the side of a giant rock.

Finally, as the darkness nearly overtook him, G.I. Elvis lashed out with one final burst of desperate energy, thrusting his knee forwards. It landed heavy, punching into Steve Clefton's groin with a dull, cracking thud.

Immediately the man released his grip, the hand springing wide open as small tears sprung in the corner of his eyes. G.I. staggered backwards, clutching at his throat and sucking in great lungfuls of air as Steve Clefton dropped to his knees, Detective Keane springing off and landing in a heap next to him.

With the two Clefton brothers down on the floor, the rest of the crowd flooded in, raining down kicks and punches in a bright, multicoloured swirl of hands and feet.

"That's enough," yelled Detective Keane, scrambling to his feet for the second time. "Back up now. Back up."

He had to physically yank one over-zealous attacker back, pulling him by his elbows as he attempted to deliver one last kick to the ribs for luck.

"Come on now," said Keane, "you've had your fun. Come on, move back."

Gradually the crowd peeled away, three brawny men needing all their strength to pull Big Fat Elvis up from a rather squashed-looking John Clefton. Kneeling down, Detective Keane pulled two pairs of handcuffs from his pocket and, as he clipped them into place with a satisfying metallic click, he couldn't help but smile as he said, "You two are fucking well nicked." It was a little more *The Sweeney* than he'd usually go with, but it seemed to fit the occasion pretty well.

******

On the other side of the car park, Les looked out at the mass of multi-coloured limbs swaying and weaving as the crowd pulled full circle around the two fallen brothers. With his dim-witted accomplices prostrate on the floor, Les was keenly aware that his chances of escape were diminishing with each passing second. The plan had always been to offer up the Cleftons as bait, should the police catch their trail, creating a very big, very visible distraction while he and the Major slid away unseen.

Unfortunately, he hadn't counted on the idiots going charging into battle in such an ill-prepared, foolhardy manner. And he certainly hadn't expected them to be defeated so quickly. Conversely, he wasn't at all surprised that the Major had scarpered so early in the proceedings. The man never had any real backbone, and was always the first to go running from a fight. The time for retaliation would come and Les would track down the lying weasel and teach him a lesson. But for now he had to focus on escape.

Tightening his grip on Alice, he aimed the pistol away from the crowd and pressed the barrel hard against Alice's cheek. Feeling the cold metal on her skin, she let out the slightest breathy squeal as her body quaked with an involuntary tremble.

"Pick up the bag, Alice," said Les, "you're coming with me. Don't put up a fight, don't struggle and I promise I won't hurt you."

Les gave her just enough freedom to move, and Alice did as she was told, bending down and hauling up the heavy green duffel bag. Les then renewed his grip on her, digging the barrel of the gun into her cheek again.

He looked down at George, crumpled on the floor, who'd turned his attention away from the brawl and was looking up at him with concern.

"Don't try and follow us, Thring," he said.

Les then started moving slowly backwards towards the door, dragging Alice along with him. George tried to push himself up onto his knees, but as he did Les pressed the gun harder into Alice's cheek, eliciting another, louder shriek.

"Don't be a hero, George," he barked. "Just stay where you are and I promise I won't hurt her."

All George could do was sit there, slumped on the floor, watching as the man he thought was his friend held a gun to the woman he loved. His heart pounded in his chest as he looked at Alice, fear engulfing him like flames.

Alice's face did not bear an expression of fear so much as anger. She was not at all fearful of Les. It was more of a resigned frustration that he'd managed to get the upper hand on her. She would have loved nothing more than to stamp on the man's foot, elbow him hard in the ribs, then wrestle the gun away as he lay on the ground wheezing.

But the cold, hard circular feel of the gun's muzzle pressed tight against her skin was a sobering reminder of just how real the situation was. There was no telling how this man might react, or how good his reactions were. Even if Alice got the upper hand, and Les gave up the fight, the gun could still go off by accident. She could still get shot, or a stray bullet could ping about and end up hitting George or someone else in the crowd.

Much to her annoyance, the best chance Alice had of getting out of this alive and in one piece was to do nothing and simply go along with Les. Until he dropped the gun, of course. Then he'd most definitely find himself on the receiving end of a good, hard kick in the nuts.

George, who was contemplating the exact same set of possible outcomes, could do nothing but watch as the two shuffled slowly backwards, crossed through the open door and disappeared into the darkness of the kitchen. And then they were gone.

He glanced round to the open car park, desperately seeking out some help or assistance, but the crowd was still consumed and swarming, huddling round the fallen robbers like a pack of dogs fighting over a discarded sausage.

No help was coming.

Pain seared in George's arms, back and legs as he slowly pushed himself up onto his knees. His ribs ached as he gripped the wall beside him and his legs shook and wobbled as he finally managed to pull himself up onto his feet. His head swam and his vision swayed as he edged his way along the wall, stumbling like a toddler learning to walk.

He crossed over the doorway and made his way through the kitchen, guiding himself through by holding onto kitchen tops, cupboard handles and any available steadying point, trudging over the faded lino flooring with tiny pigeon steps.

"I'm coming Alice," he said to himself. "I'm coming."

******

With the two thugs subdued and handcuffed, Detective Keane rose and glanced over to locate Thring and the rest of the gang. Instead he found a wide open door and no trace of anyone.

In all the fighting and confusion he'd completely forgotten about Thring, not to mention the older man who'd been waving a gun about. It was a miracle neither he nor any of the Elvises had been shot in all the fuss.

When the brothers had come running at him he'd planned to try to side-swerve them and head for the armed man. But getting himself punched in the face and thrown on his arse had somewhat hampered that plan. He'd then spent the next few minutes fighting to get back onto his feet, leaping on the back of one the attackers, then brawling to get the men down and the handcuffs on them.

Now that the two were subdued, cuffed and definitely going nowhere, Keane suddenly realised he had no idea what had happened to Thring and, most importantly, the old guy with the pistol. He scanned the area, checking off all the people in the crowd surrounding him, looking for any sign of Thring or the other men. They were nowhere to be seen.

He checked all the parked cars, stared into every dark corner of the car park, trying to pick up some trace of them. Still nothing. There was only one way they could have gone – back into the hotel.

Keane quickly bent and double-checked his prisoners' handcuffs, making absolutely certain they were sturdy and inescapable. He then issued orders to the crowd, telling them not to follow him into the hotel, and to make sure they held their position at the end of the car park to block off any escape routes. Should anybody else come, they were absolutely not to engage them, but simply to make enough noise that Keane would hear and come running back.

Finally, he took G.I. Elvis to one side, giving him sole custody of the brothers and asking him to keep an eye on them. He was to do nothing more than ensure that they stayed flat on their faces on the ground, and weren't allowed any opportunity to escape. And most importantly, no matter how he or the rest of the mob felt, he was to ensure that no further harm came to the brothers. The gang had taken their revenge, and now that the prisoners were incapacitated, that was to be the end of it. An audible sigh of disappointment echoed through the group as G.I. Elvis reluctantly agreed.

With the situation contained, Keane took a long, deep breath and headed off across the car park to the open door.

CHAPTER 62

IT took George a lot longer than he'd have liked to make his way through the kitchen, holding onto the counters and stumbling along like an old man desperate for a pee in the middle of the night. Every single inch of his body ached and throbbed, and every time he moved the pain pulsed and radiated through him, shuddering his bones and threatening to send him tumbling to the floor.

He thought of those ludicrous action movies where the hero took a severe beating, got hit by a car, fell off a building and took three bullets to the chest, yet somehow managed to race off after the bad guys and rescue the damsel in distress. From his own limited experience, he could say that was complete bollocks. He'd taken a fairly reasonable beating, though nothing compared to what it might have been, and he was struggling even to stay upright let alone move his feet one after the other. And that was only the outward physical symptoms. He dreaded to think what kind of kidney damage, organ failure and internal bleeding he was no doubt already suffering.

As he struggled to inch his way along he thought of Alice. His heart pounded as he considered the possibility of not making it in time to save her. He'd come so far over the last few days. He was so close to having everything he'd ever wanted and now his battered, ragged, beleaguered body threatened to let him down just as he was able to reach out and grab it. He couldn't let Alice be harmed. He had to save her.

He pushed himself on, urging his limbs to move quicker, trying to find that extra bit of strength buried deep down inside himself. His knees cracked, his muscles screamed, his back felt like it was barely threaded together. On he stumbled.

Finally he made it across the room and through the door to the main hallway. Letting go the stabilising support of the counter's edge he literally had to throw himself forward, whistling through the air like a falling tree, reaching out and catching hold of the doorframe's edge.

He pulled himself out through the door and caught sight of Les at the other end of the hallway. He was moving backwards, still with Alice gripped tight, the gun still pressed hard against the soft, reddened flesh of her cheek. Her eyes widened as she saw George, anger burning in them.

"Stop Les," wheezed George, fighting to catch his breath. "Just give it up."

"Piss off, Thring," retorted Les, glancing back to seeing George in the doorway. "I told you not to follow us. Didn't I tell him not to follow us?" he said to Alice.

Alice didn't reply, she just rolled her eyes and George could imagine the bad words she was saying inside her head.

"Come on, Les. There's no way out of this. Nowhere to go."

Les said nothing. Holding the gun in position, he released his grip on Alice, reached out behind him and gripped hold of the door handle.

As he pulled it open, a buzz of activity exploded in the street outside. Red and blue lights flashed and whirred, illuminating the large windows at the front of the building, slicing in through the gap in the door and cutting across the room. High-pitched, squealing sirens blared in the still evening air, echoing just out of sync, and bouncing off the walls and houses outside.

A loud screeching sound followed as two police cars skidded along the road, coming to a halt directly in front of the hotel, blocking any potential escape route. Doors flung open on either side of the two vehicles and uniformed officers came bundling out, racing round and huddling behind the now stationary cars.

"What the hell?" said Les, peering through the thin slit between the door and the frame.

"This is the police," came a voice from outside the building. "We have you surrounded."

"Oh for God's sake," said Les, slamming the door shut. "Oh Jesus fucking..."

"Les, why don't you just give up before somebody gets hurt, eh?" said George. "You can't get away now. The police are out the front and all the Elvises are out the back. There's no way out. And you can't hold us here forever."

"Bloody Hell, Thring, why did you have to go and call the bloody police? I was practically out of here."

"Call the police?" screeched Alice. "Call the police? You were going to kill us, Les. *Kill* us. Damn right he called the police!"

"Just give up Les," urged George.

Les groaned with frustration, shifting right and left, looking this way and that, desperate for some hidden escape route.

"We don't have to tell the police you were involved, Les. Do we Alice?"

George looked at her with desperate, pleading eyes. She looked back at him, her face etched with contempt for the idea. Then she shrugged her begrudging approval.

"We could say... you helped us escape. Nobody needs to know the truth. We'll say the others followed us back here, held us hostage and you helped us escape... Or we could say that you just got caught up in it by accident... you were just another hostage..."

"Nice try, Thring," said Les. "But it won't work. Aside from the fact that your detective friend out the back saw me pointing a gun at him – not to mention about fifty other witnesses – how long do you think it'll take those two morons out the back to start pointing fingers at me? And once they catch up with Charlie, he'll grass me up quicker than a fat man running to a buffet table."

"Well, no, okay… but… I mean, we could…"

"It's no good Thring." Les shifted slightly, pulling Alice closer and tightening his grip on the pistol.

"You don't have to do this, Les. Just let Alice go," said George, panic pinching his vocal chords, making his voice raise by one or two octaves. "Please Les, don't hurt her. Take me instead if you need a hostage. I've got money. You can have it all. We'll take my car. I'll go with you, if you want, until you get away. I can be your hostage. Just let her go. Please."

Les's eyes narrowed and flickered, his mouth tightening, like he was considering the idea.

"No," he said, "it's no good."

His hand shifted on the grip of the pistol and he pulled it back from Alice's face.

"No!" shouted George, releasing his grip on the desk and throwing himself forwards in a desperate leap, his arms outstretched.

Everything moved in slow motion. George hurtling forwards, his arms slowly swimming through the air in a demented front crawl. The gun in Les's hand pulling back, inch by slow inch, the barrel still pointing at Alice's head. His other arm released its grip on her, moving deftly behind to grab her other shoulder and slowly spin her round.

Fear and panic finally inched its way onto Alice's face, the sudden movement jolting her, making everything instantly so real. But just as she expected to see the gun raised to her head, Les slowly took a step back away from her. And she noticed that Les's arm was not moving towards her, but actually lowering, pointing the gun towards the floor.

Her fear turned to confusion as Les released his grip on her arms, letting go of her completely. She stopped in front of him, looking deep into his eyes, shame and embarrassment staring back at her.

Somewhere behind her, George hit the floor with a loud, dull thwack.

"I'm sorry Alice, I really am," said Les. "You know I never would have hurt you. You do know that right?"

"I… erm…" said Alice, stunned.

"I just panicked. When I saw the copper and the… well, you know. Back up against a wall, type thing. I just had to get out and grabbing you… well, it was just the old instincts kicking in. I was gonna let you go as soon as I got out the front door. You have to know I would never have hurt you."

"No, of course not. You were just going to let those other idiots kill me and George," she said indignantly.

"What, that?" Les chuckled. "Don't be daft. You didn't think I would…"

He laughed again, a deep, raspy giggle coughing in the back of his throat. "I wasn't really going to let that lot hurt you. Honestly. I was just trying to get them all somewhere quiet. Then I was gonna let you two go and pinch all the money for myself."

"What… but?"

"Hey, they were gonna do it to me too, you know. All three of them had plans to shoot me and do me over."

"So what now?" said Alice.

Les looked to the front door. Red and blue flashing lights buzzed and flickered, making the windows glow. A hum of activity raced outside, frantic footsteps clopping on the pavement, the police moving into position.

"Well... looks like it's all over," said Les mournfully. "Like Thring says, there's no way out of here. And it's only a matter of time before the Old Bill come knocking the door down."

He looked down at the gun, his mouth spreading into a melancholy smile.

"They've got me bang to rights, haven't they? No getting out of this one."

A silence hung in the air between them.

"Looks like there's only one thing I can do."

He tightened his grip on the pistol, his skin creaking against the handle. He stared at it intently, slowly rubbing the trigger guard with his finger.

Alice's face whitened with shock, her mouth falling wide open.

Les lifted the gun, turning it upwards as he raised it slowly towards his face. His hand shook slightly as a pale, ghostly look came over him, the merest hint of tears glinting in the corners of his eyes.

"No!" cried George from his crumpled position on the floor. "Don't to do it, Les. You don't have to kill yourself."

"What?" said Les, freezing suddenly and looking down at George in confusion. "I'm not gonna kill myself, you berk. I'm handing myself in. There's only one thing left to do – hand myself in."

With that he spun the pistol round, gripping it by the barrel and passed it handle first to Alice.

"I'm sorry Alice," he said. "I really am."

Alice dropped the bag to the floor and took the gun, gripping it lightly between finger and thumb, holding it far away from herself.

"Honestly Thring," said Les, laughing, "you do have some funny ideas. Kill myself. Why would I kill myself?"

"Erm... well, I thought... you know, rather than go to prison..."

The old man erupted into fits of laugher, bending forwards and gripping his knees.

"You thought I'd rather kill myself than go to prison? Oh, that's classic..."

"Er... well, I... erm..."

"Come off it, Thring. I'm not exactly quaking in my boots at the thought of a long stretch. At best the police can only do me as an accessory. I was nowhere near the bank when it was robbed and I have half a dozen witnesses that'll say so. They'll probably do me on conspiracy to commit robbery, but they can't prove exactly what I did or how much I knew."

"Well... what about the kidnapping?"

"Hmm..." he said, thinking. "Well, it wasn't me that kidnapped anyone, it was the other lot. As for this bit just now... well, it's really only your word against mine. And there are plenty of different ways to construe exactly what happens and who did what in a struggle. I mean, I was fearing for my life, wasn't I? I come out the back of the pub and there's all these nutcases threatening me."

He paused to think again, playing out a possible scene in his head.

"So... I... picked up a gun in the struggle... panicked... and in all the confusion I accidentally pulled Alice along with me... I mean, I was just doing what I had to do in order to escape. It's borderline self-defence."

"You can't honestly think you'll get away with that?" said Alice.

"No, I won't get away completely Scot free. But with the right lawyer... best bet, they'll probably give me a three to five. I'll be out in 18 months at the most."

"Oh..." said George, discombobulated at the revelation.

"Kill myself," Les chuckled. "Honestly. It's not even a real gun."

"What?" shouted Alice, spinning the pistol round and inspecting it. It looked real enough to her.

"No, just a replica, I'm afraid. A pretty good one, but fake all the same. You very rarely need a real gun nowadays. It's the threat that gets most people scared, much more than the actual bullets. You can't be walking round with a real gun, Thring. Someone might get shot."

"You mean to say that I was scared you were gonna shoot me... no, *kill* me..." said Alice, exasperated. "And it's not even a real bloody gun?!"

"Sorry," said Les with a shrug.

Alice looked at the weapon in her hands. She twisted it one way, then the other. Then she took two steps towards Les, shook her head in disappointment and kicked him hard in the balls. His face turned bright red as his hands instinctively flew to his groin and he dropped to his knees.

Alice looked down at the crumpled man, satisfaction glinting in her eyes, then suddenly remembered the other crumpled man in the room and rushed over to his side.

"Are you okay, George?" she said, kneeling down beside him. "Did they hurt you?"

"No, no, I'm okay," George lied.

Aside from the searing pain his back and legs, likely cracked ribs, potentially broken bones, cuts, scratches and possible internal complications, the thing that hurt most was his dented pride. He'd wanted to be the one to make the daring rescue. He'd wanted to come riding into battle, slay the villains and ride away with the rescued damsel in his arms. Instead he'd been thrown over a table, beaten half to death, collapsed in front of her, stumbled through a kitchen like a decrepit old man, and was now laying battered at her feet. All in all, it was far from a textbook rescue.

"Oh, God, you're really bleeding," she said, tentatively stroking his face, careful not to touch the bigger, uglier cuts and bruises. "Oh, and your eye. Does it hurt?"

Yes. It was incredibly painful. "No, it's not too bad," he lied.

"Don't worry, you'll be okay. We'll get an ambulance."

"I'm sorry Alice," he said, suddenly looking away from her.

"Sorry? For what?"

"For getting you into all this. For putting you in danger. For... for not being able to rescue you properly?"

"Rescue? Oh don't be daft," she said, smiling and turning his head so that he looked at her. "You did a very good job of rescuing me, George. If you hadn't called the police, God knows what would have happened to us."

"But it was all my fault in the first place. If only I hadn't grabbed that bag... I never should have come here."

"It certainly wasn't your fault. You didn't know what was going to happen. And you're not responsible for a load of lunatics robbing a bank."

Her face turned slightly stern. "And as for never coming here... well... maybe you're right."

George's face dropped. Alice again turned it back so that he was looking at her. She was smiling again.

"But if you hadn't come here, I'd never have met you."

She leaned forward and kissed him on the lips. It was the warmest, sweetest, most tender kiss he'd ever experienced. And because of his bruised nose, battered cheeks and bleeding lips, also the most painful. He did his best not to wince too much and hold back from shrieking like a girl.

"Thring?" said a muffled voice from the kitchen. "Thring? What's going on out there? Is everyone okay?

George and Alice looked over to the kitchen door to see Detective Keane peering cautiously around the edge of the frame. He had his back pressed hard against the doorjamb, hunkered down with his knees slightly bent, gripping a rolling pin in one hand and a large fish slice in the other.

"It's okay," George called back. "You can come in."

"Are you in danger?" he called.

"No, it's okay," said George. "Danger's over. You can come out."

Keane swivelled further, poking his head fully round into the room, glancing round all the angles, checking the potential hiding spots. He saw the old man collapsed on the ground, holding tight to his groin and whimpering slightly. He saw George battered and beaten, grounded on the other side of the room, Alice knelt down and tentatively stroking his head.

"Where's the gun," called Keane. "The old man had a gun. Where is it?"

"Don't worry," said Alice. "We have it."

She held up the gun showing it to him.

"Jesus," he cried back, flinching and trying to hide behind his fish slice. "Be careful with that."

"It's okay," said Alice, "it's not real. Apparently."

"Show me," said Keane. "Slide it over."

Alice slid the gun over to Keane, who stopped it with his foot. He bent over and picked it up, inspecting it to determine that she was telling the truth. When he was satisfied there was no real danger, he tentatively stood up, placed his fish slice and rolling pin on the side and walked into the room.

He noticed the red and blue flashing lights streaming in through the windows. "Oh, who called that lot?"

"The police?" said George. "I assumed you brought them."

"Me? No, I brought the Elvises." Keane sighed heavily, shaking his head. "Well… that's just brilliant," he said, like a petulant little boy who'd lost his favourite toy to a gang of bullies. "So what the hell's happened here, then?"

"Long story," said George.

"I like stories," said Keane.

"In a nutshell," interrupted Alice, "those two out the back and another one who seems to have disappeared were working with this one."

She pointed at Les.

"The other three robbed the bank; this one was involved, but we're not sure how much. George accidentally took the money from the robbery, panicked and hid it. The other three kidnapped me to force George to give it back, at which point I assume he phoned you."

Detective Keane went to speak, but Alice raised a finger to indicate that she wasn't finished.

"The other three thugs dragged me to the pub so they could exchange me for the money. Then they dragged us out to the woods to try and kill us."

Again Keane opened his mouth to speak. Again Alice stopped him.

"We get out to the woods and Sergeant Collins, the local policeman, turns up. He beats up these three, and we think we're rescued. Only it turns out Pete wants the money for himself, and now *he's* going to kill us. Only he has a heart attack and dies on the spot. His body is probably still out there.

"George and I manage to escape, and we run back to the hotel. We get here, and the next thing we know this one…" She pointed at Les again. "This one is in on it all. The other three turn up, they decide they're going to try and kill us again, beat up poor George, and drag us out to the car park. And that's where you come in."

Keane stood silent for a moment, thinking and trying to take it all in.

"That's a very inventive story, Miss…" He looked like he was trying to think of her name then simply gave up. "But it doesn't explain Mr Thring's part in everything."

"Oh, for God's sake," said Alice, "you don't seriously still think George had anything to do with this, do you? We've already told you what happened. George had nothing to do with the bloody robbery."

"He's already admitted being in the bank when it took place. And you've just confirmed that."

"Okay, well not nothing, exactly. He was just in the wrong place at the wrong time. He somehow ended up with the money, panicked and ran away. Okay, he acted like a bit of an idiot…" She looked down at George with raised eyebrows, and again softly stroked his hair. "But he's not a bloody bank robber."

"Yeah, well, I'm not buying it. Until I've interviewed all of you, and until I make up my mind about what really happened, you're all under arrest."

"Don't be a bloody fool," coughed Les from the other side of the room.

He sat up slowly, wincing with pain and still clutching his groin.

"Thring had nothing to do with it. And neither did Alice. They were just in the wrong place at the wrong time. The two out the back robbed the bank with another man named Charlie Robson. At least, that's the name I know him by. He also goes by Major Charles Fairview and about a hundred other names. And he's currently getting away while you're arresting the wrong bloody man. Just leave Thring out of this. You can take it from me that he had no part in any of this, and he's done nothing wrong."

"Really? And what exactly was your part in all of this?" asked Keane.

"That's something I'm not prepared to discuss until my lawyer is present. Now, if you don't mind, let's get this arrest over with. And then can someone get me some ice for my fucking testicles?"

Keane stood thinking again. He looked suspiciously at George, beaten and mangled and barely conscious. He looked down at Les, red-faced and tear-streaked, hands still gripped tightly between his legs. Then he noticed the dark green duffel bag on the floor beside him.

"So," said Keane. "I guess this is what all the fuss was about, eh?"

He crossed the room, bent down next to the bag and carefully unzipped it.

"So, how much money did you actually get away with then?"

He dipped his hand inside to inspect the contents. His brow instantly furrowed in confusion. "What the hell?" he said

He pulled his hand back out of the bag, taking with it a sticky handful of crumpled brown leaves and mud.

Les's eyes widened at the sight. "That cheeky fucking bastard," he said.

CHAPTER 63

SATURDAY

GEORGE Thring woke at exactly 7.13am. Despite the drama, chaos and bodily damage he had endured over the past few days, and despite having been kept at the police station until nearly 2am, his internal clock was annoyingly still set to rouse him two minutes before his alarm was due to start buzzing in his ears.

He lay there, half between sleep and wakefulness, as the events of the previous day flickered through his mind. He remembered the sheer panic at waking to find that he had accidentally fallen asleep rather than planning Alice's escape. He thought back to pacing the room, desperately trying to come up with a rescue plan and then carefully putting the various elements in place. His mind raced with images of confronting the criminals, attacking them and trying to get away. Then the embarrassment of throwing up in front of the crowd.

George's bones ached and his bruised face throbbed as he relived the fists and boots of the two thugs clattering into his legs, arms, back and head. He felt a sickly swirl in his stomach as he thought of the gun pointing directly at him, fearing not only that he was going to lose his life, but that he had also nearly caused the death of the woman he loved.

He thought of Alice. An image of her smiling face came to the forefront of his mind. The pain seemed to ebb away slightly, and he smiled back.

He yawned and stretched, the metallic bed springs tinkling beneath him, poking up and digging hard into his delicate skin. He was glad to be waking up in that bed. He was lucky to be waking up in any bed, rather than a police cell or, even worse, finding himself dead in a shallow grave in the woods. Thankfully he'd had the good sense to call for Detective Keane's help. And luckily the man had come through.

******

There had been a certain amount of confusion and arguing when Keane had finally opened the front door of the hotel and allowed the rest of the police to enter the building. At first they had wanted to arrest Keane, assuming he was one of the criminals. It had taken several minutes of the detective furiously waving his warrant card, spouting references and phone numbers they could call to confirm his identity before the arresting party finally believed him.

George, Alice, Les and the two Clefton brothers were all taken to the local police station for questioning, while a number of officers were sent out on foot and in patrol cars to search for the Major. They would later come back with accounts from various witnesses who had seen a shifty-looking man running off down the road with a green bag under his arm. Unfortunately no-one saw where he had run to and the trail soon went cold.

After two hours of questioning, and personal assurances from both Les and Detective Keane that they were not guilty of breaking any laws, George and Alice were released. Detective Keane actually put in more than just a word on George's behalf, working hard to convince the local force not to pursue him for the charges of accessory to commit robbery, interfering with a police investigation and wasting police time. Himself finally convinced of the man's innocence, Keane felt it unnecessary to punish him any further.

There then followed a good deal of debate between Keane and the local police as to who exactly would get to take credit for the arrests. Technically, Keane was miles out of his jurisdiction. A very angry, red-faced Detective Inspector with a crumpled black suit and greying hair was at pains to remind him that he should not even have been present in the town, let alone running around arresting persons of interest in such a high profile investigation.

His own force would not even have been present to act as back up had it not been for local community support officer Tony Clamp. Concerned at the disappearance of his commanding officer, and suspicious at having seen a small army of Elvis Presley's marching up the hill towards the hotel carrying an array of weaponry, he'd been the one to call for the reinforcements.

Then there were Keane's methods to take into consideration. The grey-haired D.I. spoke at length about how dangerous it had been to involve members of the general public in such a situation; how he'd never seen such a level of gross misconduct in over twenty five years on the force; and how he had half a mind to arrest Keane himself for incitement to riot.

Keane countered this, arguing that he should be given some credit for using his initiative and employing the only resources available to him at the time. And how if he hadn't acted as quickly as he had, the robbers would be miles away with a trail of dead bodies in their wake.

The Inspector came back at Keane, saying that he should have contacted the local police force with any information he had as soon as he had it; that having kept his leads secret in the hope of making the arrests himself had been wildly irresponsible. It was a wonder nobody had been killed. Keane again countered, saying that the local force had not exactly done a sterling job with their own investigations. Without him no arrests would have been made at all.

After a good twenty minutes of arguing, the two reached an impasse. Naturally, Keane was aware of the various penalties likely to await him on returning home, and was eager to avoid them. Similarly, the local D.I. was keen to keep things as quiet as possible. It would not reflect well on him were it noted that not only had his own force failed to apprehend the criminals but they were eventually foiled by an out-of-town D.C. and an army of Elvis Presley vigilantes. Not to mention the fact that they had not recovered any of the stolen money. As such, it was decided that they would make a formal statement that Keane had been working with the local force to take down the gang and they would share the credit over the arrests.

As for the Elvises, they would simply not mention too much detail and hope to avoid too many searching questions.

Keane was less than happy about giving away half the credit for his first major arrest, but some was better than none. He knew he would still score plenty of points back home for having followed what had seemed like such a spurious lead but which had finally led to the taking down of a major armed criminal gang. And, most importantly, the Detective Inspector agreed to smooth things over with his bosses back home, convincing them to overlook Keane's disappearing for three days and various other breaches of protocol.

George and Alice were finally released at just before 2am and told that no charges would be brought against either of them. Alice tried to convince George that he ought to go to the hospital, but the paramedic who had attended him had seemed to think that his injuries were not too serious and that he could go home if he wanted.

With George's assurances that he 'felt fine really' and just wanted to get back and go to sleep, Alice had finally relented. Detective Keane even gave them a lift back to the hotel, offering his own stern version of an apology for having hounded the man so determinedly – although still asserting that had George been straight with him from the start, things may not have spiralled so far out of control.

George listened to his words of warning, fighting the urge to retaliate, and promised the detective faithfully that he would be staying out of trouble in the future. And should he decide to go off on one of his jaunts again, he'd at least let somebody know what he was up to.

Finally George made it back to his room, flopped down onto the bed and was asleep within seconds.

******

As the fog of sleep lifted and he slowly came back to life, George opened his eyes. He looked at the dark brown stain on the wall. He took in the meagre dimensions of the tiny room. He looked down at his cold feet poking out the end of the duvet.

As the events of the previous few days continued to whirl through his mind, George tracked back to the very first night that had brought him there. He thought of his little grey car, his little grey house. He thought about his little grey job and his little grey life.

It was all over now. George's moment of madness, the protracted adventure that followed. It was Saturday. The weekend. Back to work on Monday. The thought made him shudder with dread. He actually felt slightly nauseous, although that could equally be attributed to the lack of sleep, the strong painkillers the paramedic had given him and the repeated kicks to his stomach the previous night.

George thought of going back to his old life. It seemed incredible to him now, how he had lived like that for so long. How had he allowed himself to live so without purpose or pleasure? He'd just been drifting along. Existing more than living. He could see that so clearly now. He wished he could grab his old self by the shoulders, shake him and scream: 'What the hell are you doing? Get out and live your life for God's sake!'

There was no way he could go back to that life. Of course he couldn't. But if he didn't go home, where was he going to go. What would he do?

He lay there thinking those two thoughts for a long time, imagining the various possibilities. It was a big world, after all. He could go wherever he wanted, do whatever he wanted to do. He was only inhibited by his own mind, his own imagination – something that had become far more ambitious of late. Where previously the world had seemed such a big, scary, unfamiliar place; it now seemed inviting, exciting, filled with possibility.

A sigh next to him. The bed creaked and wobbled as Alice rolled over, sleepily stretching an arm around George's middle and squeezing him tight. George's bruised ribs screamed with excruciating pain and, try as he might to hold it in, he couldn't prevent a tiny yelp from escaping his lips.

"Oh God," said Alice, waking at the sound. She sat up on her elbows, looking down at George's bruised face. "Sorry. Are you okay?"

George smiled up at her. "I am now," he said.

Alice lay back down, nuzzling her face into George's shoulder. Again it was incredibly painful, but this time he managed to refrain from whimpering. They lay there for a while, cuddling.

"So… erm… what now?" Alice asked hesitantly.

"Now?" replied George.

"Now," said Alice. "Life. You. Me. What happens next?"

"Erm, well, I…" said George. He looked down at his hands, the fingers tightly entwined and the thumbs bouncing off each other at a furious pace.

A silent tension drifted between them like a cool wind.

"I mean, this has been great, of course…" said Alice, filling the void with nervous energy. "You know, aside from the kidnapping, armed robbers and nearly being murdered. But I mean… you know… what are your plans now? What about your job, your life? What happens with…"

She hesitated, building up the courage to ask. "With you and me?"

"In all honesty, I really don't know," said George, still looking at his fingers.

Alice's face dropped, disappointment glinting in her eyes like the merest hint of tears.

"I mean," George continued, "this is all still a bit… well… unexpected. I don't really know what to do next."

He turned to face Alice, gazing deep into her eyes and beaming with an excited smile.

"But I know what I'm *not* going to do. I'm not going back. I'm not going back to that life. I'm not going back to that house. And I'm certainly not going back to that job. I've been thinking about what you were saying the other night. About the world being a big place, and not settling for things. About how life should be more of an adventure. Well... I think I fancy a bit of an adventure."

"An adventure?"

"Yes. I think I might go on an adventure. Just get in the car and drive. And see where I end up. So far it seems to be working for me, so I thought: why not just keep going?"

Alice gave an understanding smile. Trying to hide her disappointment, she said, "Well, that sounds great. I think you deserve to do something fun. You deserve an adventure."

"As for you and me..." said George.

He suddenly went very sheepish, not sure where to look.

"I was... erm... I was wondering whether you might like to come with me?"

"Come with you?"

"Yes. I know we've only known each other for a few days, but... well, I really like you. And I can't think of anyone I'd rather share an adventure with. If you're not busy?" said George, hopefully.

Alice went quiet, her mouth parted slightly.

"I mean," said George, looking back to his erratic thumbs, "it's okay if you can't. Or don't want to. I know you have your own plans... Your own adventures... It was only an idea, really..."

"George," said Alice, taking his chin in her hand and turning his face to look at her. "I'd love to go on an adventure with you."

She smiled and kissed him.

George's heart raced. His lips stung and his bruised ribs creaked with pain, his cheeks buckling under the weight of his smile.

"You will?"

"Yes, George."

"Great. Well, that's just great."

"I'll have to tell Mum and Dad, of course. But they'll be fine. How long do you think we'll be away for?"

"Until we get bored, I suppose."

"And where will we go?"

"Wherever. I don't care. As long as we're together, let's just go and see what happens."

The pair sat up in bed, grinning at each other.

"I probably will need to go back home briefly," said George, reality suddenly sinking in. "I need to sort out a few things with the house. And pick up my passport."

"Passport?" said Alice.

"Yes. Well, you never know. You'd better pack yours too, of course."

"Might as well."

"I suppose I should probably quit my job, too," said George. "You know, formally, so they know I'm definitely not coming back. Oh, and I should probably pick up some other clothes."

George looked over at the pale blue Elvis jumpsuit hanging over the back of the chair.

"Actually, you know what, maybe I'll just keep wearing that," he said. "It's done me okay so far."

Alice looked at the jumpsuit. She looked at George to find that he did actually seem to be serious. She looked at the bedraggled jumpsuit again.

"Hmm," she said. "Maybe we could buy you some new clothes."

She looked over at George and he was already fast asleep again.

******

Four hours later, after a little more sleep and another heavy, fried breakfast, George Thring climbed into his small grey car and slid the key into the ignition. He looked over at Alice sitting next to him and smiled.

She was leaving her family, her home, her job – her whole life – all to run away with this mysterious man she had met only a few days before. But the decision had been so easy for her. She didn't really like her job and she wasn't particularly keen on living at home with her parents. Neither had she any real affinity for her hometown – God knows she'd been desperate to leave for as long as she could remember. And it wasn't as if her life was going to become exponentially better if she stayed.

But strangely, none of that had much to do with her decision. Somehow it just felt like the right thing to do; as though she was supposed to go with George. She had no idea of where they were going, or even how they were going to pay for any of it, but somehow she just knew that she had to go. She wanted to be with George – this funny, cute, charming little man that had washed up into her life like a half-drowned cat and somehow made her feel more alive than anyone else she'd ever met.

She had spent about five minutes packing a bag, throwing in only the bare essentials – toothbrush, clean knickers for five days, a couple of tops and a spare pair of jeans – so desperate was she to get her new life under way.

She'd said a teary farewell to her parents – her father eyeing George suspiciously and not saying a word the whole time – and promised to send postcards and emails. Then they'd climbed into the car.

A giddy, nervous surge of energy pulsed through her as she placed her hand on George's on top of the gear stick.

"Are you ready?" he said.

"Ready as I'll ever be," said Alice.

"Let's go then," said George, starting the engine.

Alice smiled at George, a quizzical, devious look suddenly flashing in her eyes.

"Did you never think of taking any of it?" she asked.

"What's that?" said George.

"The money," laughed Alice. "You had all that money. Did you never think of taking any of it for yourself? Not even a little bit? It would certainly come in handy now. I mean I have my savings, but they won't last long. And adventures don't come cheap."

"Oh no," said George. "I couldn't have taken any of it. That wouldn't have been right."

"Well, no. But no-one would have blamed you if you'd kept just a little bit."

George gave a short laugh. "Hmm, maybe. But I wouldn't have felt right. Besides, I don't really need it. I'm actually quite wealthy."

"What's that?" said Alice.

"I have just over seven million pounds in the bank."

Alice sat stunned, her eyes wide and her mouth half open.

"Seven million pounds?" she managed to blurt out in shock.

"Yes, seven million. My parents were eaten by a lion. I'll tell you about it on the way."

With that, George lifted the handbrake and pressed down on the accelerator. The little grey car pulled out into the road, drove up the small hill and off out into the world.

THANK YOU

Thank you very much for deciding to buy my book. In a world where there are so many books being published on a daily basis, it means a very great deal that you decided to buy my quirky, silly, little book.

Since I started reading at a young age, it has been my dream to write a book and to have it published. I've truly loved writing this novel, and I hope you enjoyed reading it as much as I've enjoyed reading some of my favourite books.

If you did like it, then please feel encouraged to leave a review or a few good words on Amazon, Goodreads.com, Facebook, Twitter, any social networking sites you regularly use... or even good old word of mouth!

And make sure to come and say hello at:
www.facebook.com/unexpectedvacationofgeorgethring. It would be great to hear from you.

Alastair Puddick

ACKNOWLEDGEMENTS

WRITING this book has been a long, fun, sometimes hard, often stressful, but hugely enjoyable experience.

The actual writing took place in quite a few different locations – with parts written in the house I used to share with my brother; my friend John Fuller's living room; the café in Slough that I used to visit every lunchtime when I snuck out of work with my notepad (and a nice lady used to give me free biscuits); the 'cupboard/office' in my flat; and countless other coffee shops where I'd sit huddled in a corner scribbling down thoughts and ideas. So a big thanks to everyone who allowed me space to work.

Of course, there are a few people I have to mention, without whom this book would never have been written. Firstly, huge thanks to Elizabeth Puddick; a pretty decent proofreader, a source of immense inspiration and encouragement, and the best Mum I've ever had. And to my beautiful fiancée Laura Adamson – thanks for putting up with my bad temper, insufferable moods and moments of self-doubt. And thanks for always helping, supporting and encouraging me.

Special thanks to Gavin Walker, Jenny Mcleish and David McLeod, who all read early drafts of this book and whose comments and encouragement helped to shape the final version. Thanks to my sister, Jenny Irwin, whose knowledge of banks and bank safes was invaluable. And thanks to my chum, Helen Brennan, for encouragement, moral support, not *always* distracting me, and many, many tea breaks.

Of course I have to thank my family and friends; particularly my Dad for giving me such a memorable surname and my brother, Stuart, for his gentle mocking of my 'wall of Post-it notes' that contained all my ideas and plot points. And thanks to Gavin 'Smudger' Smith for his frank advice to stop talking about writing a book and just get on with it.

A very big thank you to Dave Lyons from Raven Crest Books, for believing in this novel enough to publish it and for helping me to get it out into the world. And finally, thanks to all the Elvis impersonators in the world – you guys rock!

ABOUT THE AUTHOR

Alastair Puddick is a writer and editor who lives in Crawley with his fiancée Laura. The Unexpected Vacation of George Thring is his first novel.

CONTACT DETAILS

Visit Alastair's website: www.alastairpuddick.wordpress.com

Follow Alastair on Twitter: www.twitter.com/HankShandy

Like or join Alastair on Facebook:
www.facebook.com/unexpectedvacationofgeorgethring

Cover designed by: László Zakariás.

Published by: Raven Crest Books
www.ravencrestbooks.com

Follow us on Twitter:
www.twitter.com/lyons_dave

Like us on Facebook:
www.facebook.com/RavenCrestBooksClub

95294221R00220

Made in the USA
Lexington, KY
07 August 2018